T0316080

How to Die Famous

BENJAMIN DEAN

SIMON & SCHUSTER

First published in Great Britain in 2023 by Simon & Schuster UK Ltd

3 5 7 9 10 8 6 4 2

Simon & Schuster UK Ltd
1st Floor, 222 Gray's Inn Road
London
WC1X 8HB

www.simonandschuster.co.uk
www.simonandschuster.com.au
www.simonandschuster.co.in

Simon & Schuster Australia, Sydney
Simon & Schuster India, New Delhi

A CIP catalogue record for this book is available from the British Library.

PB ISBN 978-1-3985-1257-3
eBook ISBN 978-1-3985-1258-0
eAudio ISBN 978-1-3985-1259-7

This book is a work of fiction. Names, characters, places and incidents are either the product of the author's imagination or are used fictitiously. Any resemblance to actual people living or dead, events or locales is entirely coincidental.

Typeset in the UK by Sorrel Packham
Printed and bound by CPI Group (UK) Ltd, Croydon, CR0 4YY

Content warning: This book contains on-page depictions of excessive alcohol consumption, death and murder.

PRAISE FOR BENJAMIN DEAN

'A scandalous thriller.' THE *GUARDIAN*

'My favourite kind of YA. Benjamin Dean is a welcome
addition to the UK YA scene and has written a royal triumph.'
JUNO DAWSON, AUTHOR OF *HER MAJESTY'S ROYAL COVEN*

'Scandalous, funny and deliciously compelling!'
CATHERINE DOYLE, CO-AUTHOR OF *TWIN CROWNS*

'All hail this exquisitely twisty, delightfully queer mystery.'
CHELSEA PITCHER, AUTHOR OF *THIS LIE WILL KILL YOU*

'A compelling thriller that stays with you long
after you've finished reading.'
KATHRYN FOXFIELD, AUTHOR OF *GOOD GIRLS DIE FIRST*

'More jaw-dropping, OMG-twists than even
the most salacious tabloid journalist could create.'
ERIK J. BROWN, AUTHOR OF *ALL THAT'S LEFT IN THE WORLD*

'One page-burning scandal after another.
Benjamin Dean is YA royalty.'
FEMI FADUGBA, AUTHOR OF *THE UPPER WORLD*

'A scandalous, twisty mystery that had me
on the edge of my seat gasping for more.'
KATE WESTON, AUTHOR OF *DIARY OF A CONFUSED FEMINIST*

'A twisty thriller that kept me guessing until the very end.'
LEX CROUCHER, AUTHOR OF *REPUTATION*

'Addictive, compelling, and utterly delicious.'
SIMON JAMES GREEN, AUTHOR OF *NOAH CAN'T EVEN*

For Mum, as always, and for Ellie B –
those therapy sessions while we were supposed
to be writing our silly little posts might
have just saved my life. Thank you.

Prologue

WHAT HAVE WE DONE?

Abel Miller / 11 August 2023 / 23:13

Nobody was supposed to end up dead. I thought the safety of fame would protect us from that. I assumed nothing could touch us. Hurt us. Kill us.

And yet, right now, there's blood on my hands. My shirt. The kitchen tiles. The cupboard door. It's splattered everywhere like a fucked-up paint by numbers. I guess I was wrong about the whole *being famous* thing. There was me thinking this blessed and gilded life was supposed to be fun. It wasn't meant to be a death sentence.

But I can't think about that. I need to stay focused on getting as far away from this crime scene as possible. I can't be caught here. Not with someone else's blood all over me. Especially now the police have arrived.

I reach the side door and take off running, pelting through the shadows of the garden, away from the flashing red and blue lights of the police sirens that seem to be chasing me. I hear the front door crash open and a loud voice demand that nobody move. I don't stop. I keep running.

History has a habit of repeating itself.

2010.

2020.

Now.

Maybe everyone was right. Perhaps this show really is cursed. The only difference this time is that I'm right in the middle of it, and I've had a big part to play.

I escape the way we got in. Through the trees, over the fence, down the mountain and back to the car. They're waiting, but the moment I appear covered in blood, their faces fall.

'Abel . . .' one of them whispers.

I nod. 'It's done.'

In a daze, I can't find any other words, but it's enough for them to understand. Four of us walked into that house. Only three of us are here now. The blood on my hands tells the rest of the story.

One of us is dead.

Part One

THE PERFECT SURFACE
AND WHAT HIDES BENEATH

THE DAILY EYE NEWSPAPER

THE CURSED SUNSET RISES ONCE MORE!

By Hannah Wilkes, CELEBRITY REPORTER

1 August 2023

AFTER MELTDOWNS, DISAPPEARANCES AND TRAGEDY, OMNI CHANNEL HAVE ANNOUNCED THE RETURN OF TEEN DRAMA SUNSET HIGH.

It's been labelled one of the most cursed TV shows in Hollywood history, but Omnificent, the famed production studio behind Omni Channel, have today revealed that Sunset High *will make its grand return to screens early next year, with filming due to begin imminently. The show follows the drama-filled lives of high-school teens at a prestigious private school in Beverly Hills, and its brand-new cast includes Omni Channel's go-to heart-throb Lucky Tate, marking his return to work following the death of his mother in a car accident last December. Tate's long-term girlfriend and fan-favourite Ryan Hudson, as well as Omni Channel's latest rising star Ella Winter have also joined the line-up.*

However, the murky past of Sunset High *shrouds its*

return in controversy. Many will be familiar with the streak of bad luck that followed the show since the original aired in 2010, with critics online dubbing it the 'Cursed Sunset'. At the time, millions of fans around the world witnessed the unravelling of twenty-year-old actress Mila Stone, who, after increasingly erratic behaviour and numerous public meltdowns, announced her retirement from the spotlight altogether. The star sensationally blamed Omnificent for 'ruining my mental well-being' and 'dragging me to the brink of a nervous breakdown'. Omnificent refuted the allegations and accused Stone of breaching her contract. Multiple on-set sources later claimed that her ego and demands made her 'impossible to work with'.

Things only went from bad to worse for the show in 2020 when it was rebooted with teen sensation Penelope Daunt leading a fresh cast. What started as a Hollywood fairy tale became a nightmare when the nineteen-year-old disappeared while on a solo sunset hike around LA's Runyon Canyon, something her friends said she often did in a bid for alone time. Daunt was last seen on the evening of 8 July that year, with door-cam footage picking up the star as she parked her car on a nearby residential street. A missing person report was filed on 10 July when she didn't show up to work. Despite a storm of conspiracy theories touted by amateur sleuths online, which persist to this day, no trace of the actress has been found. The case remains open more than three years later.

News of Daunt's disappearance came on the heels of

a tragic accident that took place at an exclusive Beverly Hills hotel frequently booked for Omnificent cast and crew. On 9 July 2020, just one day after Daunt was last seen, it was reported that a junior assistant working for Omni Channel on the Sunset High *reboot had plunged to his death after falling from the hotel's roof, leaving members of the show badly shaken. A source with direct knowledge of the situation, speaking on the promise of anonymity, told Page Six at the time: 'The show can't go on. After the rooftop fall and Penelope's disappearance, nobody feels safe.' Omnificent were quick to scrap the reboot following the incidents, with the show's creator and director, Lake Carter, stating everyone needed 'time and space to grieve and heal after such tragedy and loss'. In response to the news, another source added: 'I'm glad* Sunset High *has been shut down. I hope it never sees the light of day again.'*

Chapter One
ON THE HORIZON

Abel / 1 August 2023

I'm walking through Heathrow Airport when I'm recognized for the first time. I feel it before I see the eyes that have found me, like an invisible hand has tapped me on the shoulder, raising the hairs on the back of my neck. Sure enough, when I turn round, there they are – a young couple holding hands, whispering frantically to each other while stealing glances in my direction. I tell myself it's not what I think, that they're not looking at *me*, but then I clock the large TV screen overhead, flashing up the latest news stories of the day.

**CONTROVERSIAL TEEN SHOW *SUNSET HIGH*
RETURNS WITH NEW CAST.**

I stop dead in my tracks. Above the headline are four pictures. Lucky Tate, every inch the white Hollywood dreamboat with ruffled brown hair, searing blue eyes and a face that looks like it's been carved from marble. Ryan Hudson posing on a red carpet, dark skin flawlessly smooth, full lips curving into a dazzling smile. Ella Winter performing the role of young starlet with effortless ease, tanned complexion gleaming as she tosses long silvery-blonde hair over her shoulder. The final picture is clearly a selfie masquerading as a professional headshot. The boy's mixed race, with short freshly faded hair and clear-rimmed glasses. He smiles but I can see the uncertainty behind his eyes.

Abel Miller.

I'm staring at my own face. Not weird at all.

I glance at the couple again out of the corner of my eye, but now I see they're not the only ones looking in my direction. A group of teens have noticed too and they're not even trying to be subtle about it – they're pointing right at me. My breath lodges in my throat like the oxygen has turned solid. I duck my head and get the hell out of there. I wasn't expecting to be noticed so soon, but news of the *Sunset High* reboot has clearly got people interested.

It takes me a minute to find the first-class lounge, not least because I've never had a reason to go to it before today. Only yesterday I was a nameless nobody who flew economy. I guess things have changed now.

I'm welcomed into the lounge by two smiling faces on the front desk. They offer to take my rucksack and hoodie, which

I politely decline, then guide me to a set of double doors that open into a world I've only ever imagined before. And, let me tell you, that shit is LAVISH! You get a whole separate lounge in the airport to chill in with food and drink and the option to take a freaking shower or a nap while you wait for your flight. There are literal *nap pods*! I've been slumming it in economy this whole time like a fool while the other half live it up like this? Wild.

I'm definitely the youngest person here, and by the way I stick to the outskirts of the room, you can tell this isn't my usual scene. I'm not even bothering with the food because what if I *think* it's free but I actually have to pay for it? I'm not about to embarrass myself like that. I should just be happy that I didn't have to pay for my own flight, because based on how my bank account looks right now, I would've had to travel to Los Angeles in the cargo hold.

I settle into a leather armchair in the furthest corner possible with a USB charging port built into the armrest, a mini desk that swivels over my lap and a view of the runway. There are worse places to mind your own business. I watch as a plane prepares to take off, bound for who knows where. It picks up speed, rumbling down the tarmac, then its nose lifts and the plane aims for the clouds, beginning its journey to a new destination . . . just like me.

With over an hour to kill before my flight takes off, I unzip my rucksack and grab my laptop. My stomach lurches when the internet tabs I forgot to close last night reappear on the screen, evidence of my last-minute research when I couldn't sleep. Even though I know the story like the back of my hand,

I can't help but read about that damn curse all over again.

The girl who broke down.

The boy who fell.

The star who vanished.

You can see why people call it the 'Cursed Sunset'. Whenever the show comes back, something tragic happens.

I swipe through the tabs and headlines, various pictures scattered underneath them. There's Mila Stone looking the essence of glamour on a red carpet before filming for *Sunset High* started; then again, this time her face blurred in anger as she lashed out at photographers days after the show aired. On another tab there's a video of Penelope Daunt accepting an award, the one she dedicated to her estranged father, Max Daunt, who was in hospital at the time. Penelope went missing weeks later.

I stop on a tab that contains a video of the door-cam footage dated 8 July 2020. I press play and watch as a rusty white car passes through the shot a minute before Penelope's Mercedes appears. She climbs out, a rucksack slung over her shoulder, and scrapes her auburn hair back into a ponytail before putting on a baseball cap. She looks . . . agitated, glancing round every few seconds like someone might be following her. There aren't many other people or cars around at that time of the evening, though. A blacked-out jeep passes by, followed by a guy on a bike who does a double-take in Penelope's direction and slows down as if he's recognized who she is. The driver of a blue BMW must beep impatiently because the cyclist gives them the middle finger and pedals away. They exit the shot just before Penelope does. She walks out of the frame, and that's it. Ninety seconds of footage. The final moments of Penelope Daunt before she vanished.

It was the celebrity story of the year, maybe even the decade. Countless front pages, news articles, podcast episodes and fan videos had been dedicated to Penelope's story, and they all asked the same question – how does one of the most famous faces in the world simply disappear into thin air? Penelope had joined Omni Channel as a teenager, and after starring in a bunch of their most successful shows, she'd become their queen. Even if you weren't a fan, it was hard not to know who she was. Surely *someone* had answers.

Various conspiracy theories had been offered up and passed around the internet like sordid secrets. The most popular revolved around the guy on the bike. He'd seemed to recognize her after all. But Porter McKay, as he was later identified, had been interviewed by police and cleared of any wrongdoing. Not that it stopped people online from calling him a murderer, even though there was no proof to even suggest Penelope was dead. For all anyone knew, she could've slipped away to a paradise island to sip on piña coladas and escape the suffocating frenzy of fame that followed her everywhere she went.

I sink into my chair, letting my head fall back and my eyes close. Even then, I can still see the tape and the headlines as if they're imprinted on the back of my eyelids. Maybe I've been too obsessed lately with Omnificent and *Sunset High* for my own good.

My phone vibrates, dragging me back to the lounge. I see

the name on the screen, then quickly glance around the room to make sure nobody is in earshot.

'Hello?' I say, keeping my voice quiet.

'Not too famous to answer your own phone yet?' Hannah Wilkes asks.

'Not yet. Give it a few days.' I take a steadying breath, ignoring the tingle of anticipation that's crawling up my spine. 'So . . . do we have a deal?'

Hannah pauses. The silence crackles in my ear, enough to spike my heartbeat. But then she says the words I've been waiting to hear.

'Yes, we have a deal.'

I close my eyes with relief, clenching my other fist. It might be the eleventh hour, but the last piece of my plan has finally slotted into place.

'You give us the stories, we publish them,' Hannah continues. 'But if you get rumbled, you leave the *Daily Eye* out of it. We can't be caught conducting an undercover investigation into Omnificent. They'll have us in court quicker than Lake Carter can yell *action*.'

'You have my word,' I say.

Hannah chuckles to herself. 'You're going to blow this shit apart from the inside. They won't see it coming.'

I remember when I first walked into her office for a meeting. I'd received the call that I'd got the role on *Sunset High* the week before after endless gruelling auditions. I was glad to see that years of being a theatre kid and drama school had finally paid off. After being told all my life that it would be almost impossible to make it as an actor, I'd landed myself a pretty sweet role – I'd be playing Rex, the best friend of Lucky Tate's character. I'd heard it was down to me and Saint Morgan. He was a Hollywood bad boy, much more established and a sure favourite for the role. But fate must have smiled down on me because he got busted for drag racing his sports car while under the influence of drugs the week of the final audition. What a shame.

But this wasn't about getting my first big break. No, I had much bigger plans than that. So I pitched my idea to Hannah – use me and my role in *Sunset High* to peel back the Omnificent curtain and see what really happens behind the scenes. She'd looked at me like I'd not only grown a second head, but like that second head had turned out to be Kim Kardashian.

Sure, the *Daily Eye* newspaper was one of the trashier tabloids, one that many wouldn't even waste spit on. But that rag also happened to have one of the biggest global readerships in the world. Any story they published would be seen by millions, which was the exact platform I needed to expose Omnificent for the liars they really were. If I was going to risk everything to do this, then I wanted to make sure that the whole damn world knew about it.

'I do have one question, though . . .' Hannah says. She clears her throat. 'Are you going to tell me why you're doing this? What do you have to gain from it?'

I weigh up which of my guarded secrets to let free and decide a little sprinkle of honesty can't hurt.

'I want the truth,' I say. 'Omnificent, Lake Carter, *Sunset High* – they've already ruined so many lives. Why should they get away with that? Why should we let them destroy anyone else?'

It's not a lie, but I'm glad Hannah doesn't push for anything more. She acknowledges my answer with a hum of satisfaction, then throws me a curveball.

'I'm sure you've already seen the latest news. Looks like you're flying straight into the eye of the storm.'

I frown. 'What news?'

I hear a faint gasp in my ear. 'Holy shit. You don't know?'

'Know *what*?'

Hannah cackles with glee. 'God, I'm so happy I get to be the one to break this to you. You're not going to believe it.' I hear some tapping on the other end of the line as adrenaline plunges its needle into my heart. 'This just in from TMZ. Check your texts.'

I swipe at my phone screen and open a screenshot sent from Hannah. It's from an article posted an hour ago. I must've missed it while checking in for my flight. The headline reads: **LUCKY TATE CHEATS ON RYAN HUDSON WITH BEST FRIEND ELLA WINTER!** I can't even hide my shock. I'm sure I haven't read that right. Lucky and Ryan have been the golden couple for two years now since meeting on the set of Omni Channel's hit show *This High Life*. They played characters who fell in love on screen, and then they fell in love in front of the world off screen too. There were even rumours a while ago that they'd got engaged. They're kind of couple goals, even though I think I might be allergic to seeing straight relationships with my own eyes.

15

Ella Winter was in *This High Life* too. She's pretty new to the spotlight, but she's quickly become an Omni Channel favourite. People are already saying they think she might eclipse Ryan. Her star is rising at an alarming pace. I see her face everywhere. I'm sure I even saw it on a billboard advertising make-up when I first walked into the airport this morning. But Ryan and Ella are supposed to be best friends. Everyone knows that. This is huge.

There's a second screenshot too, this one including a couple of pictures clearly taken at a distance. I inspect them properly, feeling my jaw drop as I see Ella's silvery hair and Lucky's brown curls. Their faces aren't visible since they're glued to each other's, but it's unmistakably them.

'Oh my fucking God,' I say as I bring the phone back up to my ear.

'Really shakes the table, doesn't it?' Hannah says, as if she couldn't be happier. 'I'm just reading E! News now. *Lucky Tate has been pictured getting close with Hollywood's newest starlet Ella Winter, the best friend of his supposed girlfriend Ryan Hudson. The intimate moment was snapped by fellow diners at a hotel bar in New York.* Blah, blah, blah, everything's terrible. Reps for Omnificent have now come out to say Lucky and Ryan broke up quietly a few months ago. Funny that they failed to mention that earlier.' Hannah tuts to herself, then carries on reading. *'Lucky hasn't been seen in public with Ryan since earlier this year following the death of his mother.* I suppose cheating on your girlfriend is one way to deal with grief.'

I flinch. Grief isn't something I joke about. I act as if I didn't hear what she said.

'It's happening again,' I say instead, thinking about the supposed curse.

'I know! Isn't it great?' Hannah says, completely misreading the apprehension in my tone. 'The scandals are already starting, and you're going to be front row for the whole thing.' She sighs to herself. 'I'd kill to watch this unfold with my own eyes.'

'I'll send you a postcard,' I mutter.

A melodic sound plays over the speakers in the lounge, followed by an announcement that my flight is ready to board. This is it then. I say my goodbyes to Hannah, who makes me promise to keep her updated on every small detail, then I hang up and start gathering my things before setting off for the gate.

As soon as I flash my ticket, I get ushered to the front of the crowded line as if I'm royalty. Once on board, a flight attendant offers me a glass of champagne or freshly squeezed orange juice. I choose the champagne. I'm not stupid. If I'm going to do this, I plan to enjoy every single perk that comes with it.

Another smiling attendant guides me to my seat, which is actually a suite with sliding panels to create privacy and a leather chair that folds down flat to make a bed. I've seen apartments in London with less space. And as if that's not enough, a first-class care package provides me with luxury bedding, a pillow, loungewear, slippers, an eye mask and a toiletry bag filled with mini essentials, such as a toothbrush and hand cream. In economy, you're lucky to get leg room and a seat that nobody's kicking from behind.

In a little cubby under the TV screen is a bundle of magazines. I barely glimpse them as I reach over to see what movies I can line up for the flight, but then I realize Lucky Tate is staring back at me from the top cover. He looks like he's just fallen off a ruffled-hair, blue-eyed, Hollywood fuckboy conveyer belt. He has this easy grin that spreads over his face, and even in print it's like he's pinning me in place with his stare, looking *into* me. I may as well admit it right now – I have a huge crush on him. To put it simply, he's hot. *Stop you in your tracks, heartbeat fluttering* type of hot. But still, I won't let myself get distracted by a disarming smile. Nope. No way. I refuse to be that pathetic. I pick a magazine with Meryl Streep on the front and cover Lucky Tate. There. Problem solved. God love Meryl Streep.

When I settle back into my seat, I think I spot Tom Holland a little further down the aisle. I can't be sure because whoever it is has a cap and shades on, clearly not wanting to be disturbed, but that mixed with Lucky Tate is enough to make me feel a little dizzy. To take my mind off the crush I also have on Spider-Man, I check my phone, automatically opening my messages. The first thing I see is the text chain pinned to the top of my screen, and it instantly wipes my mind of anything else. It's probably not wise to keep it there, so visible, but I can't let go. It's a reminder of what I've lost. And now it's a reminder of why I'm doing this.

Thu 9 July 2020

Adam
I know you're probably still asleep
but can you call me when you wake up?
I don't care what time it is here, just
call me straight away. It's about Omni
and it's urgent. I don't know what's going
on but it's fucked up. Call me asap
06:04

No worries, false alarm!
Love you bro x
06:17

Me
Since when do you call me bro 😴
Just woke up and called you but
no answer. Everything okay?
08:38

You must have crashed. I'm heading
to school. Call me when you wake up
09:02

I'm seeing stuff online.
Someone fell from a hotel roof in LA?
Isn't that where you're staying?
What's going on?
10:29

Adam, please pick up
10:31

Please . . .
10:36

My brother was only twenty-two. He'd gone to LA to pursue the job of a lifetime working on the reboot of *Sunset High*. He'd said it was going to be his big break because he never believed in maybes. For him, it was a matter of fact, written in the stars. He wanted to be a director. He used to always say, 'Hey, Abel, I'm going to write a script someday. You'll play the lead and we'll win an Oscar. Two Black brothers standing up on that stage together in front of all them white people, mad that we even got a foot in the door. You in?' I used to laugh because it seemed like a daydream to me. But I always said yes. He had it all mapped out, and nobody was going to stop him from getting there.

Nobody except Omnificent.

They said it was a tragic accident, and my brother's death was quickly swept under the rug when it was announced twelve hours later that Penelope Daunt had gone missing. Adam became nothing more than a nameless victim to a supposed curse. But I haven't forgotten. His last texts have played over and over in my head for three years. He wanted to tell me something about Omnificent, and I won't stop until I know what. I won't stop until I get the truth.

The plane begins to rattle as it sets off down the runway, and before I know it we're in the sky, climbing into the clouds, beginning our journey to LA. Possibility lingers on the horizon. Fear too. But so does revenge.

Chapter Two

TRACES OF HEARTBREAK

Ryan Hudson

If you'd asked me how I wanted to spend my Monday night, I might have said a nice hot bath, a good book, a new script to sink my teeth into or a trashy romance movie that plays into every cliché but in the best possible way. What I got instead was a stalker leaving me a 'gift' outside my home, the cops being absolutely useless and the news that my 'doting boyfriend' has cheated on me with my 'best friend', something I discovered at the same time the rest of the world found out. I know they say bad things come in threes, but *come on*, universe, give me a break.

'So you're saying you've seen this man outside your property before?' The officer sits on the edge of my couch, legs crossed at the knee and a notepad in hand. He has yet to take any notes, despite the fact we've been talking for ten minutes already.

'I've already reported this,' I say, trying not to lose my patience. '*Three times.* This man has been outside my gates every other day for the last few weeks since my address got leaked online last month. Whoever it is won't go away.'

'Has he approached you or tried to gain entry to your property? I mean, he's technically not breaking the law by standing on the street.'

I briefly close my eyes, an intense pain at the front of my brain kicking the inside of my skull over and over again. I point to the box wrapped in a red ribbon on the coffee table between us.

'Is this not enough proof that I have a stalker and you need to do something about it? That was left outside my front door for fuck's sake.'

The officer bristles at my tone. 'Thank you, miss. We're very aware of that.'

I force myself to remain calm. I might be famous, but this officer and the sour-faced colleague behind him couldn't give less of a crap. In fact, they look like they despise me because of it. Telling them I have a stalker isn't getting me any sympathy.

'With all due respect, how do we know that this is a stalker? Could a friend not have left it for you?' the officer continues.

I bolt up, swiping the lid off the box and grabbing a fistful of the *Sunset High* posters inside. They're all from the scrapped 2020 reboot, Penelope Daunt front and centre. Her face has been scribbled out in red marker pen on every single one.

'I arrived home to find these on my doorstep. It's the same show I've just been cast in. Do you not think this makes it pretty obvious that I've got a stalker?'

'Ah, you mean the *cursed* show,' the other officer says, ignoring the actual problem here. It's hard to miss the sarcasm oiling his words. 'A kids' show, isn't it? So you think one of them might be stalking you?'

I don't get why they're both so intent on being useless. It's like I've got to prove that I'm the victim here. Not that proving myself isn't something I'm used to. I've had to do that my whole life, especially in this industry. People used to say I'd never make it as an actress. Some said I was too brooding, too awkward, too miserable. Others thought I wasn't girly enough, not happy enough, not *grateful* enough. Let's talk facts, though – a lot of their criticism was just an acceptable cover for people being pissed off that I was a successful Black girl who dared to follow my dreams and make it in a business that hadn't always wanted me in the spotlight.

Still, I'd made it. The house I'd bought was proof of that. The foundations, the bricks, the walls and everything in between them was mine, paid for with the money I'd earned off my own back, having started with nothing. So I'm not about to let these two dumbasses get the better of me.

'For the last time, this man has been outside my house for weeks, he's now left me a threatening package, and I no longer feel safe. Is that not enough for your investigation?'

'Can I ask how many people have access to your home?' the first officer asks, as if I haven't even spoken. 'Maybe one of them simply left this behind as a joke.'

I'm about to lose my shit, even though I know that's not wise, when I hear the front door open. I jump half out of my skin, thinking the stalker has come back, but my manager, Brad, comes striding round the corner. The officer gives me a sharp look, as if this proves his point.

'Are you okay?' Brad asks, coming straight to my side. He opens his arms and pulls me into a tight hug. 'I'm going to sort this out, don't you worry.'

I let myself feel safe for just a moment in his embrace. Brad's the only man I even vaguely trust. We've been through a lot together since he signed me to his management company back when I was only just starting out. Omnificent had held open auditions for supporting roles in some of their Omni Channel shows, and I'd rocked up on my own, a thirteen-year-old with nothing but hopes and dreams. They signed me and I met Brad soon after. He was more than a manager to me. In some ways, he was the only family I'd ever known.

'You've given the cops a statement?' Brad asks, pulling away.

'Yep. They were just being super helpful by asking some follow-up questions.' I plaster a smile on my face and turn to face the officers.

Brad understands my tone and shoots them a glare. 'If you'll give us a moment,' he says. Then without waiting for their answer, he guides me out into the hallway where he hands me a set of keys. 'I'll pick it up from here. Take these and head for the house in the Hills. Nobody will find you there.'

'I don't want to be scared into running away.' Fear laces my words, but I try to stay calm. 'This is everything I've worked for all these years. This is my *home*. Leaving feels like letting this stalker win.'

Brad nods his understanding. 'I know, but it's temporary, okay? Just until we sort out better security here. And besides, Omni have booked you a suite at the hotel from tomorrow until filming wraps up, so you can stay there instead. I want you to be safe, Ry.'

I feel defeated, but I know I don't have another option. Staying here alone won't prove anything to anyone. I take the keys and give Brad a quick peck on the cheek, then I glance towards the living room to check the officers aren't listening in.

'Have you heard from Omni?' I ask softly, already tensing.

I'd been on my way home earlier, blissfully unaware that my stalker was leaving me a gift, when Brad had called to break the news. My relationship with Lucky had been over for a month now, not that the world knew it yet. I was sure Omni were waiting for the reboot announcement in order to get the most press. Instead, Lucky – the boy everyone thought I was still in a happy relationship with – had been pictured out for lunch with Ella in New York. That was odd enough in itself, but then TMZ dropped the clanger that in one of the pictures, they'd clearly moved on to dessert.

Brad shifts uncomfortably. Great, *more* bad news then. 'Just know that I'm fighting this every step of the way.' He hesitates, then lets it spill. 'I'm told it's not serious right now. Apparently it was just a casual date.'

'A casual date?' I splutter. 'Did you *see* the pictures? They were all but dry-humping the table, and in broad daylight too. They *knew* they'd be seen.'

Brad grimaces. 'Yes, well . . . Omni aren't saying much. Have you heard from either of them?'

'They're not picking up my calls.' I shake my head in disbelief. 'This has Omni's fingerprints all over it. They never wanted me as their star, and this is their perfect opportunity to phase me out.'

I squeeze my eyes tight shut as if that will stop it from happening, but despite my best efforts, I feel my heart drop. Sure, my relationship with Omni is hardly perfect. I don't think they ever really planned for me to become as successful as I did. They cast me in my first show as a supporting character with six lines of dialogue. I acted my ass off and took those six lines straight to the bank. The show was critically panned, but every single review highlighted me as one to watch. Omni called it a happy accident. I called it damn hard work. But I've always known I don't fit their usual lead actress mould. For a start, I'm not white or some all-American girl next door. I'm not like Mila Stone or Penelope Daunt. And I've always felt like they were keeping a close eye on me, biding their time, waiting for me to fuck this up.

'None of this is confirmed yet,' Brad tries, but even he sounds less optimistic than usual. 'You just focus on doing a good job on *Sunset High* and let me figure out the rest. Everything will be okay, I promise.'

But I know in my heart that's not true. Lately I'd started to clash with Omni more and more. It all seemed like silly stuff on the surface – what I wore, how I looked, how I styled my hair, how I answered interview questions. I stood my ground instead of simply wilting on the spot like a dying flower. They didn't like that I did things my own way. They wanted to put their claws in my back and control me like a puppet. And maybe I was over being controlled, or maybe I was just *growing the fuck up*. Either way, I'd started to step outside the lines they'd drawn for me, and they didn't like it.

Ella Winter was a different story.

She came into my world like a flash of lightning when she was cast as my best friend on *This High Life*. Ella had been Omni's latest hire, and they were keen to introduce her to the world. We quickly became close. Maybe too close. She was magnetic in a way that celebrities should be – charismatic, talented and beautiful, with these wide blue eyes the colour of a summer sky that hasn't seen a cloud in days. I was mesmerized by her, and we'd quickly struck up a friendship, one that had outgrown the show with every passing day, hour, minute spent in each other's company. Everyone thought she was pure sunshine. I did too.

So, of course, it would only be a matter of time before Omni replaced me with Ella. Why wouldn't they? She was exactly what they were looking for – new blood, and therefore easily mouldable. They could make her into anything they wanted her to be. She was the perfect target.

I finally acknowledge the thought I've been pushing away ever since I saw the pictures. 'There has to be some kind of game plan here. There's no way Lucky and Ella wouldn't have known cameras were watching them.' I shake my head, utterly helpless. 'This is my life. This is everything I've ever worked for. They're going to take it all away from me just like that, and they didn't even warn me.'

I'm not sure I'm talking about Omni any more. Yes, their betrayal hurts, but it's Lucky and Ella that kills me the most. I thought they'd have my back. Apparently I was wrong.

Brad tries to talk me off the ledge, but all I feel are the last traces of control deserting me. Still, when one of the officers pops their head round the door and gives a pointed look at his watch, I put a smile on my face, then head upstairs to pack a bag while Brad deals with Dumb and Dumber.

It might seem silly to cry, but I can't help it as I load up the car trunk, give Brad a hug and then edge the vehicle along the driveway. I look at the house, my home, in the rear-view mirror – a symbol of my wildest dreams and everything I've worked so hard for – and the tears come quickly. I will come back; I promise myself that. I won't let anyone take this away from me.

I pause as I hit the street, glancing at the screen on the dashboard for the directions that will take me from Holmby Hills to Brad's safe house in Hollywood Hills. That's when I see the notification that tells me *Famous Last Words* has posted a new podcast episode. Brilliant, just what I need. That show is gossip personified into two hosts who love to talk and bitch about nothing but celebrity scandal. Omni once asked if I'd do an interview for the podcast since they bring in millions of streams a week. I said *no fucking way.*

I know I shouldn't listen to it, especially when I see the title: *What the Hell is Going on with Lucky, Ryan and Ella?* But I can't help myself. It'll keep my mind from thinking about the stalker at the very least. I press play and start the drive, letting Hattie and Devin fill me in on what the world thinks about my private life.

'So what do we make of these Lucky Tate and Ella Winter pictures, Devin?' says Hattie after introducing the show as *an emergency episode.* She sounds solemn, but I can literally hear the grin spreading across her face. I want to punch the steering wheel. 'It's got to be the scandal of the year already, right?'

'Oh, absolutely,' Devin responds, not even trying to hide his excitement. 'At best, you've got the golden couple of the moment breaking up in secret before the ex-boyfriend moves on with her best friend. Or, at worst, you've got Lucky Tate *cheating* on Ryan Hudson with Ella Winter over a Caesar salad in broad daylight. It's pretty juicy whichever way you cook it.'

I smirk to myself, despite the sting of being reminded of my situation. Devin and Hattie clearly scrambled to record the episode before they saw the statement from Omni admitting my relationship with Lucky was already over. Not so *finger on the pulse* as they claim to be.

A flash of headlights appear in my rear-view mirror, another car joining me on the dark and winding road. I glance at it, hoping it's not paparazzi . . . or my stalker. It keeps a fair distance, and I tell myself to relax and concentrate on the road.

'Omnificent have never looked after their actors,' Devin

is saying. 'They pluck these kids out of obscurity, often from poor homes because they know they'll be easier to manipulate, then they offer them the world on a plate, work them to the bone and spit them back out before replacing them with the next kid on the conveyor belt. And there's always a thousand little wannabes waiting for their big break once Omnificent has tired of their latest toy.'

I feel my rage bubble. For once, Devin's right.

'But you can't deny that if you're an actor and you land a role on one of their projects, you're set for life – even more so if it's *Sunset High*,' Hattie muses. 'It's their biggest show by far. Wouldn't you take that opportunity?'

'And risk waking up in heaven days after the curse comes for me? I'll pass, thanks,' Devin responds.

'Heaven is where you think you're going, is it?' Hattie asks pointedly.

Devin cackles and calls her a bitch.

But I'm hardly paying attention now. I'm too busy looking in my mirror at the car behind that has crept closer. I frown. Something feels off. I press on the gas a little, and the car behind speeds up too. I slow down, and it mirrors me, always keeping just enough distance away. I start to panic, my breathing sharp and shallow.

I'm being followed.

'All I'm saying is if that curse is coming for any of them, then God help them all,' Devin says.

My hands grip the wheel as the fear in my chest flutters. If I can just make it to Brad's house, I can call the cops. I take a steadying breath, then floor the gas once more. My car shoots through the dark as gated mansions and looming trees bear down on the road. The car behind speeds up too, gaining on me.

'I just hope they make it out alive.'

I pull hard on the steering wheel, veering dangerously before I slam on the brakes and skid to a stop outside Brad's house. The other car doesn't slow down. I can just about make out that it's a dark-coloured truck, but then all I can see are its tail lights as it pulls away, glowing neon red, like a sign of danger.

On shaky legs, I let myself into the house, turning on all the lights. Devin and Hattie are now playing through my phone, but two grown adults bitching about my private life is the least of my worries right now. I call Brad, who tells me to lock the door and hold tight while he notifies the cops. I can hear the edge to his voice.

I lock it and slide down to the floor, back to it like that will keep me safe. Drowning in panic, I don't know who else to call. There's only one person I want to talk to. I find the number and bring the phone to my ear.

'Pick up . . .' I whisper. 'Please pick up.'

Hi, this is Ella. I probably won't call you back, but y—

I cut the call, and before I can stop myself I launch the phone with all my might at the opposite wall. Then I bury my head in my hands and begin to break.

Chapter Three

BEHIND THE MASK

Ella Winter

The pictures with Lucky weren't my idea. But, okay, I admit I knew there was a photographer posted outside the restaurant. I'd spotted him straight away, lurking behind a car on the opposite side of the street. Omni hadn't said anything about that, but you develop a sixth sense for picking up camera lenses when you spend your entire life in their crosshairs. Lucky had spotted him too.

'I guess we've got company,' he'd muttered under his breath. 'Just what you want on a first date.'

Omni had known we were both in New York, of course. They were the ones who'd called my manager – also known as Mom – to tell me that, now Ryan and Lucky were over, Lucky was wondering if I was available for lunch. Mom said yes without bothering to check with me first. She didn't even blink. She hung up the phone and told me that I had a date to get ready for.

I wanted to tell Ryan straight away, I swear on my life I did, but it all happened so fast. I was pushed into a meeting with Omni, then whisked off to lunch, before being pulled into a car that took me to a meet-and-greet and finally a photo shoot booked to promote *Sunset High*. I didn't even have my phone. Mom had it the whole time, saying it would only be a distraction while I got on with work. I didn't put up a fight. Instead, I hoped Omni would tell Ry and that she'd understand.

'Hey, Ella? Everything all right in there?' my assistant calls.

It's midnight in New York City. The photo shoot has already stretched hours past its scheduled wrap time, and we haven't even started the interview part yet. Once that's done, I need to sign off on a lipstick and eyeshadow collaboration, then run lines for *Sunset High*, which might just be my biggest break yet. I'll get a few hours' sleep before I have to be up for a radio interview at seven, followed by yoga, running lines once more and then packing for my flight back to LA, where all hell is waiting to break loose. I'm already dreading the mob that'll no doubt be waiting at the airport.

But if there's one thing I've learned in this industry, it's to never complain. That's the first sin of Hollywood if you want to keep a good reputation. A bad attitude one moment can seep like poison into the rest of your days. Suddenly you're branded *difficult to work with* or, God forbid, *a complete bitch*, a label so impossible to shift that you may as well pull the plug on your own career. I have to remind myself that I'm lucky, right? I'm the luckiest girl in the world.

'I'll just be a second,' I call, trying to make my voice all light and airy as if I'm not on the verge of a full-blown panic attack from being dragged this way and that.

I have my back against the door, like I can lock myself away from everything in this cupboard that's acting as a dressing room. I hear the hesitation in my assistant's silence, but Natalie eventually gets the hint and steps away. She quietly tells the photographer to start setting up for the next shot. Panic attacks can wait. Photo shoots can't.

I take a deep, shaking breath, then another and another, trying to steady the beat of my heart and stop the walls from closing in around me. I shut my eyes, let my head lean back against the wood and try to breathe, to escape for a second, to forget the hurt that I'm leaving in my wake by trying to keep everyone happy.

Against my better judgement, I decide to check my phone, which Mom eventually gave back to me when we arrived on set. There are three hundred and forty-eight unread messages. The total never goes below two hundred these days, but I have the important ones pinned to the top. Several are alerts telling me Mom has added or shuffled events around in my calendar. There are a few discussing a potential new contract with Omnificent. They want me exclusively. If I accept, I'll be theirs. I know what that did for the likes of Lucky and Ryan – it took their careers to a whole new level, with leading roles and multiple projects. It's a big deal, one that's guaranteed to catapult me into a much bigger spotlight. Mom is basically already spending the money, even though I haven't officially accepted yet. I keep saying I want to read the contract thoroughly to buy myself some time, but the truth is I haven't made up my mind. Something about Omni, the power and control they have over everything, scares me a little. Signing a new contract will only keep me in their clutches. Do I really want that?

There's a text from Lucky reminding me that he's there if I need him. We had a good chat over lunch once the photographer had got what he wanted and disappeared. Lucky's been doing this a lot longer than me – a couple years shy of a decade, and he's still only eighteen. He's a genuinely *nice* boy, a rare thing. There are worse things in the world than being photographed with a heart-throb who just so happens to be a sweetheart too.

I'm worried about him, though. He wasn't quite slurring his words, but I noticed over lunch that he definitely wasn't sober. I could smell the vodka on him from across the table. I suppose it's understandable after what happened to his mom last year, but still. Before the accident, he was more of a one-glass-and-done at parties. He used to always say he wanted to keep his wits about him because you never knew who was watching. Now he doesn't seem to care.

And then there are a dozen messages from Ryan. My hopes that she won't feel betrayed by this are clearly way off the mark. There are a bunch of missed calls too, but the last message, sent thirty-three minutes ago, is enough to punch me in the gut.

Ryan

Ella, how could you do this to me?

23:34

I don't have an answer because she's right – how could I?

I'm distracted from my gloom by a notification that slides into view. Mom set up Google alerts on my phone for my name because she said it was always good to see what other people were saying about me. I didn't agree *at all*, so I'd turned them off. Mom noticed because it's a shared account and turned them back on. I haven't found the energy to fight her on it since.

THE CURSED SUNSET STRIKES EARLY? AS OMNI CHANNEL ANNOUNCE NEW *SUNSET HIGH* REBOOT, ARE THE CAST ALREADY AT WAR?

Ugh. Trust the *Daily Eye* to twist the story into a narrative that'll help them get clicks. At *war*? I mean, come on. I already know that if I open the article, there will be some wild claim about how a *source with direct knowledge of the situation* knows for a fact that I've buried Ryan in my back garden so I can date Lucky. One thing I learned as soon as I landed in the spotlight? *Never* trust what you read in the press. It's only ever half the story, if that.

As for this *Sunset High* curse or whatever they're calling it? It isn't real. That's what I'm telling myself anyway so I can hold on to just a shred of my sanity. I know what happened to Mila Stone and Penelope Daunt. I heard about the crew member who fell from the hotel roof in a freak accident. I've been told about the dramas the public don't even know about, little fires that have been put out before they became wild and untamed. Rehab stays, blacklisted actors who didn't play ball, on-set fights. And, sure, it's all been playing on my mind lately. You can't deny that whenever *Sunset High* starts up again, something bad happens. But still. It's not a curse. It's nothing more than bad luck and tragic coincidence. So long as I stay in line and do as I'm told, no devastating fate will be able to touch me.

'Baby girl, we need to get this ball a-rolling!' Mom sounds loud and cheery on the other side of the door, but I know her well enough to decipher the warning that's coming. She lowers her voice just enough so only I can hear her next words. 'You'd better get out here, Ella – you're embarrassing us in front of these fancy folk. I'm not messing around. Get in front of that camera. Now.'

When she gets like this, I know there's no reasoning with her, no matter how I might be feeling. Sometimes it paralyses me with fear how much my parents rely on me and what I do. The pressure to never put a foot wrong sits in my gut like a dread I can't shake. Mom puts my work, success and wealth before anything else. If I'm not earning more money or landing the next big role, then I'm simply not doing enough in her eyes. Realizing that you're a meal ticket first and a daughter second is a tough pill to swallow.

I sigh, but I'm already stepping into the character everyone wants me to be out there. The all-American sweetheart, the wholesome girl next door. Whatever any of that even means. I've become an expert at wearing this character like a coat. Or maybe as more of a shield, armour to protect me from the world watching my every step. I've got so used to Ella Winter, actress and rising star, that I've started to forget who Eleanor Grayson even is.

Despite the hammering in my chest that refuses to subside, the pounding in my head and the constant peck of intrusive thoughts, I pull myself together and put on my best *good girl* smile. One more deep breath and I go to open the door. But before I do, I catch a glimpse of myself in the mirror. I'm not sure I recognize the person looking back.

Chapter Four

THE GENTLE ACHE OF MEMORIES NEARLY FADED

Lucky Tate

One shot.

I don't even know what the alcohol I'm trying to find solace in right now is. It could be vodka. Maybe it's a gin or tequila bottle nestled inside the brown-paper bag that I'm swigging from. I don't know and I don't care. My tongue can hardly taste it. I'm too focused on numbing everything out, blurring my senses so I can't feel anything any more.

The streets of New York are barely alive at five a.m. on a Tuesday morning. The humid air of a summer's night flirts with the city, holding it in its warm embrace. I'm grateful for the quiet. Too many people make me nervous these days. They're always out to get something from me. But not tonight. My phone might still be lighting up in my pocket, but in the real and physical world, I'm all alone. I like it that way.

Two shots.

Although I'm trying not to think about anything specific, the image of home materializes in my head. Not LA, the place I've lived since I was eleven. No, I think of the two-up two-down, seen-better-days house back in Chicago with its ramshackle porch and weather-beaten fence. I used to play soccer in that front yard, dreams of being *someone* still so far out of reach that I hadn't decided which way I was going to achieve it yet. I'd kick that ball against the garage wall while Mom sang in the kitchen, moving her hips to the rhythm of the radio. I'd never been happier, before or since.

Three shots.

A teacher in elementary school described me as outgoing, always the centre of attention and everyone's friend in class. She'd told my mom that I'd auditioned for the school play and had blown everyone away. I remember the look on Mom's face as she listened, then the way she'd dropped her gaze down at me, full of love and pride. In the car ride home, she'd turned off the radio and looked at me in the rear-view mirror. Somehow I can still hear her now, even after all this time.

'You're going to make Mommy really happy one day,' she'd said. 'Whatever you decide to do, whatever dreams you have, you're going to make it happen. I can feel it in my bones. And I'll always be so proud of you, no matter what. You know that, right? You'll always be my perfect little dreamer.'

Little me nodded in the back seat, knowing I'd do anything to make Mommy happy. I'd have moved mountains if I could.

By the time I was eight, I knew that I wanted to be one of the people on TV. Their lives seemed so perfect, and they were always having so much *fun*. But as I grew up and started booking commercials, I realized that I wanted this for more than just myself – I wanted to be able to give something back to my mom too. It had always been the two of us, and we'd never had much, but now I had the opportunity to look after her the way she had me, and she deserved the world.

Four.

Somewhere between one block and the next, I start to cry. I don't notice it at first, so lost in my own head, but then I feel the sting of tears escaping and soon they're coming thick and fast. They won't stop. They haven't stopped in months behind closed doors. Will they ever? I can feel the gentle ache of memories calling out to me from the darkest parts of my mind. I chase their voices, but every time I grasp one, it slips through my hands like a ghost. I can feel the edges of myself crumbling, each brick falling faster than I can rebuild it. I must make a noise because someone hurrying past turns round. But I don't care. I'm just trying to hold on. I'm just trying not to remember any more.

Five shots.

The anger that always follows these thoughts is a friend. Or maybe it's the opposite, but would an enemy fill me with such comfort? When I think of it, I imagine it as a red poison simmering in my gut, slowly getting darker until it's almost black. It should make me sick with its potency, but instead its burn feels familiar, like a balm that soothes the destruction

41

that tears and memories leave behind. I don't want to feel anything, but if I have to, I choose this anger that sets my insides alight. It reminds me that there is someone to blame for what happened to Mom.

Six shots.

And then, after that, all that's left is fear and a raw anxiety that eats at me from the inside out as more thoughts tumble through my head like a crushing waterfall. Will I ever be able to get back up from this? Will I ever be able to face the shadow of grief that haunts me? Will I ever be the same again, or am I forever changed by cruel misfortune, a stranger I no longer recognize? Unlike the comfort of anger, these fears are parasites, worming their way deeper and deeper, making a home within me.

Seven shots.

Emptiness. Finally the alcohol numbs it all. There is nothing left in me. No fight or will to swim to the surface for air.

Somehow I find myself back in my hotel room. The sun hasn't risen yet, but, like me, the night is breaking apart. Soon it will relinquish the dawn. Will my darkness do the same? Will it let in the light?

Floor.

I don't make it to the bed. In a few hours I have to be up to fly back to LA. I try to unlock my phone to check the flight information, but I can't see the screen properly and I must open Twitter or another app because an audio clip from some podcast starts playing and they're talking about me, Ella and Ryan, but that's all I hear before the plush carpet grazes my cheek.

I start to fall and keep on falling, this conscious world mercifully slipping away.

You're going to make Mommy really happy one day, a memory says in my head as the dark begins to close in. *You know that, right? You'll always be my perfect little dreamer.* It's creeping round the edges of my vision, threatening to swallow me.

I will, Mommy. Just tell me how.

I finally give in to the dark and let myself fall into a place where nothing can hurt me. I just want to forget. I just want . . .

Chapter Five

A CITY OF ANGELS AND DEMONS

Abel

I'd always wondered how I'd feel landing in LA, edging ever closer to Omnificent and their secrets. Would I be scared? Filled with adrenaline and nerves that made me sick? Would I be ready to do whatever it took to get to the truth? Now I'm here, I feel it all at once.

I hop off the plane at LAX with jet lag and a splitting headache. No dream and a cardigan here. All I can think about is my brother, *Sunset High* and the reputation that precedes it. I wonder if Adam thought about that too when he landed. Was he worried about what people were saying about the show, or was he just excited, blissfully unaware of the tragedy that loomed on the horizon? I guess I'll never know, which hurts me to my core. I just hope that now I'm here,

I can find the answers I'm looking for.

The moment my phone gets signal again, it almost flies out of my hand from the notifications. The banner at the top of the screen is a blur of social media alerts – new followers, likes, comments. My phone begins to crash under the weight of them all, so I quickly turn all notifications off and try to settle myself. The rising number sitting inside small red circles in the top right-hand corner of my text, WhatsApp, Twitter and Instagram apps isn't helping. Begrudgingly I leave the safety of my first-class compartment and step out into the early-afternoon sunshine of LA.

A guy dressed in a sharp black suit and shades waits for me at arrivals holding a sign with my name written on it in neat letters. He waves as soon as he lays eyes on me, reminding me that I'm no longer able to blend into the background. He greets me with a warm handshake and a drawling American accent, swiping the luggage from my hands before wheeling it towards a blacked-out SUV.

We're not even halfway to the car, however, when a guy in a hoodie with a raised camera jumps out of thin air, shouting my name as if I'm not a metre away from him. I'm not sure what's going on at first, and I flinch as clicks like gunshots pepper the air around me. Then I hear the guy yell a question about *Sunset High* and I realize what's happening – my first run-in with the paparazzi. It's not exactly a swarm of cameras with their flashes lighting me up like fireworks – it's just a guy with straggly hair pulled back into a ponytail.

For a split second, it's almost exciting. Isn't this what

people dream of? But all too quickly, it becomes invasive. The photographer is so close that I can smell cigarette smoke and the weak hint of gum trying to mask it on his breath. I try to step round him, but he mirrors my movement as if we're connected to the same piece of string.

'Aw, come on, kid. Smile for the camera,' he says sarcastically. His tone has a mocking edge to it, as if he's taken personal offence to me even though we've never met.

The guy with my suitcase steps in between us, ushering me towards an open car door. I dive inside and slam it shut behind me. The photographer, undeterred, thumps his camera up against the tinted windows. I can hear him shouting, louder now.

'HOPE YOU'RE NOT WORRIED ABOUT THAT CURSE! IT MIGHT BE COMING FOR YOU NEXT!'

The driver jumps into his seat and starts the engine, speeding away and leaving the paparazzo in the rear-view. My body sighs into itself, the brief spurt of adrenaline leaving me shaking.

'Welcome to the City of Angels, sir,' the driver says brightly in an attempt to pop the bubble of tension lingering after the . . . attack? Can you call it that? It certainly felt like it.

I murmur a thank you and try to smile like I'm loving every minute. It's supposed to be my big break after all. But in my head I don't think of angels. I think of the demons that lie in wait instead. I don't know who that guy was, but I think I just met one.

*

Omnificent's go-to hotel is nothing short of luxury. It's in the heart of Beverly Hills, complete with doormen who take your luggage and wheel it up to your room so you don't have to, a large swimming pool that's perfectly heated, a menu of spa treatments and a restaurant that may or may not have had Zendaya seated in the far corner. It certainly beats a Premier Inn, anyway.

The white man at the front desk is pretty young, maybe a few years older than me, and is handsome in an old Hollywood, Marlon Brando kind of way with slick combed-over hair and an easy confident smile. His name badge says: Casey Beck.

'Abel Miller,' I say when he asks for confirmation of my name. A gentle frown creases Casey's brow for a second, but he quickly busies himself by tapping some keys on the computer.

'You'll be on the thirteenth floor,' he says, handing me a small wallet with two metal swipe cards inside while I pray that the floor number isn't a bad omen. 'Omnificent have thirteen and fourteen all booked out for cast and crew. I believe your co-stars will be staying with us too.'

I don't know why I'm surprised by this. I'd just assumed that the others would have homes in LA. In fact, I know for sure Ryan does – I saw pictures of it when her address was leaked online.

'Please do call us at the front desk if you need anything,' Casey continues. 'The restaurant closes at midnight, but room service is available twenty-four hours. The pool, gym and spa close at ten, although special exceptions can be made for our most important guests.' He winks with a laugh. 'And, of course, I must remind you that staff quarters and the roof are out of bounds. You'd be surprised at how many guests try to make it up there for a better view.'

I offer a strained smile at the mention of the roof. Casey seems to notice. His eyes narrow for a moment, sweeping my face and taking me in properly. I feel like I'm about to be busted before I've even had a chance to check in. But he shakes his head with a breathy laugh.

'Forgive me,' he says, all business once more. 'I hope you enjoy your stay with us.'

I shuffle uncomfortably. 'Thanks for the welcome,' I say, pulling my cap down a little lower.

I scarper up to my room without a backwards glance, hoping Casey's eyes aren't following me. I only start to relax when I'm safely behind the closed door of my hotel room, which . . . well, it's hardly a *room*, let's just say that. The junior suite is more of an apartment fitted with plush white and beige furnishings, a super king-size bed and a small balcony looking out over the city. The shower, made of marble and partitioned off from the rest of the bathroom by a sheet of glass, is bigger than my entire bedroom back home.

I dump my case and flop onto the bed, which instantly enfolds me with a level of comfort I've never experienced before. Damn, rich people *really* be living, huh. I can't bear to look at any of the notifications I've received since landing, so instead I send a quick message to Hannah to let her know I've arrived safe and sound. Then it's time to get my investigation underway.

In all honesty, I don't have many leads to follow. I know I want to speak to Mila Stone, especially because she appeared on the original series of *Sunset High*. She could have some useful information about the show that might link back to my brother. But there's another lead I want to investigate first. I unlock my phone and find my text chain with Adam.

It was a couple of weeks shy of 4 July 2020, which happened to be the same day as Adam's birthday. I'd messaged him to ask for an address that I could send his gift to, and he told me he'd be spending the weekend at a friend's house in Echo Park. The friend was called Hope Waters, another junior assistant on the show. I find her address in our texts now, along with the picture Adam sent from the party of him with a bunch of friends, including Hope. She's white, has short reddish hair, freckles and large square glasses. Hope seems like the best place to start.

As I book an Uber and head out of the door, I see a couple of news notifications on my phone. The first reads: **ELLA AND LUCKY LAND IN LA TOGETHER; UNFAZED BY NEW YORK CHEATING RUMOURS**. There are pictures of Ella and Lucky holding hands as they make their way through a mob of photographers to a waiting car. Both of them are hiding behind dark shades, Lucky going the extra mile in a cap and hoodie, while Ella raises a hand to her face like that will protect her. Even through still pictures, I can feel the claustrophobia, as the cameras encircle them.

But the second one gives me pause for thought: **RYAN HUDSON STALKER LEAVES SUPER-CREEPY GIFT ON**

DOORSTEP AS RUMOURS OF THE *SUNSET HIGH* CURSE SWIRL. I click the notification and pictures of old *Sunset High* posters with faces scratched out appear on my screen. It *is* pretty fucking creepy. If anyone thought this *Sunset High* reboot was going to be any different to the others, I guess they'd be very, very wrong.

I double-check the address to make sure I have the right number. I think I'm standing outside the house of Hope Waters. But for all I know she could have moved, leading me to a dead end. There were no social media profiles attached to that name that matched the picture I had, so this is my only shot. If she isn't here, I don't know how I'll go about finding her.

If she *is* here, then I plan to tell her the truth. Well, I'll leave out the part about Hannah, but there's no use telling a friend of my brother that I'm someone else. How else will I explain how I had her address and why I'm here asking questions about someone who isn't alive any more? I take a deep breath, sending up a prayer to Adam if he's watching. *You'd better be looking out for me. This is for you.*

I knock on a dull blue door, the ensuing silence ticking in my ears. There's no movement at all for a few seconds, long enough that I raise my hand to knock again, but then I hear steps on the other side and the door opens. I'm disappointed to find that I'm not faced with Hope Waters, but a slim-built white guy giving me a quizzical up and down like he wants to know who the hell I am. He has shaggy brown hair, sunken cheeks and is wearing a polo with a hammer and spanner logo.

He looks like the exact type of guy who knows how to ride a skateboard.

'Can I help you?' he asks. His tone isn't rude but it's definitely guarded.

'Yeah, I'm looking for someone called Hope. Does she live here?'

The guy glances over me again. I can't be sure, but was that a flicker of recognition? Or am I making myself the main character in a situation where he's simply wondering what a stranger is doing on his doorstep?

'Nope, never heard her of her. Sorry.' He goes to close the door.

'Wait!' I say and the guy pauses. 'Maybe she lived here before you? Do you have any information on the last tenant? It's kind of important.'

The guy shakes his head, seemingly keen to get rid of me.

I frown as I look at his face again. My adrenaline spikes.

'Nope, sorry.'

He begins to close the door and this time I don't stop him. I get a brief look at the guy one more time and a peek at the hallway beyond before he's gone. I force myself to put one foot in front of the other and walk away, as normally as possible. It's not until I'm round the corner that my thoughts form into two questions.

First of all, why did that guy lie? Behind him, hung on the hallway wall, was a collection of photo frames. I might've only seen them for a moment, but one definitely showed a red-headed girl smiling at the camera. It sure as hell looked like Hope Waters to me.

And weirder still – Porter McKay had been the man at the centre of baseless conspiracy theories online accusing him of murdering Penelope Daunt. He was the guy who'd cycled past her in the door-cam footage on the last day she was seen. He'd been cleared of any suspicion by police and retreated back into anonymity.

But of all the people in the world, why was he the one who'd answered the door?

Chapter Six

STARS DON'T SHINE AS BRIGHT IN THE DAYLIGHT

Abel

The Omnificent headquarters is an incredible curved design made of metal and glass that reflects the sun like a rare jewel. If you look up close, it seems to glitter, throwing a rainbow of colours over the grey floors. In the lobby, there are three-metre posters of Omni Channel's most famous TV shows and movies plastered on the walls, alongside portraits of their biggest stars. Amongst them is Lucky Tate, running a hand through his hair and smirking at the camera. He looks confident, like he's got the whole world at his feet. I suppose he does. I almost want to blush just staring at the picture.

It's late afternoon, and I'm all but on the floor with jet lag. I'm running on pure adrenaline and vibes right now. But I've been summoned here to meet the rest of the cast so, for now,

I have to put that and thoughts of Porter McKay and Hope Waters aside. To be honest, I'm terrified. Fear is no longer snaking its way through my body and has instead settled like a dead weight in my stomach. The anxiety is still simmering, though, making me itch. This is it.

I'm taken to a large corner office on the eleventh floor, with floor-to-ceiling windows offering uninterrupted views over LA. I'm left alone for a few minutes, which only makes my fears multiply, but I don't have to wait long before Ella Winter arrives.

She storms into the room, ethereal and thoroughly pissed off. Her silvery platinum hair frames a perfectly tanned heart-shaped face, high cheekbones and a slightly pointed nose. A white woman whose expression is completely frozen from a little too much Botox is by her side looking equally annoyed, while another girl, a few years older than Ella, trails them both, dark brown eyes flitting around the office with interest before assessing me.

'I'm going to lose the part because I don't have mutant lungs and a high fucking ponytail, aren't I?' Ella fumes, throwing a Prada bag down onto the conference table.

She's so wrapped up in her own world that she doesn't even see me sitting there. Instead, she closes her eyes in the middle of the room and takes a deep breath like she's trying to meditate or something.

The woman, who I know from my research is Kate Grayson, her mom and manager, huffs. 'Well, you'd better hope you've outdone Ariana's audition is all I'm saying on the matter. And apparently they're looking at Jacob Elordi to play Hercules.'

Ella opens one eye to check she's not being pranked. When she sees her mom is being deadly serious, she immediately closes them again and begins to pray. I mean, she literally starts praying. In her defence, I would too if I got the chance to be Jacob Elordi's love interest.

'God, I know I haven't been to church since I was like, six, but please give Ariana Grande tonsillitis. I promise I won't ask for anything else ever again.'

'You said that when you asked him to capsize Kylie Jenner's birthday yacht because it clashed with your own party,' Kate snaps. 'If you'd taken singing lessons as a kid like I told you to then we wouldn't be in this position. You'd be able to whistle note her under the table.'

Ella opens her eyes, incredulous. 'You had me in six acting classes, four dance rehearsals, beauty pageant prep *and* piano practice every week! Where would singing lessons have fit in?!'

Kate folds her arms. 'You'd better watch your tone when you're talking to me, missy.'

The other young woman, who looks kind of similar to Ella with blonde hair a few shades darker and two phones in hand, clears her throat politely and murmurs something about *company* under her breath. Ella and her mum finally look past their own first-world problems and see me sitting in an armchair, observing the whole scene in amazement.

'Oh. Hi. I didn't see you there!' Ella says, her tone changing so quickly that it completely throws me. 'You must be Abel!

It's so cool to finally meet you. I'm Ella, this is my mom, Kate, and that's Natalie, my assistant.'

I meet her smile with one of my own, standing up to shake her hand as Kate and Natalie step out of the room to leave us to it. She bats it away with a grin and throws her arms round my neck instead. 'We're supposed to be best friends now, right?'

She pulls away and throws a glance over me, taking me in properly and making up her mind about something in half a moment. 'Cute,' she says. I don't know if she means me or my clear inexperience in this new world, but I can feel myself blushing under her stare.

I'm fighting to keep my cool, but I'm a little starstruck to be honest. Here's Hollywood's 'next big thing' standing right in front me saying we're supposed to be best friends now. Surreal doesn't begin to cover it. I'm busy thinking about how even Ella's perfume smells rich when the door opens again.

God am I glad I'm here to witness this.

Ryan Hudson strides into the room with the confidence of a star who's been doing this for a long time. She's comfortable, both in this setting and in herself too. She's taller in real life and could've easily been a model if the whole acting thing hadn't work out. Her black locs have been swept up into a ponytail with a few strands left loose. She has a small gold hoop in her nose and is wearing a diamond choker round her neck. I'm stunned into silence by her presence.

I'm sure this is the first time Ella and Ryan have been in the same room as each other since the photos with Lucky were published. I don't know what I'm expecting. A screaming match? A literal fight? Should I alert security?

But instead, Ryan offers me a warm smile as if her day is going perfectly. 'Ryan,' she says as way of introduction. 'Nice to meet you.' I stammer my own name back and limply shake her hand.

Her eyes flit to Ella for a brief moment, but she doesn't say anything. She simply walks straight by her, face smoothed of any emotions, and takes a seat in one of the armchairs, scrolling through her phone, completely unbothered. Ella's bubble of confidence is punctured, but only for a second. She straightens up and the girl who first walked into the room is back in the building.

'You're not even going to say hello? Are you really going to be that insufferable?'

Ryan doesn't raise her eyes from her phone. 'You have no idea how insufferable I'm about to be,' she says, as if she's bored. Ella is stunned into silence, which I know must take a lot. In the few seconds I've been in her presence, I just know she's a talker.

After an eternity of awkwardness has me ready to dive out of the window head first, a middle-aged white woman with a severe blonde bob and tortoiseshell glasses enters the room, a small trail of people behind her. She carries a thick folder stuffed with papers, which she slams onto the conference table before spreading her arms in our direction with a huge smile on her face.

'If it's not the most famous teenagers in the world!' she sings. Her eyes flit over the three of us, realizing that one is missing. She sighs. 'Or most of them, anyway. No Lucky?' She glances at an assistant, who shakes his head.

'I guess we can get this show on the road without him,' she murmurs, gesturing for us to join her at the table while she takes a seat at the head of it. For just a second, she looks annoyed, but then she claps her hands together and beams. 'You have *no idea* how excited we are to have you guys on board for this new reboot of *Sunset High*. It's going to be *huge* – a truly pivotal moment in Omni Channel's history.'

It's a pretty grand statement, but I'm drawn in and intrigued all the same. The original *Sunset High* and the subsequent reboot have been pivotal for Omni Channel too, although for all the wrong reasons.

Her eyes flick towards me, and I feel my heart thump in my chest. She gives me a big grin, which doesn't quite have the relaxing effect I'm sure she's hoping for.

'Hi, sweetie. Sorry, I should have introduced myself properly – I'm Jill Anderson,' she declares in my direction. I assume the others must already know her since they're Omni Channel staples. 'I'm the head of publicity and brand image for *Sunset High*. This is my team.' She vaguely gestures at the people standing in a loose semicircle round the table. 'And it's our job to make sure we get you guys and this fantastic TV show in front of as many eyes as possible. We'll be in charge of interviews, photo shoots, appearances. We want every single person in the world to know your names, and we won't rest until they do.'

I glance at Ella and Ryan, sitting on opposite sides of the

table and refusing to look in each other's direction. Neither of them seem overly impressed. They must've heard this spiel a million times before. But I'm low-key starting to freak out. Or is it excitement? I can't tell, but there's a strong chance I might puke.

Before Jill can tip me over the edge, however, the door opens for a final time, and in walks Lucky Tate. Straight away I know that something is wrong.

Sure, I don't know him. All I know is what I've seen through the lens of a camera. But still, the golden sparkle that we all expect from those who have been blessed with the filter of fame, that confidence and bravado and maybe a hint of arrogance, is nowhere to be seen. Gone is the charismatic movie star. Instead, Lucky mooches into the room in an oversized black hoodie. He has dark circles under his eyes, his cheeks are sucked in and his mouth is a grim line that turns down slightly at the edges. To put it bluntly, he looks a mess.

'Nice of you to join us, honey,' Jill says brightly.

Lucky ignores her, and everyone else for that matter, crashing down into a chair next to me. He doesn't raise his eyes to the room, and instead seems to be studying the floor. Exhaustion? His schedule must be pretty busy, especially if he's just landed back from New York with Ella.

Ryan only briefly shoots a look at him, narrowing her eyes slightly before turning away again. Ella does the same, stealing glances every few seconds. Her knee bounces nervously. For two people who are apparently risking it all to date each other, they don't even seem able to say hello. I put it down to awkwardness in front of Ryan, who is doing a great job of remaining unbothered by any of this – on the surface at least. I wonder how she feels on the inside.

'As I was saying, we have lots lined up for you guys, and we're starting right away. No time like the present!' Jill checks some notes in her file. 'If we want to capitalize on the announcement, then we need to get you out there as soon as possible, so you'll be doing an interview on *The Late Late Show with Jeremy Love* tomorrow night.'

She goes on about commitments and appearances, all of it to make people fall in love with the show before a single second has even been aired. One thing is clear – Omnificent are sparing no cost when it comes to making *Sunset High* a triumph. I can't help but wonder if they're hoping a successful reboot will eliminate, or at least cloud, its past.

When Jill's done listing the schedule and arrangements, she removes her glasses and looks at each of us in turn. 'I can't stress enough to the four of you how important image will be to this show's success, and therefore *your* success. Your careers will be built off this. Everything you've ever hoped for and dreamed of could be waiting on the other side of this moment. But only if you don't step out of line. Stick together and stick to the script. For the good of the show and for the good of your futures.'

'Tell *her* that,' Ella mutters under her breath, glaring at Ryan like she's the one who made out with Ella's boyfriend behind her back. I almost feel mad on Ryan's behalf, but she stifles a yawn and examines her nails.

'Tell me yourself if you're brave enough,' she says flatly. Ryan meets Ella's stare head on, daring her to say something. Ella opens her mouth to bite back, but Jill cuts in.

'*Girls.*' It's a simple warning, but one that makes Ella fall back.

Ryan smirks. 'That's what I thought.'

Lucky just sits there staring at the table. It's like his body is physically present but completely empty. Wherever his mind has wandered to, it's far away from here.

'If you're quite done, let's talk rules.' Jill smooths down her suit jacket as she toys with the words in her head. 'Whatever you do in private is up to you, but it absolutely cannot breach the public wall. Out in the open, there's to be no drinking, no drugs, no excessive partying.'

She seems to be directing this at Lucky in particular. I peek at him out of the corner of my eye. Is he hungover? He doesn't respond, but a humourless smirk briefly pulls at his lips.

'As for any personal feelings, I don't care what's going on behind closed doors, but in public you play by the rules. We need to present a front that appeals to as many people as possible. I don't care if you want to drown each other in the Pacific. I don't care if you want the world to turn vegan, or you suddenly have the grand realization that you're actually gay. *Nothing* can rock the boat.'

'Basically, don't have an opinion or say anything of real value, regardless of what you do or don't stand for,' Ryan mutters. 'Just have an empty head. No thoughts, just vibes.'

Jill levels Ryan with a glare. 'That's exactly what I mean.'

61

She shrugs, leaning back in her chair. 'Let's say, for example, you suddenly tweet that you hate the president. You might despise him and his morals. You might think that he's a danger to marginalized communities. And you might well be right. But millions of people in this country voted for him to be in that position of power, and if you go out there running your mouth, every one of those people who voted *for* him now turn on *you*, and as a result, the show. That's millions of viewers, gone in a click, because you couldn't keep your opinions to yourself.'

Ryan doesn't blink. 'And bigots who *are* a danger to marginalized communities, and who will probably hate me anyway because I'm a successful *Black* girl in this industry, are my problem because . . .'

The air seems to leave the room for a moment. Jill falters, but she recovers quickly, smiling tightly. 'I'm not telling you that you can't have those opinions. And I'm not telling you that you're wrong.'

'Funny, because that's what it sounded like.'

'What I *am* saying,' Jill ploughs on, 'is that I'm trying to protect not only this show, but *you*. I've seen stars come and go, their careers cut short because they got off the fence. And what does it achieve in the end? You're left blacklisted. The thing you worked so hard for is taken from right out of your hands. And the people you stood for? Where will they be in a week, a month, a year's time? Will they still be patting you on the back? Will their gratitude give you what you crave, or will the light from their applause dim until you're left in the dark with nothing?'

Ryan goes to give a response, sitting up straighter with the bit between her teeth, but Jill beats her to it. 'It's only for a few months, okay? It's for your own good. I'm trying to protect you all – I'm on your side.'

I can tell Ryan isn't buying it, and neither is anyone else in the room. Ella and Lucky have disgusted looks on their faces, which echoes the exact way I feel right now. How can Jill say the only thing that matters is that the show doesn't suffer? Her words leave more than a bitter taste in my mouth. But she doesn't even notice. She takes our stunned silence as agreement, smiles and moves on.

Chapter Seven

A LIE, A WHOLE LIE AND NOTHING BUT A LIE

Ryan

I don't believe in the *Sunset* curse or whatever you want to call it, and I won't be scared by it either. What, am I meant to believe that there's some ominous fate written in the stars, plaguing a TV show about kids in high school? Please. If a higher power existed, they would have better things to do with their time than worry about which TV show gets renewed for another season.

However, when I'm given my room key at the hotel check-in desk and I realize I've been put on the thirteenth floor, the curse is the first thing I think of. 'Unlucky for some,' I mutter under my breath.

The hotel manager behind the desk, an older white guy called Stephen who has been only slightly less than rude while checking me in, suddenly beams. 'Ah, Miss Winter! And of course, Mr Tate. We've been awaiting your arrival,' he says, looking straight through me to the couple who have just walked through the doors.

I feel my heart drop to my stomach, but I force myself to maintain a blank mask. There's no way I'm going to let anyone know how I *really* feel. Hell would have to freeze over first.

Ella and Lucky stroll into the lobby, hand in hand, a huddle of paparazzi nearly crashing into the glass doors with their cameras as they try to snap some pictures. We all jumped into separate cars upon leaving Omni's headquarters, except Lucky and Ella, who climbed into a blacked-out SUV together while I tried not to seethe with absolute rage.

The paps have clearly been following them all the way here and are reluctant to let them out of their sight, but hotel security quickly jumps into action, forming a human barrier and pushing them back. They don't leave, though, and instead set up camp on the opposite side of the street, where they'll no doubt wait for the next glimpse of the new and happy couple.

The moment Lucky and Ella are safe from the prying eyes that hunt for them, their smiles slip, replaced with relief to have got inside and away from the cameras. Their hands immediately unlink, Ella removing a pair of Chanel shades I know for a damn fact are mine with one hand and shaking out her silvery hair with the other. She offers Stephen a beaming smile, which quickly falters when she sees me standing there too.

'These are for you, madam,' Stephen says, interrupting

the awkwardness by producing an enormous bouquet of grotesquely coloured flowers with a flourish. 'A welcome gift from Omnificent.'

'Oh, how *gorgeous*,' Ella says brightly, cradling the flowers and smelling the petals with a deep sigh. I know she's lying – white roses are her favourite. I clamp down on a surge of fury, but it's only made worse by what Stephen says next.

'Here are your room keys. You both have superior suites on the fourteenth floor.'

Is it a big deal on the surface? No, of course not. There are worse things in life than being given a junior suite on the thirteenth floor of a luxury hotel. However, I see that, and the flowers, for what they really are – Omni putting me in my place. I've been in this game for too long not to know how it works. We're all chess pieces for Omni to move wherever they please, and, right now, they're making it clear that Ella is currently the queen on this board.

'You good?' Lucky murmurs in my direction as Ella happily signs an autograph for Stephen's daughter.

'Just fucking peachy,' I snap back. 'Not even a *text* to tell me? Are you serious?'

Lucky holds up his hands, guilt forming a grimace on his face. 'I know. I'm sorry, Ry. I . . . had some shit going on. I wasn't in a good place. I should've called and told you first, but I thought Omni would've given you the heads-up.'

'You mean you expected them to show a shred of decency and respect for the lives of their puppets?' I snort. 'You should know that's asking too much.' I soften slightly when I take a proper look at him. I know him well enough to see he's not doing good. 'You look like shit, by the way.'

Lucky laughs. 'Thanks. I feel it too.'

'I'm serious. You're drinking?'

Lucky ducks his head. 'I'm getting by as best I can. Give me a break.'

'I'm trying to look out for you.' I move myself into his eyeline so he has no choice but to look at me. 'How are you doing? *Really?*'

He huffs a bitter laugh. 'Being back in the eye of the storm, you mean? Like you said – just fucking peachy.'

I give him a knowing smile. 'I know it's shit, but I'm glad you're here. This way I can make sure you're looking after yourself. Well, if you ever decide to respond to my texts, that is.'

He gives me a sheepish smile just as Ella comes over to join us. She's uncertain of herself for once. 'Can I talk to you?' she says to me.

'Ah, attempting to get your knife out of my back?'

Lucky swallows a laugh as Ella glares at him. When she looks back at me, it's with softer eyes. 'Just a minute. Please.'

I sigh like this is an inconvenient chore and nod. Like I was going to say no. I already felt my resolve wavering the second she walked through the hotel doors. We step aside to a quieter spot in the lobby as Lucky heads up to his room.

'Play nice,' he says with a smirk over his shoulder.

'So . . .' I say pointedly. 'My sunglasses? My *boyfriend*? What do you want next? The keys to my closet since you want to be me so bad?'

67

Ella rolls her eyes. 'Oh, come on, stop being dramatic. I wanted to tell you myself, but Omni had me on a photo shoot. You know I would've called if I could.'

'You couldn't pick up just once? I tried your cell a million times and only got that irritating voicemail I told you to change because you sound like an obnoxious brat.'

Ella at least has the respect to look guilty and a little ashamed. 'I'm sorry, okay? I was wrong, and I should've told you. Can we move past this? I don't want it to come between us.'

She looks me in the eye, and I hold her stare. I know enough of Ella Winter to see the honesty there. Any last trace of resistance I've built up dissolves.

'No more lies?' I say.

'I didn't lie!'

I fold my arms.

Ella concedes. 'Sure. Let's just move on.'

We hug it out, holding on to each other for a second too long, then head up to our rooms. I've hardly closed the door when my phone rings. I see the caller ID and roll my eyes.

'And to what do I owe this pleasure?' I mutter, not bothering to say hello.

Jill laughs. 'Let's put the handbag down, sweetie. I'm not here to fight. I'm here to help make things better, remember?'

I've always been good at pushing the emotions that I'm really feeling far down, sometimes to places I can hardly reach myself. As a Black girl in this industry, I've had no choice. You can't ever let them see you as weak or ungrateful or it's game over. Right now, I want to snap, let my frustration fly.

But I take a breath and bring myself back to centre, just like I've done every time before.

'Of course you are,' I say instead. 'But if you wouldn't mind skipping the pleasantries and getting to the point? I'm scheduled to watch paint dry this evening and I would hate to miss it.' A *little* attitude can't hurt. Jill laughs some more, but I can hear that I've touched a nerve.

'I have the press on my back trying to add some salt and pepper to the Lucky and Ella story.' Jill says it casually enough as if it's not a big deal. Like it's just business. 'We want to control this narrative as much as possible and not let the story get away from us, so I need you to jump on a call with a reporter and tell them the truth – you and Lucky were already over and there's no hard feelings between you and Ella.'

'Oh, I'm allowed to tell people we're over now that it's good timing to boost the *Sunset High* announcement? Thanks for the permission. I'm *so* glad I've got you looking out for me.'

Jill doesn't say anything for a second. When she talks again, her tone is clipped. 'Just say that things are perfectly fine and everyone's moving forward. The usual spiel.'

'You want me to lie, you mean.'

'Call it whatever you want, honey, but I've got Page Six telling me you're currently hospitalized for heartbreak and TMZ in my ear ready to run a piece about your pregnancy.'

'My *WHAT*?!' I splutter. I've been at the centre of my fair share of the press' spiteful stories before, ones designed to paint me in unflattering lights, but these lies are a whole hop, skip and jump past the line. 'I've never been pregnant. You know that's bullshit. And I'm *certainly* not pathetic enough to be hospitalized with fucking heartbreak.'

'Exactly, sweetie, but you try telling them that. So give a brief comment to a journalist to explain you're doing fine and can't wait to start work on *Sunset High*. I'll leak a few quotes from "sources" to help spread the story that everything is great behind the scenes. Then we'll have control over the narrative once more.'

'Or it'll just make everything worse,' I mutter.

'Nonsense, angel,' Jill says with a condescending laugh that makes me want to smash my second phone of the week. 'It's all about redirecting the fires. You know how to play this game by now. This is what we want. If they're talking about you, they're talking about the show. You don't fight the rumours – you just mould them into something else that puts you in a better light. It boosts your profile, the show's profile, and everyone wins. We just need to make sure that the seeds we plant in the press don't get out of control. All publicity is good publicity, right? So what do you say?'

'Isn't it your job as my representative for the show to give the quote on my behalf?' I ask in a last attempt to avoid this. I'd rather sit on a cactus while juggling knives than talk to a journalist right now.

'You know I usually would, but a rep quote never quite has the same effect. If it comes straight from your mouth, it'll pack a more powerful punch. Just don't mention the pregnancy or hospitalization rumours. Best to leave them alone. If you shoot them down, something else just as spiteful will grow in its place. People will have forgotten by tomorrow.'

I roll my eyes so hard that I'm surprised they don't come out of my sockets altogether. Of course she doesn't want me to mention the rumours that will be getting the most attention. That would be killing the buzz before Omni can wring it for all the press it's worth. But even though I hate to admit it, I know Jill's right. I can fight these stories as hard as I want, set the story straight a million times, but like some fucked-up version of whack-a-mole, you bury one story only for several more to pop up straight away. It's better to have my say while I still can.

I inwardly groan, falling into a chair by the floor-to-ceiling window of my suite and dragging my knees up to my chest. The sun is beginning to set over Beverly Hills, basking LA in a lavender haze.

'Fine, whatever. When?'

'I've got Hannah Wilkes from the *Daily Eye* on hold – I'll pitch myself out of the window before I give Page Six or TMZ the exclusive after the stunts they've tried to pull. They can have the sloppy seconds. I'll patch the journalist through to you.'

Of course Jill already has the reporter waiting. She'd framed the whole conversation as a question, knowing full well it was an order. I resign myself to getting this done and out of the way, because what's the point in fighting it?

'Okay, they'll be on the line in a moment. Keep it brief. I'll stay on the call just in case. Oh, and I've booked for you and the others to go for dinner tonight. The car will pick you up from the hotel at eight.'

71

Before I can say another word, there's a beep and a new voice joins the call.

'Hi, Hannah, honey. I've got Ryan for you,' Jill says, so sickly sweet that I feel my entire body cringe.

Whoever the hell Hannah is, she clears her throat and jumps in with an overexaggerated greeting that I can smell is fake from a mile off. Talk about a kiss ass. Then again, I shouldn't be so hypocritical – I'm about to join the club.

'Hey!' I say brightly. I sound so cheerful that you'd think I was sunning myself on a beach in Hawaii instead of straight up lying through my teeth.

'Ryan, it's so nice to speak to you!' Hannah sounds like she's about to take off and hit the moon with the energy she's putting into her words. 'I won't keep you for long. I just wanted to get a quote on how you're feeling, and if you can tell me anything more about the situation from your perspective. I know it must be a really hard time for you right now . . .'

She's trying to lead me to the water, hoping that I'll drink the poison. Framing the question as if I'm the victim and this is my moment to get my side across? *Nice try, Hannah.*

'Oh gosh, don't be silly!' I actually throw my head back and laugh. I'm an actress after all, I don't do things by halves. 'I'm doing just fine. You know, in life, things happen, relationships don't work out. Lucky and I mutually decided a while ago that we were better off as friends. We're still really close, and, of course, we'll be working on *Sunset High* together, so I can't wait to dive into that and have a friendly face on set.'

'That's great. I'm so glad to hear it,' Hannah says in a tone that makes it clear she's far from happy about any of these updates. She chuckles to fill the dead air, but I know she's circling, thinking of a way to prod for a better response. She's getting ready to attack, but my guard is steely. 'Of course, you'll have more than one friendly face on set, though. Unless you're saying that your friendship with Ella isn't what it once was . . .?'

Jesus Christ. She sounds like she's breaking the news of a dead hamster to a five-year-old.

'Oh, you *know* that's a lot of gossip and not a whole lot of truth,' I say. 'Ella and I are best friends. As if we'd let something as inconsequential as a *boy* break that up! Ella is and will always be my rock. We're all adults here, and we can't wait to work together on this new project.'

Hannah wants to press for more but Jill jumps in. Timed to perfection. You give them just enough to run a story, but you cut it short before you say something you'll regret.

'We've got to run, Hannah. Let me know when the article goes live, won't you? Bye, sweetie!'

Without waiting for a response, Jill boots Hannah from the call and gives it a few seconds to make sure she's gone. 'Asshole,' she says. 'But perfectly handled, angel. That should keep the dogs at bay for a while longer. Just remember not to call Lucky *inconsequential* in future – he is our leading man after all! Anyway, enjoy dinner tonight. And remember to smile for the cameras, won't you?'

Before I have a chance to reply, Jill hangs up. I'm muttering a two-word response of my own into the silence when I see a text.

Ah, because someone leaving me a gift-wrapped box of old *Sunset High* posters with Penelope Daunt's face scratched out wasn't evidence enough. Gotcha. I crawl onto my bed and let my body sigh into itself, suddenly exhausted. The last thing I want to do tonight is go out and face the world. I just want to lock myself away and sleep.

The hotel phone by my bed rings.

What now?

'Hello?'

'Hi, Miss Hudson – it's Casey from the front desk. We have a Brad Bolton on the line?'

I frown. Why didn't he just call my cell?

'Thanks, you can put him through.'

There's a click and a moment of silence. Then another, and another.

'Hello? Brad?' No response. 'Brad?'

Nothing. Bad connection? I'm about to hang up when I hear something on the other end of the line – a rustle, like someone moving. Silence again. Then the sound of slow and measured breaths. Realization dawns, and my skin prickles. This isn't Brad.

'Who the fuck is this?'

There's no answer. Just breathing. Then the drone of a dead line after the call is hung up. I slam the phone down, forcing myself to stay calm. *It's just a prank or something. I'm safe here*, I tell myself. *Nobody can reach me.* Up here, I'm like a princess in a tower. Except it occurs to me that princesses in fairy tales are usually trapped.

I shake my head. Not me. I never believed in fairy tales anyway.

Chapter Eight

WINTER

Ella

I'm not scared of many things. Sure, I'm not a fan of spiders or clowns, nor am I particularly fond of horror movies, even though *The Ghost of Halloweens Past* was the first role I booked in a feature film when I was twelve years old. But if there's one thing that scares me, it's my mom.

I'm not quite sure when I first realized I was scared of her. When I was a little kid, just barely walking and out of diapers, I remember how she'd sit me on the chair in front of her vanity mirror and swipe make-up brushes across my face. She'd coo and laugh while she did it, and it made me giggle too. I knew in those moments that I was making her happy, even though I didn't know how or why.

My dad, Mitch, was an alcoholic. He and Mom used to

argue a lot when I was growing up, huge screaming matches becoming the backdrop to my childhood. Mom's temper exceeded my dad's by a clear mile. She'd pick up an ornament from the mantlepiece or a book from a shelf and throw it in his direction while I hid behind a door, watching it all unfold through the crack between the frame and the wall.

When Mom wasn't mad at him, she'd turn on me. She'd say I was a daddy's girl, which wasn't strictly true as I never felt entirely loved by either of them. But there was no telling her that. She was convinced that if I ever did anything she didn't like – asking Dad to take me for ice cream, not wanting her to brush and style my hair – I was doing it on purpose to spite her.

The only time she felt otherwise was if I did exactly what she told me to. That was the only way to please her, so I drilled it into myself that if I listened and went along with her wishes, everything would work out. She only wanted what was best for me after all. That was what she said, and why would she lie?

I won my first beauty pageant when I was six, and Mom was thrilled. I don't think I'd ever seen her so happy. She kept pulling me into these long and hard hugs, telling me that she was so proud, and that one day, if I kept doing pageants and auditions like she told me to, I'd make lots of money and we'd all live happily ever after.

We already lived in California, so it was easy for Mom to drive me around for auditions. She dyed my hair blonder, put blush on my cheeks, read lines with me instead of bedtime stories. I did it all because every time something went right, Mom was so happy it was as if she'd floated up into the sky

77

and touched the stars. I think it made me happy too, although I couldn't be sure that I wasn't just mirroring her. Was I proud of my success, happy that I'd booked another job? Or were my mom's feelings so all-consuming that they seeped into me until I had no choice but to believe they were my own?

I only had a small part in *The Ghost of Halloweens Past*, but I must've done a good job because I booked another role, and then another, and another. With each pay cheque, we were able to better our situation. At first, we paid off debts and bought a new sofa to replace the one that had springs poking out of the cracked leather. Then when I booked a recurring speaking role on TV, we got a new car. By the time I'd turned fifteen, my parents had divorced, and Mom moved us into a bigger house in a better part of town – one where the neighbours looked down on us because Mom said they were posh snobs. But the work kept coming in, and my career was going from strength to strength.

Still, Mom always wants more.

We're rich now. There's no doubt about it. The family bank account, where all my earnings are kept, has more zeroes in it than we could've ever possibly imagined. My parents would have had to work four lifetimes over to earn even half of it. We have a large house in Calabasas, and Mom travels with me around the world as my manager. If I sign the new contract with Omni, I could be the biggest star they've ever had.

And yet, it isn't enough.

'You've lost us *millions* of dollars!' Mom yells, not bothering to keep her voice down. 'The *Hercules* job was worth more than anything you've ever done before. Being offered the role of Meg would've catapulted us to a whole new level. We could've used that to negotiate better contract terms with Omnificent, but instead you let a singer named after a Starbucks drink beat you to it!'

I'm sitting on the bed, clutching a pillow. The darkening sky beyond my window reflects the mood in my hotel suite. My eyes sting, first from crying triggered by rejection, then from the ugly feeling in the pit of my stomach that tells me I've let my family down. Now the tears have dried and I'm left almost empty, nothing but dejection eating away at me.

'She was always going to be the front runner,' I try, but my voice is weak in the face of Mom's fury.

Her face is so flushed with rage, I can hardly stand to look in her direction, scared of what I'll see there. I look at the door instead, worried her anger will burst through the cracks and find ears not meant for this conversation.

'You're lazy and *selfish*,' Mom continues. 'If you cared for me *at all*, for how hard I've worked to get you to this point, you would have nailed the audition. Now we don't have a leg to stand on with Omnificent. They'll know they haven't got any competition. If we don't sign their contract soon, they'll lower their original offer or take it off the table altogether.'

Is that such a bad thing? I don't dare say that out loud but . . . Yes, the new contract with Omni is a great deal on the surface. However, I still have my reservations about it. If I sign on the dotted line, my fate will be sealed. Omni will own me. Plus, I still have to find a way to tell Ryan about it. If they're offering me leading roles, that means she'll get pushed down the pecking order. That isn't going to be a fun conversation. I know it's kill or be killed in this industry, but this doesn't seem fair.

'I need a bit more time to think about it,' I murmur.

'What is there to think about?' Mom snaps, her mood souring more by the second. 'We can't afford to lose what they're willing to give us. God knows you seem incapable of booking other roles right now.'

I sniff, trying to rein my emotions back in. 'I can't book every job. There are a million other girls out there all going for the same thing. I won't win every time. But I'm trying my best, I promise.'

'YOU ARE NOT TRYING AT ALL!' Mom roars. In a fit of rage, she picks up the large vase of flowers from the side table and launches it across the room. It shatters, leaving the flowers to wilt on the floor. I flinch at the sound.

'Mom, please, stop! Someone will hear.'

'AND SO WHAT IF THEY DO! Let them hear what a disappointment you are! They should know that they can take any job from right under your nose because God knows you won't put in any effort to book it yourself!'

Mom finally takes a deep breath, letting her rage turn from crashing waves into lapping water, just like the shrink told her to. She closes her eyes and massages her chest.

'All this stress will bring on another heart attack. And you know what? It'll be your fault. Hopefully this one finishes me off, huh?'

The words punch me in the gut, just like they were supposed

to. The guilt they unleash is almost unbearable. But Mom doesn't stay to see their effect. With one last look of disgust, she marches out of the door, slamming it for good measure.

Alone, I let my walls down, the immense sadness I've bottled up finally pouring out. But I only let it last for a few moments before I start to piece myself back together again, like always. I have a dinner to go to tonight, and I won't let the world see me as weak. I won't let them see that anything is wrong.

There's a knock at the door and, panicking, I quickly dab at my eyes. When I answer with a smile on my face, my assistant Natalie is there, half a dozen expensive dresses sent to me for free by various designers draped over her arm. The second she sees me, she sighs apologetically. I clearly haven't hidden my crying well enough. She quickly shuffles into the room and drops the dresses on the bed, then glances at the vase in pieces on the carpet.

'It was an accident,' I say quickly. 'I knocked it off the table.'

Natalie thinks twice about letting it go. She knows better than anyone else what goes on behind closed doors. She's been with me for a year now and has seen a lot of it first-hand. But she never says a word. She just makes sure that she's there when I need her most. She's older than me, in her early twenties now, and in a way she feels like the big sister I never had.

'The dresses can wait,' she says. 'You look like you need a hug.'

She opens her arms wide with a warm smile. I only hesitate for a moment, and then I fall into her embrace, holding on tight.

Chapter Nine

THE LION'S DEN

Lucky

You only go to The Big Kid if you want to be seen. It's a high-end restaurant and bar with a who's who of the Hollywood elite on the guest list and paparazzi who notoriously camp outside waiting to see who will turn up. A car door opens, a big name bows their head as a frantic flurry of flashes chase after them, and then those pictures appear online almost immediately before being splashed all over the next day's newspapers. The routine was the same every time and it never failed. Just one way in a million to get free press. That's why Jill booked it.

From the window of my hotel suite, I can see the commotion unfurling on the sidewalk below. A crowd of mostly restless teenagers have caught wind that we'll be leaving the premises soon, a whisper I'm certain must have come from Jill. No doubt she slipped an anonymous message to one of the many Omni Channel fan accounts online. There's no such thing as a simple coincidence in this fame game. The crowd have been separated into two and pushed behind metal barricades on either side of the hotel's entrance. A huddle of photographers waits amongst them too, cameras in hand, poised to jump into action at a moment's notice. I never used to fear them, but now they only trigger bad memories and unrelenting grief.

I down a shot from the minibar to soothe my nerves, then think twice and shoot another. It's not exactly a cure, but it helps to numb everything, for now at least, and it gives me the hint of bravery I lack when I'm sober to face those monsters.

My thoughts are interrupted by the vibrating of my phone. I know there's little point in ignoring it. She'll only keep calling.

'What trouble am I in now?' I mutter when the line connects.

'Oh, sweetie, don't be silly,' Jill says. 'I'm just checking in to make sure everything's okay. I know this is your first time back at work since . . .' She trails off, leaving an awkward silence to fill in the gaps.

'Since my mom died in a car accident after being chased by the photographers that Omni called so they could get a picture of me and Ryan together, even though we weren't in the car? Oh yeah, I'm doing just fine. Being back in this circus is *exactly* what the doctor ordered.' I clutch the phone tightly to my ear.

Jill switches tack, her tone softening. 'I'm sorry, Lucky. I really am. I know this is hard on you, and we really appreciate you coming back to us so soon.'

'Did I have a choice? Or was I forced to come back because of a contract I signed when I was thirteen? One that Omni waved in my face while telling me the schedule couldn't be changed for personal reasons.' I snort in derision. 'But, hey, at least they offered to put a grief counsellor on set so I've got someone to break down to in between takes. I forgot to say thanks for that. Gratitude must've slipped my mind.'

'I understand why you're angry, Lucky,' Jill starts. 'I know the world doesn't seem fair right now.'

'Oh, Jesus, spare me the spiel,' I snap, trying my hardest not to let my anger explode. 'We both know those are empty words. Why don't you tell me the reason you really called so I can get on with this sham you're calling *good publicity*?'

There's a brief pause. 'I wanted to make sure you were prepared for this evening.'

'Not my first rodeo, but thanks for your concern.'

'I'm being serious. There will be a lot of eyes on you tonight. People want to see you back out there. They miss you!'

'Do they miss me, or the person I've been forced to pretend to be all this time?'

'Lucky . . .'

'Forget it. I already know the answer. Now if that's all you called for, I've got to get ready to look the part for this fucked-up fairy tale you've created.'

'There is one more thing actually,' Jill says quickly. I can tell by her tone that it's serious. 'There's no easy way to say

84

this. I know you're struggling, and I understand. Truly, I do. But . . . we need you to stop the excessive drinking.'

It winds me for a moment. I start to splutter a defence, but Jill jumps in to stop me.

'I hate to be the one to deliver the news, but it didn't go unnoticed that you were . . . a little worse for wear earlier. You were late, and I could smell the alcohol on you. People higher up than me, all the way at the top, have had it brought to their attention too.'

'How?' is all I manage to say, the word scraping against my throat as it leaves me.

'A pap in New York got a picture of you swigging from a bottle in the street. He said it was five in the morning and you were swaying all over the place, completely out of it.'

I flinch. How could I not have seen that I was being followed? But as soon as I think that, I already know I was drunk enough to walk entire blocks without seeing anything at all.

'We had to cough up seventy-five thousand dollars for the rights to the pictures so he wouldn't be able to sell them elsewhere, but this can't happen again. You're not just anyone, Lucky – you're a role model that kids look up to.' Jill sighs, as if she's reprimanding a child. 'If you need anything, you only have to tell me and I'll sort it. But this needs to stop, or else we'll have no choice but to take action.'

I try to ignore the whispers of rage echoing in my mind, telling me to fight back against being controlled, but its pull is more irresistible with every word that sinks in. The only reason I'm drinking in the first place is because

Omni got their claws into me. It's because of *them* that my mom is dead.

'What do you mean *take action*?'

'Rehab, Lucky. If this problem continues, we'll intervene. Please don't make me do that. We just want you to be okay.'

'If you wanted me to be okay, Jill, you wouldn't have got my mother killed.' My voice breaks. 'Fuck you. Fuck rehab. Fuck Omni.'

Without waiting to hear another one of Jill's empty words, I hang up and hit the shower. The water is searingly hot, almost unbearably so, but the burn on my skin makes me feel like I'm washing my problems away. The Lucky Tate who smiles and winks for the cameras, who never puts a foot wrong, who is adored and almost worshipped – that's the Lucky who needs to be front and centre, tonight and for evermore. The broken boy who can't free himself from the maze of grief in his head must always stay hidden. The real me, whoever that even is now, has to remain in the dark.

There's a knock at the door of my suite a minute later. I think about ignoring it – it's probably just someone from the front desk letting me know that the car is here – but then the knock comes again. I tut and turn the water off, grabbing a towel from the heated rack before wrapping it round my waist and going to answer the door, still dripping wet.

It's Abel, dressed up in a tailored black suit over a fitted white tee, paired with crisp white sneakers. He'd look effortlessly cool . . . if his expression wasn't so awkward having laid eyes on me.

He immediately starts to blush, dropping his gaze and then quickly realizing that he's now focusing on my towel. He's cute when he's nervous. He starts to stutter, mentioning something about a package. I raise my eyebrows, enjoying every second as Abel hears the clumsy phrasing with his own ears. He looks up to the ceiling like he's ready for the heavens to open up and claim him. Finally he raises a hand that's holding a small box gift wrapped with a silky black ribbon that's been tied into an intricate bow.

'You shouldn't have,' I tease.

'Someone at the front desk delivered it to me by accident,' Abel murmurs. I can tell he's trying so damn hard not to let his eyes go wandering again, but I find myself thinking that I want them to. 'It's addressed to you. Thought I'd bring it up since we're, like . . . neighbours, I guess?'

'Neighbours?' I ask, trying to contain my amusement so as not to embarrass him any further. I shouldn't be flirting right now, but it's a pretty good distraction. 'Aren't we supposed to be more than that?'

'M-more than that?' Abel asks.

I smile innocently. 'We're meant to be best friends now, right? That's what Jill said.'

'Oh. Yeah, of course.'

There's a silence. Abel looks like he can't decide if he's supposed to leave. I nod at the package in his hand.

'Can I have my gift then, or are you going to keep holding it hostage?'

He apologizes without needing to and all but throws the

present in my direction. I hold the door open for him to come in, then assess the box, unwrapping the bow and lifting the lid. Inside is a thin gold chain. *Fitting.* A handwritten note is attached, welcoming me back. It's signed: *With love, from Jill and all at Omnificent.* I remove the chain, letting it dangle from my hand. It's a bribe to buy my co-operation and it makes me feel sick. I'd rather walk out into the lion's den naked than wear it myself.

'Here,' I say. 'A welcome gift from me to you. It'll look better on you anyway.' I unhook the clasp and hold it out to Abel.

'Oh, you don't have to do that,' he says.

'I know I don't. But I want to. Or are you going to decline a gift . . .?'

Abel frowns a little. 'Technically *you're* declining a gift by giving it to me in the first place.'

I laugh. 'Touché. Here, let me.'

I step round him, placing a gentle hand on his shoulder. He instinctively tenses up, but then he relaxes under my touch as I drape the chain round his neck where it settles along his collarbone. I fasten the clasp, my fingers grazing the back of his neck. I let them linger for just a moment, enjoying the flush of his warm skin beneath my hands. When I turn him round to get a better look, we're standing so close he fills my entire vision. His lips have parted slightly, his breath quickening. My own races to meet it. I examine the necklace, nod to myself, then step back.

'I told you it'd look better on you than me.'

Abel glances in the large gilded mirror leaning against the

wall, his hand touching the chain. He smiles. 'I guess it doesn't look so bad.'

'Trust me, I know what I'm talking about.' I smile back. 'Well, I guess I'll see you down there, *neighbour*.'

Abel tries to hide a small smirk, then lets himself out. I watch the door for a moment after it's closed. I kind of wish he hadn't left – a thought that surprises me. But just as quickly my smile begins to fade, and I start to prepare myself for what lies in wait outside.

Chapter Ten

ALL THE WORLD'S A STAGE

Abel

NEIGHBOUR?!

I don't want to be dramatic, but I can't believe I stood in front of Lucky Tate while he was dripping wet with nothing but a towel on, stumbling and fumbling over my words like a clown, and then called him my *neighbour*. What am I, a twelve-year-old kid with a crush at their first school disco?

My ego is saved a bruising though as my mind entertains something else. I'd been about to knock on the door when I'd overheard Lucky on the phone. I could only hear his side of the conversation, but what it revealed gave me food for thought. First of all, Lucky blamed Omni for his mom's death. I knew she'd been in a car accident and that paparazzi were involved, but the public details were otherwise vague. What did Omni have to do with the accident?

Not to mention that the person on the other end of the line, presumably Jill, had seemingly brought up the idea of sending Lucky to rehab. My guess was for alcohol dependency, since I'd noticed an open bottle of tequila on the bar in his suite, but it could be for anything. I think about the way Lucky looked when he walked into the meeting earlier, just a shell of the person the world knew him to be. I'd assumed it was as a result of a hectic schedule and his flight from New York. I could definitely relate – my own jet lag had forced me to take a nap before dinner. But could Lucky's state have been a sign of something more serious?

With plenty to think about, I make my way down to the hotel bar, where the pandemonium outside is reaching fever pitch. The fans, restless from waiting so long, are chanting for Lucky and singing songs to raise their spirits. It's mayhem. My adrenaline is skyrocketing, coming to the boil, and threatening to spill over.

Ella sashays into the bar looking glamorous in a Versace dress and impossibly high heels that demand attention as they clack on the marble floor. Her hair has been blow-dried to perfection, falling in loose curls over her shoulders, and a dark blue stone cut into the shape of a heart sparkles at the base of her neck. She looks immortal, like a goddess who dazzles with the force of a thousand suns.

'Ready to put on a show?'

'As I'll ever be,' I say, standing to receive the air kiss Ella sends my way.

She perches on the edge of a stool, flicking her hair over her shoulder so she's shielded from the onlookers in the bar. I hadn't even realized that they'd started taking pictures but, as if she has a sixth sense, Ella's noticed.

She offers me a smile, one that seems genuine and warm. I don't know why I'm surprised. I guess I'd made up my mind about her already – a slightly bratty star used to getting her own way. But she places a reassuring hand on my arm and gives it a squeeze.

'Just remember to keep walking. Don't stop or they'll literally devour you. Oh, and smile! Look like you're having fun out there. Even if you're not, don't let them see that.'

Ryan is next, strutting into the hotel bar like it's a catwalk. She's wearing a black minidress that looks like it's been poured onto her body to create a metallic second skin, with strappy Louboutin heels and a row of spikes that cuff her ear.

'Besties for the night then,' Ryan says. She links arms with Ella, which is news to me since I thought they were fighting. But whatever's going on, they hold on to each other tightly as if they're protecting one another.

'Shall we get it over with?' Ella murmurs. There's a hint of excitement underlining her words, and it must be contagious because I feel it too. 'We'll go first, and then Abel, you wait for Lucky?'

'Sure thing.'

Ella and Ryan turn on these megawatt smiles, then stride for the entrance holding hands. They're met with screams as the hotel doors open, white-hot flashes lighting up the night.

They giggle and laugh, not stopping for a second until they reach the car.

'Waiting for me? What a gentleman you are.'

I turn round to find Lucky watching too. He's no longer wearing a towel (unfortunately), but he still looks just as good. He's changed into some fitted trousers and a printed shirt that's open just enough to reveal the curve of his chest. It's like he's turned on a switch and dialled it up to a million. No cracks are visible in his veneer. Right now, he's Lucky Tate at full power, all smiles and confidence. Still, when he gets closer, I smell alcohol. It's mostly concealed by his intoxicating aftershave, but it's there all the same. He clearly isn't worried about Omni's threats, or he simply doesn't care.

'So they've made up?' Lucky asks.

'It seems so.'

Lucky chuckles to himself. 'Of course they have. Shall we? On your six.'

I fight a smile as we start walking. Even with all those people waiting, it feels like I've got a shield round me now.

'What's with Ella and Ryan anyway?' I find myself asking, desperate to know more of the story. 'Besides . . . well, *you.*'

Lucky bursts out laughing. 'Oh, I'm nothing to do with it. Believe me, it's best if you don't ask questions and just go with the flow. It makes everything a *lot* easier.' He slings an arm over my shoulder like we're a couple of frat bros.

'Whatever I say next, throw your head back and laugh for the cameras. Trust me.'

I don't have time to react as the hotel doors are opened once more and we're met with a wall of screams so loud that I think my eardrums might burst. Exhilaration rises until the thrill is almost unbearable. Then, as Lucky leans in so his lips are just a breath away, it consumes me all at once.

'That chain looks real good on you.'

The words leave their trace on my ear, sending a ripple of – lust? Desire? Some stupid schoolboy crush? – through me. For just a second, every part of my body feels it. But then the flashes and screams bring me back to the moment. I throw my head back and laugh, just like Lucky said to, and he does the same, pulling me in close like we've known each other for ever.

And I wish we had. I want to know everything there is to know about Lucky Tate. I want to pick apart his exterior and find out what lives there, because behind his guard there are darker shadows lurking. He hides them well, but now that I've stepped through the illusion, I know all three of them are hiding their demons, hoping they remain unseen.

I want to meet them all.

Dinner is an odd charade that unfolds like a movie. As we're ferried in the back of an SUV with tinted windows from the hotel to the restaurant, it feels like filming for *Sunset High* has already begun. It's as if real life has ceased to exist and we're all just living in some version of *The Truman Show*, the eyes of the world on us.

In the car, everyone's in good spirits. We laugh together like any other teenagers. A bond has instinctively formed between us, built on the common ground of the unique position we've all found ourselves in. We're a team. But, I remind myself, as I joke along with them, I'm an intruder who's managed to breach their ranks, and they have no idea. Maybe it's dark-hearted, but a small part of me relishes this secret. I'm here behind enemy lines, ready to find out the truth about my brother and Omni. I hope revenge will taste sweet.

As soon as we arrive at The Big Kid and our car doors open, there's what can only be described as a wave of sound that erupts and then rolls towards us. The flashes from the cameras, the scream of fans, the pushing and shoving and jostling to get closer to us. It feels like water sweeping me up and then yanking me under the surface. I can hardly breathe, and it's only once we clear the restaurant doors that every emotion starts to cascade through me at once. I have to hold the wall to ground myself.

'You okay?' Lucky asks, coming up behind me as the doors close and drown out the sound. He steps in front of me as Ryan and Ella surround me too. I realize they're trying to shield me from view so I can have a moment to reset.

'Yeah, all good,' I say, shaking it off. 'The attention is just . . . a lot.'

'Don't worry about it,' Ryan says kindly. 'We all feel the same way.'

I frown. 'You do? But you all walked through that fire like it was nothing.'

Ella laughs softly. 'We've had a lot more practice at hiding how it really makes us feel.'

Lucky puts his hands on my shoulders and breathes in through his nose, then out through his mouth, nodding for me to follow his lead. I do, and as I look into his eyes, I start to feel—

No.

I shut down the thought quickly. This was *exactly* what I'd been worried about in the first place. Being immune to Lucky's charms was always going to be a longshot, but I'm here for a reason. I'm not throwing myself in front of the world just to start crushing hard on him. I have to keep focus. I can't afford a distraction like Lucky to throw me off course.

'You good?' Lucky asks.

I step out of his reach and nod. 'Never better,' I say, avoiding his gaze. 'Shall we?'

Lucky takes Ella's hand as a suited waiter guides us past the other diners, some of whom start taking pictures of Hollywood's latest golden couple without even trying to be subtle about it. We're shown to a booth in the back where nobody else can see us before the waiter departs so we can settle in. Even here, huddled round a private table in an exclusive restaurant, the glances and stares don't feel far away.

The moment the waiter disappears, Ella lets go of Lucky's hand and goes straight for Ryan. I think she's . . . I don't know, going to fight her? Which doesn't make sense considering I now know they've made up. But, instead, she wraps her arms round Ryan's neck and gives her a long, deep kiss on the lips before nestling into her. My eyeballs nearly fall out of their sockets.

'Sorry, Lucky,' Ella says with a grin when she finally extricates herself from Ryan's embrace. She leans over and gives her one last peck.

'Don't be,' Lucky says. 'Who am I to stand in the way of true love?'

Ryan takes one look at my dumbfounded expression and bursts out laughing.

'We forgot to tell him,' she says, linking hands with Ella under the table. 'No time like the present, I suppose.' She points to herself. 'Gay.'

Ella flicks her hair over her shoulder. 'I would say I'm, like, fluid? I draw the line at dating an Aries, though.' Ryan rolls her eyes and laughs before planting a kiss on the hand she's holding. Lucky pretends to throw up.

'Also gay,' he says. 'Unwillingly so, but gay all the same.'

'Unwillingly gay?' I ask, my mind still trying to grasp all this new information. Ella and Ryan is a plot twist I wasn't expecting, but *Lucky Tate* stepping out of the closet is a whole different ball game. It feels like Christmas just came early, Mariah Carey appearing from her grotto to sprinkle some festive joy over me.

Lucky scrunches up his nose. 'Do you think I'd actively choose to like *men*? Evil creatures, the whole lot of them. I have some self-respect, thank you.'

'You do? Could've fooled me,' Ryan teases, giving Lucky a wink. He shows her the finger, then locks eyes with me. My gut clenches.

'So, welcome to Hollywood, where there are plenty of

queers and just as many closets to go with them.' He shrugs. 'Just assume everyone's a little bit gay unless they say otherwise.'

I laugh and place my hand over my chest like I'm taking an oath. 'For the record, I'm totally gay.' Not one of them so much as raises an eyebrow.

'We guessed,' Ella says, no hint of judgement in her tone. 'Just like Lucky said, right? Gay until proven straight.'

'I'm happy to hear you say it anyway,' Lucky adds. He doesn't break eye contact.

The way he says those words, as if there's a hidden message between them, makes me want to blush right there and then. The smirk flirting with his lips pulls me in closer, making me wonder how they'd feel on mine. Telling myself I don't have a crush on him isn't exactly working out very well.

Ryan digs out her phone and raises a perfectly arched eyebrow. 'And just like that . . .'

She flips the phone round so we can all see the screen. Pictures of us leaving the hotel are already online, circulating with hundreds of comments attached. There's Ella and Ryan holding hands, proving to the world that they're best friends. Only now I know a different story – they're much more than that. There's a picture of Lucky running a hand through his hair as people reach for him like he's the second coming of Christ. And then there are some of me too, introducing Abel Miller as the newest member of the fold. One caption calls me a 'rising star', which feels ludicrous. Is that what people think of me now?

'You've got yourself a fan page already,' Ella muses, pointing out one of the accounts that has posted pictures of me and Lucky in the hotel lobby. We look like best buddies.

The name of the profile is, originally, @AbelMillerFans. It blows my mind. I'm a nobody. And yet when Ella clicks the profile, it has a couple of hundred followers already.

'You're a natural,' Ryan says with a smirk. 'You'll be at the centre of your own *love triangle* before you know it.' She punches those two words with derision.

'So what's the deal then?' I ask, not missing my chance to start gaining some intel. 'Why pretend you're in a relationship with someone else?'

The three of them share a sigh and an eye-roll. 'Omni call it a *mutually beneficial agreement*,' Ryan explains. 'If there's one thing that will boost the profile of a TV show or movie, it's two co-stars starting a romance off screen, especially if their characters play love interests. It drives fans, and therefore the press and box office, wild.'

I recall *This High Life* and how Lucky and Ryan became an item during filming. Sure enough, Hollywood's golden couple was all anyone could talk about. Ryan and Lucky were everywhere, holding hands on red carpets, posting cute pictures at Disneyland. The world loved them, and the show was a huge success. I can see exactly how the relationship benefited Omni Channel.

'But . . .' I start. I glance at Lucky, then Ella. My question is clear, awkwardly lingering over the table. If Omni Channel wanted Ryan and Lucky together originally, why do they now want Ella in the picture with Lucky instead?

Ella blushes a little as Ryan looks down into her lap. A sore subject? Before tension can envelop us any further, a group of waiters descend on the table, taking orders and pouring drinks like we're royalty on a state visit. I nearly choke when I look at the menu and see the prices. Even the cheapest meal would pay half a month's rent on a standard family home. The others don't seem fazed in the slightest. Ella tells me Omni will pick up the bill. The perks of being rich, I guess. Suddenly everything is given to you for free. I order a truffle burger while the others add pastas, pizzas, oysters and desserts. Then the waiters disappear just as quickly as they came, expertly melting into the shadows.

'They're talking about the curse already,' Ella says when they're gone, looking down at her phone. Her tone is underpinned with a vague tinge of nerves.

I immediately sit up a little straighter. 'This curse is real then?' I ask tentatively.

The three of them share an uncomfortable glance.

'I mean, *curse* is a bit extreme,' Ella says, flicking her hand as if she's attempting to get rid of the palpable energy settling over us. 'Some headline called it that and it stuck. It makes it sound like a tacky Halloween movie where one of the characters is sticking pins in a voodoo doll with our faces on. It's gross.'

'They actually think it's *exciting*,' Ryan says with disgust. 'People love waiting to see what will happen, and they're *especially* thrilled if things start to go wrong. There's this morbid curiosity, like it's a TV show that keeps running when the cameras stop rolling. It's sick. People think we're not *real*. To them, we're just characters. Even when the show is over, that's all we are to them.'

'Sometimes I even believe them.' Ella's voice is small but measured and thoughtful. 'There are times when I feel like I can't even see myself. I can only see the character everyone else projects onto me.'

Ryan nods in agreement. 'It completely fucks with your head and blurs the lines so you can hardly tell where the real you ends and the person they think you are begins. And then in some twisted way, that character becomes the thing you hide behind to protect yourself. But in doing so, you're feeding into the narrative that you're not a real person, which makes the idea of a curse more palatable and entertaining to them. It's such a toxic cycle.'

'But calling it a *curse* makes a mockery of the bad things that have happened to real people.' We all turn to Lucky. There's a quiet rage boldening his words. 'Mila Stone was a real person. Penelope Daunt was a real person. The guy who fell from the roof was a real person. They all had families, friends, people who loved them.'

My eyes instantly blur with unshed tears. I duck my head to try to collect myself, hoping nobody has noticed. Fortunately Lucky keeps talking.

'Saying that any of them were victims of a curse makes it sound inevitable, like it's a script that someone has written. But this is *Real. Fucking. Life.* Not some TV show where there's a happy ending and a second season. Every day people watch videos on their phones of the most terrible things and they don't even blink. They watch as people literally *die*, but they're so desensitized to it. And I think it fools them into believing that it's not real. Or that it's at least removed from reality because they're watching it in the same way they watch their favourite shows. That's the reason people enjoy calling this a curse. In the most morbid way, to them it's entertainment. Then, when they're done, they turn off their phones, close their laptops and they're back in their own world, where what they've just witnessed seems incomprehensible.'

A heavy silence bears down on us all. It's uncomfortable and raw, affronting, but it's honest.

'There's no curse,' Ryan says eventually. 'But there is blame.'

I want to ask what she means and start unravelling the web of lies that Omnificent have hidden in the dark behind a glittering disguise. My brother was a part of this. I *have* to know. But then a waiter suddenly reappears to replenish our drinks, and, just like that, our tiny bubble is popped. The real world – or the fake one, where everyone plays a character and the whole world is a stage – seeps back in. I'm overcome with this crushing wave of dejection, because no sooner had all their walls come down, they'd quickly, instinctively shot back up like the conversation had never happened.

Lucky slips a crisp bank note into the waiter's hand, who nods discreetly and brings over a dark bottle. He pours the golden liquid into glasses and shares them out round the table. None of us are the legal drinking age in the US, but that doesn't seem to matter when you're rich and famous.

'A toast,' Lucky says, raising his glass. 'To Hollywood lights and scandalous nights.' He pauses, then lays his ocean blues on me. 'And to Abel,' he says, locking me in place with his stare. His knee brushes mine under the table, and, just like when his fingers grazed my neck in his hotel room earlier, I feel my world tilt a little.

Ryan grabs my arm with a grin, saving me from straight up blushing in response. 'You're one of us now.'

'Yep, welcome to this fucked-up club,' Ella chimes in, raising her drink too.

We clink glasses and take sips. Lucky throws his back in one.

The evening is going perfectly, full of laughs and gossip that has my jaw on the floor. They weren't lying when they said everyone's at least a *little* gay, and hardly hiding it either when they're on the right side of the Hollywood curtain.

It's all good fun, but then Ryan's phone pings, and she flicks her eyes down to read the notification. Ella does too and immediately tenses up. Ryan's face falls. When she looks at Ella, hurt and betrayal are clear to see. Ella reaches a hand out for hers, but Ryan shrugs it off and storms to the bathroom. Ella is only pinned to her seat for a moment before she jumps up and follows.

'What now?' Lucky mutters with a sigh. He digs his phone out and checks his notifications. He doesn't have to go far to find the article.

A NEW DIAMOND IN THE OMNIFICENT CROWN?

By Gordon Wright, CELEBRITY REPORTER

1 August 2023

ELLA WINTER SET TO SIGN AN EXCLUSIVE OMNI CHANNEL CONTRACT AS THE STUDIO CONFIRM THAT SHE'LL TAKE THE LEAD ROLE IN SUNSET HIGH.

'Oh, shit,' Lucky says. He whistles. 'That's low, even for Omni.'

'This is bad?' I ask, feeling slightly stupid that I need the situation spelled out for me.

Lucky nods. 'That headline all but says they're replacing Ryan with Ella. It wouldn't have been published without Omni's say-so. Jill leaked this for sure.' He reads it again. 'I didn't know anything about Ella's new contract. And I sure as hell didn't know she was taking the leading role for the reboot. By the look of it, Ryan didn't either.'

Well, there's no way I'm missing this. I was going to get my investigation into Omni underway properly tomorrow, but I guess there's no time like the present.

'Nipping to the bathroom,' I murmur, but Lucky's too busy pouring another drink to pay much attention.

I slink towards the back of the restaurant where the toilets are nestled in a quiet nook. The small corridor is empty. I creep slightly closer to the women's bathroom, crouching down and pretending to tie my laces just as I hear the first raised voice.

'I wanted to tell you!' Ella says, her voice straining to keep itself at a reasonable volume.

'Like hell you did!' Ryan shoots back. 'If you were going to tell me, then you would've done it before the rest of the world found out.'

'I haven't signed the deal, I swear. I wanted to talk to you first when everything else had died down. I didn't know Omni were going to leak the story before I made a decision.'

'I thought we had each other's backs!' Ryan almost yells, the hurt in her voice echoing off the bathroom tiles. 'Maybe that was expecting too much. I should've known that you'd put yourself first, just like Mommy told you to.'

'Don't you dare,' Ella says, wounded. 'How can you throw that in my face after everything I've told you? I didn't think you'd stoop that low.'

'And I didn't think you'd stab me in the back after all I've told *you*, but here we are.'

There's a beat of excruciating silence. And then . . . my phone starts to vibrate.

I dig it out of my pocket to see the name Hannah lighting up the screen. I'm torn between answering the call or listening to the rest of the argument, but I think I've heard enough. I can't get caught eavesdropping. I step away into the shadows and hit the green button.

'How's my favourite celebrity?' Hannah asks before I've even managed to get the phone all the way to my ear.

I murmur a laugh, turning my back on the restaurant. 'Enjoying the high life. The perks of being famous are pretty good so far. Shouldn't you be asleep at this time?'

'Spin class. No rest for the wicked. Besides, it's past six here in London.' Me, on the other hand, I could fall sleep on my feet right now. 'But never mind that. I just saw the news about Ella's new contract. Tell me everything.'

I quickly fill her in on the earlier meeting with Jill, the threat of sending Lucky to rehab and what just happened over dinner. I also tell her that the new relationship between Ella and Lucky is fake, as was the relationship between Ryan and Lucky, but I stop short of telling her that it's actually *Ryan* and Ella who are a thing. It feels wrong to out them like that.

'Interesting,' Hannah muses. 'I did hear rumblings that Ella had already signed a new contract, but it sounds like Omnificent have jumped the gun. Maybe they're hoping it'll push her into signing it. But Lucky potentially going to rehab? Now that's a story. I haven't heard anything about it on the grapevine, so Omnificent are keeping a lid on it. That kind of scoop would be huge for us.'

I chew my lip. It feels like I'm betraying Lucky by telling Hannah, but I quickly remind myself why I'm here – for Adam. Everything, including Lucky, comes second to that.

'I'll start writing up a story on Lucky and his drinking,' Hannah says, oblivious to the tug of war battling in my head. 'It'll take an age to clear through legal, and we'll need to reach out to Omni for comment, but give it a few days, maybe a week or so, and we'll have something to publish.'

'You think that's a good idea?' I ask, trying to conceal the panic in my voice. 'A story like that could only come from the inside. What if it blows my cover?'

Hannah mulls it over for a moment but sticks firm. 'There are so many people a story like that could come from: assistants, producers, runners. You'll be fine. This is a great start. But I do have a lead for you to follow up.' A light shiver of adrenaline skims over me. 'I want you to pay a visit to Barb Harrington's house. I'm texting you the address now.'

'Barb Harrington?'

'Ugh, you Gen Z kids wouldn't know a legend if they slapped you in the face,' Hannah grumbles. 'She's a big-deal journalist, used to interview all the stars back in the day. Her sit down with Michael Jackson was sensational. She officially retired last year, but here's where things get interesting. There was a rumour floating about between journalists a while ago that Penelope Daunt had gone behind Omnificent's back and set up a tell-all interview with Barb before she went missing.'

I'm stunned. That would've been huge, especially if it had anything to do with Omni Channel.

'It was just a rumour, and it might be bullshit, but something tells me it could be close to the truth. And, listen, Barb's one to talk. I met her at an award ceremony once – anything you'd done, she'd done better, and she sure as hell was going to let you know about it. That's celebrity journalists for you. They *really* want you to know two things – who they've interviewed, and all the secret celebrity gossip they know about but can't legally report on in case they're sued. Affairs, feuds, fights. They love to tell you all of it. So get out to Barb's house, appeal to her ego and get her talking.'

'Barb Harrington, got it.'

I say my goodbyes and hang up before checking the address in the text Hannah sends me. It's in Beverly Hills, not far from the hotel. I might be able to get there tomorrow morning.

Happy, if not slightly apprehensive, to have a plan, I turn round only to find Ryan watching me a few metres away. The door to the women's bathroom gently closes behind her, so I know she hasn't been standing there long. But what, exactly, did she hear?

'Everything okay?' She asks it casually enough, but is there a hint of suspicion to her tone?

'Yep. Just . . . a call from home, checking in.'

Before Ryan can interrogate me further, I give her a tight smile and start for the table. If I'm going to be undercover for the *Daily Eye*, I really need to get better at lying. When Ryan and Ella rejoin the booth, they refuse to look at each other, subtle traces of tears leaving a mark on both their faces. But as we prepare to leave and face the crowds outside, their perfect smiles are once again in place.

Lightning flashes from the cameras bathe us in cold spotlights as soon as we step out of The Big Kid. I climb into the car, jet lag well and truly kicking my ass. As I doze in and out of sleep, I go over what needs to be done. Tonight I've enjoyed playing celebrity, but tomorrow the real work begins.

Part Two

AGAINST ALL HOPE

Chapter Eleven

AND THE WORLD KEEPS SPINNING

Abel

Barb Harrington's house sits in the exclusive zip code of 90210. It's not the most expensive place in the neighbourhood by any means – just a casual four million dollars according to Google – but it sure is stunning. The terracotta-tiled roof, cream-coloured walls and palm trees in the front yard that gently sway in the breeze give it the feel of a Mediterranean villa. Rich people really do be rich people-ing.

I'm rehearsing everything I want to say when an older white woman comes pottering round the side of the house. She has perfectly coiffed white hair and bejewelled spectacles attached to a crystallized chain round her neck, with muddy gloves covering her hands and dirt-splattered trousers. It seems that Barb Harrington has taken up gardening in her retirement.

Seeing her right there in front of me throws me off and my mind goes blank. I'm standing there like a complete doofus, head empty of any thoughts, when she spots me.

She frowns, her eyes giving me a once-over. 'Can I help you?' she asks. Her tone is polite enough, but there's a shadow of suspicion underneath it. Each word is crystal clear from years of conducting hard-hitting interviews in front of the camera.

When my jet lag woke me up at stupid o'clock this morning, I used the time to watch a few YouTube videos of her. She might look harmless, but she was a bulldog when she got the bit between her teeth, and she wasn't afraid to ask the tough questions others might have shied away from. That was what made her so successful.

'Just admiring the garden,' I say, scrambling for an excuse as to why I'm staring like I don't know how to mind my own business. At least I remembered to put on a Californian accent – the cast announcement made a big deal of the fact I'm British. If she hears my real voice, she might put two and two together and realize I'm the new kid on *Sunset High*.

'Well, don't just stand there looking gormless. Grab that sack of fertilizer and bring it over here for me.' She turns her back like she knows damn well I'm going to follow her orders without question. She's not wrong. I pick up a large heavy bag from the other side of the garden, trying to pretend like it's not about to break my back with its weight, and drop it down beside her. She gives me a glance that tells me she's ready to dismiss me from her property, so I let the first thing in my brain spill out into the open.

'Oh my God, you're Barb Harrington, aren't you?' Not my finest work, but, just like Hannah said, appealing to her ego might get her to talk.

Sure enough, Barb lights up with pride. She assesses me again and chuckles to herself. 'You're far too young. Your mom a fan?'

'We both are! She'd freak out if she knew I was talking to you right now. We used to sit down and watch your interviews together all the time. I kind of always hoped you'd do a *Sunset High* special, though. All that stuff about the curse? It would've made such great TV! Especially now it's coming back.' I shrug and sigh a little, really putting those acting skills to work. 'I suppose getting the cast to agree to an interview would've been hard for anyone – they were pretty famous.'

It's a gamble. I know I sound like a complete tool, but if Hannah was right about celebrity journalists, then . . .

'I'll have you know, *actually*, I interviewed the likes of Michael Jackson, Oprah, six presidents and even royalty. A little TV show for kids was *not* out of my reach.' Piss her off so much that she recites her CV? Check. But would her ego stop there? Of course not. 'And for your information, I already had an interview with Penelope Daunt in the pipeline. She just happened to disappear on the day.'

I can feel myself reacting and try to put a lid on it, but my thoughts are racing ahead. Barb's interview with Penelope was not only true but was scheduled for the same day she went missing. Coincidence? I'd bet my life to say otherwise. I pick up another bag of fertilizer in the hope I can keep Barb talking.

'It's so sad what happened to her. She must be . . .' I shake my head and lower my voice. 'Well, you know what people say. If she was still alive, they would've found her by now, right?'

Barb purses her lips, disapproving. 'I'm not a fan of conspiracies. I have my own theories about what happened, all based on fact, of course.' She taps her nose smugly. Ugh, time to kiss butt again.

'I'd trust your theories over some randomer on the internet! I've read people saying that Omnificent could be to blame. Ridiculous, isn't it, how far-fetched some of these theories can get?' Barb raises her eyebrows and tilts her head pointedly, saying a lot with no words at all. '*You* think it too?!'

She chuckles to herself. 'I'm not saying a word. Except . . .' She shrugs. I can tell she's enjoying being cryptic. I wonder if she misses her old lifestyle, knowing things that others don't, collecting secrets and gossip like currency. 'Let's just say I'm sure the last person Omnificent wanted Penelope talking to about her time on *Sunset High* was me.'

I grin. 'Omnificent would know better than to mess with you, though. You'd kick their ass.'

There's that pride again. She wears it like a medal. 'Didn't stop them from trying, but, of course, I came out on top of *that* encounter.'

'They did? I bet they regret that so bad.' I cringe internally.

'They sure did. Threatened to sue me and the network if I kept poking around. *Pfft.*' Barb snorts, wielding the notion of nearly being sued like a badge of honour. 'Like that was going to stop me. They forgot I'm not one of their scared little actors – I'm Barb fucking Harrington. They were right to be scared about what I might get out of Penelope Daunt.'

Barb looks down at the flower beds, lost in their beauty and her own thoughts. When she talks again, her confidence is replaced by sincere sadness.

'I'm sure they would've done anything to keep her quiet. And they got their wish. I just hope that whatever they did to poor Penelope haunts them for the rest of their days.'

My head and heart are heavy. Penelope *was* going to talk. It sounds like she was going to tell Barb everything. But Omni caught wind and put a stop to it? I don't know what happened, but the world only knows a snippet of the story, that's for sure.

Barb shuffles uncomfortably, like she knows she's said too much. I'm about to open my mouth, but she beats me to it, and I know I've been busted.

'Who *are* you?' She levels me with a glare and my heart starts to race. 'You ask too many questions, and I know an interview when I see one. Who sent you here?'

'N-no one,' I stutter. 'I'm just a fan, that's all. I'd better be going.'

I don't wait to see if Barb buys my excuse. I already know she doesn't. I wheel round and get gone, keeping my head low. I don't stop until I'm a few blocks away, pulling out my phone to message Hannah.

But as I do, questions emerge from the shadows of my mind, appearing like bad omens. The night after Penelope was last seen alive, my brother text me saying he had something to tell me about Omni. *It's fucked up. Call me asap.* He fell to his death shortly after, and then Penelope was publicly announced missing the following morning.

Is it purely coincidence? Or is it connected in some spiderweb of lies and deceit? Did my brother stumble upon something to do with Penelope Daunt's disappearance? And if so, would someone kill to keep it a secret?

'You don't belong here,' says Ryan, a snarl in her voice. 'So why don't you do us all a favour and run home to whatever backwards little town you came from. While you still can.'

Ella shrugs. 'I must have missed the memo that says I take orders from you. Who died and made you Queen Bitch?'

Ryan's confidence falters but only for a moment. 'You'd do well to stay on my good side. You don't want to piss me off.'

'Leave it, babe,' Lucky says. 'She's not worth it.'

Ella turns on him, a smirk on her face. 'Not worth it? That's not what you said yesterday.' Ryan looks furious. 'Oops, did he not tell you about our little introduction? He sure knows how to make a girl feel welcome around here.'

'Aaaaaand cut!' Lake Carter takes off his glasses and shuffles his script into a neat pile. He looks pretty happy with himself. 'Perfect, I think that's working great. Love the animosity between you two – could've fooled me into thinking it's real!' Lake bellows a laugh, oblivious to Ryan and Ella's blushes. They're still refusing to look at each other properly after last night. 'Okay, let's take a break and come back for another table read this afternoon. Good job, guys.'

The two dozen people round the table – actors, assistants,

script editors – all stand up and stretch. The first table read is out of the way and things are going well. On the surface anyway. Ella and Ryan haven't so much as uttered a word to each other since we got here, Lucky looks like he's trying his best to hide a hangover behind his shades, and I can't stop thinking about what Barb Harrington had to say about Penelope this morning. That, plus trying to keep my head above water on the set of a TV show for the first time, is fucking with my head.

I step outside for some air, although it's hardly the relaxing environment I want. People rush around me, carrying all manner of strange things – a dragon's head, some kind of medieval weapon, a giant plume of pink feathers. Three people jog past wearing green onesies made of Lycra. A London classroom, the packed streets of Manhattan, the front of a Parisian hotel, even the White House – they're all here somewhere on this enormous lot. Here, you can visit the world in a single day, no passport needed. Welcome to the sound stages of Hollywood.

> **Hannah Wilkes**
>
> Great job on Barb. Keep going. Have you thought about trying to get in contact with Mila Stone? I heard she's holed up in a house somewhere on the coast, but might be worth a try. If she hates Omnificent as much as I think she does, she could start talking.
>
> 10:12

I scan the text, then open Google and search Mila's name. It's been thirteen years since she retired from the spotlight after starring in the original *Sunset High*, but it seems that nobody is willing to let go of the past. With the reboot happening now, the press has dredged up every story they can. It's nothing new, but that's hardly stopping them. There are old pictures of Mila's run-ins with paparazzi, headlines wondering where she is now and speculating on her current mental health. I feel a jolt of disgust. Why won't they leave her alone?

I nearly drop my phone as the door I've just come through is thrown wide open, and I doubly panic when I see who it is. Lake Carter. He's the king around here. Creator. Writer. Director. Producer. *Sunset High* is his brainchild. In fact, it's because of Lake and this show that Omni Channel are even alive now. In 2008 they were close to bust. Many had already counted them out, marking their days. Omnificent was going to become nothing but a memory. Then came Lake and *Sunset High*, reviving the studio and giving it a new lease of life. Now Omni are the single biggest entertainment studio for kid and teen shows in the world. They literally owe him everything.

'Ah, Abel. Glad to finally meet you properly.' Lake thrusts a hand out to shake mine. He's a white man in his fifties, tall and wide-shouldered. He has an easy confidence about him, one that can only be exuded by someone in charge. 'Loved the audition tape. Real talent you've got there. A few more years at the craft and you'll be a pro.'

I don't know what to say, especially considering the compliment seems . . . kind of backhanded? 'Thanks for believing in me.' I manage a weak smile.

Lake doesn't notice, clamping his hand on my shoulder as if

he's about to impart some fatherly wisdom. 'Course we believe in you. I mean, sure, it helped your case that Saint Morgan got arrested for a DUI before we made our decision, but you were pretty good on your own merit. I'll make a star of you yet.' He booms a laugh, gives me a thump on the back and heads off in the direction of the catering tent.

He seems nice enough, like a grandparent who means well but puts their foot in it by saying something controversial from time to time. But I'd be lying if I said he hasn't put me on edge. Maybe it's because I know the power and control he has. Or maybe it's his link to the other iterations of *Sunset High*, and therefore his degrees of separation from Mila Stone, Penelope Daunt and, most importantly, my brother.

'You've met the big boss then?' Lucky says, materializing by my side. His curls are particularly unruly today and he doesn't seem to have slept much. Still, unlike the rest of us who'd have had the respect to look like shit with a hangover, he appears as though he's preparing for a Calvin Klein photo shoot.

'Seems like an all right guy,' I murmur. 'Heading for the trailers?'

Lucky nods, and we start towards the back of the lot.

'How are you finding your first time on set then?' he asks.

The set itself is still being put together by members of the crew. When it's done, there'll be a school hallway lined with lockers, a classroom fitted out with desks, a cafeteria, basketball court and bleachers, and the bedrooms of our characters. A whole world created out of nothing.

'It's so strange,' I respond honestly. 'I've been on small sets and stages before, but this is something else entirely. It all looks so . . . real? Is that stupid to say?'

Lucky laughs. 'Of course not. I still find it pretty cool seeing the magic that goes into bringing a script to life. It's the little things like this that I love the most. I'd happily leave the rest of it behind.'

I glance at him out of the corner of my eye, but Lucky's face is neutral. I wonder how high his guard is right now. This is his first job back after his mum's accident after all. I want to peer inside his head, unspool his thoughts. The crowds of crew members start to thin out a little as we move through the lot, ducking under light rigs and out the way of props.

'What don't you like about the job?' I ask, genuinely curious.

'The obvious – paparazzi are annoying, the constant attention can get overwhelming, and feeling like your entire life is on display for everyone to pick apart and judge is tough.' He sighs. 'I don't know. It's hard to complain when I've put myself in this position. I think other people see us in the spotlight and think that if we've stepped into it of our own accord, then we've basically put the target on our backs.'

I don't know what to say to that because . . . well, I thought the same. Not with any ill intention, but I'd always seen celebrities complaining about people observing their lives and thought: *Isn't that what you signed up for?* I've only been on the other side of the curtain for a minute, and I can already feel the claustrophobia. How must someone like Lucky feel when he's been doing this since he was a child, growing up with the whole world watching his every step, judging every mistake?

'I suppose we *have* put ourselves here, and we live privileged lives because of it. But . . .' He lowers his voice a little, as if he's suddenly realized that he's speaking so openly. 'I understand that having a career like this comes with a certain level of exposure, but just because I've chosen to do it, it doesn't mean every tiny detail of my life should be laid bare for judgement. Sometimes it feels like no matter how much you give people, they always want more. They want to know my address, my blood type, how I'm grieving my mom . . .'

We reach the back lot, where a bunch of large white trailers are parked in neat lines. Each member of the core cast and crew has been given one as a personal dressing room. Lucky lingers by the steps that lead up to a door with Abel Miller written on it. His shoulders are tensed and a shadow has crossed over his face.

'They even want *pictures* of it,' he says. His voice cracks a little. 'Some piece-of-shit photographer caught me the day after my mom's funeral. I didn't see him – thought I was alone. And I . . .' He hesitates, thrown back into that memory. 'I was breaking. I couldn't hold myself together any more. I was tired of trying to and I just let go.'

I feel awful because I know exactly what pictures he's talking about. Everyone with a social media account had seen them.

'I heard the pictures were bought by some tabloid for fifty thousand dollars. I thought there would be outrage that my grief, something so *personal*, had been photographed without my knowledge and put out into the world. But no. When they

121

were published, everyone lapped them up. Even the people who call themselves fans were sharing them.'

Lucky ducks his head, snapping out of his rant and wiping his watering eyes with the back of his hand. When he looks up, there's shame embedded there too. It breaks me a little. He might be eighteen, but I can see the kid hiding behind the character of Lucky Tate.

'Sorry,' he says, his voice wobbling slightly. 'I didn't mean to offload that on you. It's been a hard few months.'

I abandon any self-consciousness and look him straight in the eye. 'Don't you dare say sorry. You have every right to feel those things.'

His words tug at my heart, at my own grief that I've tried to bury over the years but never successfully moved past. I know what it's like to feel as though you're falling apart and can't do anything to stop it.

'Can I give you a hug?'

I'm almost surprised at my nerve. But I no longer feel like I'm dazzled by Lucky's light. Sure, it's still there, and it still burns just as bright, but a stronger urge has taken hold instead – one that tells me he needs someone right now, just like I needed someone back when Adam died.

Lucky breathes a laugh, and for a second I think he's going to decline or tell a joke to lighten the mood. But instead, he moves in close, and we wrap our arms round each other. We're just two boys standing together, sharing each other's pain while the world keeps moving around us.

Chapter Twelve

LEADING LADY

Ella

I'm chatting through my schedule with Natalie in the packed-out catering tent when her phone lights up with a message. I wouldn't normally have paid it any attention, except I see the name 'K' with a love heart next to it and she immediately blushes upon seeing it, snatching up her phone as quick as lightning.

'Ohhhh, I know *that* look,' I tease. 'Who's the guy?'

'Nobody,' Natalie mumbles, throwing the phone in her bag.

'Natalie Trenton, you tell me right this second!' I protest. 'Come on, you know everything about my life; it's only fair you give me some gossip about yours too.'

'It's early days. I don't want to jinx it!' Natalie hesitates and I pounce.

'But . . .'

She gives me an embarrassed smile. 'I suppose he *is* pretty great.'

I squeal with delight. 'Tell. Me. Everything.'

What a shame that Lake Carter interrupts us by announcing in front of the whole tent that he wants to see me in his trailer. There's a palpable awkwardness as everyone stops what they're doing to search me out. It feels like even the walls are holding their breath. And I know damn sure why – everyone's surprised that I've been given the leading role over Ryan. I can sense they're all talking behind our backs. I even heard Macy Diaz, one of the supporting actresses, bitching about it in the toilets earlier.

'She's only been here five minutes. How the hell did she land the lead already?'

When she saw me leave the cubicle, she went pale. I gave her my nicest smile and told her maybe if she had more charisma than a plank of wood, she might get a leading role one day too, but then again, she shouldn't hold her breath.

I stand up and Lake gives me a big grin like he couldn't be happier to see me.

'I think we should discuss your role as *leading lady* in a bit more detail,' he calls out. 'Whenever you're ready.'

I nod and follow him out of the tent, but not before I see Ryan sitting on the opposite side with some of the hair and make-up squad. She's the queen at masking her true feelings, but right now, under the stares of cast and crew, she looks humiliated. Whether Lake meant to or not, a hierarchy is being formed, and *very* publicly.

I want to speak to Ryan so badly but I don't know what to say. I threw her under the bus pure and simple. Sure, I haven't signed the contract yet, but Omni Channel and Lake giving me the lead role is their way of trying to force my hand, which leaves me in a sticky position. If I don't sign it now that they've leaked the story to the press, they'll get rid of me to save face. And that's the best case. At worst, they'll make sure I never work in this industry again. Omni have enough power to take my entire career away from me. I've heard rumours that it's been done before. Some whispers even say that that's what happened to Mila Stone – blacklisted in the business for not playing ball. I can't let that happen. If Mom was angry about the *Hercules* job, she'll go through the roof if I lose this contract too. But if I agree to it, I'll lose Ryan, and that's only if I haven't already. I'm well and truly fucked.

Lake leads me to his trailer, closing the door behind us. It's identical to mine, laid out like a small apartment with a kitchen, living and dining area, a bathroom, a tiny study and even a bedroom in the back. Pages of a script are scattered on the table, defaced with notes and annotations in barely legible scrawl. I feel a little awkward in the cramped space, so I point to a framed photograph of Lake holding a puppy in his arms.

'So cute,' I say just to break the silence. 'What's its name?'

'His name was Ripper,' Lake answers. I catch the past tense and grimace, ready to apologize, but Lake waves it away and gestures to the table. 'Why don't you have a seat?' I do as I'm told. I've heard he can have a short fuse, although I've yet to see it for myself. I glance at the top page of the script and see that it's an untitled project.

'Water? Coke? Maybe a tequila to give the day a boost? I won't tell if you don't!' He laughs, then hands me a water without waiting for my answer.

I try to relax into my seat, but I'm too on edge, wound tight from the stress of last night and today. Lake cracks open a beer for himself before sitting opposite me.

'So you're going to be our new leading lady!' he starts brightly.

'I guess so,' I say. 'Thank you so much for giving me the opportunity. I'm really grateful to be a part of something this big.'

'Big?' Lake shakes his head with a glint in his eye. 'No, no, no – this show is going to be *huge*, the most talked about show in years. And I've specifically chosen *you* to lead it. If you play your cards right, this could be your making.' He raises his hands over the table, as if he's putting my name up in lights. 'Ella Winter, the next big thing. You want that, right?'

I nod because . . . well . . . I don't know. I *do* want this. It's everything I've ever hoped for. Right?

Lake looks happy with my answer and places a hand on the stack of papers between us. 'This script will be my new masterpiece, a movie that's going to set the world alight. I'm going in a different direction, straight for the Academy and the Oscars. Omnificent have my back, but I'll need someone with real talent to front it.' He pauses, enjoying himself. Then, as if he's handing me a gift on Christmas morning, he adds: 'I want that person to be *you*.'

126

A seed of excitement blooms inside me. For just a moment I can see what I think are my dreams coming true – standing on the biggest stage of them all, accepting an award, my mom in the audience bursting with pride. If we could get there, we'd have made it. Surely then Mom would want nothing else for me. *From* me.

Lake's smile drops, and he looks down at the table as if he's preparing to break bad news. I feel a shift in his energy. 'But first, I need someone I can trust. I want to give you the future you deserve, Ella, I really do. But if there is something, or someone, holding you back . . .'

His voice is warm, friendly even, but all I can hear echoing in my head is that one word – *someone*. I want to make myself smaller somehow, so small that I disappear altogether.

'I don't know what you mean.'

Ryan and I had been careful to keep our relationship away from Omni because we knew they wouldn't exactly approve. It would go against the script they wanted us to follow when we were out in front of the world. They'd rather we were pitted against each other than in love with each other. But somehow Lake knows.

He holds his words for a moment, then gently unleashes them like a nightmare unfurling.

'I get the sense that your *friendship* with Ryan is what's stopping you from signing the contract.' He shrugs. 'I understand that you're young and you don't know all the ways the world works just yet. But . . .' He sighs apologetically. 'Ryan would do the same if she was in your shoes. How do

127

you think she's stayed on top for so long? This business is cut-throat. Everyone is out for themselves. Do you really want to get left behind?'

He lets his question hang over me, sucking all the air out of the room, then he reaches across the table, placing his hand over mine. It's clearly meant to be a caring, protective gesture, but for some reason his touch makes my skin crawl.

'I'm looking out for you,' he says. 'I want your future to be as bright as it should be. But if Ryan, or anyone else, is holding you back, then I'll have to take that as a sign that you're not serious about your career and . . . well, I'll be forced to look elsewhere. I'd *hate* to do that. You're so talented. You deserve this. But there are a million Ella Winters out there waiting to step into your position. Ryan would be one of them. And if she really cared for you, she wouldn't stand in the way of your dreams. Right?'

I don't know what to say. I feel bound by my silence, drowning in it, but a guttural scream rages inside my head, begging to be heard. Lake, however, isn't finished.

'I met your mother earlier,' he says lightly. 'Kate, isn't it?' I clench the fist Lake isn't holding so tightly under the table that my knuckles feel like they're trying to pierce the skin. 'We had a lovely conversation. She seemed so happy when I told her about my big plans for you. I'm certain she'd be incredibly proud to see you succeed. Don't let her down over some silly little friendship.' Lake pats my hand with a smile and sits back, rolling out his shoulders with the confidence of a man who always gets what he wants, one way or another.

128

'You shouldn't wait too long to sign the contract, Ella. It won't be there for ever.'

I nod and smile through the rest of our meeting, mask firmly on as we talk about my *Sunset High* character and her progression through the show. But the moment I leave, I feel myself begin to crumble.

I head straight for my trailer, hoping to hide away from everyone, but Natalie's there at the table, sorting through emails on my laptop. She doesn't raise her eyes at first, concentrating on the screen.

'Your mom's signed off for the day,' she murmurs. 'Something about a massage and lunch.' When she looks up, her eyes flit over my face. 'You need anything?'

I think of telling Natalie about what happened. Maybe she'll offer some advice, like a big sister would. But, instead, I smile and say nothing. Just like always.

Chapter Thirteen

A TALE AS OLD AS TIME

Abel

Mila Stone is the next lead I need to follow down this Omni Channel rabbit hole. There's just one teeny-tiny problem – I have no idea where she lives.

We get back from set in the early afternoon and I spend some time googling all I can about her. But every headline and picture – even ones posted yesterday – are stuck in the past. To say she's kept a low profile since stepping out of the spotlight would be an understatement. There is *nothing* about Mila Stone's current life to be found. She seems to only exist as a ghost of the girl she used to be.

I find some old interviews and watch as a smiling bubbly teenager gradually becomes a shadow of herself. Long honey-coloured waves are chopped shorter and dyed darker.

Her startlingly green eyes, once wide at all the attention, are guarded and restless by the time she turns nineteen. A polite demeanour is traded for a no-nonsense attitude and a sharp tongue. By 2011, when she eventually retired, she'd become an entirely different person.

I check the time. Past three. If I'm going to find Mila and see if she'll talk, I need to move fast. The car that's taking us to the studio for *The Late Late Show with Jeremy Love* is picking us up in a few hours. I'm actively choosing to ignore the fact my live TV debut is tonight, so what better way to distract myself than by seeing what Mila has to say – if she has anything to say at all. But first, I need to find out where she lives.

'Hey,' Casey, the guy who checked me into the hotel yesterday, says when I step out of the lift and shuffle over to the front desk. He flashes me a bright smile, inquisitive eyes sweeping over my face. 'What can I do for you?'

'I'm wondering if you could help me with something . . .' I lower my voice as if the hotel might be bugged and Omni can hear every word I'm saying. 'I was wondering if you know where Mila Stone lives?'

Casey glances around nervously. I can tell the question has not only caught him off guard but made him paranoid.

'Why?' he asks, a little more bluntly than I expected.

'I, uh . . . she invited me for lunch. And I, uh, need to . . . get there.'

Casey raises an eyebrow. 'Mila Stone, the woman who has barely left her house since 2011 and who owns four guard dogs to ward off visitors, has invited you over for lunch. *That's* the lie you're going with?' Casey seems to remember he's at work and talking to a guest, so quickly adds, 'No offence, but I can tell you're lying.'

I sigh and decide to try the truth instead. Or a version of it at least.

'I want to talk to her. I'm new to this world and everything to do with *Sunset High*. I just . . . I don't know. I want to hear what she has to say about it.'

I try to give Casey my best puppy-dog eyes, but I can't be sure that I don't just look constipated. He must feel sorry for me because he sighs and gives in.

'She lives by the beach out in Malibu. I don't know any more than that. It's about an hour away if the traffic's not terrible.'

'An hour?' I moan. 'Please tell me you have good public transport out here.'

'In LA?' Casey snorts. 'Be for real.' He groans under his breath, then digs out his phone. 'Hey, Ronnie? Can you do me a favour? I've got someone here who needs to go out to Malibu . . . Mila Stone's place? . . . Are you good to take him? . . . Great, he'll meet you out back in a minute.' Casey hangs up the phone. 'You're welcome.'

'First of all, who's Ronnie?' I probably shouldn't ask any questions, but I'm also not about to get into a stranger's car without knowing who he is first. Do Americans no nothing about *stranger danger*?

'He's the best driver this hotel's got. Old Ronnie's worked here for over twenty years and escorted just about everyone

132

you can think of around the city. If he's driven there once, he remembers the way for ever. He's discreet too. I assume you want to keep this under wraps, right?' I nod and Casey raises an eyebrow. 'Well, he'll pick you up from the back entrance where there aren't any cameras. But if you get caught snooping around places you shouldn't be, you leave my name out of it.'

I nod and thank Casey for helping. I start to leave, but he calls out my name.

'Abel . . .' The rest of his sentence eludes him, as if the words are stuck in the back of his throat. 'Good luck with Mila,' he manages. 'You're probably going to need it.'

I'm sure that what Casey *really* wanted to say is on the tip of his tongue – or maybe I'm overthinking – but another member of hotel staff joins him at the desk before I can say a word.

Instead, I head for the back entrance, where a black SUV is waiting to take me to Malibu. The driver waves. I'm about to climb into the back when I glance down the alley towards the street.

I freeze. Porter McKay is looking right at me, rooted to the spot a few steps into the alley with a phone to his ear. His face pales, draining of all colour. He doesn't hang around. Without a backwards glance, he turns on his heel and runs.

The house by Malibu beach is modest and stunningly beautiful. A small white picket fence borders a freshly cut lawn, with neat paving stones leading up to a door that's been painted forest green, an old white car sitting in the driveway. There are gorgeous flowers in every colour lining the path and a small tree off to the side. When I arrive, I can hear the gentle lap of the waves beyond. It's idyllic. The perfect escape from a place that drove you to the brink of your sanity.

Before I start up the path, I pull out my phone and take a picture of the house just so I have *something* in case this all goes south. If word is to be believed, Mila doesn't accept visitors. That's what the four guard dogs are for. She's lived out here for more than a decade, minding her business and waiting for the world to mind theirs. But with *Sunset High* starting up again, she must be on edge.

The whole way here I've tried to push Porter from my mind, instead going over what I want to say to Mila so I don't trip over myself like I did with Barb this morning. I might not get this opportunity again, so I need to make sure I get it right.

'You'd better have a damn good reason to be standing on the sidewalk snapping pictures of my house,' a sharp voice says.

I nearly drop my phone, whirling round to find Mila Stone coming up the street and holding a leash. Great, I'm about to get eaten alive before I've had the chance to ask any questions. Except . . . the four formidable guard dogs are actually two cream-coloured Labradors who jump up to lick my face. I laugh, despite my nerves.

'I was told you had four guard dogs to keep away unwanted visitors,' I say, stroking both Labradors behind the ears once they settle back down.

'Glad to see my rumour is working then. Or *was* anyway. It clearly hasn't stopped you from coming out here to bother me.' Mila looks me up and down. She's tall and slim, with pale skin, perfect posture and jet-black hair that's been cut short and spiky. She looks casual in jeans, trainers and a plain white T-shirt, a world away from the Hollywood glamour of thirteen years ago.

'I don't want to bother you,' I say, holding my hands up to show that I come in peace. 'My name is—'

'Abel Miller,' Mila finishes for me. 'The latest rising star to join the Omnificent ranks, destined to have all your dreams come true.' The words are bitter, bursting at the seams with contempt. 'I know who you are, and I know why you're here. Believe me, you're not the first. But I can't help you. Now please leave.' She starts off up the garden path.

'Wait!' I call after her. She gets to the front door and unlocks it, stepping inside, ready to close it in my face. I panic. 'I think they killed my brother!'

I blurt it out by accident, but it's all I've got. I can't reveal who I am to many people, but if there's one person who isn't going to snitch on me to Omni, it's the person they fucked over first.

Mila pauses in the doorway, her back to me. I can see she's breathing heavier. When she turns round, her expression hasn't changed much but it's softened slightly.

'I'll give you ten minutes,' she says eventually. Relief unspools within me, and I go to follow her inside. She shakes her head, blocking the doorway, and points to a white gate at the side of the house. 'You can wait out back. You sure as hell aren't coming into my home.' Without waiting for a response, she closes the door in my face. I suppose if the past that nearly ended my life kept coming back to haunt me, I'd feel the same.

I do as I'm told and find myself in a small back garden. There's a hammock, flower beds and, just beyond, a low white fence, the beach and rolling waves of the ocean. I stand still and take it all in, breathing in and out, nice and slow. When I close my eyes, it feels as if the water is lulling me to sleep, cradling me in its melody.

Mila steps outside to join me, taking a seat at a wooden table and lighting a cigarette as one of the dogs settles by her feet. At least I thought it was a cigarette, until I catch the smell of weed on the breeze. I sit opposite her, wondering where on earth to start.

'I'm sorry for coming out here and—'

'Interrupting my peace?' Mila takes a drag, blowing a plume of smoke up into the air.

I shift in my seat, uncomfortable at her brisk tone. This is a woman who has tried to move on. I hate that I'm now one of many anchors who refuses to let her.

'Who's your brother?' she asks, eyes searching my face as if she can find the answer there.

'Adam Miller.' I can see the name doesn't ring a bell. I doubt it would for many people. His name was largely left out of the coverage about his death, and then it was completely overshadowed by Penelope's disappearance. 'He was the crew member who fell from the hotel roof in 2020.'

Mila raises her eyebrows but doesn't say anything.

'I *am* sorry,' I try again in an attempt to make her understand that I regret having to be here. 'I just . . . I don't know where to start. I'm looking for answers and I thought it would help to know more about your story. You lived through this too.'

'Why does my story matter? Nobody cared then. They sure as hell won't care now.'

'*I* care. Omni deserve to pay for what they've done to you, to Penelope Daunt, to my brother. They can't be allowed to do it again.'

Mila levels me with an unflinching stare, as if trying to get to the heart of my intentions. I meet it head on because I need her to know that I'm not here to satisfy a thirst for scandal. I'm here for the truth. She doesn't look convinced. Would you if the world had laughed in your face when you'd pleaded for help? I'm almost out of ideas to earn her trust, but I have one last card to play.

I take my phone from my pocket and open my text messages, clicking on Adam's name. My heart skips a beat as I look at those words again. I turn the screen round so Mila can see them too. Her eyes slide over the phone for a few seconds. Even though she's protected herself well, I know the text must dredge up memories of her own. Painful ones that leave scars nobody else can see.

'He sent me those messages the night he died. Was it a coincidence that he clearly knew something about Omni and then fell off a roof not long after?' I swallow my fury, trying to keep a level head. 'Omni might have told the world it was an accident, but I'm not buying it. I think they murdered him.'

The admission robs the oxygen from my lungs for just a moment, then breathes new fierce life back into them. It's the first time I've said it out loud, but I believe it with every fibre of my being. My brother was *murdered*. There's no other explanation.

Mila bows her head, then lets go of a breath. 'I used to think they'd kill me too.'

Her words are quiet, mingling with the notes of the ocean, but I hear them, and I know she's going to talk. Not because she wants to – she probably wants nothing less – but because maybe telling her story to someone who will listen might just free her from its shackles.

'Omnificent promised me every dream under the sun,' she begins. 'And I was stupid enough to believe them. I had nothing before they plucked me out of nowhere. That's always been a part of their game plan – take a young kid who *needs* something and offer them their hopes and dreams on a platter. It makes them particularly compliant, because what kid who's just trying to survive will say no? Omnificent know that, and they use it to get what they want.'

I'd somehow never seen it from that perspective before. Lucky came from nothing. Ella came from nothing. Ryan came from nothing. They were celebrated as kids who had made it despite the odds stacked against them. But in the light of Mila's words, something I'd once seen as inspirational now looks more calculated. I feel stupid. How could I have assumed that Omnificent were generously looking to bring up new actors, to give them a chance in a world that's almost impenetrable from the outside? It might look like a selfless gift, but the ribbon it's wrapped in hides a more sinister purpose.

'I was fourteen when I signed a contract with Omnificent. They offered me everything I'd ever wanted. Money. Fame. Success. A way out. I grew up in a tough place, relentlessly bullied for years, and that's *all* I wanted – to get out. Omnificent gave me a way to do that.'

A cloud of resentment settles over Mila as she recalls a time she's tried so hard to forget.

'Things started going wrong when I signed on to do *Sunset High*. Sure, there were things I didn't like about Omni Channel before then. They were obsessed with me looking a certain way to fit the American sweetheart template, so it meant things like dyeing my hair or getting piercings was pretty much banned. Somehow it didn't seem so controlling at the time.' She scoffs thinking about it now. 'But if I thought Omni Channel were bad, they were nothing compared to Lake Carter. He's the cruellest man I've ever met.'

I frown. '*Lake?*'

I think of the overly friendly if not slightly boisterous man I'd met earlier on set. There were many words I might've used to describe him but *cruel* wasn't one of them.

Mila expels a dark laugh. 'Ah, he's giving you the nice-guy act, is he? Yeah, he does that at the start to get you on side. Quite the actor himself. But he can switch just like *that*.' Mila snaps her fingers to make her point. 'Lake Carter was the beginning of the end for me. He ruined every last scrap of dignity I had left, robbed me of my self-esteem and my confidence until I was an empty shell. It seemed small at the time – little comments about how I wasn't doing enough, how my acting wasn't up to scratch, how he could replace me with any girl in a ten-mile radius. One comment alone wouldn't get to me, but weeks of it – months even – and they all started to pile up. I felt so worthless that I eventually had no choice but to believe what he said. Maybe I wasn't good enough. Maybe I didn't deserve any of this. Lake broke me down bit by bit every day and nobody stopped him. I was just a twenty-year-old girl trying desperately to stop myself from drowning in the self-hate he inflicted upon me.'

Mila pauses to take a long pull of her joint. She's not sad about any of this and she talks about it as if it's something that simply happened. She's been hardened by it. The things she must have endured are almost unspeakable. And yet it happened in front of the world, and all the world did was watch.

'Omnificent themselves weren't any better. No matter where I went, photographers followed me. I couldn't hide from them. And when I gave them the satisfaction of lashing out, they became sharks in the water, thirsting for my blood. They always wanted more. I asked Omnificent, Lake, Jill Anderson, anyone who would listen, to make it stop. I *begged* them for help, but I soon realized it was them calling the photographers to follow me in the first place.' A sour pent-up fury coats her every word.

'Every time I landed on the front page, Omni Channel saw it as good publicity, hoping the millions of people analysing my life would also tune in to watch *Sunset High*. They were stirring the pot for their own gain. They didn't care what damage it did to me, so long as they got what they wanted.'

Mila glances out over the ocean, gathering herself together. The guilt I feel is heavy. I'd watched every sensationalized clip over the years – was I not part of the problem too?

'Have you ever felt like someone was watching you?' she asks, still looking out at the water. 'Try living that experience every hour of every day. It made me paranoid about everything. It was like an itch. I wanted to claw the skin from my body, step outside myself and run. But I didn't have anywhere to go.'

Mila flicks her eyes back to me. She doesn't cry. She's past that now. 'When I started to act out, people laughed. They called me crazy. Stories were made up about me in the press to paint me in a certain light that would better fit the narrative that I'd lost my mind. They saw a young girl, desperate to be saved, and they turned their backs. It's a tale as old as time. Nobody ever leaves this industry unscathed, but the young women in it are forced to bear more scars than anyone else. The world compares us, pits us against each other, picks at our faults, highlights our insecurities. They tell us to smile more but not too much in case we look fake. Wear something sexy but also wholesome. Don't be too frigid and definitely don't be a slut. Say yes, never no. Don't gain weight but don't lose too much either. Be grateful. Relatable. Funny. And accept that people will still hate you, even if you give them everything they want from you.'

Mila balances the joint on her lips and takes her phone out of her pocket. She types something, clicks, then places the phone down on the table so I can see the screen. It's a picture of me, Lucky, Ryan and Ella leaving the restaurant last night. Mila

141

points to Ryan, striding through the doors with a confident smile on her face.

'And history is about to repeat itself.'

My heart starts to beat quicker. 'What do you mean?'

'Omni Channel want her gone,' Mila says simply. 'It's obvious. They gave the leading role to Ella Winter, offered her a new contract, paired her up with Lucky Tate. I might have left Omnificent and Lake Carter behind long ago, but I know how they work. Ryan's no longer the innocent little kid who will blindly do what they ask of her. If I were to guess, I'd say Omni Channel see the benefit of playing out a love triangle to get more press for the show, but it doesn't matter if they throw her under the bus later down the line because they have their new princess. And then the cycle repeats itself. They mould you until they break you, then they replace you just like that.' She looks down at the picture and nods to herself. 'Mark my words – Ryan Hudson is next.'

'Is that what happened to you? To Penelope Daunt?' I ask.

There's a crash from upstairs inside the house that makes me jump in my seat. Mila whips round, panic written all over her face. She eyes the dog by her feet and gives a sharp whistle. 'Max!'

A few seconds later, the second dog comes padding outside from the kitchen. Mila strokes him behind the ears, still staring into the house. She glances back at me, then stands. 'Time's up,' she says briskly.

The remnants of late afternoon are slipping away, and I need to get back to Beverly Hills, but I have one more question.

'Thanks for your time, Mila. And I really do mean it – I'm sorry I had to come out here.' She acknowledges my gratitude with a nod. 'One last thing, though. Penelope Daunt . . .'

I almost don't know how to phrase a question so big. But I feel sure she's the missing piece of the puzzle.

'You said I wasn't the first to come here and ask for help. Did she? Do you know what happened to her?'

Mila holds my stare for a moment, the silence between us overbearing.

'Her story is not mine to tell,' she says finally. She walks to the house, steps inside and turns to close the door. 'I hope you find out the truth about your brother. But please – don't come back.'

Chapter Fourteen

DIVIDES

Abel

We're chauffeured to the set of *The Late Late Show*, and the whole way there I'm shitting myself. We're talking *deep breaths in the back of the car* shitting myself. The anticipation of being on a live TV show that's watched by more than two million people, with a few million more watching the highlights online, is enough to make me pass out. This is the complete opposite of my comfort zone. If my comfort level is Earth, then this moment right now is Pluto. In fact, those planets might not even be far enough apart.

The conversation in the back of the SUV hasn't exactly been plentiful. We've sat in complete silence except for the radio the whole journey. The tension between Ryan and Ella has settled over everything, neither of them looking like they'll be the first to break it. As for Lucky, he's in a world of his own, earphones in and eyes closed.

I'd try to crack the awkwardness if I wasn't so busy wondering whether I'll be the first person to faint on live TV, replaying what Mila said over in my head or thinking about what the hell Porter McKay is up to. I'm desperate to follow that lead but, for now I have to play the part of a celebrity.

The driver pulls up to the back entrance. 'On your guard. Paps straight ahead.'

I lean round the driver's seat and look through the windscreen. Sure enough, there's a fence about ten metres away with half a dozen photographers straddling it. Security is stopping them from hopping the barrier, but they're poised to catch our picture.

Lucky shakes himself awake and sees them too. He sighs, then lifts up his shirt slightly and retrieves a small flask from his waistband, taking a quick glug before hiding it again. Ryan and Ella both look at him with the same concern I feel.

He shrugs it off. 'Dutch courage,' he mumbles.

Without waiting for a response, Lucky jumps from the car first, jogging round to open Ella's door. There's a flurry of clicks from the photographers, who all start yelling our names. I watch Lucky and Ella hold hands, giving a brief smile and wave before slipping through the open back door. Ryan beams for the cameras too, linking arms with me. I take her lead, and smile and wave like I'm some kind of royalty. Inside, Lucky and Ella have already disconnected, smiles dead on their lips.

'There you are!' Jill says, rushing up the hallway to greet us.

'Ella, honey, I've had Natalie put some options from the stylist on the rack in your dressing room. I think you should go with the white mini. It's perfect – fresh off the runway, and it gives off a real angelic vibe. You'll look like the nation's sweetheart.'

'And the rest of us are supposed to look like what, her entourage?' says Ryan, unimpressed.

'Oh, sweetie, don't be silly,' Jill says. 'There'll be something just as gorgeous for you to wear too. But wait for Ella to have a quick look through the options first, okay?'

'So long as the princess gets her first choice,' Ryan murmurs.

Jill doesn't notice and turns back to Lucky and Ella. 'Now we'll have you two leading the interview, so let's make sure we're all on the same page about everything. The questions have been vetted in advance, so I can prep you on the right direction to take when answering them. And don't worry, you two,' she adds over her shoulder to me and Ryan as she guides Ella and Lucky into a separate room. 'We won't need you for this. Feel free to relax in your dressing rooms and a runner will come grab you when it's time. Break a leg!'

Ryan offers a middle finger to Jill's back as she closes the door, which makes me laugh. She giggles too, although it's laced with a defeated exhaustion.

'I guess I'll see you out there then,' she says when we reach her dressing room. 'Give me a knock if you need anything. And don't worry about the interview. It's honestly not as scary as you think. You'll be great.'

'Thanks, Ryan. I appreciate it.'

'Any time.' She gives me a peck on the cheek and closes the door.

Over the next hour, people drift in and out of my dressing room to prepare me for the night. First, it's make-up, whose job it is to make me look like I'm wearing nothing at all, while also giving me a flawless complexion for the cameras. Studying myself in the mirror, I swear I look like a wax doll, but the artist promises I'll look perfect on TV. I take her word for it.

Then comes the stylist, who gives me a Gucci suit paired with some expensive trainers and gold rings for my fingers. All of it is rented, a fact the stylist reminds me of a dozen times since she needs it back without a scratch or stain by the end of the night. Now I understand Cinderella's struggle. The stylist nearly has a heart attack when she sees me go to chomp down on some food once she's got me all buttoned up.

Jill briefly drops in during the stylist session to prep me for one or two questions that will be asked in my direction. Apparently there'll be a joke about my British accent – I'm not sure what's so funny about it, but whatever – and a follow-up question about how I'm finding being on the show so far. Other than that, I'm free to do nothing but sit and smile until the interview is over. Sounds simple enough.

There's a final knock at my door a few minutes before showtime. By this point, I've pushed my nerves so far down into my gut I've managed to half convince myself that I'm excited. I mean, come on, there are worse things in the world than pretending to be a celebrity. What's the big deal? When

I answer the door, Lucky's standing there, wearing what can only be described as an artist's painting coat. On closer inspection, it *is* a suit that might've once been off white but has since been splattered in various colours like Lucky's been redecorating his house. Smiley faces, stars and squiggles have been doodled onto the material at random as if a toddler was in charge. I take one glance at him and the look on my face must be clear. He groans as I let him in.

'Does it look as bad as I think it does?' His tone tells me I should either lie or . . . No, there's no other option. It's lie or nothing.

'It's, uh, pretty cool,' I try, laughter burrowing into my cheeks. 'It's a statement, that's for sure.'

'You're supposed to be an actor, at least lie convincingly.' Lucky glares at me and I cave, letting my laughter burst out.

'Okay, fine. It's not exactly my cup of tea. Then again, I think white suits are hideous. But I'm not a stylist, so what do I know? Why are you wearing something you clearly hate anyway?'

'*Jill*,' Lucky spits, as if that's all the explanation I need. 'Omnificent have this partnership with the designer – they pay Omni and Omni make sure we wear their stuff. I'm basically a walking billboard.'

'Rather you than me,' I say. Then quickly add, 'No offence,' when I see the look on his face.

He abruptly changes the subject. 'I thought I'd come and check in on you,' he says, crashing onto the sofa and stealing some of the snacks that were laid out for me. On the flatscreen

TV, Jeremy Love is about to give his opening monologue. 'Ready for your TV debut?'

I realize there's the faintest slur to his words, and his eyes are slightly glazed too. It might not be noticeable from afar, but up close I can see the shield he's tried to put up. It's not like this is the first time either – his hotel room, the restaurant, just now in the car. I think about the conversation I overheard between him and Omni. He can't be taking their threats of rehab all that seriously if he's still drinking. Maybe he thinks they're just empty words? My guess is grief. He has nobody now his mom's gone. Millions around the world adore him, and yet he still seems so lonely.

'As I'll ever be,' I say. 'Any tips, from one pro to a slightly lesser pro?'

Looking at him laid out on the sofa as if he's going to ask me to paint him like one of my French girls, I don't even mind the suit any more. Sure, I'd prefer him out of it. Wait, that sounded wrong. But you know what . . . I said what I said!

'Hey, guys, it's time to get this show on the road,' a runner says, popping their head round the door.

Lucky gets up, much to my dismay. He throws an arm round me, and maybe it's the adrenaline or maybe I'm just *that* pathetic, but his touch burns through my clothes and heats my skin.

'Top tip – laugh. Don't have anything to say? Laugh. Want to get out of an awkward question? Laugh. Someone makes a joke that's not even funny? Laugh anyway. And if you feel like you're going to faint, let me know. I'll stand up and drop my pants to distract everyone. I'll do anything to get these damn things off me.'

I hope I don't pass out before I see that. The thought enters my mind and I quickly bat it away.

'I guess this is it then,' Lucky says. He wobbles slightly as we leave the room.

'Hey, are you all right?' I reach out to steady him. He's clearly had more to drink than I thought. Now I really am worried. We're about to go out on stage.

'Never better,' he says, although his tone suggests otherwise. He looks down at my hand, then up at me. I catch a breath. He smiles. 'On your six, neighbour.'

A flush of elation is thwarted by a darker thought. I'm not the one who needs protecting here. He is. He's slipping, and I don't know what I can do to help. The only thing I can do is tell him, in his own words, that he's not alone.

'On your six right back.'

I say it like I mean it – *really* mean it – because I do. Despite my best efforts to separate my own personal feelings from the job at hand, I want to make sure Lucky knows that much.

We're ushered down the corridor towards the set and left behind a large screen. On the other side of it, Jeremy Love is doing the introductions just as Ella and Ryan join us, both in skyscraper heels that make them look like towering goddesses. Ella has her hair pinned into an up-do, wearing the short white dress that Jill suggested. Ryan looks like a model in a belted leather jacket that's styled as a minidress and accessorized with gold jewellery.

One of the runners starts glancing at us with a look of concern on her face. She murmurs something into her radio and steps towards Ella, but quickly backtracks when she hears Jeremy Love say, 'Please join me in welcoming to the stage the brand-new cast of *Sunset High*: Lucky Tate, Ella Winter, Ryan Hudson and Abel Miller!'

The screen lifts up to reveal us, and I don't even have time to catch my breath before I'm met with the lights and the cameras and a feverish audience. Lucky leads the way, striding with confidence onto the stage and towards the long sofa positioned next to Jeremy Love's desk. Ella gives the audience a wave and blows them a kiss, while Ryan flicks on a switch and offers a winning smile.

Well, here goes nothing.

I wave and smile too, hoping I don't look like a complete dork. I'm lightheaded and trying to concentrate on putting one foot in front of the other until I'm safely sat down in my spot beside Ryan, furthest away from Jeremy. Well, as safe as you can be when there are half a dozen cameras pointed at you, beaming your every movement out into the world.

'Welcome!' Jeremy Love says, holding his hands wide and showing off two rows of impossibly bright teeth.

He's a white man with a salt-and-pepper beard and a thinning comb-over. He's supposed to be a comedian, but I can't say I've ever laughed at one of his jokes before. Still, it's beyond surreal to see him in real life, in this setting, with all eyes on us. Jeremy beams.

'I have to say, guys, I'm *so* happy to have you here! The *new* cast of *Sunset High*. That's huge! How does it feel to be a part of something so big?'

Lucky leans forward as if he's conspiring with his best buddy. I know he's drunk, but he's doing a good job at hiding it. The Lucky Tate Show is in full effect. 'Well, you know, we're all so grateful to be given an opportunity to work on something that holds this much impact. Everyone loved the original *Sunset High*, and we're just super excited to try to bring you a fresh take on it. It's going to be a lot of fun.'

'Right!' Ella says, practically bouncing in her seat. 'When we got the call that this was happening, we all jumped at it, didn't we?' She places her hand briefly on Lucky's leg. It's just for a second, but I know it will set Twitter ablaze. I'm sure Ella knows it too. For a fleeting moment I feel a pang of . . . jealousy? *For the love of God, Abel, pull yourself together.*

Ryan nods enthusiastically so I do the same. I don't want to look like a spare part that's accidentally wandered onto the stage.

'Yeah, it was such an exciting moment. I called you straight away and said, "Can you believe this is even happening?"' Ryan says to Ella, and they burst into giggles like they're besties all over again. All this whiplash, I can't keep up. 'I'm so glad we get to do it together, with friends.' Ryan links arms with Ella and me. 'Old *and* new. We get to welcome Abel into our crazy little world, and it's been so fun getting to know him.'

Ryan turns to me, and it feels like the entire world does too. There's a painful, almost deafening silence that fills the room as everyone waits for me to talk. The studio lights feel like fire burning down on me. My mouth is completely dry.

Say something for fuck's sake.

'Yeah, fun,' I say and . . . that's it. Nothing more comes out. I'm completely frozen on live TV in front of an audience of fans and millions of people watching across the country.

Fortunately Lucky comes to my rescue. 'You see, we're such a wild bunch that we swore Abel to secrecy before we stepped on stage. He's bound by an oath, so don't go trying to get him to crack, Jez. I know your game!' Lucky winks at Jeremy, and they both throw their heads back and laugh.

'Oh, I wouldn't dream of it! But you *are* having fun, Abel? This is your first big role, right?'

This time, I'm a little quicker. 'Yeah, my first big role. You could say I've jumped in at the deep end, huh?' The audience gives me some polite laughter, which Jeremy adds to with his booming roar as if I've just told the world's greatest joke. Okay, sir, calm down. 'But it's been really fun already, and the guys have all been super welcoming. I'm loving every minute of it.'

'And forgive me for stating the obvious, but you're *British* too?' The crowd *woos*, which makes me blush a little. I laugh and nod. 'I LOVE IT!' Jeremy bellows.

'A real British heart-throb, isn't he, Jez?' Lucky chimes in, turning his eyes on me as if he's not outright flirting on live TV. I'm sure it looks like friendly banter to everyone else, but to me it feels like a secret only we know about. At least I hope he's flirting with me.

'You must be really popular with the ladies,' Jeremy says to me with a chuckle.

Ugh, what a creep. I flash a grin and shrug. 'If my accent is all I've got going for me over here, then I'd better start talking like I'm on *The Crown* instead of *Sunset High*.'

More laughter, and then Jeremy moves his attention back to Ella and Lucky, just as rehearsed. It seems so spontaneous watching from home, but it's as carefully plotted out as a novel. Ryan gives me an encouraging smile while the heat's off us, which I translate to mean I'm not totally fucking this up.

The rest of the interview passes by in the blink of an eye. Lucky and Ella take the lead just like Jill wanted them to, both of them in full celebrity mode. Their charisma is charming, their banter funny, and, for a moment, I begin to forget what goes on behind the scenes. They're the perfect couple. If *I* think that, the world must be completely hoodwinked.

Jeremy wraps things up and then it's done. The show goes to a commercial break and Jeremy leans over the desk to thank us. 'Great job, you guys. Thanks for coming on the show. I hope you've got me a couple of tickets for the premiere reserved – my daughter will never forgive me if we don't get invited.'

Ella giggles. 'Of course. But you can just say it's because *you* want to come and watch the show. We won't judge.'

We all stand up and get ready to leave when Jeremy notices something. 'I think you've got something on the back of your dress, Ella,' he says. 'I doubt the camera picked it up bu—'

Jeremy stops, eyes widening as he gets a proper look. Ella is trying to see over her shoulder but can't quite crane her neck round far enough. A member of the audience in the front row gasps and points. The person next to them already has their phone out, snapping a picture. Sensing something is wrong, we all hurry off stage and into the wings.

'What is it?' Ella asks, beginning to panic. She rushes ahead to her dressing room where her mom and Natalie are waiting, and as she paces ahead I see it for myself. On the back of Ella's dress, written in red lipstick, are six small words.

THE ANGEL IS A CHEATING SLUT!

Lucky sees it too, his jaw dropping. 'Holy shit,' he says, just as Ella lets out a blood-curdling scream. She storms back out into the hallway, eyes wild and furious. She barges past us and flies straight into Ryan's dressing room.

'YOU DID THIS!' Ella screams.

Lucky runs after her and I follow, shutting us into the room. I have a feeling this is going to be an argument that's best kept behind closed doors.

'Did what?' Ryan says. If she's acting, then give her an Oscar now. She seems genuinely clueless, but Ella isn't buying it. 'Want to fill me in so we're on the same page?'

'You're an evil *bitch*, that's what,' Ella retorts with as much fury as she can muster. 'I know you did this.' She turns round so Ryan can see the words on the back of her dress.

Ryan raises an eyebrow. 'First of all, I'd call you a cheating slut to your face if I really wanted to. Secondly, I'd rather be an evil bitch than Omni's bitch. And third . . .' Ryan pauses, then folds her lips to stop a smile from spreading over her face. 'I owe whoever wrote that a drink.'

Ella lets out a guttural scream and runs in Ryan's direction, but Lucky is one step ahead and grabs her round the waist, moving himself between them.

'Oh, let her go. What is she going to do? Good girl me to death?' Ryan rolls her eyes, looking every bit unbothered.

'I swear to God, Ryan, I'm entirely done with you,' Ella hisses, struggling in Lucky's arms. She gives up the fight, smoothing out her hair and dress, but she still looks furious. 'And to think I used to feel sorry for you. But now I realize that maybe it's *you*. Maybe *you're* the problem.'

Ryan's bravado slips slightly.

'Ella . . .' Lucky says in a warning tone, but she snorts in derision.

'What, she doesn't want to hear the truth now? Is that pill too tough to swallow?' Ella steps to the side of Lucky so she can lock eyes with Ryan. 'All this time I thought you were the victim. I thought you had it hard and everyone was out to get you, just like you said. But no. *You're* the problem. You're a hateful, spiteful bitch. And to think I've been missing you and wanting to make things right again!'

Ryan *almost* has no reaction to Ella's words, but she blinks and her jaw tenses, a small dent in her armour.

'Maybe if you dropped the act and let people in for once, if you stopped blaming the world and took a proper look at yourself, then people would *stay* in your life,' Ella says. 'That's why you can't keep a friend or a relationship, because you push them all away until you're left with nobody. And do you know what? That's *exactly* what you deserve.'

The silence in the room is taut with tension. I don't know where to look or what to do. Lucky doesn't seem to know either and stands defeated between them. Even Ella suddenly seems apologetic, but she doesn't take it back and she doesn't say sorry. It's Ryan who breaks the silence.

'Well, thanks for telling me how you really feel,' she says. There's a catch in her voice, but she shrugs it off, stepping in close and pushing the hand Lucky extends to keep them apart aside. 'I hope you remember this when Omni are finally done using you. When they throw you in the dirt as if you never existed in the first place. It's a long way down from the top, and I can't *wait* to watch you fall.' Her words are quiet and dark.

Ella stands her ground as Ryan storms past, leaving us all behind. But I see the hurt and heartbreak etched into her face. It's only there for a moment, though, and then she's gone.

Chapter Fifteen

IN THE HILLS, NOBODY CAN HEAR YOU SCREAM

Ryan

I'm going home, back to the place I once called a sanctuary before a stalker with personal boundary issues ruined it for me. Maybe I should go back to the hotel, or to Brad's safe house, but, right now, I just want to be home. I can't stand to stay another second under the hand of Omnificent and their games. And if I have to see Ella's face one more time, I might break apart completely.

In a way I'm glad Ella has shown her true colours and told me how she really feels. It hurts, but better to find out now than later. It confirms everything the little voice in the back of my head has always told me. *Don't open yourself up to anyone. Protect yourself because nobody else will.* I've known it my whole life, but it stings all the same. In fact, if

I dared to look within myself properly, I'm sure I'd find the devastation has cut deep. But I won't look that far. I'll throw my emotions into a box and lock it up tight. There's no room for them here. Not now.

I don't bother waiting for Jill to come and berate me for something I didn't do, as she surely will once she sees that the pictures of Ella's dress, taken by someone in the audience, are already circulating online. It's all anyone can talk about. *Good*, I think, locking my phone and punching the soft leather seat of the Uber I've hailed to take me away. They can all choke as far as I'm concerned.

If Omni want to replace me with Ella, and Ella wants to be a bitch about it, then they're both welcome to each other. Omni can try to fire me, but it would cost them a truckload of money to breach the contract they manipulated me into signing. Luckily this stupid show is the last project I have under my current deal. Once it's over, I'll be free of them.

The Uber pulls up outside the gates of my house. It's late, already past midnight, and the road is drenched in darkness, only broken by the amber glow of the street lights. I thank the driver and climb out of the car, the silence absolute all around me. I haven't been back since the *Sunset High* posters were left on my doorstep, but I'm glad to be home, away from the world, safe.

I let myself in and instantly feel relieved when I close the door behind me. I lean back against it, not even reaching for the light, just letting myself breathe. For a moment, the torment I'm trying so hard to fight against gets an upper hand, taunting me with my own memories, breaking me from the inside out.

I remember last summer, when Ella and I first started dating. We both had a rare day off and had decided to take a road trip out to a secluded beach for a picnic. We were still so unsure of ourselves and each other, if this was what we thought it might be. Until then, it had been traded glances, lingering touches, a close friendship that *could* be something more. But that day was when things shifted. We both knew it, even if we didn't say it. I knew, in my heart, that I wanted Ella. But I told myself she'd never want me. She had too much riding on her career, a family who relied on her not to fuck this up.

We laid out a blanket, the sun warming our skin as if it was bestowing its blessing upon us. We laughed, I remember that. *So much laughter.* We swam in the ocean. We talked about things that didn't really matter because we could, and it felt good to forget who we were. It was like, just for a second, we'd stepped outside our own crazy worlds and found that we were the only two people left on Earth. And when we laid down next to each other in the sand, our fingers gently brushing, I looked over at her. Her head was tilted back, eyes closed.

'I know you're looking at me,' she said.

I laughed. 'And so what if I am?'

She opened her eyes and a smile lit up her face, like a blooming flower unfurling its petals. I wanted to see that smile every day, and I wanted to be the reason for it.

She propped herself up on one elbow and I did the same. My heart hammered in my chest as we looked at each other – *into* each other – asking, without words, the question we both needed the answer to.

If I jump, will you jump too?

I leaped first, leaning in closer. I'd never been so scared in all my life. I could literally feel my heart opening itself after so many years living under a steely guard. I felt like I was taking it out of my chest and placing it in her hands, begging her not to break it. But she did the same, giving hers to me, and our lips came together, sealing a pact.

The memory disintegrates before my eyes and I'm back home, in the dark, alone once more. I feel like I have nothing left in me but shattered pieces of the heart I begged not to be broken.

'Fuck them all,' I whisper. 'Fuck every single one of them.'

I take a deep breath, then start for the kitchen, dropping my bag and keys on the side table. I fill a glass with water, humming to myself to keep my mind from wandering too far. I have to keep it under control so it doesn't splinter my defences again. I can't think about what I've lost. I refuse to.

I remove my shoes and climb the stairs, letting the light spilling out from the kitchen guide me as I scroll through my texts. One from Brad, asking me what's going on and if I'm okay. A call from Jill interrupts before I can reply, but I don't even let the first ring finish before hitting the red button. *No, thanks.* I put my phone on do not disturb and place it on the dresser just inside my bedroom as I pass the doorway.

A gentle glow begins to slowly illuminate the bathroom as soon as I step onto the snow-white marble, triggered by my movement. I turn on the taps of the large, curved bathtub and begin to tie my hair up, then slip out of my dress and wrap myself in a thick white robe hanging from the back of the door. When I'm done, I lean on the counter, hunched over as I take deep breaths, trying to find myself in this nightmare.

I look up into the mirror.

It's another moment, a single beat, before I see the hooded figure standing behind me in the doorway.

I whip round, a scream trapped at the back of my throat, completely paralysed by fear. The man doesn't move. He just watches me. He's dressed all in black, his eyes the only thing I can see. The rest of his face is covered by a cap, a hood and a scarf wrapped round his mouth.

He takes a step closer.

I scramble backwards into the counter. I'm trapped. I think of my cell on the dresser in my bedroom. I begin to scream but the windows are soundproofed, and even if they weren't, would the neighbours hear my cry for help? Would they be too late?

The man doesn't move towards me again. He watches me scream, seemingly enjoying my vulnerability. He puts a finger to where his lips are under the scarf, then turns and runs. I hear him go down the stairs and out of the door. I begin to hyperventilate but quickly realize I have to pull myself together.

Because what if he comes back?

I don't dare go downstairs to try to escape, so instead I dash for my bedroom and lock the door, turning on the light and grabbing my cell. I dial the cops, the phone shaking in my hand.

'911, what's your emergency?' a calm voice says.

But I can't speak. I look all around me, horrified by what's been left behind. My bedroom has been trashed, pictures smashed in their frames, clothes ripped from my closet, a chair overturned. And there, on one of the walls, is a message spray-painted in red.

YOU'RE NEXT.

All around it are posters from the original *Sunset High* TV show, the same ones delivered to me in the gift-wrapped box, stuck to the wall and fluttering in the breeze from an open window. I feel the gasp leave my body.

'Hello? 911, what's your emergency?'

Tears leak from the corners of my eyes. 'Please help,' I whisper. 'I think someone is trying to kill me.'

The *Famous Last Words* Podcast

Hattie Wilson: Hi, everyone, and welcome to a brand-new emergency episode of *Famous Last Words*. My name's Hattie Wilson . . .

Devin Taylor: And I'm Devin Taylor . . .

Hattie Wilson: And *[sighs],* unfortunately we're here to reveal some pretty dark breaking news.

Devin Taylor: Honestly, when I first heard about this, my heart dropped.

Hattie Wilson: Same. I literally can't believe it. So, for those of you who might not be aware, we told you in the last episode that Omni Channel have announced the reboot of *Sunset High*, which was met with . . . well, a lot of excitement to be honest, but also some scepticism, right, Dev?

Devin Taylor: Absolutely, not least because of the curse, run of bad luck, whatever you want to call it, that has previously followed the show around.

Hattie Wilson: We're talking the public breakdown of Mila Stone in 2010 leading to her retiring from the spotlight in 2011, and the disappearance of Penelope Daunt in 2020, as well as a junior assistant working on *Sunset High* tragically falling from the roof of the cast and crew hotel that same year.

Devin Taylor: I guess you could say that this curse has been haunting Omnificent and *Sunset High* for a while. Which brings us to last night, when it was revealed in quotes and pictures leaked by an anonymous source that Ryan Hudson, one of the cast members of the show, had her home broken into last night. Not only that, but she actually *returned to the house* while the intruder was still inside. It's absolutely terrifying reading the details about this, isn't it, Hats?

Hattie Wilson: It really is. In the article posted by the *Daily Eye*, a source, who we believe to be a part of law enforcement since those details are so confidential, leaked the story, while pictures of the scene also managed to leak online too. In one of the snaps you can see Ryan's bedroom has been completely trashed and a spray-painted message can be seen on the wall that reads: *You're next.*

Devin Taylor: It sends shivers down my spine hearing that again. Those pictures are horrifying. I can't imagine what Ryan must be going through right now.

Hattie Wilson: Well, Omnificent have since released a statement about the break-in. It reads: *Last night, Ryan Hudson was the victim of a heinous and heart-breaking crime. Thankfully Ryan is safe, and we will continue to look after her as she begins to process what has happened. Although production will be paused for a few days so we can ensure the safety of our cast members, Ryan would personally like to thank her fans for their concern, and also let them know that she will* not *be stepping down from her role in* Sunset High. *We support and applaud her courageous decision and look forward to bringing the best show we can to screens around the world soon.*

Devin Taylor: It's a pretty run-of-the-mill statement, but that last part was pretty powerful, don't you think? I feel like Ryan is telling the world that she won't be scared into quitting. I really admire her for that because – *me*? – I would have handed in my notice and got as far away from that damn show as I could.

Hattie Wilson: Honestly, same. I *hate* the way it's always women who endure this kind of shit, you know? Like, I'm sure male A-listers and whatever get stalkers all the time, but we only ever really hear about *women* having people turn up at their houses, breaking in, having to get restraining orders on creepy men who won't leave them alone. It's so fucked up.

Devin Taylor: And, like, at the end of the day, Ryan is an *eighteen*-year-old girl. She's still a kid!

Hattie Wilson: There's this insane amount of attention that gets thrust upon girls and women in the spotlight, which I don't think helps the whole stalker situation. It's literally fact at this point that we hold female celebrities to a higher standard than male ones, but it's like people think they have some kind of *ownership* over them? It's really uncomfortable to think about. My heart goes out to Ryan Hudson. I really hope she's being looked after.

Devin Taylor: Me too. Now . . . can we talk about the *CHEATING SLUT* dress?!?!

Chapter Sixteen

SIMPLE MATHS

Abel

I didn't want to leak the story about Ryan's break-in. I felt like a piece of shit for kicking her while she was down, but I had to do it. This whole *thing* has become a tug of war inside my head. On the one hand, I know I have a job to do – find out what happened to Adam, and give information to Hannah that might be useful to the *Daily Eye* so I can keep them on side to expose Omni. But, on the other, Ryan, Ella and Lucky are real people. I don't want to hurt them for my own gain, especially after hearing about what Mila went through. I just hope this will all be worth it in the end.

The one thing I *didn't* do was leak the pictures of the scene. Somehow they'd ended up online, which only amped up the frenzy. Had the intruder taken snaps of their handiwork so they could taunt Ryan even more? The idea made me feel sick. But for now I try not to focus too much on that question – I have a lead to follow up.

It's the day after the break-in, and Porter McKay has been a constant thought simmering in the back of my mind. Until now I haven't had time to do anything about it, but with production of *Sunset High* on pause for a couple of days, I have nothing to do but look at the hotel walls. There's no better time to find out what his deal is.

I start by heading back out to Echo Park, and what I'm almost certain is Hope Waters' house. However, when I get there and knock, nobody answers. I try to peer in through the front windows, but the curtains are drawn. If anyone's home, they're purposefully avoiding me. Fine. Plan B. If Porter thinks he can elude me for ever, he's got another thing coming. I might not be able to find anything else online to help me locate Hope, but Porter is a very different story. After all, the internet already told me everything I need to know.

I set myself up in a local café a few streets away from the house and start digging. I don't exactly have to go far. In the first few frantic weeks after Penelope Daunt went missing, Porter McKay was the one name on everyone's lips. At first, when the door-cam footage was released to the public, he'd been a nameless nobody who'd potentially been one of the last people to see Penelope before she vanished. But like so many mysterious cases that go on to capture the public's attention, idle gossip became baseless accusations spread by armchair detectives. All too quickly the gossip snowballed until it was an all-out witch-hunt accusing Porter of murder.

His name was revealed by someone who recognized him from high school. From there, his social media accounts, job and even the neighbourhood he lived in were outed for all to see. He was cleared by police of any suspicion, but the damage had already been done. His life had been smeared all over the internet.

I haven't even taken three sips of a coffee by the time I've found what I need. McKays' is a family-run hardware store owned by Porter's dad not far from Echo Park. It was where Porter worked when Penelope went missing. But I don't have to find out if he's still employed there – the spanner and hammer logo on the website is the same one that was on Porter's shirt when he answered the door and lied to my face. I down my coffee and hail another Uber, ready to get some answers.

Thirty minutes later, I'm pretending to browse aisles of tools and paint while searching for any sign of Porter. I think I might be out of luck, but then I spot him coming through a side door carrying a couple of heavy boxes. Now he *definitely* can't run.

'Need a hand?' I ask politely, stepping into his line of sight. Porter nearly drops everything. He tries to walk in the opposite direction, but I jump into his way, hands up to show I come in peace. 'I just want to talk.'

'What do you want, man? I already told you; I don't know a Hope Waters.'

Checkmate. 'That's odd – I don't recall giving you Hope's last name when I knocked on her door and asked if you knew who she was.'

Porter scrunches his eyes closed for a second, his jaw rigid. I can almost hear his brain saying: *Fuck*. He groans under his breath. 'Look, I'm not sure what you want, but I don't know anything.'

'Then this won't take long,' I counter. He goes to open his mouth, but I beat him to the punch. 'Please don't make me follow you around town trying to get answers. It looks creepy.'

'You're telling me,' Porter mutters. 'Fine. Whatever. My break is in ten. I'll meet you outside if it means you'll leave me alone when we're done.'

I head out the front, almost certain he'll find a way of escaping my clutches once again, but ten minutes later he follows me out, lighting up a cigarette with a scowl on his face.

'What do you want?' he snaps. 'Aren't you too busy being famous to be chasing me around?'

So he *does* recognize me. No point beating around the bush then. 'I know who you are, and I know you lied about Hope.'

'What does it matter? You the FBI or something?'

'No, just someone who wants answers. I *need* to talk to her. So if you know where she is . . .'

Porter rolls his eyes. 'She skipped town, all right? You think she was going to stick around now your little cursed circus is back? She went home to visit her mom in Arizona. I'm a friend who's looking after her place while she's gone.'

I deflate. Can I not catch a break? 'Why would she leave LA because of *Sunset High*?'

Porter makes a face like it's obvious and I'm stupid as hell. 'Uh, you know she worked on it back in 2020, right? She knew

171

the guy who fell off the roof *and* the girl who went missing.'
He steps round Penelope's name like it's bad luck to say out
loud, but I'm too busy biting the inside of my cheek at the
mention of Adam to care. 'That whole show is bad vibes. She
didn't want to be around when it came back.'

'So why would you lie and say you didn't know her?' I push.

'She doesn't want *anything* to do with *Sunset High*. You
included, dude. I was trying to protect her peace. Why are you
so caught up on her anyway?'

'She was friends with someone I used to know,' I say, half
twisting the truth. 'I wanted to ask her about them.'

Porter's expression changes, his suspicions raised. It feels
like we're circling each other. I need to strike first. Hope might
not be in town, but I have other questions.

'Why were you lingering round the back of my hotel
yesterday? And why did you run when you saw me?'

'I was taking a call and wanted to get off the street. How
was I supposed to know it's the hotel you're staying in? And
I ran because *Sunset High* has already ruined my life once.
In case you missed it, those assholes tried to accuse me of
murder, probably to wipe their own hands clean,' Porter states
matter-of-factly.

'Wait, back up – *they* accused you? I thought that was the
doing of random internet detectives?'

Porter shrugs. 'All I know is Omnificent were more than
happy to push me to the front of the investigation into Penelope
Daunt's disappearance. The cops who brought me in for
questioning as good as said it was them who'd pointed the

finger. Sounds like a guilty conscience to me.'

'You think Omni framed you to cover up their involvement?'

'Look, man, all I did was do a double take when I saw a celebrity in the street. That doesn't exactly qualify as murder. It's Omnificent who've got a whole lot of blood on their hands. They're behind at least one person's breakdown, then years later someone else falls off a roof and another disappears without a trace. And *I'm* supposed to be the bad guy?' He scoffs. 'I'd watch my back if I were you. One of you guys will probably be next.'

A shimmer of apprehension ripples through me. I want to ask more, but Porter is done.

'I've answered your twenty questions. Now will you *please* leave me alone? I want to get on with my life without Omnificent or anyone involved with their shit ruining it. I'm sure Hope feels the same.' He stubs out his cigarette and starts to head back inside.

'Wait!' I call out. 'I know Hope probably doesn't want to talk to me but . . . if she changes her mind, can you give this to her?' I hastily pull a scrap of paper from my rucksack and scrawl down my number. 'I wouldn't ask if it wasn't important.'

'Whatever stops you from coming back here again.' Porter snatches the paper from my hand and leaves.

I head back to the hotel, thinking of the people I've spoken to so far. Every single one of them has laid blame at Omni's door. Barb Harrington said Penelope went missing on the day she was going to give a tell-all interview. She also said Omni had tried to scare her by threatening legal action. Porter thinks

Omni tried to frame him for Penelope's murder. Hope is so scared of them that she's left town altogether. And Mila said they drove her to the brink but pointed the finger at one person in particular.

Now maths has never been my strong suit, but if I add all that information together, it only creates one suspect in my head – Lake Carter, the king of Omni Channel. And if Penelope's disappearance is linked to my brother's death, that puts Lake in the centre of the spotlight. But let's say all of that is true, then there's an even bigger question that I'm still no closer to answering. If Lake is involved in Penelope's disappearance and Adam's murder . . . why?

Chapter Seventeen

A LUXURY PRISON

Ryan

I've been better, let's say that. It's not very often you come home in the dead of night to be faced with an intruder, especially one that leaves a threatening message on your bedroom wall that looks like it could've been painted in your own blood. Now, whenever I close my eyes, that's all I see. Those words, taunting me.

YOU'RE NEXT,

It's been two nights since the break-in, and I've yet to leave my hotel suite. I've kept the curtains drawn and the door locked, only opening it for room service. Movies play out on the TV, but my eyes barely see them. And even when I've managed to fall into a restless sleep, it's only because I've left the light on.

Lucky and Abel both tried to call and text as soon as they found out, but I couldn't face reliving the memory, not when it was so fresh. Ella sent a text too, apologizing and asking if I was okay. I'm sure she feels guilty – if she hadn't accused me of defacing her dress, I wouldn't have gone home that night. I haven't replied to her because I don't know what to say. The stubborn part of me is still so mad at her. Or maybe the emotion I'm looking for is betrayal. She went behind my back with Omni, knowing full well she'd be leaving me hung out to dry. That hurts, because if she's capable of that, did our relationship ever mean anything to her? I'm choosing to ignore the other part of me that wants to be safe in her arms.

Brad texts to update me on security at the house, which hadn't been implemented after the first break-in since I'd been staying at the hotel. He tells me the cops are investigating but have very few leads, which fills me with joy. I'm not sure I'll be able to go back to my home again. How will I ever feel safe there? Right now, it feels like I've lost my house, my job and the only person I really cared about. What else can possibly go wrong?

And then, as if fate is answering my question, Jill calls.

I ignore the first three attempts, but by the fourth I know she'll only keep ringing if I don't pick up. Clearly there's something she needs to tell me, which fills the pit of my stomach with dread.

'Sweetie, hi,' Jill says in the same kind of voice I imagine a parent uses to tell their kid that Santa isn't real. 'Just calling to check in and see how you're doing after that *awful* incident.'

I roll my eyes. 'Perfectly fine. Never better actually.'

Jill either doesn't hear the bite of sarcasm in my tone, or she chooses to disregard it. 'I'm so glad to hear it, angel.'

'I forgot to thank you for the statement you put out in my name. You did a real good job on that – it almost sounded like you'd consulted me on the matter,' I snap.

Jill's tone tightens a little. 'Yes, well, I didn't think it was wise to bother you after such a distressing event. I was trying to help get the press off your back so you could start healing.'

She *almost* sounds convincing. But she forgets I've been under Omni's thumb for years now. I know their games. The statement they publicized was designed for sympathy – a better angle in order to garner as much exposure for *Sunset High* as possible. It had about as much heart as a corpse.

'While I have you on the phone, honey, there's something I wanted to run by you.' Here we go. 'There's a premiere tomorrow night a—'

'No fucking way,' I cut in. I can't believe she's trying to push me back out into the spotlight already.

'Now, sweetie, think about this. It's a huge opportunity to show the world that you're not going to be defeated by the jackass who violated your privacy.'

'*Or* it's a way for you to use my name and the break-in for as many clicks as you can get. No, I'm not doing it.'

Jill sighs. 'I hate to remind you, but there's the small issue of your contract. You know what it says, of course, but there's a certain clause that states you'll fulfil *all* promotional obligations required of you.' My eyes nearly fall out of my skull. Fire licks the back of my throat. She cannot be serious. *Oh, but of course she is.* She jumps in before I can explode. 'I'm really sorry, sweetie, but we need you. Do it for your fans. Prove to them that you're strong and that this won't break you. Think about what a great message it will send to all the kids who look up to you!'

I want to yell FUCK THEM KIDS at the top of my lungs. This isn't about being a good role model. This is my *life*. But I'm too stunned to put my rage into words, and Jill takes that as an agreement.

'I knew you'd be strong about this. You're an angel. I'll make sure the stylist has some options sent over tomorrow. Oh, and filming will resume the morning after the premiere. Lots of love!' She hangs up.

I throw my phone into the pillow and let out a scream, but a knock at the door tells me someone has overheard my frustrations. I think about ignoring it, but then I hear Abel's voice.

'Hey, Ryan? Sorry if I'm interrupting. I just wanted to make sure you were okay. But if you want to be left alone, I totally understand.'

Well, it's talk to Abel and have some company for the first time in days, or wallow in my feelings for the rest of the night. Based on the thrumming in my veins right now, the latter will only make things worse. I open the door and let him in, but I'm immediately embarrassed by the state of my suite. Nothing says *I'm potentially having a breakdown* like a comfort movie playing at low volume on the TV (in my case, *Mean Girls*), an unmade bed that has clearly been used for hibernation and the remnants of room service littered all around. If Abel notices, he doesn't outwardly react, which I'm grateful for. I settle on the sofa, tucking my legs up to my chest, while he puts his phone down on the table and joins me.

'I hope I'm not bothering you,' he says. 'But it, uh . . . well, it sounded like you needed someone to vent to.'

'Sorry you heard that. Jill has a certain effect on people.'

Abel grins. 'Really? She seems like such an easy-going kind of person. Not at all infuriating.'

I laugh, feeling the tension I've been holding on to loosen slightly. 'You've heard about this premiere tomorrow night?'

He nods. 'Jill gave me the heads-up earlier.'

'Well, *apparently* I'm required to attend because it's in my contract. Never mind the fact I just faced an intruder who broke into my house and may or may not have wanted to kill me. So long as they can parade me up and down a red carpet for some sympathetic press.'

Abel shakes his head in disgust. 'They can do that? Despite what you've been through?'

'Of course they can, because we're just pieces in Omni's game. They make the rules, and they don't care who gets hurt in the process. They're probably happy about that scumbag breaking into my house. Jill will think she's won the lottery with the publicity it's received.'

'You really think that?' Abel asks, apparently floored by

179

the idea. 'Surely they draw the line at using your trauma to their advantage?'

I shrug. 'They've done worse. Me and Lucky, for example. His mom died in that terrible accident because paps were chasing the car trying to get a picture of the two of us together. But it was Jill who whipped them up into a frenzy in the first place by leaking rumours that we were engaged, even though it was a complete lie.'

I probably shouldn't be saying all this, but I'm so mad at Jill and Omni that I no longer care about keeping their filthy secrets.

'That day, there were twice the number of photographers than normal, all willing to do anything to get a shot of a ring that didn't exist. Me, Ella, Lucky, his mom and a few others had a private room at a beachside restaurant to celebrate his birthday. Super low-key, nobody really knew about it. Except Omni, of course. Once the engagement rumour leaked, the paparazzi showed up in droves. My manager Brad went out to try to calm things down, get them to leave us alone, and they laughed in his face. One of them said Lake Carter had called them in especially.'

Abel's jaw drops. '*Lake* called the photographers?'

I nod. 'Yep, he was in on it with Jill and told them exactly where to find us. The engagement bullshit was a cover – they leaked the story to draw people in, then made sure to include rumours that *Sunset High* was coming back. Omni were in the middle of auditions and wanted to get the word out there. Lake loved the hysteria our relationship caused, and the extra publicity caused by a fake engagement was the perfect way to get people talking about the show again. So, of course, he called the paps. And we all know how the story ends once we left the restaurant.'

'Lucky's mum . . .'

I bow my head. What happened had been so *avoidable*.

'Me and Lucky had agreed to this relationship so, in some way, we kind of thought we were to blame for what happened. It was all one big mess that his mom should've never been caught up in. She was such a good person, always looking out for him. For both of us actually. She knew our relationship was all business, but she still treated me like I was her stepdaughter. That's why she volunteered to drive the decoy car that left the restaurant first, to keep us safe and get the photographers off our backs. We knew they'd follow her, thinking me and Lucky were in the car, and then we'd be able to sneak off when the coast was clear.'

I think about how Rachel Tate had given us both a big hug and kisses on the cheek, wishing her son a happy birthday for the last time as she picked up her car keys and prepared to leave. 'Don't forget about dinner next week!' she'd called back to me and Ella as she got to the door. I remember her smile so clearly. 'I promise not to give you all food poisoning! I'll see you tomorrow, Luck. Love you!'

And that was the last time we saw her. We got the call less than an hour later. She was already dead before Lucky could get to the hospital. I know that's what pains him the most – the fact he didn't even get to say goodbye.

When I look up, Abel seems choked by grief, as if he knew

181

Rachel too. But he blinks quickly and I'm sure I've imagined it.

'Do you think Lucky's okay?' he asks instead. 'Stupid question I suppose, but . . .'

'His drinking,' I finish. Abel nods. 'He's never been like this before, and I don't know what we can do to help him. He's lost his mom and he's looking for comfort. I just hope that he finds peace soon. All we can do is be there for him in the meantime.'

A sombre mood hangs over us, but eventually the conversation moves on and finds lighter ground – the new Beyoncé album, our gripes with the *Famous Last Words* podcast, how *Mean Girls* is movie excellence at its finest. By the time Abel stands up to leave, I feel lighter.

'Thank you, by the way,' I say when we reach the door. 'I really appreciate you checking in.'

'Don't sweat it,' Abel says, giving me a quick hug. 'If you ever need someone to talk to, I'm just down the hall.'

He's about to go when I see his phone still lying on the table. 'Hey, you left this,' I say, picking it up to hand over to him. As I do, the screen lights up automatically, and I can't help but glance at the notifications on his home screen. The text at the top is from someone called Hannah Wilkes. The name jogs a memory in my head. Where have I heard it before? Abel takes it from me, pockets it and heads back to his own room with a final goodbye.

It's only a few minutes later that I hear another knock at the door. I wonder if Abel forgot something else, but when I look through the peephole, my heart stops, then thunders in my chest with aching desperation.

Ella.

She's standing in the hallway, arms wrapped round herself, restless and unsure. Seeing her there retrieves every emotion I've tried to barricade away. They rattle against the lid of my defences like the evils in Pandora's box. If I remove the lid, will I live to regret it? That's the risk of opening yourself up to love and be loved in return – hurt and heartbreak hide in the dark, waiting for their chance to step into the light.

'Ryan?'

My name on her lips is a divine symphony I want to hear over and over again. I'm so close to letting myself fall back into blissful oblivion with her, but the question of *us* gives me pause. Can my heart bear to be shattered by Ella Winter all over again? Can the trust between us, cracked like a mirror, ever be repaired?

She gently sighs, closes her eyes and places her hand on the door.

'I'm sorry, Ry. I hope you know that.'

I watch her back as she leaves, my hand against the door where hers had just been.

Chapter Eighteen

JOYRIDE

Abel

I can't be sure that Ryan didn't see Hannah's name on my phone. I try telling myself that even if she did, what reason would she have to know who Hannah is. I'm letting my paranoia pull me into uncertainty. I need to relax. But I also need to keep my phone in my damn pocket.

The text from Hannah tells me that the *Daily Eye* are going ahead with the story about Ryan and Ella fighting backstage at *The Late Late Show*. The only reason it hasn't run yet is because the break-in story took priority. I'd fed back the details days ago, but now I've just spent real one-on-one time with Ryan and genuinely enjoyed her company, I feel even more guilty.

I take solace in the fact that I'd kept the specifics of the argument vague. All I'd said was that tensions were rising after the headlines about Ella's new contract, and then I lied and said the argument had happened behind closed doors so I wasn't able to hear it. Then I let Hannah connect the dots. It doesn't take a genius to see the pictures of the lipstick message on Ella's dress, hear about their raging argument backstage and assume the two are related. As I thought she might, Hannah had quickly jumped to the conclusion that Ella blamed Ryan for the fiasco. It's not like a tabloid needed to confirm it was true, especially if it gave them a scandalous headline.

When there's a knock at the door of my suite, I frown. I'm not expecting anyone. I check the peephole and see Lucky standing casually in the corridor, wearing a T-shirt that has no business sculpting his chest like that, with his hands stuffed in his pockets.

'What's up?' he says when I open the door. 'This place is starting to feel like a prison. Want to get out of here?'

It sounds like he's looking to get into trouble – the good kind, nothing too scandalous – and there's a glint in his eye that says I might be right.

'What did you have in mind?' I ask, even though I know for damn sure that whatever his plans are, I'm so in.

'The sun's about to set. My car's parked out back. What do you say we sneak out for a night drive?'

It's not breaking any rules, but it almost feels like it. The very concept of sneaking out means you don't want to get caught after all.

'Besides, you can't come to LA and not break your In-N-Out virginity,' he adds.

Like I need any further persuasion – I'm already stepping out into the corridor.

'Milkshakes on you then,' I say over my shoulder, heading for the lift.

Lucky grins and follows.

For just a moment, I *almost* forget we're famous. We grab the keys from the valet and slip out of the back entrance into the city's evening traffic like we're any two teenagers in the world, albeit in a blacked-out Ferrari and not a second-hand Ford falling apart with rust. The small huddle of photographers that are camped outside the front of the hotel in the hopes we'll make an appearance don't notice our great escape. It's like we're invisible – a feeling I've missed. The pressure is huge when it feels like the whole world is watching.

I can't explain what it is, but the way Lucky drives is having *An Effect* on me. He slips the car through the streets of LA with confidence, the Ferrari rumbling and roaring under his control. He sits back in his seat, relaxed and at ease, slightly leaning in my direction, with one hand on the steering wheel. He steals glances at me as we talk, and every time he does this hot flush sears up inside me. I'm not supposed to be a crush-struck teenager right now, but I don't think I can help it.

We pull up at In-N-Out and see the long line for the drive-thru. Lucky shrugs and smoothly slides the car into a parking space instead, cutting the engine and climbing out.

'You sure this is a good idea?' I say, following him. My adrenaline is already pumping.

'We're grabbing burgers and milkshakes,' Lucky says, nonchalant. 'What's so bad about that?' He holds the door open for me, briefly pressing a hand on my back as I pass him. I keep walking and try to pretend my knees haven't just gone a little weak.

Nobody notices us for a minute or two as we join the smaller queue at the counter. But then I hear excited whispers and, out the corner of my eye, I see a group of teenagers in a booth gawping. The whispers snowball, spreading around the restaurant until it feels like everyone is staring. But Lucky acts as if nothing's happening and simply asks what flavour milkshake I want instead, fighting a grin. The girl behind the counter looks ready to either faint on the spot or shoot her shot when Lucky lays his eyes on her.

'I give it . . . five more seconds?' Lucky murmurs, leaning closer to me. His whisper brushes my ear, sending a tingle down my spine.

'Until what?'

'Any time n—'

'LUCKY!!!!!!'

The scream comes from one of the teenagers in the booth who has finally given up trying to control themself. Then, as if that one word has given everyone else permission, the masses descend on us. I look to Lucky in panic, but he seems perfectly relaxed.

'Can I have a picture?'

'Will you sign my top?'

'Sign my arm. I want to get it tattooed!'

'Will you call my sister? She loves you so much!'

Lucky doesn't hesitate and starts signing, taking pictures, laughing and joking with them all. I'm so swept up in the moment that it takes me a second to realize they're asking *me* too. It's completely bizarre – who would want *my* autograph? But at the same time it *is* pretty cool.

I catch eyes with Lucky, half a dozen teenagers between us now, and he gives me a wink. We're pushed and buffeted in this sea of people, and when we find ourselves next to each other again, he murmurs, 'You're a natural.'

We spend a few minutes making sure we get to everyone, then Lucky grabs our order and subtly puts his hand on my lower back again, guiding me to the exit. The crowd follows, snapping pictures as we get into the car. When the door closes, we're both laughing.

'That was fun,' Lucky says, revving the engine. The crowd screams with delight.

He nudges the car forward, separating them, and edges us out onto the road. Some of the teens run along the pavement after the car as far as they can until Lucky puts his foot on the gas and we shoot off into the LA night.

I switch on the radio and Lucky cranks up the volume as a Spice Girls classic blares out of the speakers. We're singing at the top of our lungs without a care in the world, the car slipping along dark, winding roads as Lucky takes us up into the Hills. We don't stop until we get to a small tree-lined nook just off the road. He cuts the engine and jumps out, leaving the door open so the radio can play. Then he perches on the bonnet with his milkshake and white-paper bag, beckoning me to join him. The city sparkles and glitters before us like a golden dream held in the palm of a summer's night.

'How's the milkshake?' he asks. His voice is husky, luring me close. It's far from cold, but anticipation raises goosebumps on my arms.

'Good. It's made coming all the way out to LA worth it.'

Lucky feigns hurt. 'That can't be the *only* thing.'

I pretend to think about it. 'You're right – the warm weather too. Other than that, I could take it or leave it.'

A car slowly passes behind us as Lucky smirks to himself. His glance slips over me, and I feel that warm fire burning just underneath my skin. He reaches out a hand, brushing gentle fingers along my throat, then hooking the golden chain he gave me on the first night.

'You still have my necklace on,' he notes, locking eyes with me.

I wonder if he can feel my quickening pulse beneath his touch; if his, too, is counting each second with reckless craving. Everything around us melts into a haze. I don't think about if this is a good idea. I don't think at all. The electric silence crackles, begging one of us to break it. But there's no need for talking now. He leans in, his fingertips still at my neck. His lips are so close to mine that my body aches with desire.

CRASH!

We both break apart, whipping our heads round.

'What the fuck?' Lucky manages.

A shadow races away from us, jumps into a dark-coloured car and floors the accelerator. It whips past, a black blur the only thing I see. We jump off the bonnet and run round to the back of the car. The rear window has been smashed, shattered glass littering the ground.

'*Fuck*,' Lucky says under his breath. He looks all around us, like the dark might reveal enemies. But I can only see one thing.

'Lucky . . . what's that?'

I carefully reach through the broken window and pick up what looks like a small colourful ball. It's heavier than I thought, and I realize it's a rock wrapped in something held in place by elastic bands. With shaking hands, I remove them and smooth out a crumpled *Sunset High* poster. I nearly drop it.

Staring back at me are the four of us, with the LA skyline behind and the title of the show splashed across the top. But Lucky's face has been circled and crossed out in red marker. I flip it over to look at the back. There, written in the same pen, are two words.

QUIT NOW.

But that's not all. Lucky hasn't even seen the poster yet. He's looking at the back of his car with wide eyes, because there's more to it than a smashed window – silvery scratches scar the paintwork, spelling out another message:

THE CURSE IS COMING FOR YOU.

Chapter Nineteen

WHAT TEAM?

Lucky

I have a target on my back. That's what it feels like anyway. Someone wants me to quit the show. I have no idea why, or how they even managed to sneak up on us. I guess I was too engrossed in Abel. But it's the scratched threat on the back of my car that's giving me the creeps.

Somehow pictures of it have ended up online. Based on the background, they were taken in the In-N-Out parking lot while me and Abel were ordering burgers and milkshakes. Did someone follow us there, leave the message, proceed to tail us into the Hills so they could throw a rock through the window and then post evidence of the ordeal for the world to see? I don't know the answers, but I know one thing for sure – I'm paranoid as fuck.

'I know we said the curse doesn't exist but –' Ryan looks uncomfortable – 'it sure feels like it does right now.'

It's late and we're once again within the confines of the hotel. Abel and I raced back after the incident, unsure what to do next. We couldn't exactly call Jill or anyone at Omni, especially when we aren't sure who we can trust, but we knew we had to get Ella and Ryan in on this. They're just as involved as we are.

Ella has the poster in her hand, her appearance paling as she studies it. 'Why is your face the only one crossed out? Who hates you this much that they'd go to these sorts of lengths to tell you to quit the show?'

I neck the shot of vodka I've poured for myself and throw my hands in the air. 'Beats me. Could be anyone, right? A deranged fan, a stalker, someone mad that I said no to signing an autograph. Hell, for all I know it could be Jill and Lake behind it, stirring the pot for more press as usual.' Abel is deep in thought. He hasn't said anything since we got back.

'You okay?' I ask him.

He doesn't hear me for a moment, then quickly snaps out of his trance. 'Just thinking. I . . .' He stops, unsure of himself. 'Do we not think this could all be connected?'

I'm not sure I know what he means, but Ella clearly does. She looks terrified but agrees. 'The message on the back of my dress. Ryan's break-in. Now this? It can't be a coincidence, can it?' She obviously doesn't believe Ryan is behind the lipstick message any more. Not now so much has happened since.

'What car did you say this person was driving when they got away?' Ryan asks faintly.

'I couldn't see it properly,' I say. 'It was a dark colour. Pretty big. Like some kind of . . .' I stop as I see Ryan's face fall.

'Like some kind of truck?' she finishes.

I fight a shiver. 'How do you know that?'

Ryan drops her head into her hands. She looks drained. 'I didn't tell you guys because . . . well, we weren't exactly talking.' I glance awkwardly at Ella. Her blush of shame mirrors mine. 'You know the night before Omni announced the reboot and that stalker left the posters on my doorstep?' She points at the one from my car in Ella's hands. 'I drove to Brad's house because I didn't feel safe at home, and on the way someone started to follow me. They tailed me all the way, then sped off when I got to the house. I didn't get a proper look, but I'm almost certain it was a dark truck.'

My body starts to tense up, like we're being watched.

'And that's not all. I received a phone call the night we checked in here. The front desk said it was Brad, but when I picked up all I could hear was someone breathing down the phone. I didn't know what to do. I told myself it must have been a prank . . .'

'Jesus Christ,' Ella whispers. I feel the same fear in her voice binding me from the inside.

'It has to be connected,' Abel says. 'Someone's playing a sick game. Maybe they want to bring the curse back to *Sunset High*, or they don't want the show to go ahead at all.'

'But wait a minute, Ry,' I say, my thoughts racing fast. 'The posters were left on your doorstep the night *before* the reboot was announced. I know there were rumours about *Sunset*

High coming back, but nobody outside the Omni circle knew anything concrete.'

'Which means the person behind this is closer than we think.' Ella finishes my thought, holding on to a cushion like it's a life jacket.

'Who knew the show was coming back?' Abel asks.

I shrug. 'Everyone in Omnificent. Writers, producers, marketing, publicity, cast, crew, probably some of *their* inner circles as well. It could be anyone.'

We lapse into silence. We're lost. But, more importantly, we're being watched. Someone wants to end the show, and it looks like they'll do anything to succeed.

The last thing that I want to do right now is set foot on a red carpet. I'd rather swim to London. I'd rather count the grains of sand on every Malibu beach, twice. I'd rather write a tweet about how Andy's boyfriend in *The Devil Wears Prada* is terrible, and you know how people feel about that.

But that's exactly what we have to do. It's all about showing the world that we're okay and stronger than ever. That's how Omni are framing it anyway. I feel the complete opposite. The number of photographers waiting outside has tripled now they know we're about to emerge, and that triggers a fear I've been trying to bury since my mom died. Not to mention the fact that I'm still on edge after last night. We all agreed not to tell anyone about our suspicions. Not yet, when we don't know who we can trust. All we have is each other.

In my hotel room, I swig from a bottle of wine to try to take the edge off, but it's not having the effect I need it to. It isn't enough to drown my anxieties, no matter how much I knock back. Still, I continue to try, because what else can I do?

Tonight is the premiere of some blockbuster that promises to have a million pairs of eyes watching our every step on the red carpet. The perfect opportunity for *Sunset High* promo. To hell with the fact that I'm still grieving my mom. Who cares if Ryan is scared for her safety? So what if Ella is beginning to crack under the pressure? I bumped into her in the gym earlier, and she looked a shadow of herself. She won't say it out loud, but it's clear that the contract, her relationship with Ryan and trying to please her mom are all eating away at her. Jill, Lake and everyone at Omni couldn't care less, so long as *Sunset High* is the name on everyone's lips.

Downstairs in the lobby, the others are already waiting for me. Ryan and Ella are avoiding eye contact. Despite last night's impromptu meeting, they clearly haven't put their fight aside just yet, which for some reason only upsets me more. Omni and this stupid show have already ruined so much. I wish we could all escape. Get away from it and start again. Maybe then we'd actually have a chance at fixing what's broken within us.

'Shall we?' Ella says, trying to feign optimism. It doesn't quite break the ice.

I sigh wearily and take her hand, ready to face the cameras. Even though it's not the hand I want to hold right now, it's easier for everyone to follow the script. What's the point in fighting back?

We're greeted outside the hotel with a rumble of sound that

builds to a crescendo. The photographers pen us in on all sides. It's all I can do to keep walking in a straight line and not curl up in a ball to protect myself.

'HEY, RYAN, HOW ARE YOU FEELING?'

'ELLA, TO YOUR RIGHT!'

'DO YOU STILL FEEL SAFE, ELLA? ARE YOU SCARED?'

'LUCKY, GIVE US A SMILE! IT COULD BE WORSE. IT COULD'VE BEEN *YOUR* HOME THAT GOT BROKEN INTO!'

Without thinking, I swing round in blind rage, eyeballing the photographer who shouted out that last comment.

'You think this is funny, do you?!' I yell, rounding on him. I step right up in his face, fury fuelling me. 'THIS IS NOT A FUCKING JOKE. THIS IS OUR LIVES. WE'RE HUMAN FUCKING BEINGS!'

The guy looks like he's loving every second. I should know better by now. This is exactly what he wants, but all I see is red. When he tries to raise his camera between us, I strike out in feral rage and knock it to the ground. The ensuing smash silences the chaos for a split second, and then it's a frenzy all over again.

There's a gentle but firm arm pulling at me, and I instinctively go to shove it away before realizing it's Abel, a concerned look pinching his face. Seeing him grounds me, bringing me back down to earth for long enough to pull my act together. I shoot the photographer a glare that I hope manages to convey just an ounce of the wrath I'm feeling. It doesn't seem to have an effect.

'Thanks for the pay day, kid,' he says with a grin.

He picks up his smashed camera and disappears into the crowd, no doubt to sell my enraged picture to the highest bidder. I'm pulled into an open car door, which is slammed shut behind me. In here, the roar sounds like I'm listening to it underwater, like I'm trapped in a bubble in the middle of the chaos. The others climb in through the second door, and the moment we set off, I groan out loud. The headlines tomorrow will be a mess. I've really fucked up.

'It's okay, just breathe,' Abel says, sitting behind me in the back of the SUV. He gently places a comforting hand on my shoulder. It works – just his touch helps to quiet the noise in my head, dissolving my fury. He leans closer to my ear so only I can hear him. 'On your six.' I melt back into the soft leather. 'I mean, I'm behind you – I'm quite literally on your six.' Despite everything, I let out a muted laugh.

Ryan and Ella are both looking at me with concern and maybe a hint of pity. I automatically want to apologize because I have no doubt that what I've done will impact us all. The attention will only intensify. Still, they have my back too.

'Thanks for jumping in to defend my honour, Prince Charming,' Ryan jokes. 'I would've paid good money to see you punch that guy in the face, though. You've got to do better next time.'

I want to laugh again, but I quickly feel my exterior crumble. 'I'm sorry,' I mumble. 'I shouldn't have done that. I've just made things ten times worse.'

Ella shakes her head quickly. 'Don't you dare say sorry! You have nothing to apologize for. If Jill has something to say about this – if *anyone* has *anything* to say about it – we'll have your back, one hundred per cent.'

Abel and Ryan nod in agreement. It's enough to bring me back from the brink, even if I'm still balancing precariously on a high ledge. Tonight will be a tightrope act that could send me off the deep end, but I'm glad I've got good people beside me so I don't have to do this alone.

'Since we're all being so nice, and I'm low-key enjoying this pity party, can I make a request?' I ask.

'I don't like the sound of this already,' Ryan says as we crawl closer to the premiere. 'I'm not promising a thing until I know what you're up to.'

'Hey, I just defended your honour out there – you said it yourself! You can do me this favour in return.' Ryan sighs, throwing her eyes up to the roof, but she nods anyway. 'No arguing tonight. No backstabbing, no bitching, no *hating* each other.' I look at Ella and then at Ryan with serious eyes, traces of a joke all gone. 'I mean it. It feels like all we have right now is each other. We're the only ones who really understand what it's like to be in each other's shoes. If the world is going to try to divide us, then we have to stand together. We need to have each other's backs.'

There's an awkward silence as everyone glances at their laps.

'I can wait all night for you to agree, but I'm not leaving this car until both of you do,' I say, just as the SUV pulls up to the Dolby Theatre, where flashing lights criss-cross in the sky, illuminating the red carpet below.

'Deal?' Ryan says, looking up at Ella hesitantly, like she fears being shot down.

Ella seems to literally glow at the truce, grabbing at it with both hands. 'Deal!'

I grin as Abel pats me on the shoulder, mirroring my happiness.

'Shall we do this then?' I say. I put my hand in the middle and Ryan literally groans.

'Are we *really* about to do some *High School Musical* bullshit? *That's* how you want to shake on this?' She tries to hide a smile.

'You know it,' I say with a wink. 'What team?'

Abel belly-laughs and throws his hand down on top of mine, finishing the catchphrase. Ella giggles and joins in, repeating after Abel.

Ryan is the last to go. 'You have *got* to be kidding me,' she says, although she's grinning now.

'You may as well put us all out of our misery or we'll be in this car until sunrise,' I tease.

'Well, that's enough to scare anyone,' Ryan counters and puts her hand on top of the others. She goes to lift it, but I stop her.

'What team, Ry?'

She rolls her eyes. 'Wildcats. Now can we *please* go and throw ourselves into this hell pit? Anything is better than this cheerleading you've got us all doing.'

'You technically didn't say, "Get'cha head in the game",' Abel adds brightly.

We all burst out laughing and the four of us climb out of the car with genuine smiles on our faces. We're met with that same chaotic rumble I feel like I've known all my life as people clock that we've arrived. Together, we step on to the red carpet and pose for the cameras, holding on to each other every step of the way.

Chapter Twenty
HOLLYWOOD NIGHTS

Abel

The lights are blinding. They're different from the ones on a TV studio set, which seem to burn hotter and hotter with every second. On a red carpet, the ceaseless flashes are cold, icily so. With every click of a camera, they rob you of your senses, so you're left like a particle of dust facing a hurricane, jostled here and there, unable to see or hear or even know where you are. It's an adrenaline gauntlet.

I hold Ryan's hand, she holds Ella's, Ella holds Lucky's, and Lucky holds hers right back. We don't break apart as we make our way down the carpet. It's an excruciatingly slow process. You start, then stop after a few paces, smile for a dozen cameras, then repeat the cycle over and over again until you've made it down the whole length. My smile feels weak, flickering at the sides, while my cheeks ache trying to support it. By the time we step inside, little orbs of light are flashing in my vision. I'm glad to see I'm not the only one dazed by the experience – all four of us release a held breath once we're finally out of the crosshairs of a camera's lens.

Lucky heads straight to a waiter holding a tray of champagne glasses and downs one. The waiter doesn't even seem to think about whisking the tray out of his reach, even if Lucky is underage. He grabs another drink and downs that too. I don't know whether it's anxiety over the photographers or what happened last night, but the boy who had been so at ease last night has gone. In his place is someone whose front is rapidly cracking.

We take our seats in the theatre, clapping for the cast as they're introduced to the stage. Out of the corner of my eye, I see Ella open her bag of popcorn and offer some to Ryan, who gives her a shy smile. Lucky sits on my other side, eyes straight ahead. But when the lights dim and the movie begins, he shifts his body so his knee rests against mine.

A couple of hours later, the movie comes to a close, and there's a polite round of applause. Then we file out, heading for the car that I assume will take us back to the hotel. Lucky, however, has other ideas.

'Who's up for a party?' he asks, a knowing smirk toying with his lips.

Ryan claps her hands with delight. 'Ugh, I thought you'd never ask. Yes, please, get me out of here.'

'I'm so in,' Ella says.

It's not like I need persuading. 'Count me in,' I say, wondering where the night will take us. We jump into our car, shielding our faces from the onslaught of flashes, and then we set off for the Hollywood Hills, debauchery on the horizon.

The house is an uber-modern mansion made of glass and grey concrete, nestled up high on the hillside with views over LA. The music pumping from inside carries out to the street on the evening breeze, along with the whoops and cheers of a party in full swing. The double doors have been left ajar, probably by the guy who's now passed out on the front steps with his mouth wide open, emitting earth-shuddering snores.

'Charming,' Ella says, stepping over him and into the house. 'Didn't he just come out of rehab?'

'Him and half the party,' Lucky mumbles.

It takes me a moment to recognize Trace, a pop star who's currently so drunk he's passed out on literal concrete like it's a five-star hotel bed. I know damn well that his whole *brand* is wholesome boy next door who wears a purity ring and encourages kids to never do drugs. That message might have got lost in translation in its delivery to himself.

I'm reminded of the conversation I overheard when it sounded like Lucky was being threatened with rehab. Do Jill and Omni know he's still drinking to excess? I assume not or surely they'd have intervened. I steal a glance at him, but his expression is neutral. I can tell, however, that he's purposefully avoiding looking down at Trace. Is he worried about what will be reflected back at him if he does?

The party only gets louder as we step through a marble-floored hall and into a large kitchen. Glass doors, which take up the entire back wall, have been pushed aside, revealing a perfectly landscaped garden fit with an infinity pool, hot tub, DJ decks and a bar. There's even a permanent beer-pong table that's currently hosting a wild game that has most of its participants losing items of clothing. I do a double take when I see a well-known actor from one of my favourite shows dropping his trousers with glee and covering his modesty with one of the cups. *Hygienic*, I think to myself. *Remind me not to drink out of those.*

'THE CAST OF *SUNSET HIGH* ARE IN THE HOUSE!!!' the DJ announces over the speakers.

It feels like every pair of eyes at the party starts searching for us. People crane their necks to get a better look, while whispers shoot off in all directions. They must have kept up with all the drama that's been following us around.

But it's only for a moment, though, and then the partygoers begin to descend, determined to claim our attention or step into our spotlight. Ryan is swept off into a group of giggling girls I recognize from the pages of *Vogue*, while Ella grabs a drink and starts dancing with the members of a girl band I saw performing on *Saturday Night Live* a few weeks ago. People start clapping Lucky on the back, trying to drag him into their own bubble, but just as I'm dreading that I might be left alone a familiar voice finds me.

'Fancy seeing you here.'

I turn round to find Casey, a cracked-open can of beer in

hand. He offers me one, then raises his in cheers. I knock mine against it and take a glug. Foul. I've never liked beer, and I don't trust anyone who does.

'What are you doing here?' I ask.

I realize as soon as I've said it that it comes out wrong, but I'm genuinely intrigued. It seems like a pretty private party packed out with supermodels, actors and pop stars.

Thankfully Casey just laughs. 'My friend's a model. I'm his plus one for the night.' He looks around, then back at me with an amused smirk. 'It's fun seeing how the other half live when they think nobody's watching.'

'Tell me about it,' I murmur without thinking.

Casey frowns, but I jump in before he can highlight my slip-up.

'You must see how the other half live all the time working at the hotel. It's basically a who's who of Hollywood, no?'

Casey chuckles. 'I suppose I see a fair share of LA Bitches – that's what we call the particularly rude ones.'

I laugh. 'Have you worked there long?'

Casey drops his eyes down to his beer, then takes a swig. 'A year or so,' he says.

The answer is short and blunt. If I didn't know better, I'd say it was a conversation-ender. But instead, he starts to . . . study my face? Maybe that one swig of beer made me tipsy, but I swear Casey is proper X-raying me. He looks like he wants to say something.

'Everything all right?'

Casey opens his mouth, then slams it shut and shrugs,

just as Lucky appears at my shoulder. 'All good,' Casey says. He raises his beer, then falls back into the crowd and disappears. Odd.

But then there's Lucky.

'I got us some drinks,' he says, holding up a bottle of wine and two cups. 'I thought we could find somewhere quieter.'

He looks me dead in the eyes and something shifts, the remnants of last night's feelings awakening once more. A faint whisper in the back of my mind tells me not to get so involved with Lucky, to concentrate on what I'm here to do, but he raises an eyebrow in question, or as a dare, and I forget what my defences were trying to tell me.

We steal away into the house, where we end up finding a spot on an upstairs balcony that juts off from an empty games room. It's just the two of us, standing over the party, a string of tension pulled taut in the small space between our bodies.

'It's quieter up here,' Lucky says, his shoulders dropping. He pours us both drinks. When he hands me my cup, our fingers brush and lust ignites inside me. 'I would've hated for you to get stuck listening to some nepo baby telling you how their next movie will be an indie because, "Acting is my passion, and I really don't care about the money." At a party like this, that's code for "I'm not very good at acting, but Daddy has promised the director that he'll bankroll the movie if they give me a leading part".'

I laugh. 'It sounds like you know a thing or two about parties like this.'

Lucky mulls it over, eyes sweeping the party below. He

points to a group of teenagers around our age. 'So first you have the Instagram babes, the ones who use their followers as clout to get in anywhere and everywhere. They're trying to bump themselves up the pecking order by being associated with A-listers and "legit celebrities".' He puts those words in air quotes, like he finds the notion of *legit celebrities* ridiculous.

He points to another group lounging by the pool, keeping to themselves. 'Then you've got the models. They're not quite your Kendall Jenners or Bella Hadids, but they're pretty big fish in their pond. They come back from their runways in London or Paris or Milan looking to unwind, and there's no better place than another celebrity's house party. It's the only time you're guaranteed some privacy. What happens in here, stays in here. Usually anyway.'

He nods to a few people amongst the throng. Each one of them is like the centre of their own Earth. They're idolized, those surrounding them hooked on whatever story the star is currently telling. It's like they're begging for a single ray of the person's light to touch them.

'Your big fry are the singers and actors. I guess people assume that since they've used "legit" talent to get to where they are, they're automatically *worth* more?' A dark shadow passes over Lucky's face. 'It's a fucked-up way to look at a person, and it's a fucked-up way to be looked at too. To know that those people surrounding you only care for material, shallow reasons. They don't care about *you*. They don't even see you as a real person. They only care about what you can do for them. Every little thing in this world is fake.'

I look out over the party. Everyone is pretty young and full of life. The beer-pong game has restarted, pulling in more players. A bunch of guests are now in the pool, some having dived in with clothes still on and drinks in hand. There's loud music pumping through every corner of the house, people bent over counters covered in snow-white trails. Laughter echoes up into the night sky. They all *look* happy to me, on the surface at least.

But even as I think it, I see a different energy. It's in the way people stand, their arms absently wrapped round their bodies as if they're trying to embrace themselves or hold themselves together. It's in the way others posture slightly, chests pumped, taking up as much space as possible. When I listen properly, the laughter seems a little too loud, a little too forced. Voices are competing to climb over each other. The more I look, the more I sense this invisible *competition*. Sure, most people appear outwardly confident, or at least they're trying to be perceived that way. But in some I see it's nothing more than a flimsy shield. Are those who seemingly brim with confidence just better at faking it?

'I'm getting the sense that you hate this life and everything to do with it,' I say, trying to lighten my words.

Lucky breathes a laugh, placing his hands down on the balcony rail just centimetres from mine. Is that a voice I hear in the back of my head again, warning me not to get this close? I couldn't tell you. I'm not listening.

He takes a sip of his drink. Then a gulp, finishing it off. 'I guess I always thought that if I got to where I am in my career now, it would fix everything, you know? I thought if I earned a ton of money, if I became somebody, if I *made* it, then nothing would ever be able to hurt me.' He drops his head, staring into the depths of the drink he's now finished. 'It hurt to find out that's not true.'

There's a weight piled onto his shoulders, one that's been trying to pull him down into darker depths that would be nearly impossible for anyone to climb out of. I think about what Ryan told me yesterday, how Lucky blames himself for his mom's accident, and looking at him now I can tell he's far from absolving himself of responsibility. A toxic fusion of grief and guilt is eating him up. He's been trying to hide it, to push it down and smother it with drink, but it's there. It might not be my place to try to help – in fact, I *know* letting things get personal is a bad idea, especially when I'm here to find out the truth about Adam – but I can't leave Lucky to drown.

'Sorry, I don't know why I blurted that out,' he says. 'I guess there's something about you that makes me feel comfortable. Maybe it's the accent.' He nudges me and smiles, trying to lighten the mood.

There are a million things I could say about how he's feeling, but instead I try to offer him a seed of hope that might, in time, bloom. I put my hand over his and say what I wish I could've told myself three years ago.

'You'll be okay. You know that right? It might take another day or another week or maybe a lot longer, but you'll get through this. You'll remember what it's like to breathe and feel free again, to smile and laugh without guilt or shame.

Darkness often feels so complete when you're in it, but light still exists, even if you can't see it right now. You'll see it soon. I promise you that.'

Lucky gives me a small smile, one that punches straight through my chest. His eyes glimmer with tears for just a moment, rippling across the blue like waves.

He lets go of a breath with a choked laugh. 'It's definitely your accent,' he jokes. Then he bows his head and nods to himself. I wonder if he can feel the first ember of hope. 'Seriously, though – thank you, Abel.'

My hand is still on his. He looks at it, then up at me. Everything falls away. It's just us. He flips his hand upside down, letting our fingers gently interlace, then he brings them up to his chest. I can feel his heart pounding beneath my palm. This time, when he leans in close, there's no hesitation or interruption. Lucky kisses me. The moment our lips meet, melting perfectly into the shape of each other, a soft growl escapes from one of us. I can't be sure who. The sound is ours together.

As if he's waited so long to do this, he clutches at my shirt, drawing me closer to him like the lack of space that's already between us is still nowhere near as close as he wants to be. His arms wrap round me, his hands finding their way to my back and pulling me into him. I sigh with a pleasure I didn't know was possible as he guides me backwards and presses me into the wall. And as his lips move from mine to my jaw, to my throat, to my collarbone, they burn into my skin as if they're leaving a trace of each kiss behind.

Chapter Twenty-One

TIGHTROPE

Ella

The party is winding down, only pockets of it still alive. Tonight I've danced until I've forgotten everything, laughed as if there isn't a trouble in my world, sung at the top of my lungs until they burned and then laughed some more. Sure, the drink has probably helped to push me into euphoria, leaving behind my worries for one night, but I could get used to feeling this free.

To save the trouble of calling the SUV to circle back and collect us, and to hopefully keep word away from Omni about how much fun we've really had tonight, I called Natalie to ask her to come pick us up. She's on her way now, but I can't find Lucky and Abel. I see the guy from the hotel's front desk talking to one of the other remaining partygoers. He spots me and gives me an embarrassed wave.

211

'Time to go?' Ryan appears at my side, checking the contents of her bag. She looks beautiful tonight. As always, but tonight a golden glow seems to emanate from her. Maybe it's the drink feeding me thoughts, stripping away my inhibitions, but it also feeds me bravery and I don't think twice about stepping into her reach.

'We haven't spoken properly yet,' I say quietly. 'About us, and where we stand.'

Ryan doesn't back away as I feared she might. She stands her ground, like she always does, unflinching. I wish I could be more like her. Whether she feels it or not, she radiates confidence. And not just for other people, but in herself too. Her self-assurance, at least from the outside, is rock solid. She puts herself first because she knows her own worth. I could do with some pointers.

We find a cushioned swing in a quiet corner at the edge of the garden. It overlooks the city, which twinkles like it's putting on a show just for us. My heart flutters at the sight of Ryan looking back at me. She looks nervous too. This feels like a make-or-break moment. We could mend what we had, or we could leave it in pieces on the floor.

'Is it stupid to ask how you are?' Even with my alcohol-infused bravado, my words are still delicate, hiding the real conversation we need to have.

'I'm good,' Ryan says cautiously. She shakes her head, looking up at the stars like she can pluck her words right out of the sky. 'I mean, I guess I've been better. Everything right now seems . . .'

'Shit?' I offer.

Ryan smiles, laughter escaping at the edges of it. 'That's putting it lightly.' She turns her eyes on me and it's like every part of my body can feel their warmth. She drinks me in, and I do the same right back. But then there's silence, and we know we have no choice but to face our ugly truths.

'You hurt me, El.' Ryan's words are a whisper and yet they cut me deep. 'Not telling me about the contract was one thing. You should've known that I'd be happy for you if you'd told me. We could've figured things out between us. But then accusing me of being a hateful bitch and scrawling that message on your dress to embarrass you in front of the world – do you really think that little of me? Of how much I actually care about you? About *us*?'

'I know I have, and I'm sorry. For everything. I am *so* sorry that I did that to you. That I let them come between us.' I reach out my hand for hers. Our fingers lock into place instinctively, pieces meant for each other. I never want to let go. 'I don't deserve forgiveness for betraying you and what we had. But I need you to know that, from the bottom of my heart, I'm sorry.'

Another silence. Ryan looks uncertain, wary of opening up to me again. And I can't blame her. I drop my eyes and let my hair form a shield between us because I can't bear to see her face, or the choice she might make written on it. It feels like we're balancing on a tightrope. Will we fall, or will we make it to the other side of this? But before I can think the worst, Ryan swipes the curtain of my hair aside and cups my face with her hands, raising my gaze to meet hers.

'I've missed you,' she says.

Her words are like pure joy to my ears, a song that I never want to end. I feel like I don't deserve to hear them, but she ducks her head, bringing herself closer to me. Her lips part, almost touching mine. I can't think of or see anything else. It's just us, overlooking LA like queens on our throne.

'Tell me you've missed me too,' Ryan whispers.

The distance between us, or lack of it, is sweet, agonizing torture. We're almost one, separated by held breaths.

'So much it hurts,' I say back.

I can't bear it any longer. I place my lips softly on hers, as light as a feather, and in an intoxicated haze I tell her a truth I've denied all this time, even to myself.

'I love you, Ryan Hudson.'

She utters it back without hesitation. My name on her lips is a drug I can't get enough of. It's ecstasy and bliss and all I've ever wanted.

Chapter Twenty-Two

I'M SORRY I CAN'T GET TO THE PHONE RIGHT NOW

Abel

Maybe it's the alcohol. Maybe it's the fact I can smell Lucky's intoxicating aftershave all over me, like his body is still on mine. Whatever it is, I've got a smile on my face as Natalie drives us back to the hotel. What a shame such bliss can be ruined so quickly.

'And this just in minutes ago from the *Daily Eye*,' a radio host reporting on the news says over the car speakers. My heart drops. It's morning back in London. Has Hannah published something new? 'It seems that a scratched-up Ferrari and last night's altercation with a photographer are the least of Lucky Tate's problems right now.'

The inside of the car goes completely dead. Lucky tenses up next to me.

'Sources close to the situation have told the *Daily Eye* that Lucky's excessive drinking and partying has led to threats of rehab from bigwigs at Omni Channel. According to those in the know, Lucky is just days away from an intervention that could see him fired from *Sunset High*.'

Lucky looks like he's going to be sick. The hope I thought I saw at the party is immediately extinguished. He looks lost again. I find his hand in the dark and squeeze, but it feels lifeless in mine. Ella quickly punches the radio off, and we drive in heavy silence until we reach the hotel a few minutes later.

'Do you want me to come with you?' I quietly ask Lucky when we step through the doors and head for the lift. Lucky shakes his head automatically, walking as if in a trance. I deflate a little. 'I'm here if you need me.'

Ryan gives him a quick hug as the lift stops on the thirteenth floor before we both step out. I take one last look at Lucky, but he doesn't meet my eyes. I turn and say goodnight to Ryan and then disappear into my suite.

The guilt unravelling inside me is leaden. This is my fault. I gave Hannah the story. She must've finally had the all-clear from the legal team to go ahead and publish it. But why didn't she warn me? There's only one way to find out. I grab my phone and call her number.

'Hello?' Hannah sounds confused as she picks up on the other end of the line.

'It's me,' I say, even though she knows that.

'You got your phone back then?'

216

I frown. 'Huh?'

'You found your phone?' Hannah says slowly. 'You said you lost it.'

I'm so confused I've almost forgotten why I called her in the first place. 'What are you talking about? My phone's right here. I'm literally calling you on it.'

Hannah pauses. 'Did you or did you not email me a few hours ago to tell me that you'd lost your phone?'

Considering I was probably tied up with Lucky then, the answer comes easily to my lips. 'No, I didn't email you anything. I don't understand what you mean.'

'Then explain why I got an email from you saying th—'

Hannah stops in her tracks and my heart does too. I'm not even sure it's in my chest any more.

'Hannah . . .'

Nothing. And then: 'Oh, God.' Her tone sends shivers through my body. 'I received an email earlier. The name attached was yours and the address matched too. It said, "Hi Hannah. I've lost my phone so emailing instead. How did the Ryan and Ella story go down? Abel".'

The room warps and spins around me. This is bad.

'I . . . I just assumed it was you,' Hannah says. 'Who else would know that the Ryan and Ella story came from you, or that there's even a connection between us?'

'What did you reply?' I ask, even though I fear the answer.

Hannah heaves a shaky sigh. '"Hey, Abel. Bad luck on the phone. Story did well – got lots of traction. The article about Lucky potentially going to rehab has been through legal and

217

should be live within the hour.'"

I fall into a chair, heart racing. 'Hannah, that email didn't come from me. My phone's right here.'

Silence stretches from Los Angeles to London as we both realize what's happened.

'Your cover's been blown,' Hannah says at the exact same time that I say, 'Someone knows.'

'They will have got my email from my *Daily Eye* profile,' she says. 'It's right there, for sources who want to send in tips on potential stories. But who could possibly know we've been working together and then email me pretending to be you?'

I shake my head, trying to think straight. I've been so careful, I'm sure of it. Nobody knows that I'm here for any other reason than *Sunset High*, except for Mila Stone, and she hardly has a reason to stitch me up. The only other conclusion is that someone close, someone *inside* Omni, saw the stories that Hannah has been publishing about the show, realized it had to be coming from cast or crew and jumped to (correct) conclusions. But it seems like a one-in-a-million chance to guess it's me. Right?

It doesn't matter. Someone knows I'm leaking stories to the *Eye*. Maybe they know more than that too. Have they figured out my connection to Adam and why I'm really here?

'You should think about getting out while you still can,' Hannah says quietly.

No doubt she's thinking of the curse and the fates that have befallen others before me. I know I am. My brother might've been murdered for knowing too much. Who's to say I won't be next? But I can't back out now. Not when I don't have answers. I won't leave until I know what happened to Adam.

'I'll be fine,' I say. 'Don't worry about me. Just make sure you call this number if you receive any more emails.'

I hang up and let the silence of my room wash over me. Things are getting dangerous. I don't feel safe. If someone knows who I am, then that means I'm being watched. By who, I don't know. But before I go to sleep, I make sure to lock my door.

Chapter Twenty-Three

A MASK SLIPPING

Ella

I'm singing in the shower. That's how damn happy I am right now. I spent last night with Ryan cuddled up in bed, her body as familiar to me as my own. It was pure bliss. It's put things into perspective for me too. Taking the leap to go for what I want is terrifying, but the exhilaration matches the fear. I'm finally going to look out for myself and not be worried about what other people think or want from me.

There's a knock at the door of my suite, interrupting my good vibes. Humming to myself, I turn off the shower and wrap myself in the fluffy white hotel robe, drying my hair with another towel as I go. But when I open the door, my heart sinks like it knows something I haven't figured out yet.

Lake Carter stands in the doorway, tall and imposing, filling up all the space he can reach. Instinctively I make myself smaller, especially when his eyes sweep over me in my robe. I fight off my uneasiness and offer him a smile.

'I hope you don't mind me popping by,' Lake says, strolling into the room without waiting for permission to do so. 'I wanted to make sure you were okay after the events at Ryan's house the other night.' He makes himself at home on the sofa while I take a seat in the armchair opposite.

'Yeah, I'm okay,' I say cautiously. 'Obviously I'm a little shaken. We all are. We just want to be safe while making this show.'

Lake nods, clearing his throat and sitting forward, elbows on his knees. 'I hear you,' he says gently. He seems to mull something over, and I feel a prickle of apprehension slither across my skin. 'We want to make sure that every single measure is in place to keep you safe from harm. And we can do that. We *will* keep you and your family safe. I'll personally look out for you. But I need something from you first.'

He reaches into his satchel and produces a wad of papers. I already know what it is. The contract. I'm cornered.

'Omnificent will look after you. I'll make sure of it.' Lake pauses, then lays down his card. 'But we need you to sign the contract. Now.'

My heart flutters in my chest. Every thought and fear races through me. I think of Mom. Ryan. Lake. *Sunset High*. Omni. My future. All of it at once. My whole career, I've never been able to forge a path of my own. I've only ever done what had already been chosen for me. I know, with every fibre of my being, that I do not want to sign this contract. For Ryan's sake, but for mine too. This isn't just about protecting Ryan, although it's a big part of it. It's about protecting *me* – Eleanor Grayson – and deciding what *I* want for the first time in my life.

'You'll notice that I've upped our offer in response to how well you're already faring with the fans,' Lake carries on. 'They love you. Signing this contract will be the making of you, Ella Winter. But . . .' He clenches his jaw and hesitates, and, right then, I see it, as clear as day. His mask is slipping. The kindness Lake's showed me, the mentorship he's promised, the *I want what's best for you* bullshit – it's been nothing more than an act. And now that he hasn't got what he wants right away, the way he's used to, his exterior is cracking.

'But . . .' I press, trying to keep my tone level.

Lake purses his lips. 'Let's just say my patience is starting to wear thin. I don't like to be kept waiting.' He must hear his tone, coloured with a trace of rage, because he quickly morphs back into that *oh so friendly* character he's been so good at portraying.

'What is there to think about, right?' he says brightly, clapping his hands together. 'It's all the money in the world, leading roles, more fame than you could ever ask for. You've hit the jackpot!'

I bite the inside of my cheek. I don't care what Lake's offering; I won't walk myself into a trap.

'I'll need to give it a proper look-over,' I say, hoping I can buy myself more time. 'With a lawyer,' I add.

Lake shakes his head and retrieves a pen from his satchel.

'Sign the contract, Ella. It's in everyone's best interests.'

His tone is darkening once more, but I raise my chin slightly and stick firm. 'I'll give it a look-over *with my lawyer* and then—'

'SIGN THE FUCKING CONTRACT!'

I jump, flinching back into my chair. Lake's face is flushed with the anger he's tried so hard to cover, but there it is, exposed in all its horrific glory. I shake my head, but before either of us can say anything more, the door to my suite opens and Natalie walks in, oblivious to what's going on.

She stops in her tracks when she sees us. 'I'm so sorry,' she says apologetically. 'I'll wait outside until your meeting's finished.'

Lake doesn't miss a beat. He hops up with an easy smile on his face and gathers his things. 'Don't be silly. I was just going anyway.'

I stand too as Lake starts to leave. At the door, he turns round. 'I'll see you back on set, Ella.' And then he's gone.

Chapter Twenty-Four

HOLLYWOOD, WE HAVE A PROBLEM

Ryan

I wake up with a smile on my face, memories of last night a warm and welcoming comfort in my mind. I haven't felt this happy in a while. It feels as if something inside me, something previously locked away, has opened up and set itself free. It scares me a little, to be so vulnerable with Ella and remove the steely armour that shields my heart. Fuck, it terrifies me, and maybe it's reckless, but I'm so tired of closing myself off from people in case I get hurt. I want to give myself chance to be happy. And, right now, I am. Even more so when Ella arrives at my suite door with a tray of room service.

'Morning,' she says, giving me a kiss on the cheek and slipping inside. She sets up the tray on the table and holds up a croissant in one hand and an iced coffee in the other. My favourites. 'Breakfast?'

I light up from the inside and feel it spread into a smile on my face. I could get used to this. I turn on the speaker system and join her at the table, ready to gossip about the party. We're just done talking about a certain actor who may or may not have been caught in the bathroom with someone who definitely isn't his new fiancée when Ella gets a text. She reads it and sighs.

'Everything okay?'

She chews her lip and shakes her head. 'Not really. Lake came over to see me this morning.'

His name isn't welcome here. I swear I feel the temperature in the room drop a couple of degrees. She quickly fills me in on what happened.

'He wants me to sign the contract. Omni have made a new offer and now –' Ella raises her phone, pointing at Lake's text – 'they're putting a deadline on it. I've got a week to decide, or they'll take it off the table, and, in his words, "look elsewhere".'

'Bastard,' I mutter.

'He's pretending this morning never even happened. And it gets better,' she says, reading the rest of the text. 'He says, "You have my support if you wish to become a free agent, but I can't promise that directors, producers, casting agents etc. won't gossip about why you've turned down such a lucrative deal. Word will spread that you've declined a generous offer and people will assume you're difficult to work with. I'd hate to see your career ruined by petty rumours.""

Ella isn't upset. She's furious. I can't blame her. Lake might be playing the *I want what's best for you* card, but we're both able to translate the threat – sign the deal or I'll make sure you never work again. People like Lake have that power in this industry. I've heard of him blackballing actors who got on his bad side, blocking them from ever working or booking roles again.

'And, to top it off, he told my mom about the new offer too,' Ella murmurs. 'She called me from the airport on her way to Hawaii. You can imagine how well that conversation went down.'

I sure can. Kate has never cared about what Ella wants. To her, it's all about how much money her daughter earns, and how much of it she can spend herself. That trip to Hawaii will have come straight out of Ella's pocket.

'I'm sorry,' is all I manage. What else can I do? Ella is as good as cornered. She has two options – agree to Lake's demands or lose everything. It might hurt me to my core, but I certainly won't be the one to ruin her career and tell her not to sign the deal. Even if it means her replacing me and leaving me with nothing. 'I'm not going to stand in your way—' I start, but she stops me before I can go any further.

'I'm not signing the deal, Ry. I won't do that to you. Not again.'

'But . . .'

She shakes her head. 'But nothing. I don't care what Lake is offering or what he threatens me with. I won't have my life

226

controlled by him or Omni, and I won't let it come between us.'

My heart swells with that word – *us*. I don't know what to say, so I don't say anything at all. I kiss her instead in the hope that it tells her what this means to me. What *she* means to me.

'How's Lucky?' I ask when breakfast is over.

Ella chews her lip. 'I tried to talk to him last night when we got out of the elevator, but he wanted to be left alone. He's struggling. That article about rehab hasn't exactly helped.'

'What did it even say?' I wonder, pulling out my phone to search for the article. I find it quickly and open it up, Ella peeking over my shoulder to read.

'Scroll down then,' she says, but I'm too busy looking at what's in front of me. Not the headline, but the words underneath it. *By Hannah Wilkes, celebrity reporter.*

'Get Lucky down here now,' I say. 'We've got a big problem.'

Chapter Twenty-Five

AND YOU THOUGHT THINGS COULDN'T GET WORSE

Abel

I get back to the hotel after a morning run to try to clear my head. I was already feeling paranoid because of the threatening messages that have been left for the others. I knew it was only a matter of time before whoever is behind them came for me too. Now they have, and my cover has been blown. I feel helpless. Watched. Stalked.

Casey is at the front desk when I walk in. He beckons me over, looking a little awkward, his eyes flitting around me but never actually landing *on* me. It sparks a sense of unease, but more than that it fires up my suspicions. I think of last night and the weird way our conversation ended. It wasn't the first time he's seemed on edge while talking to me.

'Hey,' he says, giving me a rigid nod. 'Ryan called down

to the front desk a few moments ago. She told me to ask you if you could go to her room when you're back. Apparently it's important.'

My pulse spikes, wondering if this is about the stalker who seems to be watching our every move.

'Of course,' I say to Casey. I turn to go, but I still can't shake my paranoia. Whenever he sees me, he seems unsettled. Even when I first checked in, he'd looked at me strangely, almost like he knew me from somewhere. He has no reason to recognize who I am. Unless he knew someone who looked a little like me . . .

'Hey, random question, but when did you say you started working here?'

I fight a prickle of adrenaline to keep my question casual, but Casey is immediately on his guard. I'm not even sure he's going to answer, but then the hotel manager, Stephen, rounds the desk at that exact moment.

'Since fall 2019, isn't that right, Case?' Stephen says. 'He's been a thorn in my side ever since.' He throws his head back to laugh but stops when he sees the look on my face followed by the burning red of Casey's. 'I was only joking; he's not so bad,' Stephen adds, looking between us. But I'm not focusing on him. I'm looking straight at Casey, whose eyes won't lift from the desk.

He lied.

At the party, when I asked him, Casey said he'd started working at the hotel a year or so ago. A lot might have been going on around me, but I know for *sure* that's what he said.

Why would he lie to my face for no reason? Unless he had something to hide . . .

But with Stephen watching, I can't outright accuse Casey of lying. I have to bide my time. One thing is for sure, though – if Casey started working here in 2019, he was present for the 2020 reboot. That means he would've seen, helped and spoken to my brother, who was staying at the hotel too. Is that why he can't look me in the eye? Does he know something?

He knows he's been caught out, so when Stephen turns his back for a moment, he grabs a slip of paper and scribbles down the name of a café and its address, as well as a time: midday. He slides it across the desk, then says under his breath, 'My break is in a couple of hours. I can explain.'

I manage to pocket the paper, but then Stephen is back, looking between us apologetically, like he doesn't know what he's done to cause such awkwardness but he's sorry all the same. I give them both a nod and head for the lift, my heart in my throat the whole way. It feels like answers are dangling just out of my reach. Maybe soon I'll be a step closer to the truth.

I make my way to Ryan's suite, wondering what this is about. I knock on the door and wait. To my surprise, it's Lucky who answers, and I know immediately something's wrong. At first, I assume it must be because of the *Daily Eye* story, which eats me up with guilt. Maybe he's worried that Omni will ship him off to rehab now that the news is out there. But when I try to give him a hug, he steps out of my reach and shakes his head in a way that royally shoots me down. He won't meet my eyes, instead turning his back and letting me follow him into the room, where Ella and Ryan are waiting. Neither of them look happy. In fact, they're furious.

'You lying little *scumbag*,' Ryan hisses, throwing a cushion at my head. I dodge it, heart now hammering.

'What's going on?' I ask, fear swelling in my chest.

'Oh, don't act all innocent now!' Ella shouts, throwing another cushion that succeeds in hitting me with a dull *thump*.

'What's going on?' I try again, although I'm feigning ignorance to buy myself more time because this can only be about one thing.

Ryan scoffs at my reply. 'You know what, I thought I recognized her name when I saw the text on your phone the other day. *Hannah Wilkes?*' I stop breathing, the room tilting. 'There are all these articles this morning about Lucky smashing that photographer's camera last night, but one reporter just happened to have a little extra seasoning to add to their story about how Omni are threatening to send him to rehab. And – what do you know? – Hannah Wilkes, she's a *journalist*, ladies and gentlemen.'

A nervous shiver coats my entire body. I can feel every part of myself alive with panic.

'And not only is she a journalist, she's the head of CELEBRITY AND ENTERTAINMENT NEWS for the *DAILY FUCKING EYE* of all places!' Ella almost yells. 'We looked up the stories she's been writing recently, and there's sure been a lot of focus on *Sunset High*. In fact, she's written about nothing else in the last two weeks!'

Ryan, brimming with fury, marches up to me until she's so

close that I can almost feel the heat of her anger on my skin. 'You've been working for them, haven't you? You've been trying to get some seedy scoop from the inside. That's it, isn't it?'

'It's not what it looks like . . .'

My words trail off as Lucky finally looks at me properly. He's wounded. His body is hunched into itself, like it can't stand up any more. '*You* leaked the story about me?'

It's worse than a slap in the face. He doesn't try to conceal the hurt in his voice. I can feel the ache of each word as they pummel me.

'I . . . I can explain.'

'Well, please, the floor is all yours,' Ryan says, stepping back and folding her arms. She gives me a murderous glare. 'And don't you dare lie.'

Ella's eyes are on me too, just as furious. But it's Lucky's face that gets me most of all. He looks betrayed, like I've shattered the delicate glass of trust between us. I don't have a choice. I have to tell them.

'It's true. Hannah Wilkes works for the *Daily Eye*, and, yes, I've been working with her to feed back stories about *Sunset High*.'

I can't tell if Ryan or Ella will kill me first. They look ready to team up and do it together. Lucky looks like I've just punched him in the heart. He turns his back on the room, and I've never felt like a bigger piece of shit in my life. I've taken his trust and destroyed him with it, at his weakest moment too.

'But it's not what you think, I swear. I never wanted to betray you. Any of you.'

232

Ella rolls her eyes. 'We said *don't* lie.'

'I'm not,' I reply, and I'm glad my voice has the strength to support those words because I need them to know that I'm being honest. 'This was only ever about finding out the truth. It was about getting answers. I needed them because . . .' I can feel my words breaking as they leave me, but I have to keep going. 'Because I think Omnificent killed my brother.'

Ryan's face falls and Ella lets out a tiny gasp. Lucky turns, his expression shattered.

'Your brother?' Ryan asks, all hint of anger gone like water through cupped hands.

I wrap my arms round myself. I don't know if can explain, but I have to try.

'The reboot in 2020? The night before Penelope Daunt was announced missing, someone fell from the roof of this hotel and died. They said it was an accident.' I drop my head. 'His name is Adam Miller.'

I flinch as I hear myself use the present tense. It still hurts to think of him as a *was*, as if he no longer exists. To me he lives on in my head and in my memories. He always will.

'Adam is my older brother.'

Their faces share the same expression of shock. It takes everything in me to look each of them in the eye and not run away from this. But I can't. Not now. I'm in too deep.

'He was offered a placement as an assistant on the reboot. He was *so* excited. It was going to be his break into the industry. His life was just beginning, and instead it . . . he . . .' I can feel myself beginning to crack.

Ryan tries to comfort me, but I gently shake her off. I have to finish this.

'The day after Penelope went missing, I got a text from him saying he needed to speak to me. He said it was about Omni. But I was home in London, eight hours ahead and asleep. When I woke up, I tried to reach him, but it was too late.'

The grief I've tried to bury for so long splinters each word. I can feel the breath shallowing in my chest, making it harder and harder to keep going.

'What did the text say . . .?' Ryan asks tentatively.

I unlock my phone and pull up the message. '"I know you're probably still asleep but can you call me when you wake up? I don't care what time it is here, just call me straight away. It's about Omni and it's urgent. I don't know what's going on but it's fucked up. Call me asap." Then he sent me another message less than an hour later that said, "No worries, false alarm! Love you bro x".'

I shake my head, trying to unroot those words that have branded me for so long. 'He never called me "bro". It was too cringe for us. When I woke up, I knew there was something wrong the second I read the text.'

'Wait,' Ella says in disbelief, 'the story was that he fell. It was a tragic accident, right?'

'Yeah, that's what they said, but—'

'It's not true,' Lucky finishes. He says it with resigned certainty. 'Your brother knew something. He must have. And I bet it was about Penelope Daunt. She goes missing, then

234

the very next day he sends those messages and dies? In an *accident*? No. Something's off.'

I'm glad to know I'm not the only one who's drawn that conclusion.

'Omni washed their hands of it completely,' I say, anger becoming the backbone of my words. 'His name was never even mentioned. They brushed him under the rug, like he never existed at all, and that's exactly what they want.' I shake my head. 'Well, fuck that. Fuck Omnificent, fuck Lake Carter, fuck Jill Anderson, fuck the whole lot of them. I've spent years with this pain sitting in my chest. It's with me for life. All I can do is carry it with me and hope that one day the weight of it doesn't feel so heavy. So, yeah, I want answers. It might not fix anything. In fact, I'm sure it won't. But maybe it'll allow me to finally start moving on with my life. And maybe I can stop it from happening again.'

Most of my cards are now on the table, but I still have to make things right. I look at all three of them, feeling disgusted with myself for what I've done in order to seek revenge.

'I'm so sorry. To all of you. I knew if I wanted to expose Omni, I needed a journalist to help get the story out to as many people as possible when I found the answers I was looking for. I've been sending Hannah stories to keep her happy, but I should have never thrown any of you under the bus for my own gain. I really am so sorry.'

Lucky shakes his head. 'I understand. You don't need to be sorry.' The others agree.

'I do,' I say firmly. 'And I am sorry. I understand if you don't

235

forgive me. It's what I deserve. But I need you to know how much I regret it now.'

Lucky doesn't absolve me of my guilt with words. Instead, he comes up beside me and wraps me in his arms. His embrace is tight, urgent, as if he desperately needs me to know that I'm not alone any more – we're in this together. If anyone can understand what grief drives you to do, it's him. Ella and Ryan step in and join the hug too. I laugh, despite the situation.

'Who would've thought we'd become, like, best friends or whatever,' I say.

'Okay, let's not get ahead of ourselves,' Ella replies with a grin.

I don't have a moment to feel gratitude though because my phone vibrates in my pocket. I pull it out and see Hannah's name. At the same time, Ella's phone vibrates too, while Ryan's lights up on the table. Lucky frowns and pulls his own out of his pocket. Something tells me this isn't good.

Hannah Wilkes
Get online now. Someone has posted pictures of you at a party last night.
10:45

My heart drops. I look up at the others to see they've had texts from people they know too. Based on their expressions, it's about the same thing. I quickly close the text and open Twitter. I don't have to go far. It's right at the top, posted from an account with a *Sunset High* poster as its profile picture. It already has a couple of thousand likes and comments, even though it was posted less than twenty minutes ago.

There are no words, just two pictures. The first is of me and Lucky at the party last night. We're on the balcony pressed up against each other, Lucky's lips at my neck. It's been taken from inside the house. I think back and only remember an empty games room. But before I can spiral any further, the second picture grabs my attention. I open it and look apologetically across the room. Ryan and Ella look like their world is falling apart. The second picture is of them locked in an embrace of their own in a shadowy corner of the garden.

'I guess the game our little stalker is playing just stepped up another level,' Ryan murmurs tightly.

She's right, I think to myself. *And whoever it is, they're closer than ever.*

Part Three

GOLIATH

Chapter Twenty-Six

BURY YOUR GAYS, OR AT LEAST THROW THEM BACK IN THE CLOSET

Ryan

The way Jill is pacing, stressed to her wits' end, you'd think we'd collectively announced that the four of us were terminally ill. She's not called one of us by a pet name since she arrived, so you'd be well within your rights to think that something *really* serious has happened. Just the small situation of her four leading stars being outed as gay. The shock! The horror! Whatever will we do?!

Okay, so, real talk – I'm terrified. Hurt. Worried. We all are. Nobody wanted this to happen, especially like this. A stranger has taken something private and posted it for the world to see way before we were ready to show them ourselves. None of us were out as queer in a professional capacity before the pictures were posted today. So, yeah, it's a big deal. A huge fucking deal. But what we need right now is care and support – not a publicist who looks like she'd rather we'd been convicted as serial killers if it meant saving the brand image she's so carefully curated.

'On that *very* first day, I warned you about this,' Jill rants, pacing in front of the window of my hotel suite. She'd arrived, all a fluster, pretty much the very second we'd had a chance to see the pictures ourselves. 'I said that if you stuck to the script and kept everything else *private*, all would be fine. And now your golden image is up in smoke.'

I swallow the fury that's trying to form words on my tongue. 'It's not exactly our fault that some heartless son of a bitch has done this. *We're* the victims here.'

'You should've been more careful!' Jill yelps. 'Acting like that at a party with hundreds of other people there. What were you thinking?'

'That, in the moment, I was pretty damn happy I could be myself for once,' Lucky says in a strained tone that tells me he's also trying to keep his anger in check too. We all nod our agreement.

Jill slumps down into her seat and sighs. 'Look, I'm very happy for you all. If you've . . . found happiness with each other, then great.' Her tone says the complete opposite. Good to know she'll be marching with us at a Pride parade soon. 'I'm all for it, honestly. Head to the chapel in Vegas and get married for all I care. Kiss under a rainbow flag. Whatever it is you want to do. But *after* the show has finished. Do you realize what kind of position you've put Omni Channel in? You've all but told the world that we lied to them.'

Ella clears her throat. 'With all due respect, Jill . . . we *have* lied to them. But now is our chance to be honest. I don't think we have much choice.' She squeezes my hand under the table. No point in pretending we're not together now.

'Honesty is the only way out of this, surely,' I add, jumping in to back up Ella. 'Sure, some people are pissed we lied, but the pictures have already been liked more than eight hundred thousand times, and they've only been up for an hour. It doesn't seem like anything is "up in smoke" to me. If anything, we've got you good and *honest* press.'

But despite the fact there's clear support for us all, there's no convincing Jill. It's more press than she could have ever dreamed of – it's just not the *right* press in her eyes. She doesn't want one bit of this. She takes off her glasses with a sigh and collects her thoughts, then tries to fix what she deems to be a mess.

'Okay, here's what we're going to do. I've got some contacts in the press who'd kill for an exclusive. We'll say that the pictures are deep fakes. That's the easiest way to get out of it. Sow seeds that the images have been doctored, and people will soon move on.'

She turns her attentions to Lucky and Ella, ignoring the fact it's my hand Ella's holding right now. 'We'll set up a couple of photo opps for you two asap. No time like the present to start twisting this back in our favour. Perhaps a casual dinner date, holding hands in the street, sources saying you're almost *unbearably* cute on set. We'll have the public eating out of the palm of our hands.'

Abel is looking at Jill like she's lost her damn mind. I don't think he's wrong.

'Jill, nobody's going to believe any of that. Not now,' Lucky says.

But Jill stands up, all smiles once more. 'Oh, honey, give me a week and I'll have them thinking you're straighter than a ruler.' She throws her head back and laughs. 'Oh, and Lucky, when you've got five, can I grab you for a second? I'll be waiting in the restaurant downstairs.'

I wonder what that conversation will be about. Jill doesn't wait for Lucky to answer and heads out of the door without a second glance.

'I guess we're back on the merry-go-round then,' I mutter.

Lucky shakes his head. 'Not me. She can set up whatever photo opp she likes – I'll be showing up in a be gay, do crime T-shirt waving a Pride flag in the air.'

There's a pause. Then we all burst out laughing. Despite everything, it feels good to know we at least have each other to face whatever might come next.

Chapter Twenty-Seven
THIS IS NOT A SAFE SPACE

Lucky

The meeting with Jill went about as well as I expected. Of course she thinks the world is ending over a couple of leaked pictures. I mean, she should be happy the picture of me and Abel only showed me kissing his neck. If it had been taken a few minutes later, it would have captured me unbuttoning his shirt and pushing him back onto the sofa. *Then* I might have agreed that we had a problem.

But all that aside, I'm wondering what the hell she wants now. Asking to speak to me alone reeks of suspicion. I don't like this one bit, but I head downstairs to find out what it's all about.

I find Jill sitting in a booth in the back of the hotel restaurant, a black coffee in her hands. She beams when I walk over, standing up to give me a kiss on the cheek as if I haven't just seen her moments before. Then she asks if I want anything to drink. When I say no, she gathers herself for a second, then rips the Band-Aid off.

'I saw the incident last night with the photographer.' She doesn't look impressed. I should've known I'd be in trouble for that, but the leaked pictures distracted me somewhat.

'It wasn't my fault,' I start to say, but Jill holds up her hand.

'I'm sure it wasn't, sweetie, but we're worried about you. All of us at Omnificent are.' She tilts her head sympathetically, then taps her phone and turns it round so I can see. The picture on the screen winds me, casting a searing light on the shame I've been trying to hide.

It's the photos from New York that Jill paid seventy-five thousand dollars to hide from the world. I don't recognize the person in them. It's like someone is wearing my skin, parading it around for all to see. I feel exposed and vulnerable, my grief encapsulated in this one moment. I ache to help that person, to protect him from the world, but I can't compute that the person is me.

'We're worried about you,' Jill repeats herself. 'But I told you on that first day we wouldn't think twice about intervening if your drinking didn't stop, and I'm afraid you've left me with no choice.'

My mouth opens but nothing comes out. I'm too stunned to speak. Is this a fucking intervention?

'There's no time like the present. We want to look after you. So I've taken the liberty of booking you in with a therapist. It'll be good for you to talk to a professional. You've been through a lot, and I think it'd be wise to start putting measures in place now that will help you. She comes highly recommended.'

I feel blindsided. Attacked, even. This has all been set up without my knowledge.

'And what if I don't go?' I say, trying to gain back any kind of control.

Jill sighs. 'Lucky, please. We really are trying to help you. But if you don't follow our plans or guidance, we *will* be forced to take greater measures. None of us want that.'

'You mean you'll fire me.'

Jill hesitates, finding the right words. 'Like I said, we just want to help.'

It's like the floor has been pulled out from beneath me. I don't want to do this. I don't want to sit in front of a therapist and start delving into things I've been trying to lock away for so long. But what choice do I have? Omni are forcing my hand. I slump into my seat, defeated, thinking of the lost boy in that picture.

'When?'

Jill downs the last dregs of her coffee. 'Right now. I have a car waiting out the back. It'll take you straight there. We'll organize for it to pick you up when the session is over and bring you straight to set.'

I feel the smallest flicker of fury that the wheels are already in motion and that I'm helpless to stop it. But, just as quickly, my energy saps and I can't find the fight in me to push back. I nod. Jill gives me a big hug when we stand up and tells me

247

everything will be fine like she's sending me off to war. Then I'm directed to the car, and before I know it I'm in the back seat being driven through the streets of LA, trying to remember how to breathe.

We're a few minutes from the therapist's office when I realize we're being followed, and I start to panic. I can see a photographer in the car behind leaning forward with his camera on the dashboard. He can't see through the tinted window, and I fool myself into thinking they have no clue that I'm inside, but I see him talking on a phone and my heart rate spikes.

'Ronnie . . .' I start to say, but Ronnie swears before I can continue, and I soon see why.

We pull up in front of the building and are greeted by a swarm of paparazzi. There's at least a dozen of them, maybe more, standing between me and the door. They spot the SUV and come charging, cameras raised, shouting my name.

They knew I was going to be here. There's no other explanation. Someone tipped them off.

I immediately think of Jill. Would she want this kind of press? Would it fit some kind of sympathy narrative she's devised to turn the story round in Omni's favour? I can't be sure, but staring out of the window at the rabid beasts pushing up against the car, I feel like a cornered animal desperately looking for a way out.

Right now, I wish I was anyone but Lucky Tate. I've thought that a lot since Mom died. I just want a safe place to hide. To *grieve*. To try to put my life back together. But so long as I'm him, I'll never be free.

Chapter Twenty-Eight

CHOOSE YOUR BIGGEST FEAR: THE TRUTH OR A GREEN SMOOTHIE

Abel

The meeting with Jill – one of the more ludicrous experiences of my life – finishes in good time for me to slip out of the hotel and meet Casey in a café a few blocks away. The others have already headed off to set, but my call time isn't for another couple of hours. I've told them what I'm doing. What's the point in keeping secrets from them now? They all wished me good luck and warned me to be careful of paparazzi. Now the pictures have leaked, they're swarming even more than usual, hunting for us. Not to mention we have a stalker on the loose too, apparently keeping a close eye on our every move. I put on a cap and shades, hoping that will disguise me enough.

The café is some uber-healthy place selling smoothies that look too green to actually taste nice. I spot Casey sitting at the back. He looks nervous. I can see it in the lines of his face when I sit down, the shifting of his eyes, his too-rigid posture. He keeps looking over my shoulder to the door and scanning the room as if Omni are about to send a SWAT team to break this up. I wouldn't put it past them to be fair.

'I guess I should start by saying I'm sorry for being so shifty,' he begins once the waitress has brought over our drinks. 'I know I'm playing this all cloak and dagger, but Omnificent aren't people you want to mess with . . . I can't risk them knowing that this conversation happened.'

I nod, not trusting myself to speak. Nervous energy is pinballing through my entire body. The answers I've been looking for, the truth I've so desperately craved, could be mere words away. Casey doesn't seem to know where to start.

I take a breath and make the first leap, hoping that I'm right. 'You know who I am, don't you?'

Casey gives one last glance around the room, then nods. Tension pulls itself tight in my chest, where a thrill of adrenaline is also sparking.

'Knew it the second I saw you,' he says. 'Same eyes and nose, same British accent I always loved listening to. It took me straight back.' He swallows, tries to smile. His eyes sweep over my face, confirming it to himself one last time before he speaks it out loud. 'You're Adam Miller's brother.'

Hearing the confirmation sends a chill down my spine, but I try to keep myself level. 'That's me,' I say.

Casey lets out a big breath. 'Man, I can't believe you're here. He used to talk about you all the time, you know?' He winces

250

when he sees the look on my face, and I realize I must've had an instinctive reaction to hearing those words. It punched me in the gut.

'He did?'

'Yep. Said you were going to make it someday as a big-shot actor. He told anyone who'd listen that you were going to make it in this town.'

I glow a little at that, even though it hurts, like salt in a wound. We both hang our heads, lost in our own private memories of Adam.

'How did you two meet?'

Casey smiles to himself. 'We hit it off the moment he walked into the hotel and said, "You're telling me *this* is how the other half live?"' I breathe a laugh. We were one and the same. Of course we'd had identical reactions to being thrust into this lifestyle. 'I thought it was hilarious. He said he didn't know anyone in LA, and I offered to show him round since he seemed pretty cool. Similar age and everything. I didn't exactly expect him to agree, but he couldn't have been more up for it. We became good buddies after that.'

I wonder what Adam was like when he was here. He'd only been in LA for a couple of months when he died. Did he love it? Did he hate it? Did he find out new things about himself? What was LA Adam like? Was he different to the one I knew back home, or was he the same brother I'd grown up with? I had so many unanswered questions about him, some that I'd never get closure on.

'Was he happy here?' I ask.

Casey gives me a small smile. 'He was *so* happy. He loved the sun, said your weather back in London could kiss his ass.' We both throw our heads back and laugh some more. That sounds like Adam all right. It feels good to think of him like this. For too long now I've only seen him one way, veiled in misery and grief, but it's like the ghost of him is sitting with us now, enjoying the happy memories and guiding me closer towards the truth.

Casey's face quickly falls, his eyes dropping into his lap. When he looks up, there's severe sadness there. 'We might not have known each other that well – we didn't have the time – but I can say with confidence that he was a great friend.' He sighs. 'Which is why I'm ashamed that I've kept what happened from you for this long.'

My breath catches in the back of my throat, as if it's become a solid object and got lodged there.

Casey drops his head into his hands. 'I've tried to tell you this so many times. Every time I've seen you, I've wanted to blurt it out, but I guess . . . I don't know. Maybe I'm just a coward.' He shakes his head. When he looks up, though, I know he's ready to start talking properly. 'I guess I should start with the night he died.'

He pauses. Then he lets the truth fly free.

Chapter Twenty-Nine

SMILE FOR THE CAMERA

Casey Beck / 8 July 2020

'Well, don't you look a million dollars?' I say with a teasing grin as Adam Miller walks out of the elevator opposite the hotel front desk. He looks exhausted, walking with a slight hunch as if sleep is sitting heavy on his back, trying to grind him down into submission.

'Ugh, don't,' Adam groans, mooching over and bending down to use the counter as a pillow for a moment.

'That bad, huh?'

Adam nods into the crook of his arm before standing up straight and stretching. 'Lake is kicking our arses on set. He wants everything absolutely perfect, even if it takes six hours to get one damn shot. We won't be wrapped until Christmas *next* year at this rate.'

'Sounds like a drag,' I say. 'Who knew living out your dreams could be so exhausting?'

'Tell me about it.' Adam glances around the lobby and leans forward over the desk, gossip simmering on his lips. I instinctively mirror him, moving closer. 'There's been drama on set, too. One of the other assistants apparently overheard Penelope Daunt on the phone to a journalist in her trailer yesterday. Rumours are flying that she's going to tell everyone what a dickhead Lake has been to her the last few weeks.'

'No way,' I say, pretty shook. A sit-down with Penelope exposing Omni Channel would be worth its weight in gold.

'I'm not sure if Lake's found out yet, but he won't be happy if he does.' Adam leans back and starts getting ready to leave.

'There's no way you're finishing the gossip session there,' I say. 'I want the full breakdown. Over drinks? I get off work in twenty.'

Adam shakes his head. 'Can't. Gotta run by the set to grab the script notes that Lake left behind and then deliver them to his house. *Not* the job I signed up for.'

'After then,' I say. I put on my best puppy-dog eyes. 'Come on, we can't let this good LA night get away from us, can we? Think of younger Adam at home in London, *dreeeeeaming* of making it to the City of Angels. What would he tell you to do?'

Adam grins. 'He'd say the first round is on you.'

I salute. 'You got it. The Playground in an hour? We might make happy hour if we're lucky.'

'Now you're talking,' Adam says, lighting up. 'I'll see you there.'

'Bring the rest of the gossip with you too.'

Adam laughs, slaps me a high five, then heads out of the hotel doors. I finish up my shift, say goodnight to Stephen, and leave for the bar in West Hollywood. I can't help but smiling. It's a gorgeous evening. Nothing could possibly ruin it.

An hour passes.

I check my texts, looking at the three messages I've already sent that have received no reply. I'm about to send another when I see the typing bubble pop up. *About damn time*, I think to myself.

> **Adam Miller**
> Meet me at the hotel asap.
> I'll be on the roof
> 21:59

The roof? Now I know something's up. It's the only place in the hotel where you don't have to worry about being overheard. I've been up there countless times, mostly with Adam so we can bitch about work in peace. Something must have happened if he wants me to meet him up there. I don't question it. I send a quick response to tell him I'm on my way, leave a tip for the bartender, then hail a cab back to Beverly Hills after grabbing some beers from a bodega.

I don't see the flashing lights at first. I'm scrolling through my phone, not paying attention. But suddenly the inside of the cab is aglow with reds and blues, and when I glance up I see chaos unfolding on the doorstep of the hotel.

'What the fuck?' I whisper, leaning forward to get a better look through the windscreen.

I pay the driver and jump out, heading straight for the entrance. But there's crime-scene tape cordoning off the whole place, and two officers tell me I can't come through.

'I work here,' I say, trying to swallow my panic. 'Front desk. Casey Beck.'

I manage to get in when Stephen sees me and tells the officers to let me pass. The lobby is deserted of guests. Instead, it's overrun with cops and paramedics. Stephen's face is ashen. He holds his hands together so tightly his knuckles are white.

'What happened?' I ask shakily.

Stephen chews the inside of his cheek. 'There's been an accident . . .' he says slowly. 'Someone fell. From the roof.'

The world around me doesn't grind to a halt. It slams to a standstill in an instant. My heart crashes in my chest, at once leaving me breathless and lightheaded. This can't be happening. I almost don't dare to ask questions, because right now I can kid myself into thinking it's someone else who's fallen from the roof. In this moment, it could be anyone. But no matter how hard I tell myself that, I already know what's happened. Stephen glances down at his phone and steps away to answer it, leaving me alone as this nightmare continues to swirl around me and that truth begins to settle heavily in my gut.

The next hour or so is a blur. I sit in the bar, unable to move or comprehend what's happening. People pass me by but I barely see them. At some point Stephen comes over with two cops flanking him.

'This is a shock for us all,' Stephen says to the officers. 'I really don't think anyone is in the right frame of mind to answer questions, particularly when it was quite clearly an accident.'

'With all due respect, sir, we're doing our job,' one of the officers says.

Stephen folds his lips together and nods rigidly.

'Did you know the deceased?' the officer asks me gently.

Deceased.

Adam Miller is dead.

I nod but the effort to do so is enormous, and I have to bow my head to shoulder the weight of it. I answer a couple more questions as best I can. I can hardly hear what's being asked, as if there's a glass wall between me and the cops, the words bouncing off it. The officers seem to realize they're not going to get much from me and turn to Stephen instead.

'We'll need CCTV from this evening if it's available.'

'Why?' Stephen asks. His tone is quick and snappy enough to make me raise my head.

'Formal procedure. We need to trace Adam's movements.'

Stephen shakes his head. I think it's in disgust at first, but then I realize it's actually in apology. 'I'm afraid there's nothing I can do. There was a CCTV glitch earlier this afternoon. Some kind of software bug, I suspect. There's no footage available from any of the cameras today, or yesterday for that matter. An engineer is due tomorrow to fix it.'

I frown and steal a glance at the officers. One of them makes a note in their pad, a puzzled expression on their face.

But Stephen folds his arms and sets his jaw. 'Now if you don't mind, we're all a *little* emotional right now.'

The cops nod politely and go to leave, but one of them quickly turns back. 'One more thing, while I remember. We received a call a short time ago from a payphone outside the hotel reporting a disturbance at a house in the Hollywood Hills.'

'What would we know about that?' Stephen asks impatiently at the same time I say, 'Up in the Hills?'

The officer ignores Stephen and nods in my direction. 'We sent a squad car to investigate and found no signs of a disturbance. It was probably a prank – someone playing up to this *curse* everyone's talking about lately – and whoever it was didn't leave a name. But I wanted to check if either of you happened to see someone using that phone in the last hour?'

I shake my head. Stephen does too.

The officer shrugs. 'Well, if you think of anything else that might be important, please don't hesitate to get in touch.'

The cops leave us alone. I look up at Stephen. His eyes restlessly roam around the lobby. He looks unsettled in a way I can't describe. On edge even. He can't seem to stay still, shifting his weight from one foot to the other and clenching his hands together.

'There was a CCTV glitch?' I ask, looking down at the grains of wood in the bar top.

Stephen shuffles beside me. 'Yep. Technology, eh? Can never trust it.' He puts his hands behind his back, then clasps them out in front of him instead. 'I'd best go see what else I can do to help,' he says, and disappears behind the hotel desk.

I glance up towards the corner of the room where one of the CCTV cameras is placed. I *know* the cameras were working earlier. I was on shift and everything was fine. I would've been alerted otherwise. What kind of glitch not only takes the CCTV out of action but also wipes the footage from the last couple of days too? It doesn't make sense.

And what about the disturbance reported from the payphone outside? It seems inconsequential, but one small detail caught my attention – why would that officer mention the *curse* unless the call had something to do with *Sunset High*? Not to mention he said it was about a house in the Hollywood Hills. Plenty of celebrities and high-profile people reside in the exclusive neighbourhood. Is it purely a coincidence that Lake Carter lives there too?

27 July 2023

We're preparing for the arrival of the new cast and crew of *Sunset High*. In a few days the whole show will descend on the hotel once more, just as they've done the last two times. I fight the feeling that nags at every thought in my mind – things didn't exactly turn out great the last time that circus was in town. But still, this is a new reboot. There's no damn curse to be scared of, only memories and questions that still haunt me.

Stephen is treating *Sunset High*'s arrival with the utmost

care. Honestly, you'd think royalty were coming to stay. All the staff have been briefed on arrivals, who and what to expect, security, how to deal with intrusive paparazzi. It's like a military operation.

One name in the cast stood out to me, though. Abel Miller. It can't be a coincidence. I haven't seen a picture of him yet, but I'd bet my last cent that I already know who he is, even if we've never met before. Adam sits at the front of my mind, where he's been living for the last three years. A day hasn't gone by where I don't think about him, not least because although the cops quickly closed the case and called his death an accident, I'm sure there has to be more to it.

I'm coming off my lunch break, heading back out to the front desk, when I hear voices from Stephen's office. I know someone from Omnificent is coming in today to discuss final preparations, so I automatically slow down when I hear them.

'. . . already settled this situation,' a woman's voice is saying. 'And may I remind you, honey, you signed an NDA when you took the money. So before you try to threaten me, I'd think carefully about what you're doing if I were you.'

Stephen snorts. 'I don't think you or Omnificent will have a leg to stand on if I break the NDA and take my little video to the press, *honey*.'

There's a beat of silence. What the fuck are they talking about? I glance down the empty corridor and creep slightly closer to the office door.

'If you give that video to the press, then the cops will get involved, and *you* will go down with the ship too. Tampering with potential evidence? You'll go straight to jail. Is that what you want?' Before Stephen can answer, the woman pushes on. 'All I'm saying is, there has to be a mutually beneficial deal we can come to here.'

'Thanks for your concern, Jill, but this isn't a negotiation. A million dollars and I'll keep quiet. I'll delete the video and never speak of it again. This will all go away. Nobody will ever know what you, Lake and Omnificent have done. You have my word.'

I hold on to the wall as my world warps. I can hear my breath rattling in my throat. I stumble away from the office door and back to the hotel lobby, trying to compose myself. When Stephen and Jill appear, they both look furious. Jill swings her bag up onto her shoulder and storms out. Stephen joins me at the desk. I pretend to tap keys on the computer, focusing all my attention on the screen, but out of the corner of my eye, I'm watching him.

3 August 2023

I'm on the front desk with Stephen. I've been replaying that conversation with Jill over and over in my head ever since I heard it. I can't think of anything else. I'm determined to know what it was all about. I mean, I have a pretty good inkling, but I want the proof. What video was Stephen talking about?

His phone sits on the counter next to the computer screen

he's working on, almost mocking me. He always places it in view so he can be alerted to anything going on in the hotel straight away. Right now, he's checking in a high-profile guest, some singer in town for a concert tonight. He chats away, kissing ass the whole time. But the minute he turns his back, I lean over. Not to grab his phone, but to wipe my thumb over the front camera. I smudge it back and forth a few times, then go back to my computer like nothing happened.

When the guest goes up to their room, I glance at Stephen. 'What songs does she sing again?' I ask, feigning innocence.

Stephen frowns. 'I thought all you young twenty-somethings had your fingers on the pulse.' He picks up his phone, raising it to his face. He frowns when it doesn't unlock and raises it higher. He mumbles something about *fucking technology* under his breath, swipes the screen and taps in the passcode instead.

1 2 1 5 1 2.

I repeat the numbers in my head, burning them into my brain as Stephen looks up the singer's discography and tells me her biggest singles. I nod and smile, all the while chanting those six numbers.

I have to wait a while longer for another guest to approach the desk for check-in. As they come through the doors, I turn to Stephen. 'Hey, can you take this one? My stomach's doing flips. I think I might be sick.'

Stephen looks horrified at the thought of me vomiting in front of guests in the lobby and quickly steps into my spot, urging me to go to the bathroom immediately. I slip past him, sliding my hand along the desk, then all but run for the toilets.

I lock myself in a cubicle and take Stephen's phone out of my pocket, typing in the passcode to unlock it – 1 2 1 5 1 2.

I don't have much time, but I already know what I'm looking for. I head straight to his camera roll, click the search bar and type *8 July*. Every picture and video taken on that date over the last few years pops up. There are some shots of Stephen and his girlfriend on holiday, pictures of dogs and beaches and sunsets. But it's not those I'm looking for. I scroll through until I find the right year – 2020.

I don't have to look far. He barely took any pictures or videos on that day three years ago. Just four, in fact. One is of his lunch. The second is a video taken inside the hotel. But it's not just any video. It's CCTV. Heart in my mouth, I press play.

The camera is angled towards the front desk, where Stephen is working alone. A few moments later, he looks up and smiles at a guest who quickly walks into shot. They keep their head down and move straight towards the elevator. I can only see the back of them, but I know without a shadow of a doubt that it's Adam. The door slides shut, and he's gone. The video ends.

Throat dry, heart racing, breath shallow, I slide across and press play on the next video. It's taken from the same angle but based on the time stamp, it's a short while later, twenty minutes or so. This time, Stephen smiles again and the new guest stops to talk to him. It's only a brief moment, then they turn their head enough for me to see that it's Lake Carter. He goes towards the elevator, and I want to reach through the screen to save Adam from what I already know is coming. The video ends.

I slide across to the last video. It's taken from the stairwell leading up to the roof's door. I'm terrified to press play, but I have to.

Adam hops up the stairs first, two at a time. He steps through the door to the roof. It's like watching fate taunt me. I want to cry out a warning, but it won't make a difference. It can't change what's already happened. I fast-forward the video, knowing what must be coming next. Sure enough, Lake Carter enters the picture.

He goes up to the roof and is there for a few minutes. I fast-forward through each agonizing one, until he bursts back through the door, breathing hard. So hard he stops for a second, bent double, dry heaving like a guilty son of a bitch. He looks at his phone, goes *back* to the roof, then comes running into the shot again. He disappears and the video ends.

There it is. As plain as day. Proof the *accident* that killed Adam was no accident at all.

It was murder.

Chapter Thirty

MURDER IN HOLLYWOOD

Abel

The video comes to an end. I can't see the screen now through the blur of my tears. I've wanted the truth for so long, yearned for it, but now I have it, the wounds that scar me have been opened up irrevocably.

I can't stop seeing Adam going up those stairs, unaware that Lake was about to follow him and push him to his death. Even though the CCTV doesn't prove that's what happened, I know in my heart that it did. This wasn't an accident. Far from it. Lake's hands have my brother's blood on them.

But why? Did they have an argument when Adam went to visit Lake's house? Did Adam know something about Lake, and Lake wanted to keep him quiet? Parts of the story still hide in the dark. I'd do anything to bring them out into the light, no matter how painful.

'I AirDropped the video to myself from Stephen's phone,' Casey says. 'I knew that was the only way to avoid leaving any evidence. Then I replaced the phone before he knew it was missing. He has no idea I have the footage. I've wanted to do something about it, but . . .' He lets go of a trembling breath. 'I'm a coward. I was scared. Lake and Omnificent aren't people you want to get on the wrong side of.'

Part of me wants to be angry that Casey kept this vital information to himself. He should've told the police straight away, or me when I arrived in LA. But even as I think it, I understand. This video is proof of more than just murder – it shows that Lake, Jill, Omni, the whole damn lot of them, will do *anything* to keep their dirty secrets buried. Of course Casey would be scared. Right now, beneath all my anger, I'm terrified too. But I can't focus on that. If I do, I'll crumble. All I know is that I can't – *won't* – let them get away with what they've done.

'Stephen's using the videos as blackmail to force Omni into paying him money – *more* money?' I ask. Casey nods. 'You know what that means, right?'

Casey swallows. 'I think it's pretty obvious at this point. Omnificent paid Stephen to make sure the CCTV from that night was wiped. He must have deleted the footage from the day before too to cover his tracks and make it look less suspicious if the cops started asking questions.'

'And now he's blackmailing them into buying his silence,' I finish. 'He wiped the CCTV but made sure he had a backup, just in case. He's probably spent the money they gave him three years ago and now he wants more. *A million dollars* more. Omni have got to be panicking.'

We lapse into silence. I can't speak for Casey, but I feel spaced out, in total shock and disbelief. Surely this is the script of a movie and a director is about to yell 'CUT' right about now? It's almost impossible that this is real life.

'The phone call must be connected too,' Casey says. 'It *has* to be.'

'Phone call?'

'The one the officers asked me about. Someone reported a *disturbance* in the Hollywood Hills using a payphone near the hotel. Coincidence that it happened roughly the same hour that Adam died?'

In all this craziness, the phone call hadn't even registered with me. And yet, of *course* it's a piece of the same puzzle.

'You think it was Adam who made that call?'

'You don't?' Casey counters. 'Think about it – Adam goes up to the Hollywood Hills to drop off script notes at Lake's house, comes back to the hotel with Lake on his tail, and then Lake pushes him off the roof.' Casey lowers his voice, leaning closer to me over the table. 'What if Adam saw something at his house? I don't know, maybe he stumbled on something he wasn't meant to see. He wanted to report it but didn't want it to come from him. He would have been scared, so he made the call on a payphone and gave an anonymous tip, then he hides out on the roof to wait for me.'

I think of the text that Adam sent me on the night he died. Had he already made the call to the police by then and didn't know who else he could talk to about it?

I look back down at Casey's phone on the table. The video is frozen on the stairwell. I rewind it and press play again, watching as my brother disappears up onto the roof, followed by Lake. Fast-forward, and then Lake comes bursting through the roof's door, heaving in the stairwell. He looks at the phone in his hand, already unlocked. Then he types something, runs back up to the roof and reappears a moment later, this time not stopping. The video ends. I'm leaning back in my chair when something jumps out at me. I click the video again and scroll to the point where Lake first reappears from the roof. I hit pause and zoom in on his hand.

The phone is screen down for a split second, the case facing outwards before Lake raises it to type a message. It's a simple phone case with a black covering, but it also has two initials in white text in the centre – *AM*.

'That's my brother's phone,' I gasp, fighting not to throw up.

Casey grabs his phone and looks for himself. His eyes widen. 'Holy shit.'

My mind is racing so fast, I almost can't comprehend what I'm thinking. But the facts are right there in front of my eyes.

'I received two texts from Adam the night he died,' I say, and I can feel my heart breaking into pieces as it all slots together in my head. 'The first one asked me to call him when I woke up. The second was just over ten minutes later. It said it was a false alarm and that he loved me, but he called me *bro*.' I shake my head. 'We never said "bro" to each other, so I knew straight away something was wrong. But . . .' I point

268

to the video. 'Adam never sent me that text. Lake did. That's him typing it right there.'

My grief is enveloping me all over again now I've realized that the last thing Adam ever said to me was never him all along. It was sent from the person who pushed him to his death, the person who took my brother away from me.

I can see a version of what might have happened playing out in my head, and I can't press pause. I see my brother facing Lake, backing away from him, scared for his life. His phone's in his hand. Maybe it's already unlocked because he's thinking of trying to call the police but knows they won't arrive in time. Or maybe he was texting me when Lake appeared. As Lake approaches, there's a struggle, and he pushes my brother backwards. Adam drops his phone and falls over the edge. Lake picks it up, sees the text to me. He runs off with the phone, then tries to cover his tracks by sending the second message.

Just like that, I feel my entire body shatter from the inside. The one thing I'd held on to all this time – that last text from my brother – was a lie. It breaks me in such a way that I know I'll carry the pain with me for the rest of my life.

Casey looks stunned, but then he scrambles his thoughts together and completes the picture. 'Adam's phone was found next to his body.' He presses play on the video and we watch Lake run back up to the roof, coming to the same realization together.

'Lake threw it off the roof so it wouldn't look suspicious,' I say, almost in a trance. He typed that message to get himself out of the shit. Probably wiped the messages from the phone too in case the police checked. Then he went back up, tossed it over the ledge, left the hotel and made sure he got the CCTV erased.

I come back into the café, out of my own head, but I still feel only half present. 'Lake did this,' I say. 'He killed my brother. But why? What did Adam know?'

We finish our drinks and I make my excuses. I want to be alone with my thoughts and grief so bad, but I don't have time. I need to get to set, although I don't know how I'll face Lake. But I can't give him, or anyone else, a reason to look in my direction. I don't think he's made the connection, but if I raise his suspicions and alert him, who knows what he'll do. My cover has already been blown by someone, and not knowing who makes this an even more precarious position to be in.

Casey interrupts my thoughts, reaching into his bag. He hands me a blank disc. My heart starts tattooing my ribs.

'Is this . . .?' I start.

Casey nods. 'Thought you might want a physical copy. I burned the video onto the disc for safekeeping.'

It feels like I'm holding a ticking bomb. I slip the disc into the depths of my rucksack and we make to leave.

'What are you going to do about all of this?' Casey asks as we step outside into the warm afternoon sunshine.

I look around me, then up to the sky. I wonder if Adam is looking down on me, watching me every step of the way. When I come back down to Earth, the answer is already on my lips.

'Make sure that Lake Carter goes to hell for what he's done.'

Chapter Thirty-One

LESSONS IN ACTING

Lucky

'AND CUT!'

Lake drops his head into his hands and heaves a great sigh. It's the first day back on the set of *Sunset High* after Ryan's break-in. The car dropped me straight here after my failed therapy session, and I was immediately pushed into hair and make-up, shoved into wardrobe, plucked and preened, brushed, lit, filmed and photographed from every angle. Sometimes on set it can feel like you're being pulled in every direction, all while you're trying to run through the script and memorize lines in your head, which can change at a moment's notice depending on what works on camera and what doesn't. It's the afternoon now and things aren't exactly going great.

Because of the three unplanned days off, we're behind

schedule. I'm sure Omni are worried about going over-budget as they're now having to pay past the previous end date for the cast and crew, equipment and studio. It's a costly job. I bet that's why Lake is straining to keep his temper in check as we mess up take after take. I guess, with everything that's been going on, we've all got a lot on our minds.

Lake is visibly frustrated. Sure, he hasn't exactly popped his top, but that front he puts on is cracking. I think it might have something to do with the leaked photos, which he's refused to mention or acknowledge, as if that will make them go away. The rest of the crew keep stealing glances at us like we're specimens in a zoo.

'Okay, let's set up for *another* take,' Lake says. 'Actors, take five. Can we try to nail it on the next one?'

Me, Ella, Ryan and Abel step out from under the studio lights and huddle together in a corner. Ever since Abel got to set just after lunch, he's been off. It's like he's running on autopilot, his head elsewhere. Whatever happened with Casey is clearly playing on his mind, but we haven't had a chance to talk about it in private until now.

'You okay?' I ask him in a low voice as some of the crew shuffle past.

Abel takes a second, then shakes his head.

'What did Casey have to say?' Ella asks gently.

Abel can't quite find the words to say what he's thinking. His eyes glaze over with tears for a second, but he quickly takes a couple of settling breaths, then blurts it out. 'He said Lake Carter murdered my brother.'

The noise of the set falls away. For a second, I don't think I've heard him right. I can see the horror on Ryan's face, the shock on Ella's, but surely I didn't just hear those words. As if he can read my thoughts, Abel says it again, each word breaking with the strain of holding himself together.

'Lake Carter pushed my brother off the roof to protect whatever it was he was hiding and he paid to have the evidence erased. That man is a murderer.'

We all turn our eyes to the set, where Lake is standing with his arms crossed, watching as the shot is set up once more. He's a large man, easily over six foot, with wide shoulders and arms bulked up from working out. He's always tried to present himself as a big friendly giant – at first anyway – but, right now, all I can see is how easily he'd be able to overpower someone.

'We can't talk about this now,' Abel murmurs. 'I'll tell you everything back at the hotel tonight. Let's just carry on as normal.'

I don't exactly know how you 'carry on as normal' when your director is apparently a murderer, but I guess we don't have much of a choice.

'We'll get through today,' Ryan says, giving Abel a supportive rub on the back. 'Then we'll figure this out, okay?'

We all nod, then get back into position for the next take. The whole time I'm trying to remember my lines, but I can't focus. *Lake* and *murderer* are the only words coming to me, and when Lake yells 'ACTION', I draw a complete blank. The words I'm supposed to say try to stumble out of my mouth, but my brain shuts down and I'm forced to improvise instead. Abel stutters, trying to save the take, but quickly clams up.

'CUT!' Lake yells. His face is flushed, his jaw set. He moves round the camera and goes right up to Abel. 'How are you making *such* hard work of this?' he shouts, spit flying from his mouth.

'It was my fault,' I say, coming up beside Abel and taking half a step so I'm slightly in front of him. 'I messed up my lines. If you're going to shout and scream, at least have the decency to do it at the right person.'

I didn't exactly mean to become the knight in shining armour, but Abel is already struggling to hold it together, and I can't stand here and do nothing. An ugly silence falls over the set, thick and all-consuming. Lake stares me down as if he's waiting for me to buckle. I stand my ground. Tension pulses in the air, counted in quickening heartbeats. Lake narrows his eyes, and, for just a moment, I see a flash of fury cross his face. It disappears quickly, but Lake and his ego need to save face somehow. He brightens up, with what looks like a lot of effort, and tries to laugh it off with a thinly veiled joke.

'Well, thank God you're the pretty boy of the show,' Lake says. 'You clearly haven't got your acting to fall back on today, eh!'

'An actor is only as good as his director,' I counter, failing to keep my anger in check.

Another silence, this one even heavier than the last. Lake's furious and is now really struggling to hide it. It gives me a lot of satisfaction. A flicker of a smile tugs at my lips. Lake sees it and looks ready to take the head off my shoulders. But, instead, he throws his own head back and laughs. The set seems to breathe a sigh of relief when he claps me on the shoulder as if we're best buddies. What they don't feel is the iron grip of his hand.

'It's clear everyone needs a proper break,' Lake calls out. 'Back on set in thirty. Lucky, can I speak to you for a minute? In my trailer.'

He gives my shoulder a tight squeeze, then walks off the set. The others all look at me, eyes wide. I shrug, ignoring the flutter of adrenaline in my chest, and follow him. I reach the back of the lot, the white mobile home that marks Lake's quarters coming into view. I pause. Requesting to see me behind closed doors? Lake's used to presenting a front when others are around, but I've already seen his mask start to slip today. Alone in his trailer, he could do or say anything. Things could turn south quickly. I check my phone, pocket it and knock.

'Come in,' Lake's voice calls.

I take a deep breath, the way I do before a director yells, 'ACTION' at the beginning of a shot, then step inside the trailer. It's tidy, with *Sunset High* memorabilia neatly set up on the shelves. I take particular interest in the posters, all from various iterations of the show, some framed, others in piles on the table. Lake is seated, annotated script pages scattered out in front of him. The smell of a repugnant aftershave fills my nostrils.

'You wanted to see me?' I ask, tone level and calm as if

what happened on set didn't occur at all. Lake has a smile on his face.

And then the door closes behind me.

He doesn't say a word. Instead, he stands, barrels round the table and grabs me by the front of my shirt, slamming me back into the wall. All trace of the character he puts on in front of people is gone. In its place is the monster he's so carefully hidden. Right now, up close, I can see just how capable of murder Lake truly is.

But, despite the rage rolling off him in fumes, I know I'm safe here. At least for the moment. He might be a murderer, but he's not stupid enough to do it here on set. Either way, my eyes water, and when I tell him to stop, to get off me, my voice is layered with fear.

'You little shit,' Lake hisses, his breath hot against my cheek. I struggle in his grasp, but he doesn't let go. 'You think you're funny, do you? You think you can make me look like a fool and get away with it? Let me remind you of something.' He gets so close I can see two of him, doubling the amount of anger. 'I *own* you.'

I squirm a little. 'Lake, please, get off. You're hurting me.'

'Good. And I'll do a whole lot more than that.' His face is so contorted with fury, it's like looking at a different person.

'Please . . .' I try again, my voice quivering. I bring my hands together and thrust them into his chest, pushing him back slightly. 'HELP!' I yell. But I know we're at the back of the lot. Everyone else is on set. Nobody will hear me.

'Shut your fucking mouth or I swear to God I'll kill you,'

Lake says, getting in my face once again.

I widen my eyes and tears begin to fall down my cheeks. I struggle some more, and this time when Lake slams me into the wall, a small glass award falls off the shelf next to us and smashes into smithereens on the floor.

'Please,' I whisper. I'm breathing hard and heavy. 'I'm begging you. Let me go.'

Lake sees my tears and the bastard smiles like he knows he's won. 'Know your place,' he says. His words are low and menacing. 'Defy me again, and watch what I'll do. I promise you'll regret ever crossing me.' He smooths out the wrinkles on my shirt and then puts his hands on my shoulders, like a father ready to tell his son that he's not mad, just disappointed. 'And if you speak a word of our little catch-up to anyone . . .'

His threat is clear. Murderous.

Then, just like that, he steps away and goes back to the script pages on the table. He smiles, his character firmly back in place. 'I'll see you back on set. I'm sure we won't have this misunderstanding again.'

I don't waste a second getting out of there. I scramble for the door and take off. The moment I'm out of sight of the trailer, I stop and take a deep breath, the same way I do when a director yells, 'CUT!'

And then I smile to myself.

I dig out my phone and stop the voice recording.

Not bad for a kid who apparently can't act.

Chapter Thirty-Two

MALIBU AGAIN

Abel

The others are stunned into silence when I tell them everything. We're gathered in my room that evening, finally back from set. Ella and Ryan are cuddled into each other on the sofa, while Lucky stays close to me. I feel comfort knowing that he's there. The way he looks at me, the way he gives me reassuring contact whether it's his knee against mine or a hand on my arm, makes me feel like I'm not alone in this hell.

'I can't believe it,' Ryan breathes, the first to break the silence. 'I mean, I *can*, because what won't Lake, Jill and Omni do to keep themselves afloat? But *murder*?'

'You don't think you should hand the video to the cops?' Ella asks. 'It's as good as a confession, right?' But even she doesn't sound so sure.

I'd already thought about that. It felt like the most obvious thing to do. But still, there's one glaring problem, and Lucky clearly realizes it too.

'If we hand over the video, all it proves is that Lake went up to the roof,' he says. 'It's obvious to us what happened, but there's no *actual* evidence that Lake pushed Adam to his death. That's what Omni will say if this ever made it to court.'

'A billion-dollar company versus four teenagers?' Ryan shakes her head. 'We wouldn't stand a chance. They're too powerful. Giving the video to the cops won't guarantee us anything other than alerting Lake to what we know.'

I completely deflate.

'I guess the question is . . . what do we do now?' Lucky asks, looking at each of us as if someone might have a perfectly logical answer.

'We?' I shake my head quickly. 'I don't want to drag you guys into this any more than I already have. I should've never got you all involved in the first place.'

Ryan makes a face, waving my comments away as if they're a bad smell. 'Oh, please. What do you think we're going to do – leave you to get revenge without us? I think we all want to get back at Omni, and Lake in particular, for something. We're in this together, dummy.'

'We are?' I know the four of us have been through a lot together already, but still, it surprises me that they want to help. 'But . . . your careers. Everything you've worked so hard for. This could ruin it all. I don't want that.'

Lucky snorts. 'Like any of that matters. Every single one

of us have been used by Omni. They've controlled us and fucked us over at every turn, and it's about time they paid for it. There's something else too . . .' Lucky pauses. 'I saw stacks of old and new *Sunset High* posters in Lake's trailer today.'

I'm confused about what that's got to do with anything, but Ryan's eyeballs nearly fall out of her head. 'Of fucking *course* it's him.'

'Have I missed something?' I ask, still confused.

Ryan shakes her head in disbelief. 'This whole time we've been worried that there's a deranged stalker watching our every move, but who would stand to benefit the most from making the return of *Sunset High* as dramatic as possible? Who would want everyone to be talking about this stupid made-up *curse*?'

'Lake . . .' Ella whispers.

Holy shit.

'Oh my God, how could we have been so *stupid*?' Ryan says. 'It's so obvious. Someone leaves me a gift-wrapped box of defaced posters outside my house the night *before* the reboot is publicly announced, and somehow the press find out. Coincidental timing, no? It got people talking about the curse straight away. *Sunset High* were the only two words on everyone's lips.'

'An Omni stylist gives me a dress that ends up having a message scrawled on the back,' Ella adds. 'People jump to the conclusion that it's Ryan getting her own back because I "stole her boyfriend", which only adds fuel to a scandal that everyone was already invested in.'

'Someone breaks into my house, trashes the place, pins up a bunch of *Sunset High* posters with faces crossed out and writes the message: *You're next. Somehow* pictures end up online again.' Ryan throws her hands up in the air. 'I literally said to Abel I wouldn't have been surprised if Jill was jumping for joy about how much press we got from that.'

Lucky nods. 'And the rock through my window was wrapped in a *Sunset High* poster, plus there was the message scratched into the back of my car. Pictures show up online, everyone talks about the curse again. It's a pattern. Whoever it is has obviously worked on *Sunset High* before, or how else would they have accessed the posters from the last reboot? And we all know that Lake would do anything to make sure this show is a success.'

I'm confused. It makes sense in parts, but I can't quite grasp why Lake would be behind it. 'But someone followed you to Brad's house that night,' I say to Ryan. 'Why would Lake want to scare you like that? Nobody knows that happened, so it can't have been done for press.'

Ryan mulls it over. 'I guess that could've been an *actual* stalker. My address was leaked online a few weeks before then, and people have been showing up outside ever since. Or maybe Lake wanted to scare me so much that I'd decide to walk away without a fuss when the show's over. Then it would look like it was my choice to leave Omni Channel instead of them replacing me. They come out looking like the good guys.'

I'm not sure all the pieces fit, but I admit the idea of Lake, Jill and Omni doing anything to get press for the show, even if it means terrorizing us, doesn't sound that far-fetched.

'So . . . what do we do?' says Ryan. 'We could go to the press. All of us together have enough sway to make them listen. We literally have a journalist in the room.'

I blush, still a little embarrassed about that. I wonder what Hannah would say if the four of us called her up now and gave her the scoop. She'd love it. Job done. Omni exposed. But I wouldn't have my answers, so that's out of the question.

Lucky shakes his head. 'It's not enough to just tell our story. Omni will throw everything they have at it to make sure they come out on top. Plus, fans hardly care when something they love turns out to be problematic. They just selectively ignore the bad stuff. We might dent Omni Channel's ego and reputation, but I don't think we're going to hit them where it hurts.'

'What about Mila Stone?' Ella says, sitting up. 'Penelope disappeared without a trace, but Mila's still around. She might have something that we could use. She always said Omni were evil. I feel bad for not believing her now.'

'We never did find out what happened to Penelope,' Lucky says. He pulls out his phone and starts searching her name as if the answer will be right there on Google.

'I already paid Mila a visit,' I say. The others all lean forward at once.

'You did?' Ryan says. 'She hasn't *ever* spoken to anyone about her story. I mean, to be fair, I wouldn't either if everyone had laughed me out of town when I tried to tell them what I'd been through.'

I shrug. 'She let me in. Well, she wouldn't let me *in* her house, but she sat with me in the garden and gave me some insight. They *really* put her through a lot. She talks about it as if it's just something that happened, but under the surface, she's still hurting.'

I grab my phone and pull up the picture I took of her house when I went to visit her.

'Cute place,' Ella says. 'Living by the beach away from this madness must be so relaxing.'

'Doesn't she have, like, a hundred guard dogs or something?' Ryan says, having a look at the house over Ella's shoulder and agreeing that it is indeed pretty cute.

'A rumour she spread herself. She has two Labradors, both super adorable. One of them is called Max. I didn't get the name of the other one.'

Lucky takes my phone and has a look for himself. A few seconds later, his eyes narrow. He pinches the screen and zooms in on something, looks back at his own phone, then shakes his head as if he can't believe what he's seeing.

'What is it?' I ask, feeling a heady mix of panic and apprehension swirling.

Lucky doesn't seem to hear me. His eyes are going back and forth between our two phones. Then they widen in astonishment.

'You're not going to believe this,' he says. We all gather round him, looking at the picture of Mila's house on my phone. 'Notice anything?'

'We could play I spy until the cows come home, or you

could get to the point,' Ryan says impatiently.

Lucky zooms in towards the driveway, where an old white car sits. He turns his eyes to us as if it's obvious. When we all just stare back blankly, he shows us his phone. The door-cam footage of Penelope Daunt's last sighting is loaded on the screen. He presses play.

'I don't understand . . .' I start to say, but Ella gasps and starts pointing. I'm not sure what she's seen to begin with. I've watched the video a million times already and know that Penelope's Mercedes won't come into the frame for another minute or so. My eyes sweep the street. And then an old white car drives past.

'It can't be,' I say, leaning in closer as if that's going to give me the information I need right now. The footage is pretty blurry. Too blurry to make out the number plate or even the make of the car.

'There's no way,' Ryan starts to say, but I can hear she's unsure of herself. 'What, Mila Stone coincidentally happened to be on the same street as Penelope Daunt at the same time she went missing? Nope, I'm not buying it.'

Lucky shakes his head. 'Who says it was a coincidence?'

'Noooo, don't tell me Mila killed Penelope,' Ryan groans. 'I liked Mila back in the day. She can't be my problematic fave now.'

Lucky shrugs. 'All I'm saying is she has to know something.'

I can't think straight. I'm so confused. But when I replay my visit to Mila's in my head, something jumps out at me. Then something else. Tiny details that I missed while sitting right there in her back garden. I want to scream up at the sky. I wonder if Adam, wherever he is, is smiling down on me now that I'm finally starting to get somewhere.

'Uh, what are you doing?' Ryan says as I grab the hotel phone and begin dialling the front desk.

'We're taking a little late-evening trip,' I murmur, just as Casey picks up the call. 'Hey, I need a favour,' I say. 'Can you organize a car to take us out to Malibu?'

When we arrive in Malibu, darkness has fallen completely, drenching everything in the inky black of night. A few street lights throw down amber pools on the pavement outside Mila's house, the waves of the Pacific Ocean lapping gently out the back. There are lights on downstairs and in one of the pocket windows set into the roof, warm glows inviting us closer.

'She's not going to like this,' Ella murmurs. 'Just know that when she sets the dogs on us, I *will* say I told you so.'

'Yes, I've heard that death by Labrador is quite common,' Ryan replies.

'There are definitely worse ways to go,' Lucky adds, as Ella rolls her eyes. 'But all the same . . . Abel, want to take the lead here? She already knows who you are. And you're still not telling us whatever it is you thought of back in the hotel room.'

I'd kept it to myself because, well, what if I was wrong? I was almost certain I wasn't, but until I confirmed it with my own eyes, I couldn't be sure. No time like the present to find out.

I start up the path, flinching when a motion sensor over the

285

door activates and throws us all under a harsh spotlight. The others wait on the path to show we're not a threat. We don't want to scare Mila before she's even opened the door.

Well, here goes nothing.

I knock, the sound echoing into the night. A TV suddenly mutes, followed by a painfully long silence. I can't bear it. My body wants to run, but I stand firm.

'Who is it?' Mila's voice calls through the door. She sounds even more pissed off than I thought she would. Then again, it's past nine p.m., and I'm sure she hadn't been expecting guests.

'Uh, hi,' I start, my voice all dry and cracked. I try again. 'Hi, Mila? It's Abel Miller. I came over not too long ago to talk to you.'

The door edges open, the security chain firmly in place, and Mila's face appears in the sliver of light. As predicted, she looks *far* from happy about this intrusion.

'Did I not make it crystal clear last time that I'm not fond of visitors?' she snaps. Then her eyes flick over my shoulder and she sees the others. The expression on her face doesn't change, but I can tell she's thinking a million things at once. 'There better be a damn good reason why you've brought *Sunset High* back to my doorstep in the middle of the night.'

I swallow. 'I was wondering if we could maybe come in for a minute. We need to talk to you.'

Mila shakes her head firmly. 'No. Now please leave before I set the guard dogs on you.' Ella squeaks behind me, muttering an 'I told you so'.

Mila's about to close the door in my face, so I pull the trump card. I don't have time for pleasantries.

'It's about Penelope Daunt,' I splutter as the door begins to shut. 'I . . . I think I know what happened.'

Mila freezes. She narrows her eyes at me as if I've just disrespected her dogs, then whips the chain off the door and flings it open. She steps outside, a dark glare on her face. I force myself not to back away.

'You don't know a damn thing,' she says quietly, her voice shaking with rage. 'Now get the fuck off my property before I do something I'll regret. The dogs might not bite, but I can do a whole lot worse.'

'Let's go, Abel,' Lucky jumps in.

I resist the urge to turn and run. 'I'm sorry. Really, I am. But I need answers about my brother. I need to know the truth.'

'What makes you think I know anything about your brother?' Mila snaps.

I shake my head. 'Maybe you don't. But Penelope does.'

The night is still. I can tell the three faces behind me mirror the shock on Mila's.

'You don't know what you're talking about,' she whispers, although her tone has now lost its edge.

'We won't tell a soul,' I say, trying to soothe the situation. 'We're not here to out the truth. Like I said, I just want answers.'

Mila is almost too stunned to speak. 'How . . .?' she says.

'You wouldn't let me into the house the last time I was here. I thought that was fair enough – you were being cautious after everything you've been through. But then my friend here –' I nod back to Lucky – 'saw your car in the door-cam footage of Penelope Daunt on the day she went missing. And then I remembered sitting in the garden with you and hearing a noise from the house. You blamed it on the dog. His name is Max, right? The same name as Penelope's dad? Max Daunt. She loved him so much once they mended their relationship that she dedicated her entire career to him.' I'd watched that very video of her accepting the award in the airport before my flight. I could kick myself for not making the connection sooner. 'One coincidence is easy to cover up. But two?'

I can see realization dawning on Mila's face. She knows I've figured things out, but still, I lay my final card on the table.

'Penelope Daunt isn't missing, is she?' I gulp.

'No fucking way,' Ryan whispers behind me, but I don't take my eyes off Mila. She looks almost distraught. It took a few years, but finally Penelope's secret has been rumbled.

Mila goes to speak, maybe to deny that I'm right, or to threaten us with more violence so we'll leave her house and never reveal the truth. But before she can, there's a quiet voice behind her, one that the whole world used to know. She appears in the doorway, haloed in the warm lamplight like a fallen angel.

'It's okay, Mila. Let them in,' Penelope Daunt says. 'I'm tired of running. It's time people knew what Omni did to me.'

Chapter Thirty-Three

THE SECRET OF PENELOPE DAUNT

Abel

Penelope Daunt doesn't look the same. In fact, she's not even called Penelope Daunt any more. Her name is Olivia, shortened to Liv. The iconic auburn hair she was known for has been dyed lighter and chopped into a shaggier style that she has to cut herself since she's too scared to risk going into a salon in case she's recognized. She has a nose ring and hoops in her ears, and she wears a pair of rounded glasses.

Sure, she doesn't appear the same, but if you look closely, you can still see her there, in the mint-green of her eyes and the shape of her face. Penelope Daunt hides just beneath the surface, out of sight of the regular passer-by who might not give her a second glance in the street. That's just how she wants it.

Liv fixes us all a drink, pouring a whisky on the rocks for Mila and herself, and homemade lemonades for the rest of us as the dogs fuss round our legs. Max and Bridie are excited to see new humans in their home. Then we all sit down round the table at the back of the house, the sliding glass doors open so the sound of the ocean can find us.

'And here was me thinking we'd got away with our big plan to hide for ever,' Liv says with a warm smile in Mila's direction, trying to break the ice. Mila doesn't look impressed. In fact, she still looks like she wants to murder us. She takes a sip of her whisky and folds her mouth into a thin line.

'Oh, come on,' Liv says, nudging Mila's arm. 'You've got to give it to them. It's very "And we would've gotten away with it too, if it wasn't for those meddling kids". I'm amused.'

'It won't be amusing when you're forced back out there to explain to the world where you've been for the last three years,' Mila retorts. Liv falls back a little and Mila's face softens. She strikes me as an older sister figure to Liv. A protector even. 'I'm sorry. I just want to keep you safe.'

'And I appreciate that,' Liv says, reaching a hand over to Mila's on the table. 'I really do. You've already given me so much. A home. A friendship. A *sisterhood*. But I owe them the truth.' She turns her eyes on me, and it's enough to make the world around me stop. 'Especially you.'

A cool spark of adrenaline, of hope, of fear, explodes in my chest all at once. My breath is short and sharp. It feels like an effort just to stay upright. *She already knows who I am*. And she knows what I'm here for.

'I promise we won't tell anyone,' I say, fighting to stay calm. 'We only want to know what happened.'

Liv nods. 'I want to start by saying I'm so sorry,' she begins. I shake my head, but she holds up a hand. 'No, I need to say it. Your brother is dead because of me. I can't pretend otherwise.'

It punches me right in the heart. I don't know what she means – not yet – but I knew Penelope's disappearance and my brother's death were connected in some way. I *knew* it.

'He's dead because of Lake Carter,' I say. 'He's dead because of Omni. You didn't push him off that hotel roof.' Lucky, Ryan and Ella all nod fiercely to back me up.

'Nobody forced Lake to do what he did,' Lucky says. 'He deserves every bad thing coming to him.'

Liv and Mila share a look, one that says they've had this conversation about what Lake deserves before.

'Even if you won't allow me to apologize, I *am* sorry,' Liv says. 'Adam was dragged into a mess that had nothing to do with him and I'll never forgive myself for what happened. Ever. I've lived with it every day since.'

Liv clears her throat, preparing herself. 'I guess I should start from the beginning,' she says, and guides us all back into the past . . .

Chapter Thirty-Four

A STAR ISN'T BORN, IT'S MADE

Penelope Daunt

I'm sitting in a large waiting room, swinging my legs back and forth under the chair. On the other side of a door, four men and two women are sitting behind a long table deciding my future with the same casualness as if they're choosing what they might have for dinner or which movie they're going to watch at the weekend.

I'm thirteen, on the older side of the other kids sitting around me. Some of them look like they're barely out of diapers. It's my first time auditioning for anything, which makes me something of an outcast in this room. Most of these kids have been doing it for years, even though they're not yet teenagers. I recognize one kid from a commercial for my favourite breakfast cereal. He sits next to someone I assume is his mom, so relaxed I'm sure he must know he's already been called back for a second audition.

When the doors open, a lady stands there with a clipboard. I sit up straighter like everyone else, trying to get a better look. 'If I read out your name, we'd like you to come back for another audition. Jacob Air.' The kid from the breakfast commercial fist pumps. The woman reads out a couple more names and starts to put the clipboard down. My heart sinks. 'And Penelope Daunt? If you could come with me, please.'

My breath catches in my chest, but I do as I'm told and follow the woman back into the room where I had my audition. The adults behind the table are still there, and they smile politely when I walk in. I gulp and stand before them.

'Hey, Penny,' the guy in the middle says. 'We wanted to call you back in here to tell you that we don't think you're right for this show.' My stomach swoops and I can feel a tingle in my jaw that tells me I'm close to tears. The man continues. 'We're looking for background actors for that show, you see. But you did such an excellent job today that we knew we had to call you back in here. The thing is, we're making a new show all about a girl called Silver who goes to school with her friends by day and saves the world from supervillains at night. It's going to be a really big deal! And . . . well, we think you'd be the perfect Silver.'

I can't believe my ears. Are they pranking me? But the guy gives me a big grin and offers me his hand. 'So what do you say?'

I don't even have to think about it. 'Yes!' I shake his hand before he can take my dream away from me. That was the first time I met Lake Carter.

I'm about to turn eighteen, and I'm in the back of a chauffeur-driven car on my way to the premiere for the final season of *Silver Rain Saves the World*. My life has changed more in the last five years than I could've ever imagined. Fans shout my name when they see me, asking for my autograph and picture. I can't quite comprehend it at times, but I'm so happy this is my life. I'm living my dream.

Lake sits next to me. He's been a mentor to me since signing me on to the show. He says if I follow his vision, I'll be the next big thing. I'm not sure if Lake means that or if he's getting carried away, but he seems to believe in me more than anyone. That's why he's offered me a new contract, one that will take me to the next level. Now that *Silver Rain* is over, we're looking to the future. Lake has it all mapped out for me. I trust him.

Sunset High.

Those are the words at the top of the contract next to my name. The show was huge when it first aired in 2010. I know what happened to Mila Stone as a result, but I'm adamant that with Lake looking out for me, I can avoid a similar fate. He says she breached her contract, drank too much alcohol and became a nightmare to work with, and I have no reason not to believe him. I'm absolutely positive that won't be how things go for me. I've worked too hard to get here to throw my dreams down the drain now.

I've already read over the contract, so have my lawyers, and now I'm ready to sign it. My pen hovers over the dotted line for a second, then I scrawl my name, binding me to Omni and *Sunset High*. I feel nothing but excitement. Lake gives me a high five, the biggest smile stretching across his face.

'I'm so glad you listened to my choice for tonight,' he says, nodding at the pastel-blue dress I'm wearing.

It's too cutesy for my liking. That, plus the headband makes me feel like Alice in Wonderland. I wanted to wear something more mature – I'm nearly eighteen after all, no longer a little kid – but Lake was adamant that this was the right kind of image for the show and its pre-teen/teen audience.

'Plans for the weekend?' he asks, tapping messages on his phone.

'I think I'm going to the movies with Grace,' I say.

Lake immediately looks up. 'Grace Hart?'

I nod. She's an actress a couple years older than me, although she doesn't work under the Omni umbrella. We met at a party a few months ago and bonded over being young girls in the industry. It's hard to make friends when you're in the spotlight, so it was good to talk to someone who knows what it's like to be in my shoes. Grace is *fun* too. She knows how to have a good time, which is exactly Lake's problem.

'Not a chance,' he says straight away. 'She's bad news. On the front of every magazine stumbling out of parties. Everyone thinks she's pure trash.'

'She's nothing like what the tabloids say,' I argue, defensive of the only real friend I've managed to make since working for Omni.

But Lake shakes his head. 'The tabloids are exactly what you need to think about. If you're seen with Grace, they'll paint you with the exact same brush. Nobody will ever take you seriously. You've got to choose your friends wisely in this business or your career will be dead in the water before you know it. We want you on the cover of magazines with the sweethearts of America. Wholesome is the brand we're trying to build for you here. Not trash.'

And that's that. I don't hang out with Grace that weekend, or ever again. But Lake just wants what's best for me. If I listen to him, I'll be just fine.

'So we're thinking your date for the red carpet next week should be Alfie Hughes,' Jill says. Lake nods next to her as if it's not even a question. I'm eighteen now and the only thing that's important to Omni these days is that I'm seen to be dating a rising star like Alfie to gain buzz before the announcement that *Sunset High* is returning to screens.

Alfie has worked on a bunch of Omni Channel shows and has been cast as a supporting actor in *Sunset High*. It makes perfect sense to Jill and Lake that we should be put together to maximize press potential. However, there's a small problem.

'I hear what you're saying,' I start. 'But I . . . well, I've kind of started seeing someone.' I try not to blush furiously.

Jill looks taken aback, her eyebrows rising. Lake's eyes have narrowed, and seeing him look at me like that raises the hairs on the back of my neck. I knew he wouldn't be happy about this, and I'm massively regretting saying anything now.

'Who?' he asks. The one word punches the air. Lately Lake's been a little . . . different. Still the same mentor who's looked out for me since I was thirteen, but he's started to lose his temper here and there. Not specifically at me, but I've witnessed him blowing his top at other people. Every time it's happened, it's shocked me. That's not the Lake I know. And yet that's the Lake who's looking at me now.

'Charlie Samson,' I say.

Before I can utter anything else, Lake shakes his head in disgust. Charlie is the lead singer in a boyband whose reputation is, well, not exactly squeaky clean. But Charlie is a gentleman when he's not on stage. Sure, the press has made him out to be a lothario with a drinking problem, but the *real* Charlie is nothing of the sort. That's just the image the band portrays to keep their success going. We met at a concert, and he asked to take me out. We went for dinner and talked for hours non-stop. He made me laugh. He was kind. In truth, I've already started to fall for him.

But Charlie is the exact type of person Lake wants to keep me away from.

'We've been over this a million times, Pen,' he says, his tone dark and stormy. 'We've spent years building the perfect image for you. You're America's sweetheart. You can't go off and date some tattooed rock star who struts around on stage with no shirt on. Nope, not happening.'

'I didn't realize I needed to ask for permission.' It slips out, and I regret it as soon as it does. I shrink under his glare.

'Alfie will be your date next week. End of story.'

The conversation moves on. I don't have to think about breaking things off with Charlie. He calls me the next day and says he thinks it's best we don't see each other again. What a coincidence.

I'm at the premiere of a new Omni Channel show. I'm not in it, but Lake said it would be great for me to be here to show my support and give it some extra buzz. I agreed to save the headache, even though I'd rather be at home.

On the red carpet, fans cheer for me louder than I've ever heard before. *Sunset High* has been announced and my star is rocketing. It scares me a little how much attention the world is already heaping on me. I thought I'd be ready for it, but it makes me nervous. Jill tells me nobody under Omni's watch has ever had quite this much frenzy surrounding them. I try to be excited about it because, once upon a time, it's exactly what I wanted. I just didn't realize then that it would feel so intrusive. Everyone thinks they're entitled to know my business. I feel like I've been cut open for the world to dissect.

Lake, too, has noticed the shift. I thought it would make him happy. Isn't this what he wanted all along? But it seems even he couldn't have predicted how fascinated the world is with me. Now he seems nothing like the Lake I once knew, the kind man who said he only ever wanted what was best for me. If anything, he seems a little . . . jealous? It's like his ego has been dented.

I walk the red carpet, laugh and smile, pose for pictures with fans, and by the time I get inside, I have this incredible buzz.

Lake is waiting inside, sipping from a glass of champagne. He's been watching the red carpet from the TV.

'Good crowd,' he says. 'They love you.' He pauses and chews the inside of his cheek. 'But remember who made you the star you are. You weren't *born* Penelope Daunt. I created you.'

By the time I start thinking about doing a tell-all interview with Barb Harrington, things have only got worse. The Lake who directs *Sunset High* is nothing like the man I knew as a thirteen-year-old when I first entered the industry. He's become jaded, bitter about my success, and he claims it as his own at every opportunity. In a bid to bring me down a peg or two, he's started to snipe at me on set in front of the other cast and crew members. He tells me he could replace me in a heartbeat, that my ego far exceeds my talent, that I wouldn't even be in this position if it wasn't for him. It's humiliating. I soon realize that he's worried I'm not only eclipsing the show, but also outgrowing Omni Channel in general. He can't bear the idea of me standing on my own two feet.

Barb has asked me for an interview before. At some event or another, she quietly asked if I'd sit down with her and talk about working on a show that had a certain reputation thanks to everything that happened with Mila Stone. I said no back then, but recently I've recognized that I've become a shadow of the person I once was. I'm nothing but a robot. A puppet for Omni and Lake to control and manipulate as they please.

So I'm planning to leave.

Sunset High is the only show I'm contracted for right now. After that, I want out. I want to prove Lake wrong, show Omni that I can do this without them. Lake might have plucked me out of the dumps, but he doesn't own me. He's spent so long tearing down my confidence that I've almost forgotten who I am. I won't let that happen. I *need* to find myself again, without the strict rules that I'm being forced to live by.

So I call Barb and say I'll do it. I want to tell her and the world my story. It's time to start fighting back.

I wind up on Mila's doorstep a couple of days before the interview is set to take place. It's strange for us to come face to face. In a way, we're the mirror image of each other, both of us having been in the same position with Lake, Omni and *Sunset High*. I'm not sure if Mila will talk – after all, she hasn't spoken to anyone in years – but when she sees me and hears me out, she decides to help.

The plan is set. I'll tell people I'm going for a sunset hike, something I often do when I want to be alone. Then I'll park my car, walk down the street and meet Mila, who will drive me back to Malibu, where Barb will conduct the interview in secret. It all feels very cloak and dagger, but I'm paranoid that Omni will know where I am if I drive my own car out to Barb's house. I don't want to risk it.

This will work, I tell myself. *I'll finally get my life back.*

It's evening and the sun is setting over LA. On a quiet road Mila arrives first, driving around until she finds the perfect parking space. I come next, pulling into the first spot I see.

Since it's a residential street, I know parking can be a bitch, so I end up a short walk away. Not a big deal. I put on a cap and start down the sidewalk. Only a blue BMW rolls past, cutting to a diagonal stop right in front of me. It all happens so fast that I don't even know what's going on at first. In fact, even though I know Mila's car is white, I think it might be her.

But then I feel hands on me – firm and strong – and before I know it, I'm being bundled into the back of the BMW by someone wearing a cap and scarf pulled up to their mouth. When the driver gets back in and takes off, I realize it's Lake.

He tells me that he found out about the interview from an assistant on *Sunset High*. Whoever it was said they'd overheard me taking a call with Barb in my trailer. I'd been so careful planning everything down to the tiniest detail, yet I'd still managed to slip up. Lake had followed me from the hotel with only one thought on his mind – to stop the interview going ahead.

I try the door. It's locked. I try to call out for help, but the windows are tinted, blocking anyone from seeing me. I pat my pockets for my cell, only to remember that I've stupidly left it at the hotel, worried that as it was a gift from Omni, they might be able to track it. But to my surprise, Lake seems . . . calm. For once, he isn't angry or trying to cut me down to size. He's talking to me the way he used to when he first took me under his wing.

'I just want to speak to you, Pen,' he says gently. 'I've been awful. I know I have. And I'm sorry. If you want to go through with the interview, I'll drive you there myself. But first, we really need to talk.'

I don't trust a word he says, but I have no choice. I bide my time, knowing that eventually he has to stop and I might be able to make a run for it.

We pull up to Lake's house, the gates already open for his return. He gets out and unlocks my door. I step out calmly and start walking with him so as not to alert him to my intentions. But when he unlocks the front door, I tear off in the opposite direction, hoping to God that I can get there before the gates shut.

I'm so close to making it out. *So* close. But the gates are closing with every breath, and when I'm only steps away, they shut completely. Lake's right behind me. He grabs me round the waist and puts his hand over my mouth to stop my screams. He hauls me not only into the house, but down into his basement den.

'You are not doing the interview. I won't let you,' Lake says. 'You're not leaving here until I can trust that you'll keep your mouth shut. Have a think about what you want to do next. If I were you, I'd start coming up with ways you can make all this right.'

Lake leaves me there, locking the door behind him. When I refuse to comply, he keeps me there for the rest of the night, only coming down to bring me food and water. I know the mansions in the Hills are too far apart for anyone to be able to hear me, but still I scream for help. Of course nobody comes.

Until the next night, when a guest shows up at the house.

Lake is downstairs in the den with me, asking why I want to ruin his life. We both hear the knock at the front door at the same time. I don't care who it is, I just start screaming. But

Lake is quick to throw his hand over my mouth, leaving only a second of my scream free to be heard. Was it enough?

'You stay quiet, or I swear to God, you'll never see the light of day again,' Lake whispers in my ear. 'You hear me?'

There's another knock.

Silence.

A third knock.

Silence.

Lake keeps his hand clamped over my mouth. I'm sure the person must have left by now, my chance to escape fluttering out of reach.

But then we hear the front door open upstairs.

'Lake?' a voice calls. 'It's Adam Miller. I have the script notes you asked for. I . . . I thought I heard a scream. Is everything okay?'

The door to the den is open. Lake doesn't know what to do. If he moves to close it, he knows I'll scream bloody murder. But if he stays where he is, Adam could stumble upon what he's done. Lake's breathing is ragged on my neck. He's scared that he's been caught.

But the footsteps stop in the entrance hall. I don't know who Adam Miller is, but he isn't moving any closer. I'm scared my one chance to escape is about to leave. I can't let that happen. I tilt my head slightly, Lake's hand against my lips. I don't know if this will work, but I have to try. I don't think about it. I just do it. In a split second, I force my mouth open and clamp down, hard. Lake gasps and his hand loosens for just a second. I pull away from it and scream.

'GET HELP!'

Lake forces his hand back over my mouth, but we both know it's too late. I pray this has worked. There's a moment of dreadful silence.

Then I hear Adam's footsteps racing out of the house.

Lake mounts the stairs, slamming the door behind him. I hear the front door crash open and Lake leave the house. When he comes back inside, there's the sound of keys jangling, then he leaves again. This time, I hear the rev of a car engine and I know he's gone after the one person who's discovered the secret he's hiding.

But in his rush to do so, I think he might have forgotten something. Heart in my mouth, I climb the stairs and push against the door. It swings open. I poke my head out, expecting Lake to appear at any moment. But the silence confirms I'm alone.

I run.

Not to the front door, but to the garage, where I swipe a set of keys for one of Lake's sports cars. And then I drive. Not home. Not back to the hotel. They don't feel safe enough from Lake. No, I keep on driving until I hit Malibu, abandoning the car a short distance away from Mila's house.

'Help me,' is all I manage to say when she opens the front door.

Mila doesn't hesitate. She lets me in, then says the only words I need to hear.

'You're safe now.'

Mila doesn't hesitate to help. She simply asks me what I

want to do next. We could call the police. We could reschedule the interview. We could try once again to bring Lake down.

But, in all honesty, I'm tired of fighting. No matter what, Lake always seems to win. Plus, I've now seen what he's capable of. There are no lengths he won't go to in order to come out on top and stamp out a threat. I know in my heart that trying to win this battle will be an almost impossible task, especially with the backing of a multi-billion-dollar company like Omni behind him.

I feel weak. I don't want to fight any more. I want my life back. It's more than Lake, although he's the driving force behind my reasoning. It's everything. I'm not just an object to him – I'm an object to the world, as if every single person can lay a claim to me. I want to start over again, and Mila is willing to help.

In a twist of good luck, I've accidentally found myself out of the spotlight. Nobody knows where I am or what has happened. I'm missing. So I make the decision to stay that way. Wouldn't you?

Chapter Thirty-Five

GOLIATH

Abel

I'm crying. We all are, each of us sharing in this grief together. Lucky finds my hand under the table on one side, and Ryan does the same on the other. I look at them both, at Ella too, and it's like a thin lining of sunshine behind a cloud. Not enough to take away my pain, but at least there's the promise of better days to come now that I have the answers I've desperately been seeking.

'Thank you,' I say to Liv, who immediately shakes her head. But I double-down on it. 'No, I mean it. Thank you. What happened to Adam, it was *not* your fault. He'd want you to know that. What you went through is awful. I'm so sorry that happened to you. And I truly do hope that you've found some peace now, to live the life that *you* want.'

Liv stands up and I do too. We both come round the table and fall into a tight embrace, clinging on to each other as if we might float away into the night sky if we don't. When we break apart, new tears replace the old ones. But even though a heavy sadness sits in my very core, I feel like the truth has unlocked something inside me. It's started to set me free.

In exchange for what Liv has told me, I tell her and Mila what I learned from Casey about what happened that night. They look disgusted, haunted even, by the lengths Lake took to keep Adam quiet, not to mention the fact that Omni paid off Stephen to wipe the hotel's CCTV. But it's when I mention the payphone that Liv's eyes widen. Her body sinks into itself, and she lets out a tight breath.

'If Adam called the cops, they would have gone to Lake's house to investigate. But when they got there, they would've found that nobody was home. I'd taken off, and Lake had gone after Adam.'

I recall the part in Casey's story where the police asked him about the call. 'They thought it might have been a prank,' I say. 'They would've got to the house, seen that it was empty, and assumed someone had tried to play up to the *curse*. The police officer said it himself when he asked Casey.'

Mila's lip curls. 'And I guarantee that even if they followed up about the disturbance at a later time, Omni would've wriggled Lake out of it. I'm sure they probably put pressure on the cops to stop looking into your brother's *accident* too, since there was no evidence to suggest otherwise.'

'You think they could've done that?' I ask. I think I

307

should be shocked and surprised, but instead I just feel grim acknowledgement. There's one thing Omni has plenty of – money – and we all know that money breeds corruption. It's the seed of greed and power, and they have endless amounts of it. Who knows how far their corruption spreads?

'Sure do,' Mila says, and Liv nods in agreement. 'I can see it now. With no CCTV or evidence to prove wrongdoing, Omni would've put pressure on the cops to close the case to stop anyone looking too closely at it. They would've said that it was a distressing time for everyone involved in *Sunset High*, and that they wanted nothing more than to move on.'

Silence lingers over the table. It's Lucky who breaks it.

'So what are we going to do about this?' He asks the question as if it's simple maths, a *two plus two equals four* scenario.

'What do you mean *we*?' Mila answers, her eyebrows knitting together. 'I've had my run-ins with Omni. In case you haven't noticed, that's the whole reason I'm almost a prisoner in my own home. They drove me out of the spotlight and nearly took my life with it. I know damn well that if you retaliate, Omni and Lake will come down on you like a ton of bricks. You have to be careful.'

'So we just let them get away with everything?' Ryan says.

'I didn't say that. But . . .' Mila pauses, looking to Liv. She sighs. 'It's a risk. I don't know you kids, and I want to help, but I feel responsible for keeping Liv safe, and I'm not putting her back in the firing line. No fucking way.'

Liv puts a gentle hand on Mila's arm. 'You've looked after

me so well. It's more than I should've ever asked of you.'

'But . . .' Mila nudges, knowing there's more to come. Liv weighs it up in her own mind first before speaking.

'But if we let Omni get away with things time and time again, it'll just keep happening. How many more people – *kids* – have to be subjected to Lake Carter's cruelty? To Omni's control? How many more people will *die* if we don't do something now to stop this?'

Mila sighs. 'I just don't think we should do anything rash. I know you want justice – we all do – but we can't act without thinking it through first. Omni are more powerful than any of us could ever imagine, and their backing of Lake makes him just as dangerous.'

'I don't want justice,' I say, shaking my head. As my thoughts have swarmed, so too has my internal rage, awakened once more now that I know exactly what Lake did. I want so much more than justice. 'I want revenge.'

'We all do,' Lucky says. I know he's thinking about his mom. I squeeze his hand, but he's lost in his own head, thinking hard.

'Okay, let's lay out the options on the table,' Ella says. 'One – we go to the cops with the CCTV footage.'

'But we don't know that Omni and Lake didn't pay off the investigators to turn a blind eye to anything to do with the case,' Ryan says. 'And even if they didn't, all the footage shows is Lake going up to the roof. Sure, people can connect the dots, but is that going to hold up in court? Probably not. Lake will walk free with a dented ego at most.'

We all agree. Ella holds up a second finger. 'We go to the press with the CCTV. Give it to Hannah Wilkes at the *Daily Eye* and let them run a sordid headline on it. That'll get the world's attention.'

Mila shakes her head. 'That throws up the same issues as the first idea. At most, it tarnishes Lake and Omni's reputation, but it's not enough to end them completely. They'll use their money and lawyers to spin their own side of the story. Not to mention they have their own journalists on speed dial who will help refute the allegations and cast the rest of us in an unflattering light. Believe me, I've had experience with being painted as the bad guy where Omni are concerned.'

Ella sighs. 'Touché. Option three . . .' She looks apologetically at Liv. 'You come forward and give your side of the story. Do the interview with Barb Harrington like you were planning to, and tell the world what Lake did to you.'

Liv looks defeated at the idea already. 'I wish I could, I really do, but, first of all, it would be my word against Lake's. It was three years ago now. There's no evidence I could use to prove he kidnapped me. Lake and Omni will turn the tables and question why, if that was the case, I disappeared and waited until now to tell my story. They'll make sure that I come across as a liar.'

Ella sinks a little lower in her chair, eyes downcast. 'That's it then. There's nothing else that will guarantee we get justice or revenge.'

I feel like we've already lost, and we haven't even tried to fight back yet. Every option leads to Omni and Lake using their power to ensure they come out on top. There's nothing we can do to topple them. We don't stand a chance.

'What if there was another option?'

We all turn to Lucky. He hasn't said a word the last few minutes, but now, when he raises his eyes, they're hardened. Determined. He thinks it over one more time, then smirks in disbelief as if he's hit the jackpot. 'I have an idea. It's . . . crazy. Pretty dangerous too. But I think it might just work. And if it does, Lake Carter will get what he deserves. I promise you that. He'll pay for every last thing he's done.'

Chapter Thirty-Six
PEACE IN BLUE WATERS

Lucky

It's late by the time we head back to the hotel. The ride home from Malibu is tense, everyone lost in thoughts of what's been learned, discussed and eventually planned this evening. There's nothing but silence in the car. Even if Ronnie wasn't here, I'm not sure anyone would be able to talk right now.

It almost doesn't feel safe to be back at the hotel, even though Lake doesn't have any idea that we're on to him. It's like we're sleeping under the eye of the enemy, and I don't like it one bit. I'm only too happy when Abel nudges me as we slip through the back entrance and asks, 'Will you stay with me tonight?' Like I'd say no.

We head up to our rooms, saying goodnight to Ella and Ryan, who break off at the thirteenth floor to crash in Ryan's suite as Natalie has been staying in Ella's second bedroom to keep her company after the break-in scare. Me and Abel, meanwhile, head up to mine.

And then it's just the two of us. Alone, together.

I can't bear the silence in the room and the questions it asks. I can feel it oozing into every crevice. I need to drown the thoughts creating monsters in my head, so I connect my phone to the speaker system and select one of the playlists I use to soothe my fears in the dead of night, when it's just me in bed, facing the world alone. I lower the volume so it's a gentle melody in the background, then sit and wait for Abel to speak.

He paces by the window, stopping to look out over the city every now and then before resuming. I can tell he's playing the night over and over in his head. I wonder if he feels better or worse for knowing what he does now. After all, we often want the truth until we realize how unbearably painful it can be.

Me? I just feel empty. I'm so tired of it all. This life of mine was meant to be a dream. Instead, it killed the person I loved most in the world, and I don't think I'll ever fully recover from that. As a result, it's turned me into a person I don't recognize any more. I've become so used to blunting my thoughts and feelings by any means necessary that I've become someone else – I'm nothing more than the broken person Jill showed me in that picture. The old me haunts my brain, begging to be let back in. I just don't know how to free myself when the world is watching. It almost feels safer to shut that part of me away for ever.

Tired of pacing, Abel eventually crawls into bed, curling

into a ball. He doesn't cry. Maybe he's out of tears, a shell of himself like me. Can two broken people help to fix each other? Or will they only break each other further? I can't decide. I shut off the light and slip into bed too, wrapping my arms round Abel and pressing myself into the shape of him. He clutches me as if I'm all he has to hold on to in the world.

We don't talk. We've done plenty of that tonight. Instead, we lay together for a while longer, letting the darkness swallow us. And then I feel him roll over to face me. I can barely see his silhouette, but the warmth of his body against mine is enough. As if we both need the same thing – to forget, to be held, to be safe – our lips find each other, delicate wanting giving way to desperate passion. His pulse beats with mine – *is* mine. We're no longer two halves. I'm him, he's me, one entity entwined together. If only time could stop now, freezing us in eternal midnight. What bliss this one moment, lived for a lifetime, would be.

We lay together, in each other's arms, until hues of blueish twilight begin to creep up the walls like water, filling the room as if we're both lost in the quiet depths beneath the waves. Here we find peace for what might be the last time.

We're woken early by a knock at the door to find Ryan and Ella with two trays full of breakfast. I rub the sleep from my eyes, stretching as a yawn takes over my entire face. Damn, I'm tired. But we don't have time to waste. If we want revenge, we have to move quickly before Lake or Omni finds out what we know.

314

Once we finish our pastries and coffee, Ella starts a video call and sets up her phone so we can all see. Liv and Mila answer after the first ring.

'So . . .' I start. 'About last night. Thoughts?'

I'd told everyone my plan round the table and we'd agreed to think about it overnight. If one person had doubts or didn't want to go through with it, then it was decided we'd pull the plug. It would only work if we were all on the same page. There couldn't be room for doubt.

'I have my reservations,' Mila says, sipping from a mug. 'It's a huge risk. If any part of your idea goes wrong, it will hurt us more than it's going to hurt Lake.'

'I agree,' says Liv, and my heart starts to sink. 'But I don't think we have any other option. It's bold, and maybe it won't work, but will we forgive ourselves if we don't try?' She shrugs. 'I guess I'm saying I'm in. Fuck Lake Carter.'

Ella and Ryan agree in unison. I'm sure they've been up discussing it all night.

'I don't think there's another way,' Ella says.

'And if it *does* work, it's the only way we're guaranteed that Lake will get everything he deserves,' Ryan adds.

Abel looks to me, searching my eyes for . . . doubt? A hint of reservation. I'm glad he doesn't find any there. He nods. 'I want revenge for Adam. I'm in.'

Mila holds out a little longer, but she eventually concedes. 'I hope the bastard rots,' she says, and clinks mugs with Liv. Then everyone turns to me.

'Lucky, are you sure about this?' Liv asks. 'I know it was

315

your idea, but we're talking breaking into this guy's house a—'

'I know,' I interrupt. 'But this is our best chance to get back at him. He'll never even know we've been there. It's a quick job. We'll be in and out in no time, and then we can all watch that asshole suffer.' There's an uncomfortable stillness between us all. I can almost hear everyone's worries. But now's not the time to back out. 'I promise you, this will work.'

Part Four

DEAD FAMOUS

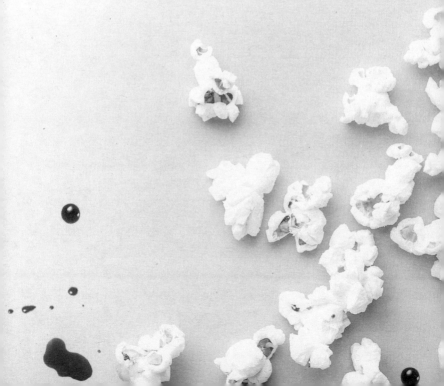

Chapter Thirty-Seven

THE HOUSE IN THE HILLS

Ella / 11 August 2023 / 21:52

The plan is set. It's already in motion. For days, we've followed the script Omni have laid out for us. Lucky and I went for a planned dinner date to keep Jill happy and throw the press off those leaked pictures, and we've all showed up to set for filming and acted as if everything is normal. Even if we've had to face a murderer the whole time. I've had to fight to keep my emotions in check so I don't crumble. We all have. Abel in particular. But tonight we get our revenge.

Right now, down the road in Beverly Hills, there's a party happening. Omni Channel executives and staff have gathered to pat themselves on the back in some exclusive bar to celebrate their recent successes. It's a fancy event, one that has special catering and private bar staff as well as an open tab.

Us? We're not celebrating. We're preparing to break into a mansion in the Hollywood Hills.

Me, Abel and Ryan are waiting in dark clothing for Mila at a meeting point on a quiet side street in West Hollywood. The second we see her car, we duck our heads and jump in.

'Nothing suspicious?' Mila asks tightly, driving in the direction of our target.

'Nope,' Ryan says. 'Everything is just as it should be.'

Following the directions given to us by Liv, we drive up into the Hills, then park up on a dark tree-lined road. The three of us jump out, checking our rucksacks, the night our only witness.

'Good luck,' Mila says.

'We'll see you back here,' Abel says. He sounds like he's trying to fake confidence, which doesn't exactly make me feel good about this. I already know that there are so many things that could go wrong. But still, I take a deep breath and force a smile on my face.

'We've got this,' I say. 'We just stick to the plan and everything will be fine.'

The others nod. We do one last check, then quickly slip across the road and into the shrubbery, where we begin the hike along uneven ground up the mountain towards a chain-link fence. When we reach the top, we find the house made of tan brick with the black-slate roof, double-checking we've located the right mansion. It'd be just our luck if we broke into the wrong fucking house.

'It's this one,' Abel says, crouching down by the fence.

My breath rattles in my lungs, and I can hear the ragged pants of the others too. Not from the hike, but from fear of what we're about to do. I check my watch. Twenty past ten. Lake is at the party right now, but for how much longer? I bring my face as close to the fence as I can and peer through the trees to see the rear of his house. For now, all the lights are off. Just as they should be.

'Let's do this,' I say quietly.

Abel and Ryan give me a boost, then Abel helps Ryan up before climbing the fence last. We're careful to stay in the shadows, alert for anything out of the ordinary that we haven't planned for. But everything is silent and still. No sound. No lights. Nobody home. Game on.

Keeping behind the cover of the trees that border the garden on three sides for privacy, we edge closer to the property until we're level with the house. I glance up, eyeing the camera perched in a high corner, facing out towards the garden, the pool and the direction we've just come from. On the opposite side there's another, facing the front of the house and the driveway. There are none facing the side of the house, assuming anyone getting to that point would've already been seen. If Lake hadn't so smugly showed off his home on an episode of the rebooted season of *Cribs* we'd be none the wiser. I'd always wondered if celebrities showing off their homes for fans wasn't just a huge security risk, which is why I'd turned down the opportunity. We paused the YouTube video more times than I could count while researching the layout of Lake's house, but it had given us everything we needed. The side door was the only way in without being caught on CCTV.

'You're up, El,' Ryan says.

I sigh but crouch down, crawl forward and start manoeuvring myself headfirst through the dog flap. It's a tight squeeze, but with some wriggling I slide through to the other side. Once I'm in, I listen carefully but the house is silent. Perfect. I unlock the side door and the others pile inside, Ryan closing it quietly behind us.

Again, we listen out for any sound that might indicate Lake, or anyone else, is here, but there's nothing except dead silence. The air crackles between us. Abel unzips his bag and starts handing out evidence – the disc with the roof CCTV on it, strands of Penelope's hair to prove she was kept here against her will, *Sunset High* posters that have our faces scribbled out, and even a doctored NDA 'signed' by Stephen, because that bastard deserves to rot too. They'll help the police piece everything together, and, once they do, Lake will pay for what he's done.

Chapter Thirty-Eight

ANOTHER CHAMPAGNE, SIR?

Liv / 22:22

It feels terrifying to be so close to the enemy that ruined my life, but there's a thrill to it too. Especially when I'm a metre in front of them and they have no idea who I am. I look nothing like the flame-haired starlet the world once knew. I'm three years older now, no longer a child. New hair, glasses and coloured contacts have taken care of the rest. I'm someone else entirely. To everyone in this room, I'm just another waitress, hired by an events company to make sure nobody's glass goes empty. Making sure *Lake's* glass never runs empty wasn't in the official job description, but, hey, what company doesn't love an employee who goes above and beyond?

Getting the job was easy enough. Once we knew the party was happening, thanks to Ella sweet-talking an assistant, all it took was a little research to find the events company in question and put forward a fake résumé. We knew they wouldn't look too closely at that, though – they just needed as many hands as possible to ensure the night ran smoothly. They gladly hired the enthusiastic girl who showed up early to the interview, and promised her that if all went well, there could be more shift work for future events. Sorry, guys, but I don't plan on sticking around.

I load up another tray of champagne flutes and slip through the crowd, smiling as hands snatch glass after glass. By the time I reach Lake, there's only two remaining. He's standing with a bunch of older guys in suits, talking about a football game. I duck my head slightly out of instinct, but Lake barely looks up as he takes a glass and places his empty one back on the tray. Of course he doesn't pay attention to the wait staff. He thinks them beneath him. Thankfully his ignorance works to my advantage.

I give it another twenty minutes, then repeat the process.

Again.

And again.

And again.

Lake takes a new drink every time, downing the last gulp when I reappear with the tray and replacing his old glass. Greed will always be a powerful man's downfall.

The night goes on, the cycle repeating, until eventually I see Lake stumble into one of his buddies, roaring a laugh when he spills their drink. Then, with clumsy hands, he takes out his phone and speed-dials a number.

'Outside in ten,' he says loudly, words slurring together. He hangs up and claps one of the guys he's standing with on the back. 'Home time, boys. Don't do anything I wouldn't do, eh!'

He starts to head for the cloakroom, but I'm not finished just yet. I want to see the bastard up close one last time. Besides, another drink can't hurt, right? Especially one with a little extra *kick* to it. As Lake fumbles for his wallet, searching for his ticket stub to retrieve his coat from the attendant, I quickly dip behind the bar and casually slip a small sleeping tablet into a champagne flute. It fizzes and dissolves in the golden liquid just as Lake takes his coat. I round the bar and step between him and the exit.

'One more drink before you go, sir?' I ask sweetly in a fake New York accent.

'Oh, go on then. One for the road, huh!' He blows a drunken laugh, then throws back the glass, downing it in three gulps. He belches and pats his stomach. Then he lays his eyes on mine. My heart stutters, then rapidly flutters.

'Pretty girl, aren't you?' he says, drunken gaze dragging over me like he's weighing me up. But before he can say anything more, his phone lights up in his hand. 'Yes, I'm coming down now,' he snaps into it.

He gives me one last leer, then heads for the door. I ditch my tray and pull out the burner phone I acquired a few days ago. We all have them so we can stay in touch without landing us in the shit. Despite the hammer in my chest, I type the text with a smile on my face. It's going to be fun seeing Lake Carter's fall from grace.

Chapter Thirty-Nine

TARGET

Lucky / 22:25

I park my car in the shadows a little way up the street from the venue, tapping the steering wheel with either impatience or nerves – I can't quite tell which. As I stare at the door ahead, I can feel every beat of my heart pulsing through my body. I clench my jaw and tense my hands, waiting.

To fill the time, I start thinking about every last thing Lake has done to me. To all of us. He's put us through hell and got away with it each time. I can't stand the thought of him walking free without consequence. I think of Mila Stone, her life left in ruins while Lake and Omni thrived; of Penelope Daunt, kidnapped for trying to free herself of the shackles that they had bound her with; of Adam Miller, pushed from a roof to save the secret; of Abel, living for years with questions and heartache; and of my mom, whose life was cruelly swept up in Omni's games and then discarded like she didn't matter.

Lake deserves what's coming to him.

Liv
He's leaving the party.
Slipped a little something
extra into his drink too 😶
22:28

My heart starts to race. I watch the door intently as a blacked-out Mercedes pulls up ahead. Seconds later, Lake comes bowling onto the sidewalk, stumbling as he does, and the driver gets out to help him into the back seat. It's a few moments more until the car starts to move.

I quickly draft a text of my own and send it to the burner phone group chat before nudging the gas and following my target.

Chapter Forty

HIDE-AND-SEEK

Abel / 22:30

> **Lucky**
> Hope you're ready to welcome the guest of honour. On his tail.
> 22:30

I check the burner phone and slip it into my rucksack for safekeeping. We don't have long, and the clock is counting down by the second. Lucky is on his way, and Lake is even closer. We need to move quicky.

Ryan and Ella head for the study in the back of the house with the doctored NDA, *Sunset High* posters and a hair tie belonging to Penelope Daunt while I race up the stairs. I reach the top and follow the corridor, peeping behind doors until I eventually find what I'm looking for – the master bedroom. Lake's quarters take up one whole side of the house, the three rooms all interlinked. A door inside the bedroom leads through to the walk-in wardrobe, while another by the bed reveals the bathroom. A third door connects the bathroom to the wardrobe, creating a neat loop. Everything is incredibly tidy, something I'm sure is thanks to a housekeeper, because there's no way in hell a man that evil and powerful does his own laundry and makes his own bed. He definitely thinks menial tasks are beneath him.

The tidiness makes it difficult to rummage through Lake's belongings since I don't want to misplace anything, but I'm looking for anything that might incriminate Lake further. Who knows, maybe I'll find the *actual* NDA Stephen signed, although I'm not counting on it.

I start with the drawers in the bedside tables, finding nothing but discarded phone chargers, Vaseline and, to my utter disgust, a pack of condoms. Now I promote safe sex, always, but the idea of Lake doing the deed makes me want to vomit on his crisp white sheets.

Stomach clenching, I move on to the walk-in wardrobe. It's a smaller rectangle jutting off the bedroom, with rows and rows of neatly organized clothes, ordered first by item and then by colour. I run a gloved hand over the white shirts, the suit trousers, the jeans, many with labels that show they've yet to be worn. I find a section for shoes and grab a pair of sturdy-looking boots, throwing them into my rucksack.

In a cupboard by his jackets, I find a safe. I tug it half-heartedly because there's no way it's going to budge. I'm right, of course. But still, this is useful. I dig out the disc Casey gave me with the CCTV footage on it from my rucksack and slide it in next to the safe alongside a stack of folders already piled there. I quickly flick through them but find nothing except half-finished scripts in various states of progress. Sure, putting the disc *in* the safe would've been preferrable, but next to it will have to do.

I keep rummaging around the wardrobe, hoping a nook or cranny might reveal something. It's only when the hair on the back of my neck stands up that I realize something feels off. I sense it before I understand it, as if the air inside the house has come alive, brimming with secrets. It takes a moment before I realize why something doesn't feel right.

There's the quiet sound of car tyres approaching the house.

I snap to attention, every fibre of my being wanting to scream out loud. I tense my body so tightly to stop a sound escaping that it physically hurts. I quickly rush to the bedroom window overlooking the driveway to see Lake climbing out of the back of a car and making his way towards the house. I immediately duck, breathing hard and fast. I didn't think he'd be home yet.

Fuck.

Fuck!

FUCK!

I try to move my body into action, but it's like I'm crawling through quicksand, my limbs slow to react. Disorientated, I get to my feet and stagger for the hallway as I hear the car reverse, preparing to leave. I'm at the top of the stairs when I hear the key in the front door. Nope. No chance. I wheel round, retracing my steps and dive into another bedroom.

I leave the door ajar, listening carefully. Lake's heavy footsteps boom through the house as he stomps into the kitchen. There's silence for a few seconds. I'm straining against the door, trying to hear any little sound, when Lake starts talking. It's muffled and incoherent, grunts building into a raised voice. *Who the fuck is he talking to?* I can't hear a response, just Lake's rambling. It goes on and on. I only catch a few disjointed words, most of them curses. He's mad at something. Or someone.

And then there's an almighty crash.

It's followed by another and another. I let out a shocked yelp, slapping my hand over my mouth. A crescendo of quick smashes ends in a final *thud*, louder than anything before. I can hear Lake shouting and swearing at the top of his lungs. I don't know what's happening, but there's a *lot* of noise coming from the kitchen. Have Ella and Ryan managed to hide safely, or has Lake found one of them? I start to panic, thinking the worst. It's only when I go to grab the burner phone from my rucksack that I realize I don't have my bag.

Shit.

I know I had it when I came upstairs, which means I must've left it in Lake's bedroom.

Double shit.

Cursing my own name, I creep out into the hallway and up the hall once more. It's only when I reach Lake's bedroom door that the sudden silence of the house sends a chill up my spine.

And then I hear the first footstep on the stairs.

I hear it as clear as day. A stomp that's joined by another on the second step, then another and another. Panic-laced adrenaline sends me careering into the bedroom, my breathing out of control. Where the hell am I meant to hide?

I make a dive for the bathroom and have barely made it inside when Lake's loud footsteps enter the bedroom, a mere wall separating the two of us. I freeze. I don't dare creep towards the door opposite that leads to the walk-in wardrobe because what if Lake walks into it from the other side, entering it from the bedroom? But if I stay put, he could just as easily burst through the bathroom door behind me. I'm stuck.

I follow his footsteps, trying to move in the opposite direction to him. I can't bear the tension I feel in my chest. My legs are weak and shaking, knees trembling and threatening to buckle. It's all I can do to stay upright. From the bedroom, he starts to walk this way, towards the bathroom door next to his bed. I edge across the bathroom tiles towards the walk-in wardrobe, but then he stops. I do too. He goes back the way he came, now stumbling towards the door to the wardrobe, and I quickly reverse. He stops again.

Silence.

Then Lake moves once more, his footsteps travelling back towards the bathroom door next to his bed. I quickly tiptoe towards the door to the wardrobe, edging it open slightly. I hear a few more footsteps and quickly slip through just as Lake enters the bathroom. My body wants to scream. On trembling legs, I move towards the door to the bedroom, hoping to make a break for it and get downstairs to the others, but, just as

I'm about to leave, Lake goes back into the bedroom. I move backwards, knocking a watch off the centre table. It lands on the floor with a dull thud, but I don't have time to pick it up. Instead, I dive for a rack of coats, slipping between them and hoping they'll be enough to hide me from sight.

Lake comes into the wardrobe.

I freeze, holding my breath.

Through a gap in the coats, I see him start to take off his blazer and shirt. He throws them into a corner on the floor, removes his trousers, and then pauses. He bends down. Picks up the watch. I hold my breath. He stares at it like it's an object he's never encountered before.

But I'm not looking at that. I'm looking at the rucksack I've left on the floor by the safe. It's a mere few steps away from Lake. If he turns round and sees it, we're done for. The plan will be ruined before it's even had a chance to get off the ground. My heart lurches in my chest.

Lake slams the watch down onto the table it came from and hunches over it before taking deep and measured breaths. A glance in one direction and he'll see the bag. But instead, he looks the other way. It should be a relief, except now he's looking right at me.

Or at the rail of coats anyway. In the shadows, I can't tell. I don't dare move. I feel like Lake is staring straight into my soul, his laboured breath slowing down time around us. He stands up straight and I fear he might be coming for me.

He takes a step.

Another.

And then he keeps on going, straight through to the bathroom, and I hear the merciful sound of Lake throwing up in the toilet. I've never been so glad to hear someone be sick. I don't waste a second. I emerge quietly from behind the coats, grab my bag and slip out into the bedroom, then the corridor. When I hear Lake flush the toilet and crash into bed, I'm already on the stairs. The immediate snores as the sleeping pill takes effect are music to my ears.

In the entrance hall, I nearly jump out of my skin when the door to the basement opens. I slam a finger to my lips as Ella and Ryan emerge from the shadows. They've been hiding too. Their faces are pinched with panic, lips parted, breath shallow. Ryan's eyes flick up to the ceiling and back to me. I nod. We stay still, listening for any sign of Lake coming back downstairs, but there's nothing.

'Everything where it should be?' I ask quietly.

Ella nods. 'NDA and posters in the study. Penelope's hair tie under the sofa in the den.'

'Did you hear that noise?' Ryan whispers. 'When Lake was in the kitchen? It sounded like . . .'

She pauses and we all look across the hall towards the kitchen door. Ella gasps, bringing her hand up to her mouth. She points at the floor, eyes wide. When I look for myself, my heart stops in my chest. Something has seeped under the kitchen door, staining the cream carpet. In the dark, it's black, but when Ryan flashes her phone light at it, it illuminates red.

Blood.

I can feel my pulse in my fingertips as I approach the door, take a deep breath and gently push it open. The place is a mess. I follow the trail of red with my eyes to the marble island in the middle. A knife sits on the counter. A shelving unit acting as a mini bar has been upended entirely, bottles of alcohol left in shattered pieces on the floor. And next to them, lying in a puddle of blood and moonlight, is the body of Lucky Tate.

The *Famous Last Words* Podcast

12 August 2023

Hattie Wilson: Hi, guys, and welcome back to an emergency episode of *Famous Last Words*. My name's Hattie Wilson . . .

Devin Taylor: And I'm Devin Taylor . . .

Hattie Wilson: And, well, we weren't expecting to be recording this episode. We weren't even sure if we could, because when we woke up to the news early this morning, it just broke our hearts. But here at *Last Words* HQ, we're all about bringing you the most up-to-date information on all things pop culture, and we can't not talk about this, so we're going to try.

Devin Taylor: That we will. We're all in this together, trying to make sense of what happened in the Hollywood Hills last night. But we've got you. We're going to hold your hand through this. Do you want to start, Hats?

Hattie Wilson: *[Takes a deep breath]* I don't even know *where* to start, Dev. *[Sighs]* So, last night, it seems the Omnificent curse returned to *Sunset High*, and it did so in the worst possible way. Breaking news reports in the early hours of this morning revealed that leading man Lucky Tate, a hugely successful actor beloved around the world, had been murdered. And the man accused of it is none other than the Omnificent director and board member, Lake Carter.

Devin Taylor: The gruesome crime scene was discovered by cops, who were reportedly alerted to an altercation by a distressed phone call pleading for help.

Hattie Wilson: Police searching Lake Carter's house found blood and DNA matching that of Lucky in the kitchen and garage, as well as on a knife they say may have been used in the attack. They also found blood on shoes belonging to Lake Carter. CCTV from the director's own security cameras apparently show his car leaving the property around the time Lucky was murdered, before returning to the property a short time later. It's believed in that time he disposed of the body. Blood matching that of Lucky has since been found in the trunk of that same vehicle.

Devin Taylor: The search for Lucky's body is ongoing as we speak, with cops combing the wooded areas surrounding Lake Carter's property. Investigators are optimistic that a body will be recovered soon.

Hattie Wilson: The remaining leading cast members of *Sunset High* have retreated from the spotlight to deal with their grief as a result of the shocking events, with Ryan Hudson saying in a statement on behalf of them all this morning: 'There are no words to describe what we feel in this moment. We're completely devastated. Lucky was an incredible man who lit up every room he walked into and who achieved so much in such a short space of time. We hope that a thorough investigation into this heinous crime is conducted, and that those who were either directly involved or stood by and condoned it, will be brought to justice.' Some real bite to that statement, huh? It sounds like she's throwing Omnificent under the bus.

Devin Taylor: Yep. And good – there's no way after everything that's happened before and now that Omnificent can continue without addressing what's happened under their noses, as well as their own involvement in certain situations. Of course, following the news, Omnificent have announced that the upcoming *Sunset High* reboot will be shelved.

Hattie Wilson: And keep it there! Jesus Christ.

Devin Taylor: Amen, friend.

Chapter Forty-One

GOODBYE

Ryan / 13 August 2023 / 16:12

I hold on to Ella's hand as if it's the only thing I have left in the world. She holds mine just as tight and, with the other, holds Abel's hand. He can't even raise his eyes. They're cast down into his lap as he takes slow and steady breaths.

'We're in this together,' Ella says quietly as our car inches ever closer to the Walk of Fame.

I can already see fans milling about on the pavement, some gripping posters with Lucky's face on them. Tear tracks stain their faces as they hold hands with loved ones and friends. I can hardly bear to watch.

'Every step of the way,' I say, turning my back to the window so I don't have to watch raw teenage grief unfurling.

'How long, Ronnie?' Abel asks.

'We're almost there, sir,' Ronnie says.

'How many people?' he asks.

Me and Ella both peer ahead through the windscreen. There are even more fans than I could've predicted. Lucky was loved. We all knew that, but this is beyond my comprehension. Endless crowds have gathered, penned in behind metal barricades, flowers and cards and teddy bears in hand. I wonder if Lucky would've wanted to see with his own eyes just how much he meant to so many people.

I glance at Ella and decide there's no point in lying. 'A lot,' I murmur.

Abel nods as the car pulls to a stop. 'Let's get this over with.'

He climbs out first, head bowed as if he can hide from the searing spotlight cast over us today. For once, when we step out onto the street, there are no screams of excitement. There's no frenzy or pandemonium. It's . . . silent, a heavy and uncomfortable kind of quiet blanketing everything it can reach. I don't let go of Ella's hand.

Someone in charge of the memorial meets us and guides us to the sidewalk, where the stars of so many beloved celebrities stretch on and on. But there's only one star right now that everyone is focused on. It's decorated with the most gorgeous bouquets and a heart made of red rose petals. A portrait on an easel watches over the proceedings. The name in the centre of the star gleams up at the sky.

Lucky Tate.

None of us want to talk. Not when everything is so fresh and raw. But I already know that it will be expected of us, so when a mic appears, I step up to bat without hesitation.

The crowd on all sides watch the three of us intently. I blank them out and raise the mic to my lips. 'Thank you all so much for coming here this afternoon,' I start. My voice shakes a little, glazed with tears. 'This is tough. Not just for us, but for all of you too. Everyone knows that Lucky Tate was loved. He was . . .' I break and duck my head for a second. Ella squeezes my hand, giving me the confidence to go on.

'He was the brightest light. The most charismatic person in any room. In a world so hard and cruel, he was giving and generous, kind and gentle. Lucky would want the world to know that, even though his life was cut short, he *lived*. And that's something we should all take away with us today. Lucky would not want us to cry.'

As soon as I say it, tears spring from eyes and I breathe a laugh at the irony. The crowd watches on, small smiles lifting their sadness. When I glance at Ella and Abel, they're both crying too. Abel gives me a nod of encouragement.

'Lucky would want us to remember the good times and laugh. He wouldn't want us to dwell in grief, but to live in the happy memories we have of him. And, oh boy, do we have many. So, yes, today is tremendously sad. And sometimes, when I think about it, I'm not sure how we'll get through this. But then I look at the people I have by my side, and I know the answer as if Lucky himself is whispering it to me.' I turn my eyes to Ella and Abel, speaking directly to them. 'We'll get through this together.'

There's a polite round of applause. Someone shouts, 'WE

LOVE YOU LUCKY!' just before another person yells, 'FUCK LAKE CARTER! I HOPE HE ROTS IN HELL!' The statement is met with a jeer of agreement. I give the mic back and fall into the arms of Ella and Abel. We hold on to each other tightly, ignoring the clicks of dozens of cameras immortalizing this moment.

'God, I'm glad I've got you guys,' Ella says quietly.

Abel nods his agreement. 'Lucky would be proud.'

Chapter Forty-Two
DROP-DEAD GORGEOUS

Abel / 13 August 2023 / 19:35

I'm standing by the edge of the ocean, back in Malibu once more, the water softly rolling into the shore. The sun is beginning to set, dipping lower in the sky, blushing it with pinks and purples that leak into the sea like a painting. Birds call overheard, and somewhere not too far away the gentle hum of the East Pacific Highway rumbles. But here, on this small sliver of beach, it's just me, Ella and Ryan, happily lost in merciful tranquillity.

'What do you think you guys will do now?' I ask as the sun sinks lower.

Ella rests her head on Ryan's shoulder, both of them staring out over the ocean to the horizon.

'Well, Omni's going under for sure. There's no way they can

recover from this.' Ryan shrugs. 'So I guess we'll do whatever we want. The world's our oyster, right?'

Ella nods. 'Maybe we could set up our own production company or something.'

Ryan looks down at her, basically glowing with the biggest smile on her face. 'You mean that?'

'Of course,' Ella says without hesitation. 'We've got the resources, the money, we know what we're doing. We've been in this industry for a long time already, and men have only ever been the one calling the shots, telling us what's right and wrong. We could start something new – a safe place to tell the stories that matter. I don't know . . . It was just a thought.'

Ryan doesn't respond. Not with words anyway. She grabs Ella's face and plants a kiss on her lips. 'God, I love you Eleanor Grayson,' she murmurs.

Ella giggles. 'And I love you, Ryan Hudson.'

I give them a second of staring into each other's eyes before I make a retching noise to bring them back down to Earth. 'Guys, still very much here. I've been through enough in the last twenty-four hours without having to watch you try to eat each other's faces on the beach. Have some respect. I'm a grieving widow, remember?'

There's a hitch of silence. Then we all burst out laughing, getting up and heading back into the house.

'Shoes off!' Mila snaps from her spot washing dishes before we've even taken a step inside. 'You'll get sand everywhere. I already have two dogs – I don't need four more bringing in their mess.'

'Oh, give them a break,' Liv says, a chuckle warming her words. She's standing by the kitchen table next to an empty chair, a bowl of light-coloured lilac paste in her hands. 'Fingers crossed it didn't turn orange,' she whispers, flicking her eyes up to the ceiling with a mischievous grin.

'I heard that,' a voice says behind us. We all turn round and, yup, because I'm nothing if not predictable, my heart skips a beat. I can feel myself smiling already like a damn goofball. Max and Bridie yap in unison and gallop over to investigate.

'Looking good,' Ryan says with a smirk. 'Or I guess you could say you look *drop-dead gorgeous.*'

Lucky throws the towel in his hand in her direction with a wry smile, then looks at his new platinum-blond buzzcut in the mirror. 'Hmm,' he muses with a shrug. 'I think death might suit me . . .'

Chapter Forty-Three

HOW TO DIE FAMOUS

Lucky / 11 August 2023 / 23:13

'Alive and well.'

I raise my arm in the air to give Abel, Ryan and Ella a thumbs up. It feels weird lying here in a pool of my own blood, so I try to make a joke about it to ease the tension. 'Death is pretty soothing. All I have to do is lie here while you guys do the hard work.'

'Don't get used to it,' Ella mumbles.

The three of them hurry into the kitchen to join me.

'Did you not think about waiting for us to help before you started making a mess?' Ryan whispers.

'You were taking ages so I thought I'd get a head start. Then we can get out of here quicker.' I nod to the upended mini bar and smashed bottles in pieces on the floor. 'Your doing?'

Ella shakes her head. 'Lake. We heard him come in, stumbling all over the place. He must've fell into it or something. I guess the alcohol and sleeping pill Liv slipped him started to kick in.'

'Yeah, well, he's just thrown up, so let's not bank on him staying knocked out for too long,' Abel murmurs.

I gingerly stand up and start to carefully strip down to my underwear, taking clean clothes from my rucksack to change into. Then I retrieve the last transparent pouch of my blood and hand it to Abel, who opens it carefully and dips the knife inside. Turns out Mila was a dab hand at drawing blood once we'd ordered the right equipment and watched a few YouTube tutorials. All I've got left to show for it is a small plaster in the crook of my elbow. I quickly change into my clean clothes, stuffing the bloody ones into my bag.

'Everything went to plan on your side?' Ryan asks, as Abel sets the knife on the floor next to the rest of the mess.

I nod. 'Collected my car keys from the hotel front desk. Every CCTV camera in that damn place will have picked me up before I left. And I made sure I told the staff member on duty where I was going.' I grin. 'I even mentioned that I thought I might be in trouble and that things had been tense on set lately, so let's hope she remembers to recount that, word for word, to the cops when they start investigating.'

Abel gives me a high five. 'And the cameras out front definitely picked you up when you got here?'

'Yup. Conveniently looked up at the stars when I arrived so they could capture my face.'

'Perfect, but can we get this show on the road?' Ryan asks, glancing nervously at the door as if Lake might appear and catch us framing him for my murder any moment now.

'Almost,' I reply. 'Just one last thing.'

I remove the gold ring from my index finger, dip it in the puddle of blood and leave it on the floor by the counter. Something for the police to find when they show up looking for my body, which they won't find, of course. I'll be long gone by then.

Abel changes into a pair of Lake's boots and purposefully steps into the pool of blood. 'Garage?'

I nod and we all follow him back out of the kitchen and through the door opposite, Abel tramping blood through the house the whole way.

Once we've closed the door behind us, Ella puts a gloved hand into the bloody bag and uses it to open the trunk of one of Lake's cars. Ryan does the same, opening the car door with it instead. I get the bloody clothes from my bag and throw them into the trunk while Abel takes one of Lake's jackets from the hook next to the door and puts it on. Then I grab both my phones. We all tense up. This is the part we have to hope works in our favour.

'Ready?' I whisper, even though we already know the garage is soundproofed. A humble brag from Lake on his episode of *Cribs*.

The others pause for a second, then nod. On my burner phone, I pull up the voice recording before I dial a number on my actual phone. I take a deep breath and press call.

348

'911, what's your emergency?' a voice says after the first ring.

I lean in close to the phone. 'Please help me,' I whisper. I don't have to worry about faking fear. It's already there, enveloping every word.

'Hello?' the operator says. 'Can you repeat that?'

I swallow. 'Please help. He's going to kill me.'

'Who's going to kill you?' the operator responds. 'Can you give me an address?'

'Oh, God, he's coming back. Please hurry.'

Before the operator can answer me, I bring the burner phone close to my real phone's speaker and press play. It starts with the sound of a struggle as Lake forces me up against the wall of his trailer.

'Lake, please, get off,' my voice says. 'You're hurting me.'

'Good. And I'll do a whole lot more than that.'

Another struggle. Then: 'Please . . . HELP!'

The operator is alert. 'We're tracing the call. Stay on the line with me.'

Lake's voice responds to me on the recording. 'Shut your fucking mouth or I swear to God I'll kill you.'

There's the sound of another struggle followed by a smash as the award falls from the trailer shelf.

'We're trying to find your location,' the operator says desperately. 'Don't hang up.'

'Please,' my voice says, 'I'm begging you. Let me g—'

Before my voice can finish the sentence, I cut the call. *Now* we have to move fast. I dive into the still open trunk. 'See you

349

guys on the other side,' I say.

Ella and Ryan turn back to head into the house. 'We'll text if anything happens here,' Ella says. 'Be quick, Abel. We don't know how long we have until they trace the call.'

'Or, God forbid, that ogre upstairs wakes up,' Ryan adds. 'Just . . . Yeah, be quick.'

They close the garage door after themselves, leaving the two of us alone. Abel looks down at me, followed by the briefest hesitation.

'We're almost there,' I say. 'We've got this.'

He nods, putting on one of Lake's caps and pulling it low over his face. 'God, I hope you're right,' he says. With one last look, he closes the trunk, plunging me into darkness.

Chapter Forty-Four

RED AND BLUE SPOTLIGHTS

Abel / 11 August 2023 / 23:24

I climb into the car and turn the key in the ignition. It rumbles to life, then settles into a patient purr. I click a button on the keys and the garage door starts to open. I slide the car out slowly. It's brand new and creeps along the gravel with a quiet growl. I don't intend to floor the accelerator until I'm well clear of the house. The gate in front of me opens up. Head low to avoid showing my face to the cameras, I push the car out onto the road, hoping Lake's clothing and the dark of night will disguise me well enough. I hit the street and speed up a little, trying not to let my mind wander too far and instead stay focused on the task at hand.

Still, I look up to the night sky as I drive along the dark roads, stars twinkling in an onyx ocean. I think of Adam, the same way I've done every day for the last three years. I wonder if he's watching, urging us on.

I find the place we agreed on. A car is already waiting. Liv jumps out of it before I've even stopped. With my gloved hand, still splattered with Lucky's blood, I open the boot and let him out. Liv dives into him, giving him a tight hug. Then she throws her arms round me too.

'Time for hugs later,' I joke. 'I've got a crime scene to clean up before the police arrive.'

Lucky pulls me in and holds me close. 'Almost there,' he whispers in my ear.

He gives me a squeeze, then breaks away. He climbs into the car with Liv while I jump into Lake's and hightail it back to the house. I've only been gone ten minutes, but who knows when the police will manage to trace the call. They might be on their way right now.

I lower my head once more as I approach the house, driving the car through the gates and back into the garage, leaving Lake's bloodied boots by the door. I creep back inside and head for the kitchen. Lucky's blood is everywhere, black instead of red in the pale moonlight. I crouch down next to the main puddle, putting one gloved hand into it and dragging the blood outwards, leaving a print behind as if a body was dragged away. Blood drips from my fingertips as I stand up, remove the glove and check the burner phone in my pocket.

One text. From Ella. Sent a minute ago. I open it.

And then I hear a footstep on the stairs.

I immediately drop into a crouch behind the kitchen island, assessing my options. I push my panic and fear away, because if we're going to get away with this, I need a clear head. The footsteps are slow and heavy. Drunken. Maybe Lake won't find me, but I can't risk staying out in the open. I need to find a hiding place. But the kitchen doesn't exactly give me many options.

Except . . .

I remove my other bloody glove, splattering red liquid all over my top in the process, and stuff them in my rucksack, then throw open the cupboard under the kitchen counter, using the cuff of my hoodie so I don't leave fingerprints. Too full. Lake's footsteps are halfway down the stairs. I edge round the island and try the next one. It only houses a broken coffee machine. There's not much room, but I don't exactly have another choice right now. I push the machine as far to the back of the cupboard as it'll go and force myself into the space. My knees are touching my head and I'm bent into the most awkward and uncomfortable shape, but that's the least of my worries. I close the cupboard door, and a few seconds later, Lake comes into the kitchen.

He turns on the light.

353

There's no sound after that click. Not for a moment or two. I imagine Lake, groggy in the doorway, rubbing his eyes, only to open them and see the blood on the kitchen tiles. Sure enough, there's the sound of his breath leaving his body in disbelief.

'WHAT THE FUCK?'

He takes a step into the kitchen, and I hug my knees even tighter to my chest.

'OH MY GOD . . .'

There's a clatter, as if Lake's dropped something. I think of the knife left on the kitchen floor and wonder if it's that. There's more stumbling and trembling breaths. Despite my situation, I'm glad I'm able to hear the fear in him. It gives me a huge level of satisfaction. Witnessing it is almost revenge in itself, although not quite enough.

Lake's footsteps fall away, back out into the hall, and instinctively I know where he's going. He's following the bloody footprints to the garage. He'll open the door and investigate the car and the blood all over it. This is my chance to escape. Once he goes into the garage, I can slip out of the kitchen, into the utility room and out of the side door.

I open the cupboard slowly, inch by inch, expecting to be caught at any moment. But the kitchen is empty. I hear the door handle of the garage as I gently manoeuvre myself out of my hiding place, staying crouched behind the island once I'm free.

I hear Lake swear to himself again. This time his voice is *in* the garage.

I make my move.

I creep up to the hallway and see the garage door ajar opposite. Light spills out onto the floor. It's white at first. Then red. Then blue. Then red again. Blue. Red. Blue.

My heart kicks up a gear, making sense of the colours before my brain catches up. The police. They've traced the call, and now they're here. The lights flash through the small window next to the door, lighting up the hall, the boot prints on the carpet, the blood spattered on my hoodie. I freeze for a second. Lake is still in the garage, unaware that his fate is about to be sealed, but I need to get the fuck out of here. Now.

I go. Holding my breath like my life depends on it, like if I breathe this whole plan will fall apart, I step past the door and slip into the utility room. Footsteps in the garage tell me Lake has heard a commotion out front and is coming back into the house. I don't look back. I open the side door and bolt through it as someone yells, 'FREEZE, NOBODY MOVE!' I don't stop. I keep going until I reach the treeline, and I don't look back until I'm away from the house and by the chain-link fence once more.

The house is aglow, lights on in almost every window. I can see movement, people rushing by, back and forth. But most importantly I can see Lake. His mask has well and truly shattered. He looks terrified, like a man who knows that, even with all the money and power in the world, it still won't be enough to protect him from his fate.

That's revenge enough for me. I turn my back on the house and escape into the night. I get back to the car to find Ella, Ryan and Mila waiting anxiously. They all deflate with relief the second they set eyes on me. Until they see the blood, anyway.

'Abel . . .' Ella whispers.

I nod. 'It's done.'

As I dive into the car and Mila sets off for Malibu, her burner phone lights up on the dashboard. Ryan grabs it and reads the message out loud.

Lucky
Did we just get away with murder?
23:49

We all glance at each other hesitantly. Nobody wants to jinx it. But even though I'm scared to confirm the answer prematurely, I *think* we just did.

Chapter Forty-Five

THE END OF EVERYTHING THAT CAME BEFORE

Abel / 13 August 2023 / 19:37

Lucky doesn't look so much like Lucky any more. The plaster in the crook of his elbow where Mila drew the blood we'd need to make the crime scene believable is still there but his perfectly ruffled brown hair is gone, buzzed off and dyed blond. It might take more than hair dye to form a whole new identity, but, hey, it's a start. And if you ask me, he looks hot as hell.

The four of us stand together in the kitchen, smiles all round, and suddenly I want to cry. The last few weeks have been so hard on all of us. But somehow we made it through. We did it together.

'I swear to God if one of you suggests a group hug, I'm drowning myself in the ocean,' Ryan says, ducking her head and pretending she's not about to cry too.

Ella grabs her hand and gives it a squeeze. 'I mean, it would be pretty fitting,' she teases. 'They do it in all the movies. Come on, let's act the part.' Ella drags Ryan into our open arms, and she doesn't exactly put up a fight. In fact, I'm sure she holds on tighter than anyone.

We settle down that evening for dinner, the six of us and two dogs round the table, hooting and hollering and laughing and joking, and I don't think I've been happier since before Adam died. But even though that grief will stay with me for the rest of my days, I can still feel his presence, like he's telling me that it's okay to move on.

That night, as the others settle down in the living room for a movie, Lucky and I step outside onto the beach. The water is playing its usual lullaby, the crest of its gentle waves sparkling with the shimmering light of the moon.

'I hope you still like me as a blond,' he says.

'Hmm, I'm not sure,' I joke. 'Jury's still out on that one, but I'll let you know.'

He laughs but it's just for a moment, and then he's fully serious. 'You're going home soon. Back to London.'

I duck my head, the sadness weighing on me. In a way, there's nothing I want more than to go home, but I also don't want to leave any of these guys behind. Despite everything, they've given me so much over the last few weeks. The idea of leaving LA makes me ache a little.

'What are you going to do?' I ask in an attempt to change the subject.

Lucky weighs up the question, looking out at the water. 'I've always wanted to do a road trip around the US. There's so much of the world out there. I want to start exploring it. I know I've got to lay low for a while, and I'll need to sort new IDs, but I think eventually I'll do that. Maybe rent a car and take it from here to New York. That would be pretty cool.'

'That sounds great,' I say enthusiastically. 'You'll see so much. I'm already jealous. Make sure you send me a postcard or something.'

Lucky looks out to the horizon. 'And I want to start looking after myself too – grieve properly without the world watching and without drink to numb the pain. Figure out who the new Lucky Tate is. I might even get myself a therapist, but on my own terms. There'll be no Jill breathing down my neck and threatening to fire me this time.' He laughs to himself. 'I'm looking forward to a fresh start.'

'Maybe one day you can hit up London,' I say. 'I'll give you some tips on how to go undercover in a new city.'

Lucky laughs. 'I'd like that.'

We go to head back inside, but a phone call stops me. I nod for Lucky to go in without me and hang back to answer it.

'Stupid question but . . . how're you holding up, kid?' Hannah asks. Her voice is soft and gentle, which almost makes me feel bad for lying to her. Then I remember that the *Daily Eye* is partly to blame for everything Lucky and the others went through. I guess I am too. We all are. Every single one of us who watched this unfold like a soap opera instead of real life. Blame is a tough question to face up to.

'As well as I can be,' I answer.

'It's a lot,' Hannah says. 'But, look, no rush on your final piece for the *Eye*. It's not like this case is going to be wrapped up anytime soon. Apparently they're looking at a date early *next* year to take Lake to court?'

'Something like that,' I say.

'Well, between you and me, I hear the whole place is on the chopping block.' My ears prick up and I hold my phone a little tighter. 'I used my contacts to get the inside scoop, and it sounds like the police are circling others at Omni too, including Jill Anderson.'

'No way,' I say. I'd wondered how Jill would try to wriggle out of this.

'Yep. Police have questioned her once already, but it's not looking good for her. Or the manager at the hotel for that matter. Stephen? He got taken into custody earlier. I'm not sure what for, but it sounds serious.'

I swear to God I nearly start singing my hallelujahs. But I hold it in and give a less incriminating response instead. We chat a little more about the final piece I'm going to write for the *Daily Eye,* something that will be published anonymously, of course, then I hang up and join the others inside.

They're all gathered round the table. Mila, Liv, Ryan, Ella and Lucky. I feel like Adam is there too, which makes my heart full. I take my place, smiling to myself as Ryan and Lucky bicker about how good or bad some noughties romcom is. I wouldn't have it any other way.

'A toast,' Liv says once food is served. 'To Lucky and

his new life away from this hellish spotlight. To all of us for actually pulling this off. And to Lake Carter too.' His name robs the buzz from the table but only for a second. Liv grins and raises her drink higher. 'May he rot in hell.'

We all cheer and clink our glasses. Tomorrow Lucky will start his new life. Ryan and Ella will begin figuring out how to take over the world. I'll go back home to London. Who knows what waits for me in the future? But right now it's just the six of us, together one last time.

THE DAILY EYE NEWSPAPER

<u>THE SUN FINALLY SETS ON OMNIFICENT</u>

By Anonymous

22 August 2023

ON THE SURFACE IT WAS A PRODUCTION STUDIO WITH A BAD REPUTATION THAT DREW THE ATTENTION OF MILLIONS AROUND THE WORLD, BUT WHAT HID BEHIND THE CURTAIN WAS EVEN DARKER THAN ANYONE COULD HAVE EVER IMAGINED . . .

Sunset High *was supposed to be like any other TV show. Before its original release in 2010, Omni Channel, the go-to place for child and teen entertainment created by Omnificent, had hopes of it being a moderate success. If things went well, they'd renew it for a second season. But we all know what happened next. The breakdown of Mila Stone. The then unexplained disappearance of Penelope Daunt. The tragic death of junior assistant Adam Miller. And now the murder of Lucky Tate.*

Each tragedy has been treated as if it was the season finale of the show, a plot twist that left viewers on a cliffhanger without answers, desperately wanting more. In a way, a portion of responsibility sits with us, the watchers. We've sat back, finding a morbid thrill in the twists and turns of celebrities' lives. They invite us in, after all, stepping with flair into this Colosseum of Fame, laying parts of themselves bare for public consumption and personal gain. But what happens when greed makes us ask for even more? What happens when we take what they give us, discard of it once we're done, and then hold out our hands, expecting the next piece of them as if it's our right? You only need to look as far as Lucky Tate to find the answer.

We treat celebrities as our property, as though even in real life, when the cameras are turned off, they're still simply acting out a show for our entertainment. The world of celebrity feels like unscripted reality TV that's there for our enjoyment, twenty-four hours a day. And yet, behind the scenes, it's the complete opposite. In the game of fame, everything is calculated, twisted, fabricated, exploited. It's a scripted show, often written by those in the shadows who will manipulate anyone and anything to get what they want. Just like Omnificent. Just like Lake Carter.

As new details emerge from the Sunset High *case, a different picture has been painted, one that outs the lies and greed of those in power, determined to bleed their stars dry. Lake Carter now sits in jail, charged with the murders of Lucky Tate and Adam Miller after previously undiscovered CCTV footage from the night of Miller's death placed Carter at the crime scene. He has also been charged with the kidnapping of Penelope Daunt as the star came forward after three years and gave a brutally honest tell-all interview with Barb Harrington. It remains to be seen what Carter's fate will be, but a lifetime behind bars is almost guaranteed given the damning evidence.*

Also exposed is the role Omnificent has played in covering up many tragic tales over the years, leading to their stocks plummeting. Experts and insiders predict the studio could go bust by the end of the year, while Hollywood itself now reckons with its own responsibility as questions are raised about how the industry can do better.

However, as these terrible crimes slowly come to light, there's one thing that we can be sure of – the sun is finally setting on Omnificent and its twisted lies.

Epilogue

THEY THINK IT'S ALL OVER

Hope Waters / 12 August 2023 / 01:10

The car slips through the LA night. I check my phone from the passenger seat for the hundredth time, looking at the map and the little icon that hasn't moved on it for an hour. The last time I took my eyes off it, the icon disappeared. I'll be damned if I let that happen again.

'She's still there?' Porter asks from the driver's seat.

I zoom in on the icon just to make sure. 'Yep. Hasn't moved.'

I catch Porter's frown out of the corner of my eye. 'What is she doing?'

It's the same question I've been asking myself over and over again. The news of Lucky Tate's death threw me for a loop when I saw it online just now, and this has added the cherry on top of a weird fucked-up cake. I don't like being out of control, which is why I feel so unsettled. I need to know what's going on.

This whole mess with Omnificent started years ago. Three, to be precise. I was looking for a way into the world I'd wanted to be a part of for so long. I told myself that if I could get a foot in the door and get someone, *anyone*, to notice me, I'd be able to make it in front of the camera. It's where I felt like I belonged, and I'd do anything to get there. Even if it meant taking a job as an assistant crew member just to get on the set of the 2020 *Sunset High* reboot. Fetching coffee and organizing schedules wasn't what I wanted to do. Far from it. But it was a start.

I didn't make friends. I made *contacts* who I pretended were friends to keep them close. In this industry, you never know who might come in handy in the future. Best to make sure no bridges are burned, just in case that person who's a nobody suddenly becomes a *somebody* – a director or a producer or a writer who can get you one step closer to making your dreams come true. It's a selfish business, but you've got to be prepared to do anything and everything if you want to make it.

That's how I met Adam Miller. We were both assistants working on the set. While I forced a smile onto my face to make it look like I wanted nothing more than to be in this position, Adam seemed to genuinely enjoy it, like *this* was his dream right here, right now. He said he wanted to be a director one day, which was enough for me to keep him on side. I doubted he'd end up at the Oscars with his little brother like he said he would, but you never know. If it *did* happen, I wanted to be right there alongside him.

But when Penelope Daunt went missing, the world I'd been so carefully building from the inside collapsed. Okay, so maybe it was my fault. I guess I moved the first brick, and like a game of Jenga, the whole thing came tumbling down. I *thought* telling Lake Carter about the phone call I overheard between Penelope and Barb Harrington would work in my favour. When I arrived at her trailer to bring her to set and eavesdropped on the conversation, I lit up from the inside. This was the chance I'd been waiting for.

Lake had taken no notice of me yet. It was like I was invisible to him. But if I told him his lead star was about to do a tell-all interview, then he'd have no choice but to fire her. I could use that opportunity to explain that I was an actress myself and that he should give me a chance. With Penelope's spot open, maybe he'd audition me there and then. I'd perform a word-perfect monologue as if it was straight off the top of my head when, in fact, I'd been rehearsing it for years in case an opportunity like this presented itself. Everything would go just as I planned.

Except that didn't happen. Lake didn't ask me to audition for him in his trailer when I told him what Penelope was planning. In fact, when I revealed my true aspirations, he all but sneered in my face and told me to 'Find a new dream instead because that one's not for you'. It broke me hearing that. It felt like the dream I'd had for so long was now in pieces on the floor, tarnished and ruined.

Once Penelope went missing without a trace and Adam

Miller fell from the hotel rooftop, the show was cancelled and I was back to square one. But I didn't stay down for long. No, I put myself back together again. Fuck Lake Carter and fuck his stupid little show. I'd make it without him.

And yet at every audition I went for over the next couple of years, I was passed over time and time again. In fact, one Omni producer for a smaller show I was trying out for pulled me aside after a particular audition, which at first I took to be good news. I'd seen him around a few other times. Was this finally going to be my proper break? But instead, the weasel-faced little shit tried to take my dream right out of my hands, just like Lake Carter had.

'I don't think this is going to work out for you, Hope. I know what the standard of talent is like. We see better actresses daily. I don't want you to waste your time. You should contemplate calling it a day. Maybe try something else. Perhaps behind the camera?'

I couldn't believe my ears. Was this little *worm* really trying to tell me that the career I was destined for, all the fame and riches that I knew were on my horizon, was never going to happen? He didn't even give me the courtesy of his full attention. He took a phone call in the middle of shooting me down and had the nerve to dismiss me with a flick of his hand.

'Tell me Ella has said yes to leading *Sunset*,' he said, turning his back on me. Once again I was invisible. He'd probably already forgotten my name.

I stormed out. By now I had passed being heartbroken. I was

furious. Omni were once again treating me like a nobody who belonged in the shadows. It stoked fires inside me and fuelled a lust for revenge. I wasn't going to let these bastards tear me down. No fucking way. It was time to get back at them, even if it meant putting my dreams on hold.

And that's when I realized that the producer had given me exactly what I needed. Answering that call in front of me had been a bad move. He'd just told me everything I needed to know. *Sunset High* was coming back, and Ella Winter was going to be its star. Perfect. If I couldn't act in front of the camera, I'd just have to make up my own character behind the scenes instead.

And that's when I became Natalie.

Of course, now that Ella was about to become a big deal, I knew she'd need a personal assistant. It killed me to have to stoop that low. I would've almost rather given up on my plans altogether. But I never throw in the towel. That's what makes me better than these people. I don't wait for things to be handed to me on a silver platter. I go out and get what I want. So I bit my tongue, gave myself a visual transformation so I no longer looked like Hope, the girl who'd wanted to be an actress so badly, and I wormed my way into the fold. But if I wanted revenge, I needed help.

Enter Porter McKay.

He was the obvious candidate. I needed someone who hated Omni as much as me and would want revenge on them like I did. I didn't have to look very far. On the list of people who'd pay to see Omni's downfall, number one was the person everyone had accused of Penelope Daunt's murder when she had gone missing.

And so the games began.

The only surefire way to see *Sunset High* fail and in turn Omni was to bring down its stars, and we started with Ryan. Porter left the box of posters outside her house, and even broke in to leave her a little message on her bedroom wall. He almost got caught, but *almost* doesn't count. He also followed Lucky and Abel, scratched the message onto the back of the car and threw the rock through their window to scare them. I was the one that scrawled the message on the back of Ella's white dress in red lipstick before I helped her put it on for the live TV interview. And I took the pictures of Ella and Ryan, then Abel and Lucky, kissing at the party when I went to collect them under Ella's orders and leaked them online straight after. Watching them all panic from the inside was quite the thrill.

I recognized Abel, of course. I'd spent enough time with Adam to know that he had a little brother back in London, and when he showed up for that first meeting at Omni HQ, I knew straight away. I planned to keep an eye on him. After all, it couldn't be a coincidence that little bro had turned up on the same set Adam was working on when he died. Maybe he was here for his own secret reasons, just like me.

Then Porter told me he had showed up at my house looking for Hope Waters. Of course, I was Natalie Trenton now – Hope was, conveniently, visiting her mom to escape the Omnificent circus. But I couldn't work out why Abel would be looking for me unless he was up to something. My senses only tingled further when Abel cornered Porter at work, again asking about me and Adam. I was starting to feel like maybe he was on to me. I wasn't sure what his deal was, but I was on my guard.

When the story leaked in the *Daily Eye* about Ryan and Ella fighting in their dressing room at *The Late Late Show*, it didn't take a rocket scientist to figure out who was behind it. A handful of people had been backstage, and only four had been in the room and knew the argument had happened. Ella and Ryan sure as hell weren't going to leak it themselves, and Lucky didn't seem the type either. I wanted confirmation that my guess was right, so I found Hannah Wilkes' email and sent her a message from a fake Abel Miller email address. Sure enough, she responded. The little shit was leaking stories to the press. Well, at least it was helping my revenge plot by shining yet more negative publicity on the show, but I didn't want Abel looking too close in case he figured me out. Leaking the pictures of them all at the party was my way of sending a warning.

So we're all up to speed? Good, because right now, we have another problem. When Ella gave me a phone and laptop linked to her accounts so we could share a calendar, I don't think she anticipated that I'd be able to track her movements through the Find My iPhone app. Usually I always know where she is and why, but when I clocked her icon out in Malibu the other day, it confused me. But before Porter and I could follow it, she returned back to the hotel.

Now she's back there again tonight. At first, Ella's location wasn't available, which struck me as odd. Was her phone dead?

Or had she turned it off? Then it came back on, signalling that she was once again out by the beach. That raises a very interesting question – on the evening one of her friends has died, why is she in Malibu? I intend to find out.

'Apparently they're in there,' I say, pointing to the only house on the street as the car passes it. Porter nods and drives a little further down the road until he finds a quiet spot to park up. We both jump out, hoodies and caps on, and creep back through the dark.

The lights are on, and when I put my eyes up against a pair of binoculars, making sure to stay in the shadows, I see people flitting past the windows. There's Ella, and, of course, Ryan too. There's Abel and, to my surprise, Mila Stone. That gives me a jolt. What the fuck is she doing there? None of them seem overly sad right now for a bunch of people whose friend has just died. Do they even know about what's happened to Lucky yet? Jeez, that's going to be a kick in the gut when someone finally looks at their phone.

I'm deciding what to do when a new person appears. She has short hair and glasses on, a bowl in her hand. I can't say I recognize her. She must be a friend of Mila. But then I see something that shakes me to my core.

Lucky Tate.

He's right there in front of my eyes. His brown hair looks a little more messy than usual, but he certainly isn't *dead*. I can't believe what I'm seeing.

'Holy shit,' Porter whispers next to me when I offer him the binoculars to have a look himself.

I take them back and watch as the woman and Lucky disappear while the others make their way out to the garden. Some time later, they traipse back into the house and the woman reappears followed by . . . Lucky? But it's not the same Lucky as before. It's a different version of him, this one with hair cut short and dyed an awful blond. I might not have known it was him at a glance if I hadn't just seen him before. He looks at himself in the mirror, runs a hand over his head, as someone who's just transformed themselves might do.

I watch for I don't know how long. Stunned. More notifications come through to my phone telling me that Lucky Tate is dead in the Hollywood Hills. People on Twitter are saying it was Lake Carter.

I have no idea what's going on, but there's one thing I know for certain. I think it as I raise my phone and open the camera, zoom in and take as many pictures as I can.

Lucky Tate is alive and well.

And I have the proof.

Acknowledgements

I still can't believe I get to make up stories for a living, and it wouldn't be possible without a whole bunch of people, so bear with me while I thank them real quick!

First of all, to my agent extraordinaire, Chloe, who's always a phone call away when I need her and is the best sounding board for all the weird ideas my brain comes up with. Thank you endlessly for always having faith in me. You're the best of the best.

This story would not exist without the care and passion of my incredible editors on both sides of the pond. Amina and Erika, I'm so damn lucky that I get to work with you guys. Thank you for all the help and insightful edits that have made this book what it is now. I hope I've done you proud. And thanks to Jennie for making the copyedit so smooth!

Also, to the dream teams at Simon & Schuster Children's and Little, Brown. To every person in every department – sales, marketing, publicity, design, production, digital, export – who have had a hand in my books. I hope you know how grateful I am to you all.

A special shout-out to my publicist Ellen. We've had a lot of fun all over the place this last year. Thank you so much for all your hard work and for keeping me supplied with snacks when I need them most, i.e. making sure I don't *actually* faint during school visits. You're an angel. I promise to bring a coat, or at least a hoodie, for events in colder climates in future.

Ellen! Thank you for nearly TWENTY years of the bestest friendship. I love you so, so much. Please do not run off to the other side of the world again. Or do, but take me with you this time. Here's to another twenty.

Ellie B. Grass Bat. Ellington Bataloo. There's nobody I'd rather send a 'Think I'm having a breakdown, wbu?' text to. Thank you for picking me up when the world seemed to be falling apart – those therapy sessions *really* got me through the panorama. I probably wouldn't be a full-time author now if it wasn't for *Paris on a Tuesday*, so thank you for THAT.

Jack! I miss you all the time, even though I text you, like, once every lunar eclipse. Reminder that I love you, but not as much as I love Marv (even though I've never actually met him).

My Goslings squad – you're honestly the highlight of my week every week. Thanks to every single one of you for letting me hit those cross-court drop-shot winners. But seriously, for all the laughs and Sunday lunches, thank you.

Thank you to my Ladies who Karaoke too – let's continue picking songs outside our vocal range. Josh, Phil, Kris and V, thank you for being such good friends. I love you all. Tessington World of Adventures, thank you for the tea and laughs. I can't wait to watch lil baby Sid grow up. And to Matthew – please move back soon, I don't care how cheap your rent is now.

To the Goven and all the friends I've made in this industry so far. Our job can be lonely and stressful at times, but you guys make it so much easier and ten times more fun. I fear naming you all in case I accidentally forget someone, but you know who you are. Thanks for all the gossip. My life would be so much more boring without it.

Fred, Will and Charlotte . . . Yeah, you guys are okay, I

suppose. Thanks for putting up with my strops when I'm in the middle of a deadline, and for letting me talk a million miles an hour when I realize I haven't actually spoken to another human being in days. If I'm ever fortunate enough to need extras for a TV or film adaptation of my books, you're first up on the call sheet. Special shout-out to my favourite tennis doubles partner Ann Carter – I promise I'll visit one day soon!

To every single person who has read, reviewed, recommended, posted, liked, loved, told a friend about, longlisted, shortlisted, taught, stocked and generally supported my books – I will never be able to thank you enough. You've made my dreams come true. I hope you know that I'm immensely grateful for all that you do. I'd particularly like to thank the teachers, librarians and booksellers who continue to fight back against hate in order to give queer stories to the kids who need them most. You shine a light in the dark. Thank you.

And to those queer kids who feel lost, alone, scared or confused right now – I was, and still am, one of you. Be kind to yourself and know that love, hope and acceptance still exists in this world.

To my gran, who believed I could do anything, and to my sister, who I love dearly, thank you. I hope I make you proud. And, as always, to my mum. I love you more than words can say. Thank you for everything.

Finally, for Alex. You were one in a million. I know you're already dancing up there. Shine bright, babes.

BENJAMIN DEAN is a London-based children's author and ex-celebrity journalist. His biggest achievement to date is breaking the news that Rihanna can't wink (she blinks, in case you were wondering). Benjamin can be found on Twitter as @notagainben tweeting about Rihanna and LGBTQ+ culture to his 15,000+ followers. *The King is Dead* is his debut YA book.

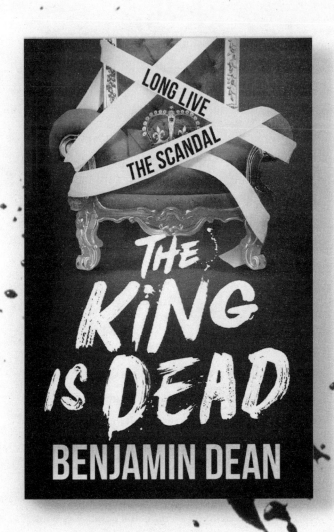

Have you read
BENJAMIN DEAN'S
scandalous royal mystery?